ENCHANTING ROLES

SOVA ERICKSON

For a moldy witch, who gave me the courage to make this tale kinky

CONTENT WARNING

This novel contains moments of dubious consent, kidnapping, graphic violence, mind control, and on page sexually explicit material. Continue at your own discretion.

CONTENTS

Prologue
The Maids of Fate

The Lady of the House was favored by fate. And so it was the fates who favored serving her.

Atropos was the fate who saw all and made sure you didn't see until she cut your life short.

Lachesis was the fate who allotted the thread, pulling at your strings to make music of your misery.

Clotho was the fate you couldn't escape. The one you met on the road to avoid her.

Lachesis stood in the midst of a cellar of shattered glass and broken chains. Her elder sister Atropos loomed over the maid being punished for causing this travesty. The poor fool cried tears from empty eyes as she used her bare hands to sweep the debris into her dustpan. Lachesis strolled around the cellar indifferently to the cruelty, acting like she was looking for a specific speck of rubble. Her younger sister Clotho was more focused on the splatter of purple blood across the floor. She dropped to a crouch like a wild beast, ran a finger along the viscous liquid, and licked it with a forked tongue. "Demon blood. Still fresh, can't be far."

"We'll have to make sure our new hire doesn't request a visit until that's solved," Atropos said curtly. Neither sister even batted an eye as Clotho pounced to the broken window like a panther and shot off into the night. Instead Atropos glared at the maid on the floor, hands bloodied and waiting for orders. In a twisted way this was her lucky day, being pushed this far meant she would be let go. Memories can be modified, but minds cannot be unshattered. Broken thralls wandering the slums invited unwanted attention. "Such a waste of fresh help. It would've been more efficient to remove the filth than store her down here."

"If we did that, said new hire will have nobody to visit. Even with our talents she may notice her sister is a corpse." Lachesis used a handkerchief to pick up the remnants of a horrid looking mushroom. Deadroot, a plant that pacified devils but turned demons into berserkers. It was such a shame Lachesis had told the servant the opposite when she was preparing their demonic guest's meal. She hid the evidence behind her back and twirled around to face Atropos. "I don't think such an act would be in line with the spirit of the arrangement."

"Spirit of the arrangement," Atropos repeated with mocking disgust as she narrowed her eyes. A look that would make even the strongest of wills crumble, but only made Lachesis smugger. "Who are you loyal to, sister?"

"The von Closen legacy, sister." Lachesis shot a look back. "The real question is, are you loyal to the legacy or just the Lady of the House?"

Atropos scoffed as she turned to leave. "There isn't a difference."

"You did always favor the prepared." Lachesis pet the head of the kneeling maid gently, already weaving a new memory of her quitting. And locking away all the bad ones, instead of just her ability to speak of them. A severance bonus for a patsy who played her part perfectly. "But I'm a romantic at heart. I favor the bold."

The Seelie Soirée

Chapter 1
A Fateful Encounter

Lia Abith swung her legs while on the couch in one of the many waiting rooms. Already her feet were tired from walking, the House was huge. It had like a million rooms, which made no sense because it was in the middle of the city. This one didn't have much besides the couch and large armchair. She'd decided that was probably where her new employer was going to be sitting, it seemed very grand and important compared to the couch. There was no clock so she had no idea how long she'd been in here. At least enough time to rebraid her hair twice out of boredom.

How did she even manage to get this job? The von Closens were very, well, closed off. She didn't think they were even still around, they basically were the first family here when Webershafen was founded. The first fae at least, she wasn't sure if humans were here yet. The only thing she knew was demons and devils came along way later. The House certainly showed age, the older architecture and brickwork could not be hidden by the well-maintained interior. The gas lights looked as if candles once sat in their place not too long ago and electric lighting was slowly taking over in a similar fashion. Even the couch she sat on now was one she'd see in antique shops but it was hard to think it wasn't brand new with how good condition it was in.

Also, what job did Lia get? Employment was nice to have, especially one that gave her a place to stay. Better than the slums so no surprise she took the deal, even if it was with the fae. But what a street rat like her was even qualified to do wasn't really coming to mind. Especially for an old money family like the von Closens.

Hair rebraid number three had finished. Maybe Lia should go find somebody to make sure they didn't forget about her? She got up from the couch and cautiously went to the door. Nervousness turned to bafflement when she found it locked. That was weird, the doorknob lock was on the other side. It could be to prevent guests from exploring the House without supervision but that didn't explain why the deadbolt would be on this side.

On instinct Lia flicked her index finger against her thumb. The tip was now sharp and thicker than before. She was always grateful she could retract her claws, even if that meant they weren't as sharp as her sister's. And they were great for picking locks, her claw already fiddling in the keyhole. It felt like an old one, barely even two notches to set, so she could be out of here and searching for assistance in no time at all.

Then Lia realized that showing off the skillset of a thief might not be the best way to start an interview for upper crusts. They're the ones who usually own the shops getting robbed after all. Not that Lia had ever used her talents for that, honestly their locks were way too good for her to even try. The explanation that Lia had only ever broken into churches would not make her sound any better. Fae already didn't look too kindly on infernals. They probably wouldn't care to let a half-demon like her explain further.

Lia retracted her claw and sat back down with an uneasy sigh. Was this an interview? She didn't remember having one but she'd already met all three head maids while they showed her the facilities. That didn't feel like something to do for somebody who hadn't been hired yet. She was trying to remember what they'd said when she asked what her job was going to be, her head was so fuzzy today.

"Your duty is to serve the Lady of the House, as we all do," Atropos had said. Her hair was tied up in a bun, and she wore glasses that sat on the brim of her nose. She was terrifying, a glare that could cut you and words just as sharp.

"To not get in the way of mine," Clotho had said. She caused a very different kind of fear in Lia. Her teeth were sharp and her eyes looked like an animal's. Her hair was messy, the only maid who seemed to be allowed to get away with that. Getting in Clotho's way felt like a mistake she'd only ever be able to make once.

"To help a troubled little bee who needs you," Lachesis had said. She reminded Lia of a marionette, drifting from strings pulling her along. She seemed nice, much more than the other two. But she was confusing, talked like everything she said meant something else. Like Lia wasn't getting a joke that the head maid kept trying to make.

Lia looked around the barren waiting room she'd apparently been locked in for who knows how long. All of this was starting to feel like a joke she wasn't getting.

Maybe there was no job and the von Closens were just screwing with her. Fae do like to mess with people without them realizing. Lia knew she was fairly gullible, her sister always joked she was so trusting she'd let the fae take her if they asked nice enough.

Wait, why *did* Diana let Lia take a job with the von Closens? That got her mind moving more than anything else. Her sister would've thrown a fit, even if she folded there would've been a lot of complaining but nothing came to mind. If Diana was here she'd say that was a sign of fae meddling. She'd also say her not being here with her was the second sign. Lia didn't need a third to come to the conclusion that she wasn't hired. Fae don't hire people, they ensnare them.

Except Lia swore she had chosen to come here. It felt like an eternity ago but she remembered walking through those grand front doors with determination. A determination that lingered even as fear questioned it fiercely, keeping her in place, this gut instinct that she couldn't leave yet. She needed to be here, not to work some stupid job but to do...what? Something was wrong. Had *gone* wrong. Her memory had been burnt and the more she scoured the ashes for answers the more it felt like arson. There had been a plan...a plan that clearly didn't work. She needed to leave. She needed to run! Run before *she* arrives to finish what she start—

The door opened as Lia shot to her feet. Atropos stepped in first with a glare that said fleeing would not be wise. Instead Lia lowered her head the way the maid did as the Lady of the House entered.

Ida von Closen, matriarch of the von Closens, was hard to describe. That wasn't true, she was easy to describe but the words were like a script Lia's brain was being fed while her eyes couldn't pick out what made it true. Ida was stunning in her emerald dress, but Lia couldn't say why. She walked with a perfect gait, whatever that meant. Her red eyes said exactly what she thought they would, not that she remembered what those thoughts were.

Lia felt like this was the most trustworthy woman she'd ever met and couldn't understand why thinking that made her skin crawl.

Her hair was odd though. It was long, insanely long, as if she'd never cut it in her life. White like a faded wedding dress, unnaturally straight for how it dragged along the floor when she walked. Ida sat down in the large armchair, as expected, and it was almost as if her hair was trained to part to the sides on its own, instead of her doing so herself as to not sit on it.

"Sit."

Lia obeyed. Atropos stood at the door as if guarding from her escape. Not that she would try that, she had no idea what had gotten into her a minute ago. She trusted Ida, she'd tell her what she was here for and all would be well. That trust didn't extend to her hair, though. The way it flowed now reminded Lia of tendrils lying in wait.

"Do you know why you are here?" Ida asked.

Lia swallowed. She already felt like she was in trouble. "Like in this room or—"

"Silence." Ida pursed her lips as Lia shut her mouth tightly. Her eyes shone like bloody rubies. Strange, red eyes were a demon trait, not fae. Although Lia's eyes were purple so maybe fae had a similar variety. "Why do you think I am meeting with you?"

"To inform me of what my new job is. You've hired me to help with something." Lia swore she heard Atropos snort from her post at the door. She was getting confused again, that question sounded like Ida didn't know either and was trying to trick her into telling.

"Ah. Of course." The lingering doubts were crushed by Ida's smile. Lia smiled back brightly, which seemed to dampen hers. "You've been handpicked for this task. I will accept nothing less than perfection in performing it."

Another snort. Lia was too nervous to stop giving Ida her full attention to glance at Atropos and check if it was indeed her. "I will do my best, ma'am."

"That brings us to the purpose for this meeting." Ida looked at her like she was judging cattle. Despite not standing it still felt as if she loomed over her. "While most of your orientation will be handled by Atropos, there is one important part that I wish to handle myself."

Lia couldn't move, by fear or magic she could not tell. Whatever fae trickery that had snuffed out her desire to run was gone but her legs would not obey her no matter how much she was internally screaming at them to flee from this hag. Ida was toying with her, letting her realize her helplessness before sealing her fate. Lia finally stole a glance at Atropos, for help or maybe just to not look her captor in the eyes. The maid stared straight ahead, her faint smirk the only implication she was a witness. The door lock clicked from behind her as if she'd waited until being seen to do so.

A tendril of white hair slithered up the seat and lightly turned Lia's head back to her glowing red eyes. "It is rude to look away when being addressed by your lady."

"You're not allowed to touch me," Lia said timidly. She hadn't meant to, it just slipped out, but the hair quickly retreated as if fearful somebody else was watching. Her memory wasn't helping so she let her instincts speak for her again. "We have an agreement. I'm off limits."

Ida's malicious joy faded as she narrowed her eyes. There was a caution in her tone now, one that was trying to hide behind a calm steel of authority. "Worry not, I won't lay a hand nor hair on you...so long as you behave, of course. The House, though, has standards and I can't make exceptions." Her smile curled further when Lia fearfully tried to return one. "Let us go over the Rules of the House, shall we?"

The only times Beatrice von Closen wished she was a winged fae was when she wanted to sneak out of her window. Of course if it was as easy as that, the windows would've had bars.

This wasn't so much a problem as it was an annoyance. Beatrice could leave the House, of course. With an escort and itinerary. It was hard to enjoy herself when her enjoyment was pre-planned and vetted by her mother.

So if Beatrice wanted to venture out on her own she was forced to do what she was doing right now, sneaking through the halls of the House moments after sunset. A task not easy in a dress, but she'd learned early on she shouldn't wear her civilian cover clothes until she had too. If a maid spotted her and she didn't notice, they'd not have to ask what she was up to. And every servant in the House was an unwitting snitch.

However, in her normal attire of aristocratic dress, if one spotted her—

"Lady Beatrice? What are you doing up so late?" a maid who'd rounded the corner asked.

Beatrice smiled as her blue eyes glowed. "I'm not. I'm in my bed. You didn't see me."

The maid's eyes emptied and she gave a faint nod. "I didn't see you."

Beatrice sighed with relief. Atropos knew everything the staff knew, but there was a buffer if she wasn't looking. "In fact, whenever

I am supposed to be in bed, you will not be able to see me unless I address you. Do you understand?"

"Yes, mistress," the maid said in a distant voice.

"Good. Wake up." Beatrice's eyes stopped glowing. The maid blinked a few times, staring straight through her with a befuddled frown before shrugging and continuing her walk.

Beatrice was a natural enchanter. That was no surprise considering she was a fae. Glamours and enchantments, to twist and trick the senses, were what fae were known for. Still, even compared to fae she had talent with enchantments in specific. Her eyes were a Von Closen family trait, she could instill a command into almost anybody with just a glance. With enough time she could lay enchantments that would give her complete control over the thoughts and will of those trapped by her gaze.

It made Beatrice feel lonely.

Perhaps that's why she was so skilled in the subtlety of enchantment. She could convince herself that her personality was what did most of the work. That her eyes and her status weren't the only reason people were inclined to obey her. It wasn't like she needed it, considering the entire staff was so heavily enchanted some probably didn't even remember their own names.

If Beatrice wanted to talk to somebody who didn't sound like they were reading from a script, she had to leave the House and unattended at that. By now she'd reached the closet near the gardens that had her civilian clothes hidden within. Getting out of her dress took much longer than slipping into the simple hood and tunic, a set that was well made but passable as poor. There was a key to the garden gate in one of the pockets, acquired after one of her attempts to climb the wall ended in her shoulder losing a battle with a garden wall spike. After being painfully taught climbing was not her forte, she'd enchanted one of the gardeners to make a copy of the key and then forget he had once it went missing.

As Beatrice slipped outside into the gardens, strolling more casually now through the maze of thick shrubbery and well-maintained bushes, she heard it. The animalistic screech declaring this was a very bad idea to try tonight.

Clotho was on the hunt.

That wasn't right, the head maid went out not but two days ago, she almost always waits a week at the least. If she caught Beatrice out on the town her mother was certain to hear about it. It wasn't a guarantee she would see her, Clotho probably wasn't hunting for fae so maybe she could try to avoid her. But why *was* she hunting? Was there a sudden need for new staff? Or maybe a specific skill set was being searched for. Or maybe Clotho was bored, it was hard enough to deduce a pattern for that fate in particular and it was even harder to avoid her if Beatrice didn't know what her hunting grounds pertained.

While Beatrice mulled over the decision of going out or giving up early, she heard rustling in the bushes. The only reason anybody would be out here this late would be to look for her.

Had Clotho smelled that hint of fear and circled back? Or maybe Atropos came across the servant from earlier and deduced her memory was just a little off. Lachesis would be able to spot her enchantment a mile away but she operated on the "I won't tell so long as you don't get caught" rule of snitching. Beatrice braced herself, preparing to put every bit of strength into an enchantment to stun whichever fate had found her. Fae enchanting fae was taboo at best and impossible at worst. Even with her gifted gaze, she'd only get a minute tops to run. And then she'd just pray it was quick enough that they wouldn't realize they'd even been stunned in the first place.

Beatrice shot around the corner and immediately tried to pull back when she was met with the eyes of a terrified maid. It was too late, a glare prepped to stun a fate only needed a glance for the poor girl. Her purple eyes glazed over and the fear drained with every other bit of emotion as her jaw went slack.

"Oh my gods, what are you *doing* out here?" Beatrice asked, completely befuddled. She was expecting sharp teeth or a deadly glare when she rounded that corner, not a random cute girl. She was a tad shorter than Beatrice so maybe that was how she had missed her amongst the bushes. Her long black hair neatly braided down her neck and under the white frilly headdress implied she was one of the house maids. Which made her extremely out of place in the middle of the garden.

"Dusting," the maid said dreamily.

Beatrice looked between the duster in her hand and the shrubbery. "The bushes?"

"Yeah." The maid nodded.

"Why?" She was fascinated now.

"I was told to dust the north side of the House."

Beatrice hid her face, she was trying not to but the idea of this girl taking such a request so literally made her laugh in a way she hadn't in a long time. The maid giggled with her as if in on the joke. "And you assumed that also meant the gardens?"

The maid nodded again. "The gardens on the north side."

Beatrice gave a sympathetic smile. This was sounding like a poorly placed enchantment. Left alone to mindlessly clean and nobody noticed her slipping outside. The green grass stains on her white apron implied she'd been out here for some time. "You must be new."

"Mhm. New." The maid smiled droopily. "I like your eyes."

Beatrice felt a flutter in her chest before remembering the cause for that coerced compliment. "I suppose they're quite enchanting."

"Enchanting." The maid's eyes were fighting to stay open. Her duster slipped from her hand and fell to the ground, forgotten. "Good word. They're...they're all..."

"All you can focus on? Getting lost in them as they draw you in?" Beatrice pulled back and smiled as the maid leaned forward like a moth to a flame. Instincts were taking over, she couldn't help speaking softer and slower. "All your thoughts drifting away. Nothing else in your mind but a desire to watch and listen."

The maid was starting to slouch. Her words now a drunken monotone. "Watch. Listen."

"Sleep." Beatrice was lucky to catch her, she went down like a tree. "That's it. Just sink and sink, deep into sleep." Her heart was racing as the maid seemed to be trying to curl up in her careful cradle. "You are quite receptive, huh?"

The maid only managed to drool onto her shirt as a response. Beatrice was embarrassed, she really went overboard with this one. "In a moment you'll open your eyes but still be asleep. You'll go to bed and when you wake up tomorrow all you'll remember is coming out here to dust and finishing up without seeing anybody."

The dreamy smile turned into a frown. "Ok."

"Is that a problem?" The sadness in her voice cut Beatrice's heart like a knife. Already she'd overdone what should've been a quick memory wipe but letting this end on a note like that was a wound she would not be able to endure.

"Don't wanna forget," the maid mumbled, "Wanna remember you. Remember your eyes."

Twice she complimented her eyes, twice it made her heart flutter. "Well, aren't you precious?" Beatrice petted her head gently and felt a very tiny nod. So adorable. "I'll compromise. You won't forget, but when you wake up tomorrow you'll think this was all just a wonderful dream. Does that sound better?"

"Better," the maid said with a faint smile.

"Good." Beatrice guided her to her feet. "Eyes open, but still deep in trance." The maid's eyes were glassy and empty. "Off to bed, darling. Enjoy your sweet dreams."

Beatrice watched as the entranced maid wandered inside like a sleepwalker. She frowned as she realized she hadn't even asked for the girl's name. Normally a pointless endeavor, by the time she learned the staff's names they'd already be gone and replaced. But now there was a sting in her chest like she just lost the chance to ever see her again because she hadn't even cared to ask who she was.

The night was young but the window of opportunity was gone. No point in going out if Clotho was out hunting. Beatrice sighed and decided to return to bed as well. She couldn't stop thinking about that last encounter though. How eager she'd been to put the girl into a trance, letting her have dreams about fateful encounters with a hooded fae with blue eyes in the garden.

Maybe that was why the maid was in her dreams that night too.

Chapter 2
A New Day

Despite not actually spending the night on the town, Beatrice was certainly failing her tests like she had.

In all honesty she'd forgotten they were occurring today. Beatrice had walked into the library to spend the morning reading and found Atropos waiting to ambush her with them. The head maid had left a proxy servant to keep watch.

Beatrice was quite aware that it was arrogant to expect results from not studying, but she was fairly certain she wasn't so daft as to not even remember the lessons these questions were referencing. She could almost feel Atropos's gaze watching her through the dazed servant, judging her poor attempt at summarizing the power shifts her family had decided to influence for the last year. Apparently a random new offshoot of studies about governance she'd suddenly decided to test her on. Or perhaps just to punish her for never caring to pay attention properly and thus not be able to call her out for being tested on something that was never taught. While her tutors were professors borrowed from nearby universities, the head maid tended to judge her progress. After all, Atropos knew everything the enchanted academics knew.

Beatrice had hoped that she would've been allowed to study abroad once she came of age a few years ago. Or at least a university that wasn't the House. She didn't exactly have ambition for any specific fine education but an excuse for relocation made the idea enviable. As both an aristocrat and fae she should've been given offers, but her mother had decided for her that the best education was one that she had control over.

Ida believed that about a lot of things.

It didn't help that Beatrice was distracted. As she tried to remember her lessons the maid from the gardens kept appearing instead. All the faces she recalled became a girl with purple eyes and a bright yet sleepy smile. Every time she pushed the image back down it nagged at her, like she had missed something in analyzing her memory's poor mockup of the cute maid. She needed to find that girl, perhaps if she had more than a passing glance in the dark she'd be able to ease her mind.

It was certainly better to think about than the disgrace of a test Beatrice had just left for Atropos.

Finding a lone maid in an estate this large was not something she was going to manage and so she was searching for the fates who could. Or fate, as it was, as Atropos and Clotho were not exactly ones she was inclined to approach for assistance. One would never tell and the other did not care to know.

Lachesis, however, was always more than glad to converse with her. It surprised Beatrice the fate did not appear the moment the thought struck, as she seemed to often take pleasure in unnerving her with such simple acts of foresight. A few more moments were spent waiting just to be sure. No sign of her.

This did not sway Beatrice's resolve, rather formed a rare occasion of needing to find Lachesis first. Luckily she had already noticed the puppeteered gait of a passing servant, a telltale sign of the enchantment being tapped into by her. She followed the maid along the corridors until reaching a large ballroom. The head maid was inside, directing a good dozen staff to carry in tables, set up decorations, a very well-coordinated preparation for an upcoming social event clearly underway. The summoned maid added herself to this trove of controlled servants, meshing in as if part of a trained team.

"Good morning, Lachesis," Beatrice said as she approached.

Lachesis turned her head and every head in the room turned with it. Beatrice never got used to that. The maid waved her hand and the staff continued as if nothing had occurred. She was a master of crowd control, even Ida had trouble directly controlling more than a few thralls at best but Lachesis could mimic a hive mind with her talents. "I'm surprised to see you awake, my lady. Did we decide to turn in early?"

Beatrice got a flutter of excitement that Lachesis had deduced her attempted outing from the very maid she was searching for. Her heart saddened when she spotted the first maid from last night, the one from the hallway rather than the garden, amongst the workers she was directing. She was now dressed as a laborer rather than a servant. "You could say that."

Lachesis smirked and turned back to her task. "Well, I'm sure you'll find a better night to catch some fresh air soon. I'd suggest waiting till after the soirée, though."

"I thought it would be a fitting distraction," Beatrice said. While Ida need not bother preparing the event itself, her schedule still should've been filled and thus a good time to sneak out unnoticed.

"Hmm, perhaps, but what I mean is you should take the time and actually prepare for it for once. Maybe you'll enjoy this one."

Lachesis whipped her hand and a servant in the distance suddenly jumped back, narrowly dodging a set of poorly stacked chairs falling on him. "Gods I was lazy last year with the cleanup. Clotho already had to overstock the staff, I'd rather not have to hear her complain about going out to collect more."

Beatrice didn't remember them hosting last year. Then again, she barely enjoyed those types of social affairs, dull conversations with other fae families who talked to her like a mouthpiece of her mother rather than her own person. It didn't shock her that she didn't care to remember the last one. "Speaking of which, what do you know about a new maid? A girl, about my age, half-elf I think?"

"Half-elf? I don't think we—" Lachesis gasped softly. Her lips curled into a devious smile as she turned so fast her skirt twirled with her. "Do you mean Lia?"

Lia. The name fit her well. "I can only assume. How long has she been here?"

"Oh she's a fresh catch. Really fresh, I think Atropos did a rush job," Lachesis said. Her sudden interest was a bit unnerving.

"I'd have to agree on that. I found the poor girl dusting the bushes last night," Beatrice said.

Lachesis stifled a laugh. "I'm not certain that was the enchantment's doing."

Beatrice raised an eyebrow. "Truly?"

Lachesis shrugged. "I wouldn't be surprised if she wasn't caught so much as just wandered onto the estate. I wager she'll last a week and then get tossed back. She's enthusiastic, sure, but Atropos can only do so much with a blank page."

Panic rose within Beatrice. She could already see Lia performing such innocent mistakes in front of Clotho or gods forbid Atropos.

They'd eat her alive. Perhaps literally in Clotho's case. "Where is she now?"

Lia hummed to herself as she swept the shelves of the library clean. Dusting was currently the only thing she knew how to do, as apparently putting on a maid uniform did not teach you how to maid. She'd assumed one of the three head maids would've taught her by now, not that she was complaining they hadn't because they were *terrifying*. Atropos especially, who did somewhat teach her a few basics after Ida taught her the rules. Lia had gathered up the courage to ask if she could see her sister after her day ended and got a scowl she hoped to the gods she'd never have to endure a second time. The head maid told Lia to keep dusting the north side until she returned. She never did.

It was unfair, Lia was supposed to be allowed to see Diana, that was the deal. Atropos hadn't technically broken the agreement but she obviously was dodging it. That didn't stop Lia from spending the morning looking for her sister, if her bosses were going to play on technicalities then she technically didn't need permission at this point. Sadly the House was so huge she got lost and ended up in an empty cellar with a boarded-up window. It must've been broken recently as she had to go get a broom and sweep up the remnants of some glass somebody had missed. It was clear she wasn't going to see Diana until Atropos caved. Maybe Lia would complain to Ida next time she saw her.

That unpleasant thought made her shudder. Lia sorta hoped she'd not have to meet with the Lady of the House a second time. She'd already blotted most of the first time from her memory.

Lia's memory in general had been really weird lately. Dusting wasn't exactly a thrilling activity but she was really good at zoning out to deal with stuff like that. Which did lead to her not always remembering things, so this wasn't too concerning. Still, she'd never zoned out so hard before she didn't remember going to bed. She didn't even take her uniform off. At least she remembered to take off her shoes.

To add to it all, Lia had a really weird dream. In it she was out in the gardens and heard a terrifying screech. It made her skin crawl and she felt like a cornered animal, looking for somewhere to hide. A shadow leapt from around the corner and she almost screamed.

Then Lia was captured by the most enchanting eyes she'd ever seen. They were beautiful as blue sapphires and glittered like a night filled with stars. Fear became a foreign concept, thinking about anything else was, well, unthinkable. The eyes drew her in until they were all she could see and all she cared about. She was willing to do anything for them, she *wanted* them to command her. Lia wanted to do nothing but watch, listen, and obey.

The eyes commanded. Lia obeyed. Then she woke up. That was all she could put together, not what the commands were, not how she followed them. Lia just dreamed that she did and it made her feel wonderful. That was ok, sometimes dreams didn't make sense.

A dream didn't explain the grass stains on her apron.

"Pardon me, but can I have a moment of your time?"

"Sure!" Lia spun around and froze as she locked eyes with...with the eyes! The sapphire eyes that sparkled like stars, they were five feet away and staring at her. Somehow her dream didn't live up to reality. In her dream she was cloaked in darkness where only her eyes shone through but now she saw a flawless face with silver hair that flowed like rich threads down her beautiful dress. The eyes weren't needed to make her stunning but with them she was mesmerizing.

The phantom from her dream made a face and Lia realized she was just standing there like a moron. She bowed her head in a panic. Whoever this was, it clearly was not a fellow servant and she was being rude gawking at them. "Sorry, sorry, uh, forgive me, my lady?" She glanced up, unsure if she was supposed to keep bowing. Or if she even addressed her correctly. "Can I...help you?"

"Yes, actually," her phantom said with a voice just as alluring as she'd imagined. She held out her hand. "I was hoping you could tell me if you are Lia."

The phantom of her dreams was Lady Beatrice von Closen, daughter of the Lady of the House. Lia asked if calling her Bea was okay. She made a face, but said she'd allow it for informal moments.

"What exactly are you doing in here?" Bea asked. In theory that should've made Lia nervous, a noble asking what one of her maids was doing, but strangely she was put at ease. She sounded genuinely curious rather than annoyed.

"That's a good question." Lia gave a tiny shrug. "I'm sorta just dusting until somebody tells me otherwise. Libraries are known for being dusty, so it felt like the right place to start. Do you know what I'm supposed to be doing?"

"Do you not know?" Bea asked with bewilderment. "Not to be rude, but I'm not a maid, how am I to know?"

"Well, it's your House, right? Shouldn't you have things for me to do?" Lia shrunk down. "Please don't make me ask Atropos, she's scary."

Bea smiled with understanding. "I would never be so cruel." She looked around. "Well, what have you done for previous assignments?" Lia wouldn't make eye contact. "Is this your first assignment?"

"This is my first job." Lia rocked back and forth on her feet nervously. "I thought I'd get some form of training. And they did teach me some things. I know the rules, I know where a lot of the supply closets are. But everyone else walks around doing things like they were all at a meeting that I didn't get invited to."

"I can try and make a list." Bea pursed her lips as if that made her think of something, but shook it off and sighed. "I know it's your job but I don't like the idea of me just giving you a list of things I don't want to do."

Lia smiled brightly. "That's ok, I'm happy to help." She gave the best curtsy she could with this oversized uniform. "I live to serve."

Bea covered her face, but couldn't fully hide her blushing. Lia didn't expect that reaction and blushed herself, maybe that was a bit too much for day one?

Before either could continue a woman, another house maid if to guess from her uniform, burst into the library with burning red eyes and a sour expression. Lia may be new, but she was certain the way she stormed towards Bea was not the proper way to address their lady. The scowl was uncannily identical to Ida's. *"Beatrice, please be a dear and visit my study. We need to have a discussion. In private."*

Lia shrunk down as the maid turned to her. She wasn't sure what the hierarchy beyond the top three was but this woman certainly glared like she was above her. "*Return to your duties. Now.*"

Lia lowered her head shamefully but Bea put a hand out to stop her from leaving. A voice in the back of her mind stirred in response.

Rule Three : Ida's authority supersedes all others if conflicting orders arise.

Lia winced as she resisted her legs trying to leave like they were late for a meeting. She wanted to listen to Bea but she couldn't break the rules. She had to obey Ida, had to return to her duties. But what *were* her duties? Nobody had freaking given her any. Well, she just told Bea she lived to serve, so...listening to Bea would be her duty. Lia sighed with relief as the solution eased her mind. No rules broken. No need to worry. No need to think about them.

What was Lia just thinking about? She shook her head, she really needed to stop zoning out. It was rude to do right in front of Lady Bea.

The scowling maid shivered as her eyes changed to green. She politely bowed with a calm tone and accent that had not been there before. "Apologies for the interruption, my lady."

"Can you tell me why she wishes to see me?" Bea asked, unphased by this very odd interaction.

The maid smiled nervously. "Any remnants left by the Lady of the House shouldn't be shared like gossip, my lady."

Bea's eyes seemed sharper for a moment, from Lia's angle she almost thought they shined brighter. "It's not gossip, just clarification."

"Clarification," the maid repeated, sounding distant. "She wasn't happy. I felt like you'd done something wrong and I wanted to strangle you for it the entire time I was searching for you."

"You were looking for me? That's odd, why didn't she just..." Bea looked at Lia as she trailed off. Not in a bad way, almost like she suddenly realized Lia had something she wanted. "You aren't enchanted by her yet."

Lia smiled, a bit confused. "Umm, no? What does that mea—"

Bea's eyes glowed and the world melted away. Every part of Lia relaxed, shoulders, legs, even her eyelids drooped but refused to close because then she couldn't keep staring. It was so wonderfully identical to her dream that she started thinking this was one. A small part of her kept asking what was happening. The eyes told her not to listen to it and the eyes were winning that debate easily.

"Go to my chambers and wait for me." Her voice was even smoother now, like melted chocolate coating her thoughts.

"With pleasure, my lady," Lia heard herself say in a blank tone. She meant it too, suddenly her entire existence was dedicated to finding Bea's room and waiting there. However, there was one small problem that rose to the top of her mind and then bluntly spilled out from her lips. "I don't know where that is."

"Oh. Right." Bea turned to the other maid and thus broke away her gaze. An unfamiliar jealousy burned within Lia, why did *she* get to look at them now? "Lead her to my chambers, then forget you took her there."

"Yes, mistress," the maid said without any emotion. More reason she didn't deserve to look at them, she clearly was ungrateful.

Although mistress was such a better word, internally Lia was stealing that.

Bea turned back and smiled at her. "She'll lead you."

"Thank you, mistress," Lia said happily.

Bea patted her cheek. "Aww, that's cute. You really are enthusiastic. But you need to run along, your guide is getting away."

The desire to stay and the desire to obey was battling harshly, but her legs won this time as they tried to catch up to the fast-paced maid. Even after they were far out of view Lia could still see the eyes, popping her thoughts like bubbles and making her giggle with delight.

What a wonderful day this was turning out to be.

Chapter 3
High Expectations

What a fascinating day this was turning out to be.

A blank page, Lachesis had said. She failed to mention not even Ida had begun to write in it. No wonder Beatrice was so taken by the girl, she was basically just a normal person who was a little confused as to how she was hired in the first place. Lia was almost a rogue element with how untethered she was.

Beatrice felt a little bad for pouncing on her like that at the end, but she just wanted to make sure she didn't end up in Atropos's lap. Otherwise the head maid would not waste any time turning the ditzy half-elf into a dull dusting doll like the rest of the staff. There wasn't any harm hiding Lia away until she could properly assess what she wanted to do with her.

What *did* Beatrice want to do with her? She was acting like she had some grand plan, but laying out her actions made her sound like she was just hiding an untrained maid in her bedroom. Sure, Lia was interesting but it wasn't clear why letting Atropos properly enchant her felt akin to turning her in. Like it would ruin what made her intriguing. Perhaps she just wanted somebody with an actual personality to talk to.

Or perhaps Beatrice wanted something else. Something more.

I live to serve, Lia had said, the flimsy curtsy she gave having been beyond adorable.

Beatrice blushed as she reached the hall that led to Ida's study. She'd heard many people, servants and loyalists alike, say those words. Most of the time they made her roll her eyes. Even the fates saying it would make her feel disconnected, a pledge to her mother rather than any earned loyalty to her. If anything it would make Beatrice feel as though she wasn't allowed to truly know them beyond their roles.

Lia said it like she meant it, joyful and genuine. It made Beatrice's face flush and ignited a flutter in her chest that she didn't quite recognize. Like her heart yearned for her to act but to do what she did not know.

Perhaps hearing it again would help her learn.

"Enter."

Beatrice opened the door to see Ida sitting behind the desk with her hands clasped underneath her chin. Strands of her hair were hard at work signing forms and some tendrils even nodded along as if they were reading them. Even with the split focus, Ida's red eyes were locked on her as she scowled with disappointment. "Sit."

Beatrice closed the door behind her. "I'd rather stand."

Ida pursed her lips. "That is quite the attitude to have. Do you know why you are here?"

"Because you called me for a private meeting," Beatrice said. Despite the obvious backtalk, Ida would be more disappointed if she gave in too soon. They were fae, their words were their weapons and this was how they sparred.

"Why do you think I am meeting with you?" Ida rephrased.

However, like sparring, endless dodging would be childish. "Atropos has spoken to you about my recent test scores."

Ida narrowed her eyes. A look that said Beatrice was wrong but was not certain if she knew that or not. "This is to discuss your recent escapades in leaving the House unattended."

Both their eyes lightly glowed as they matched gazes. Externally she was as still as a statue, but within she was in a mad scramble to build a new defense. The scripted answers explaining her poor academia were useless. She feigned ignorance to buy time. "I am unsure of what you are referring to."

"Oh? Would you like Clotho to create a list of how many times she spotted a little fae in the wild while on her hunts?" Ida sneered at her. "Or perhaps have Lachesis describe the amount of work it took into repairing your shoulder after a strange encounter with a garden wall spike? Maybe even Atropos recounting having to vet the entire staff to uncover how many of them have been unwittingly enchanted to not be able to see you after dark?!"

Beatrice was starting to wish this had been about her failed tests. "I'm a grown woman, I have a right to leave the House."

"You're also an heiress who's too valuable to risk being offed by a random street rat." Ida leaned in. "Why do you fight the idea of simple supervision?"

Because it was hard to enjoy a night on the town with the uptight killjoy, the rabid dog, or the attention whore. "Why do you feel threatened if you cannot see me at any given moment?"

The battle of fae eyes was strong. Ida conceded first and turned her focus to a letter on her desk. Her hair put a pen in her hand as she resumed writing where she'd left off. "Given the dip in your academics, I suppose it doesn't quite matter what my opinions are. You are in dire need of an attendant. Perhaps having some personal attention will encourage an end to these unwarranted absences as well assist in your education."

Beatrice cursed herself, that earlier admission had been used to seal her fate. An extension of her mother to lurk over her shoulder and report everything back to her. First her freedom, now Beatrice was about to lose her privacy.

Unless... "I think that is a point we can agree on. I've actually already taken one of the recent catches to be my new handmaiden," Beatrice said with an innocent look. Now she knew exactly what she wanted to do with Lia, the idea fit so perfectly it was like she'd planned on it from the start. She could accept her mother's proposition and uproot her underhanded intentions at the same time. "I'd appreciate it if you didn't interfere with my enchantments by having the fates implant the normal routines." *Or you implant yours.*

"Really? I'm glad to hear you're finally taking an interest in a personal thrall. Which one did we go with?" Ida didn't even look up, the smug tone of victory slipping through her facade of indifference. She'd asked as if Beatrice had just chosen a new hobby.

"The one I was talking to before you summoned me. Lia, I believe her name was."

The tip of her pen broke against the parchment. "*No.*"

"No?" Beatrice frowned. That wasn't a response so much as a reaction.

"No, you shouldn't choose her." Ida regained her composure. Her indifference couldn't hide her contempt. "There's a dozen better candidates amongst the last catch, I'd rather you picked somebody who's going to last longer than a week."

Beatrice smirked. So, she was correct, Ida didn't have a direct line to Lia yet. And she couldn't stop her without admitting that's exactly what she had planned on. "I think she's perfect. A challenge is good for the soul after all."

Ida stood up, her hair hoisting her over the desk so that she now stood in front of her. "I hope you realize that being your handmaiden will not shield her from von Closen standards. We have rules, you know; with ourselves, the courts, and the city. Personal feelings are not enough to overturn those."

"Of course not." Beatrice held her ground. This was just fear-mongering, once somebody was on their property they *were* their property, the courts of the fae declared it and the city agreed with them. "But as her lady, it will be my judgment as to whether she is upholding them."

Ida's red eyes glowed. "Where is she now?"

"Awaiting further instructions," Beatrice said, but she could already feel her mind being broken into like a parent disrespecting a closed door to search their child's room. It was both painful and humiliating, memories being tainted by false additions of judgmental red eyes. It didn't matter, Beatrice had long since learned how to hide things from such brutish tactics. Just like a bedroom, a mind can be organized and private thoughts can be hidden under the metaphorical bed. Her own eyes started fighting back. "Her training and enchantments will be left to me."

Ida slapped her. Or rather a tendril of hair did it for her. Even without puppets she preferred her strings. "Don't you *dare* try to use your eyes on me, young lady!"

Beatrice stepped back, closed her eyes, and bowed. In a way, she'd won. Ida always said physical violence showed a lack of control. "Apologies. My emotions got the better of me."

A moment of silence lingered between them before Ida huffed and her shield of indifference returned. "As did mine." Her hair carried her back over the desk. "It's been a long few days. For both our sakes, don't make the next ones longer."

"Is something giving you trouble?" Beatrice asked. Outbursts like that were rare but it was rarer for her to admit fault so willingly. Something else was going on.

"Nothing for you to concern yourself with. Unless you wish to explain to the Deburios why they cannot bring an entourage of nameless into *my* House for the soirée." Ida glanced at her. There was still suspicion in her eyes, but by now it was clear she wasn't going to tell her why. "I suppose I should be glad you finally have taken a handmaiden, even if it's not one I prefer. I'll be quite busy so if anything...out of the ordinary occurs with her, please don't hesitate to ask Atropos for assistance. The mind is a delicate thing, after all. We don't want you to break hers."

Beatrice entered her chambers, groaned, and ungracefully flopped back onto her bed. That was awful. And strange. Her mother wasn't usually this contradictory, but every time she was about to bubble over with rage she overcorrected to indifference. Perhaps the preparations truly were getting to her, but why Lia would incite that she couldn't quite figure. Perhaps she'd ask Lia herself.

Wait.

Beatrice shot to her feet. "Lia?"

"Yes, mistress?" Lia was standing off to the side, smiling brightly with her hands clasped in front of her but still had the dazed eyes of an enchanted servant.

"How long have you been standing there?" Beatrice had completely missed her when she walked in.

"I don't know." Lia closed her eyes as if calculating in her head. "The clock in the library said twelve fourteen when I saw it last."

That was hours ago. Beatrice wasn't sure what she was more shocked by, the fact Lia was still in a trance or that she'd been standing at attention the entire time. "You must be exhausted, you should sit down."

"Yes, mistress." Lia did not find a chair and instead just sat on the floor. She looked up at her like a lost puppy.

There was no way in hell Beatrice could let Ida anywhere near this girl.

Still, why Ida acted so odd about her wasn't clear. She was young, much younger than most of the staff. She wasn't very maid-like either. Not to say she was unkempt, she wore a more simplistic version of the maid's uniform. It just looked like a costume on her. In proper lighting her dark hair almost looked like a shade of violet, matching with her eyes. And she smiled a lot, Beatrice had noticed that when she met her. Even now, entranced and uncaring that she was basically being judged like a show cat, she had a contagious bright smile. It was hard to resist returning a grin from such an unrelenting expression.

Not that Beatrice didn't enjoy returning it. It was nice to have a reason to smile. "Lia, is there anything important about you?"

Lia didn't answer for a fairly long time. Her brow furrowed as her feet very faintly tapped against the floor. "I'm a good artist?"

Beatrice hid a laugh. "Noted." She sighed. It didn't matter, she should focus on protecting her from her mother before worrying about the reasons she'd even care to meddle. It wasn't like either of them were going anywhere anytime soon. She held out her hand. "As cute as this is, I think we should have a proper discussion. Would you mind getting us some tea?"

Lia's smile was brighter than ever as she took it. "I'd be happy to, mistress."

"Thank you. Please, have a seat."

Lia found herself placing two cups of tea down on the desk Bea sat at. A second chair had been pulled up for her. She blinked a few times. "You're welcome?" She sat down and pretended she remembered what she was in Lady Bea's room for. Or when she had gotten tea. "Am I in trouble?"

"Far from it. I'm in sudden need to fill a vacant position." Bea took a sip. "You're quite new. I thought it might be best to start with a fresh hire rather than have to break old habits."

Lia sipped at her cup to be polite. She didn't like tea and her face couldn't help but show it. "So, you have a specific job for me?"

"Indeed." Every glance from Bea seemed like it contained a thousand thoughts. It was like this was a test of some kind but Lia had no idea what she needed to do to pass. Or if she even wanted to pass. "I would like you to be my lady-in-waiting. A handmaiden, as it were."

"Really? Like, my job would be just to be around you all day?" Lia definitely wanted to pass.

Bea hid her laugh. "I suppose that's one way to put it." She took another sip. "Companionship is a main duty. Your chores will also revolve around my needs rather than the House's, but I'd rather go over that later. Right now, I want to learn about you."

Lia tapped her feet nervously. "To test if I'll be good at the companionship part?"

Bea nodded with approval. "Precisely."

"Well, can I ask a question first?" Lia asked.

"Interesting strategy, but I'll allow it."

Lia almost asked if she was in the garden last night. "Why me?"

Bea put her hand to her lips to ponder. "Truth be told, I've actually never had one. The head maids acted in a similar fashion, so the only reason for a handmaiden would be my own desire. I never found the right person, you may say. So this will be a learning experience for both of us." She moved her hand to hide her expression. "I suppose you could say I just found you interesting."

Lia blushed with embarrassment. "Don't see my kind often in high society, do you?"

"While you may be the only half-elf currently on staff, I've certainly seen them before." Bea took a sip of her drink. "I've met many types of creatures, darling. I'm more interested in who you are, not some commodity of what you are."

"Oh. Well, thank you." Not that Lia wasn't actively trying to hide her demon side, she just assumed Bea could tell what she was. Sure her horns were so small that her hair could hide them if she did it right but her ears were more batlike in their curling than elven. Apparently even fae were prone to not noticing the difference off hand. Her heart was starting to race, she didn't know what her lady was focusing on. Bea was way more interesting than her. Looking elven but a hint of etherealness implying something even more surreal. A silver hair color that no human could have, sapphire eyes that shone with sharp intelligence. What about Lia would a girl like that be interested in? "At least somebody is interested in me, Lady Ida—sorry, the Lady of the House doesn't seem to even want me here."

"Truly? Curious that you still are then, her wants are usually not ignored." Bea raised an eyebrow. "Is there a reason you're here?"

Lia nodded. "Yeah, I need to be here."

"Need to?" Bea tilted her head. "May I ask why?"

Lia frowned. She'd said that so confidently but the reasons all but hid from her as she tried to remember specifics. "Because...I'm a good maid and belong to the House?" She winced at her strange response. That wasn't untrue but it didn't feel like the right answer. "I mean, better than the streets. It's nice to have a roof over my head."

Bea held her gaze for a moment, then softly smiled. There was an unmistakable disappointment that hurt Lia's soul to think she caused. "I see. Well, I can assure you that if you serve under me, you will be protected from both Ida and the streets."

Lia was comforted by the casual offer of such protection. She'd actually been worried Atropos wanted to toss her to the streets even more than Ida. The agreement made it clear they weren't allowed, but fae were tricky. The lack of training certainly felt like the head maid trying to get her sacked for incompetence. Even Bea hadn't been quite sure what Lia had been doing in the library but luckily instead of firing her she offered to help.

That alone made sticking to Bea seem like a good way to stay safe. Now she was offering to actively look out for her and Lia was smiling even brighter than normal at the generosity. "Thank you, my lady. That sounds like a dream come true." A familiar thought rose at the mention of a dream and she couldn't stop it from tumbling out. "Were you in the garden last night?"

Beatrice raised an eyebrow. "That's an interesting question."

"Sorry, it's probably nothing," Lia said in a panic, "I just had a weird dream."

"Indeed?" Bea put her hands on her lap and leaned in. "Do tell."

It wasn't clear why telling Bea made her heart race, like admitting to having a scandalous dream about her before she even knew she existed, but Lia couldn't back out now. "It's sorta dumb. I must've just dusted a lot yesterday because I dreamt I was dusting in the gardens, but that's silly. And there was somebody who looked like—well, no, I didn't see what they looked like but they had the same...eyes? Except I didn't see anything else. So maybe there wasn't anybody there." She was stumbling over herself with embarrassment and wishing she hadn't brought this up. "Sorry, it's hard to put into words. Just meeting you gave me—"

"Deja vu?" Bea said.

"I don't know what that means, but probably?" Lia cringed. She was messing up this entire thing by being weird. Her new role was slipping out of her clumsy grasp.

"Deja vu, like you've felt or seen something before but can't recall why," Bea kindly explained.

"I guess that's it then, yeah." Lia was glad she didn't seem to be making fun of her for not knowing that. "Sorry, it was just a strange dream. I shouldn't have brought it up."

"No, no, this is good talk. I love hearing about dreams. The House does seem to invite strange ones." Bea's eyes glowed. "I'd just enjoy them instead of questioning them."

All this talk of dreams must've been making Lia tired, it was suddenly much harder to keep her eyes open. Her smile started to droop. "Yes, mistress."

Bea pursed her lips. "Just a glance and you're already slipping under." She set down her teacup. "I'm curious, how do you feel?"

"Calm. Relaxed. Entranced." That last word felt right but she didn't know why she knew it. It was hard to describe, probably because it was hard to think at all. Like she was perpetually falling asleep. "I like your eyes."

"You said that last night too." Bea smiled to herself like it was a memory she was fond of, then sighed. "I do apologize for my forwardness, but if I don't enchant you, my mother will. And we don't want that, do we?"

"No, mistress," Lia said. She much rather it be Bea than Ida. It was against the rules for Ida to enchant her.

"Good girl." Bea hid her face as Lia shivered. "Did you like being called that?"

Lia gave an enthusiastic nod. "Yes, mistress."

"I see." Bea reached out and lifted her chin. Lia hadn't even realized she'd been leaning closer. "From now on, hearing 'good girl' will make you feel twice as good as what that just felt like. Do you understand?"

"Yes, mistress," Lia said.

"Good girl." A shameless moan escaped Lia as a jolt of pleasure shot through her body. Bea herself was blushing, but quickly regained her composure. "I'm getting ahead of myself. Those little things should be saved for after we lay the groundwork enchantment."

"Yes, mistress," Lia said, unsure of what that meant but ready to do whatever was required. "Does this mean I'm your handmaiden?"

Her cherishing smile was almost more alluring than her eyes, at least until the glow suddenly increased tenfold. "Almost, darling. You've certainly caught my eye. All you have to do is keep staring into them. Just watch my eyes and listen to my voice until it's all that is left in your mind. Then you'll officially be mine."

Lia was all but resting her head in Bea's hand. Her body slumped against the table as she leaned even further than she already was. She didn't even react when she accidentally knocked her teacup onto her lap. Nothing else mattered but those sapphire eyes. All she could focus on was being as close to Bea as possible. Even now they were close enough to share a kiss.

"Letting my words become your thoughts. Letting my will become yours."

A kiss would let her be closer. She wanted to be closer.

"Sleep."

Lia's eyes fluttered shut and sunk deep into empty bliss.

Chapter 4
Enthralled

Luckily the apron caught most of the tea.

Beatrice felt a bit guilty for not preventing that but she had been too caught up in the act. Truth be told, she'd never actually enchanted somebody like this. Oh sure, she'd entranced people to give suggestions or instill subtle commands, mostly just to help not see her sneaking out. She'd had meetings with those already under their thumbs in what she could only describe as maintenance of puppets. The art of enchantment was a skill she was quite proud of and yet the act of instilling her will to create a thrall was something she'd never done for herself.

Lia was, as it were, her first. And she was finding the experience much more intimate than she expected.

Perhaps being surrounded by those already far gone past the first stages had skewed her perceptions, but the staff always felt stiff and lifeless. Enchantment and just demanding was no different. Lia on the other hand was like putty in her hands, open and almost eager. Enchanting her was invigorating. Perhaps a fae instinct she'd never truly been able to act upon until now.

Beatrice guided the deeply entranced half-elf in taking off her apron and using it to clean up the parts of the mess it hadn't caught. Given the circumstances she had her sit down on the couch.

"Sleep," Beatrice whispered into her ear and caught her as she went limp. No drinks to spill this time. "Deeper and deeper. Sinking so deep that nothing but my voice can bring you back up."

Lia smiled as though she was having a wonderful dream. Beatrice was going to lay her next to her but she couldn't get herself to let go. The only contact enchantments needed were the eyes and never had any other servant inclined her to go beyond that. Yet her yearning heart demanded she continue cuddling with the entranced girl. To hold her close, make her feel safe and secure both in mind and body.

Protect her from what, though? Perhaps from Ida, Lia seemed to have some inkling of her mother's dislike for her as well. She was very light too, Beatrice worried she was malnourished. That was a sad possibility, the types not to be missed were usually not in the best of circumstances and her mention of fearing the streets implied such a fate. Beatrice made a mental note to make sure she received proper meals to mitigate that.

Still, those were tweaks for later. For now Beatrice needed to set a baseline, a foundational enchantment as it were. Nothing too overbearing, the more she thought about it the more she decided she didn't want a thrall. She wasn't her mother. She gently stroked Lia's hair as she began to whisper into her ear. "Now, I want you to repeat after me. I am a handmaiden."

"I am a handmaiden," Lia obediently replied.

"My purpose is to serve my lady."

"My purpose is to serve my lady."

"I live to serve and obey my lady."

"I live to serve and obey my lady."

"My lady is Beatrice von Closen."

"My lady is Beatrice von Closen." She swore Lia sounded more delighted to say that than the others.

"You may stop repeating." Beatrice stifled a laugh as Lia cut herself off halfway through repeating that. "These are important parts of your being. If anything conflicts with them, I want you to tell me immediately. Even a hint of doubt will give you the urge to inform me. Do you understand?"

"Yes, mistress."

Not much of a protection as she but it would let Lia warn Beatrice of any enchantments from outside sources without incurring the wrath of resisting them. It would not be good to have Lia telling Ida no to her face. "Now, let's go over some rules. First, when you are in trance, I am your mistress. When you are not, I am your lady. You will address me accordingly. Do you understand?"

"Yes, mistress," Lia said. While obvious at the moment, it was best to have a separation between her awake and entranced self. Beatrice had noticed she already seemed to be doing it naturally so she just cemented the idea.

"Good girl." Beatrice got a rush as Lia squirmed in her embrace. Good to see that suggestion took hold. "Do you remember how you felt when you slipped into trance?"

Lia paused, then lightly nodded. "Yes, mistress."

"Tell me."

"Calm. Relaxed. Entranced."

Beatrice nodded with approval. "I'm going to start to bring you up. You're not going to surface, but instead reach that level feeling right beneath it. Do you understand?"

"Yes, mistress."

"Okay, let's begin." Beatrice frowned as Lia whimpered. She had a feeling as to why. "Did you wish for me to compliment you?"

"Mhm," Lia muttered, "Was I not good?"

"You're doing great, don't worry. Don't think. Just listen to my voice." Beatrice was glad she caught this early. That whimper hurt to hear. "That phrase is a reward. That doesn't mean you aren't doing well if you don't receive it, ok?"

"Okay, mistress," Lia said softly.

Beatrice pet her head. "Repeat. Obedience is pleasure. Serving is my reward."

Lia sighed. "Obedience is pleasure. Serving is my reward."

"Good. Now, what is your purpose?"

"To serve and obey my lady." Lia was taking her suggestion well, she sounded proud saying that.

Beatrice nodded. "And what is fulfilling your purpose?"

Lia's face scrunched as her muddled mind clearly tried to connect the thoughts instilled. She sighed as if a revelation hit. "A reward and pleasure, mistress."

"Precisely, darling." Beatrice smiled as Lia was beaming now. Still, even after fixing it she couldn't help herself as she leaned in to whisper. "Good girl."

A very small moan escaped Lia from the surprise praise. Beatrice was glad she didn't have to try and hide her face heating up. She didn't quite intend for *that* to be the feeling that phrase induced, but she didn't exactly wish to remedy it. She just needed to make sure she didn't say that when others were around.

Although, that sounded tantalizing. Lia standing at her side, embarrassed as she unable to resist a small moan from just a whisper of praise from her Lady. Beatrice never had such desires before. Now she had a cute girl in her lap, her mind at her mercy, and it was stirring things within her she did not know she could feel.

Beatrice buried the scandalous thoughts. She needed to focus. "With that settled, tell me again what you felt when looking into my eyes?"

Lia smiled. "Calm. Relaxed. Entranced."

"Exactly. Now, feel yourself rising to the surface, your thoughts returning but still fully asleep. All you feel is calm, relaxed, and entranced. Up and up," Beatrice sat Lia up to match her words. She turned her head towards her. "And open your eyes."

Lia obeyed. They were dreamy, as if already lost in the eyes that were waiting for her. Otherwise she looked mostly back to her normal self. Just in a light trance.

As much as Beatrice enjoyed seeing the girl go under, she wanted to make sure there was consistency to how deep she fell. She couldn't have Lia collapsing from a glance. "This is the state you'll return to from my eyes alone enchanting you. Every time it'll become more seamless, not even a trance but a reflex of your obedience. When in this state, everything I say is the truth. When in this state, everything that occurs is normal and when you leave it you will not feel any concern. Do you understand?"

"Yes, mistress," Lia said with a bright smile, only a hint of it drooping.

"Let's test it, shall we?" Beatrice stopped enchanting her.

Lia blinked a few times. She looked around as she patted her uniform. "Where did my apron go?" She glanced over at the table. "And weren't we sitting over there?"

Beatrice noted she seemed confused but not concerned. Perhaps she should work on altering her perception when leaving trance entirely to not question things. Tweaks for later, for now her eyes glowed. "No, we were sitting here the entire time. Don't worry about your apron."

"We were sitting here the entire time. I won't worry about my apron," Lia repeated with a glassy look that lasted a few moments after her eyes stopped glowing. She then smiled brightly. "So, did I pass?"

Beatrice couldn't help but give in to that infectious smile she had. "Yes, darling. You are officially my lady-in-waiting."

"Great!" Lia said with excitement. She stood up and gave a flimsy curtsey. "I'll try to do my best. I live to serve you now, my lady."

"I'm excited to see where this journey leads us." Beatrice's eyes glowed. This was testing the limits but also she was just having fun now. "However, you are not a half-elf. You are a cat."

"I am a cat," Lia repeated blankly. She blinked, staring with a very uncertain silence that made it unclear if she was fighting the suggestion or confused by its broad nature.

At least, until she meowed and then licked the back of her hand.

Lia knelt down onto all fours, her posture and attitude adorably accurate to a feline. She rubbed her face against Beatrice's dress, meowing again, then jumped onto her bed. She yawned widely and even kneaded the blanket as a cat would before laying down.

Beatrice sat down next to her and gently petted her. Her heart was yearning again and while she still could not precisely pin what it desired from her, the warmth from this was sating it for now. Lia was so cute, leaning into her hand and smiling with enjoyment of her mistress's attention. Although her uniform didn't quite match up with her new feline identity. Of course no uniform would technically fit a cat.

The thought lingered as her mind started to wonder what kind of body that ill-fitted outfit hid. She gently stroked along the resting maid, running her hand along the curves of her body. Lia rolled to the side with her arms tucked in, allowing Beatrice to discover her chest certainly did not feel malnourished. She blushed as she realized she was all but feeling up her new handmaiden and yet the scandalous follow-up was already rising in her mind; Why leave it to the imagination? It wouldn't even take more than a glance at this point, Lia would easily accept the fact cats don't wear clothes.

Except if she was told this, would she just start acting annoyed as a cat being forced to wear clothes would, or would she quickly remove the clothing that made her reality inaccurate? Suddenly the scandalous thought had curiosity to hide its intentions behind and her eyes started to glow. "Lia—"

The moment was rudely ruined by a knock at the door. Beatrice rolled her eyes, somehow she knew exactly who this was. She tilted Lia back to her original resting position, causing her eyes to slightly open with droopy confusion. "Enter."

As expected, Lachesis walked in and smirked at the maid curled up next to her. "Enjoying ourselves, are we?"

"What I do with my handmaiden is my concern alone," Beatrice said. Lia perked her head up with her eyes locked on the maid and an expression of accusing suspicion. It was interesting to see what was most likely Lia's feelings coming through the animalistic responses. She must have a wariness towards Lachesis. "Is there something you need?"

"Well, I heard through the grapevine about Lia's new position and hoped to borrow her to get a proper set of outfits in the works. Seeing as the Seelie Soirée is upcoming, I would like to get a rush on making your pet presentable."

"If you're willing to put resources into that, I assume your prediction for how long Lia will last has extended beyond a week?" Beatrice asked. She pet Lia's head, causing her to lean into her palm.

"Oh certainly. Now that she's in your hands, I wonder if she'll ever leave." Her tone implied that was her plan all along but then again, she always implied that. Lachesis could make decisions as innocuous as butter or jam sound like something she influenced. "May I borrow her tomorrow for a fitting?"

Beatrice was uneasy despite it being such a simple request. "So long as she doesn't leave your sight. She's still fresh, I don't want Atropos to break her out of spite."

"Of course, it should be her lady that breaks her in," Lachesis said with a mischievous smirk.

Beatrice narrowed her eyes and put a defensive hand on Lia's shoulder. Not as intimidating as she'd hoped as the enchanted handmaiden licked it in response. "May I ask what you are trying to invoke me to do?"

"Isn't it obvious? You need to practice those fae eyes you have and that girl is receptive. A perfect test doll." Lachesis smiled coyly. "Think of all the things you could do with a pretty girl like her wrapped around your finger?"

Beatrice hid her face. She couldn't know. She was certain Lachesis couldn't read minds, she couldn't possibly know her fantasizing. "That would be quite immoral."

"Interesting choice of words considering the state of your pet right now, but you always were a spoilsport," Lachesis said, "Still, you need to practice building enchantments, even with your talent of coercing to the core so smoothly. You can only improve so much in the mirror and I doubt you're the type to go hunting like Clotho. Or tormenting the staff like Atropos."

"Or pretending you're not holding the strings, like you?" Beatrice asked.

"The Lady of the House holds all our strings, my lady. I'm just practiced in seeing the threads." Lachesis eyed the window as the faint screech of Clotho echoed. She sighed, gave a bow, and began to leave. "Enjoy your evening. I'll set up a fitting for tomorrow."

"Oh, and Lachesis?" Beatrice said before she closed the door. "Don't call Lia a pet in front of her. Or me, now that I think about it."

Lachesis looked like a wave of fatigue hit her. She raised an eyebrow. "Is that a *command*, my lady?"

Beatrice hadn't even realized she was trying to enchant her. It was hard to describe how she used her eyes, usually it was akin to the feeling of glaring. She knew her eyes were glowing, albeit a rare moment she hadn't intended to and thus closed them. "A request."

"Hmm." Lachesis turned away. She sounded disappointed but in what it wasn't clear. "Very well, I shall keep it in mind."

Beatrice would've been more off put if she wasn't used to her tendencies. It was just Lachesis's nature to be indirect. Growing up she'd always be dusting shelves containing novels she clearly thought would interest Beatrice or ask leading questions that usually helped her avoid her mother's wrath. Considering Atropos was Ida's lady-in-waiting, perhaps Lachesis had hoped Beatrice would take her in a similar manner.

That would explain her interest in Beatrice taking Lia as her handmaiden. It did not illuminate if that interest was out of love or jealousy, though. Maybe she *should* have made that request an order.

Or perhaps that comment was meant to invoke her to think about the distinction between commands and requests, thus making her more wary of something else. This was the dangerous rabbit hole that was trying to follow the threads woven by Lachesis. It was always better to not stress about where they led and instead make sure none were wrapped around your neck.

Lia was staring out the window with a pout. She looked worried, scared even. Clotho was on the hunt again, the hunting call must've spooked her. That was so odd for her to go out twice in a row, did the staff really need that many extra bodies for the upcoming soirée?

"It's okay, darling," Beatrice whispered as she stroked her hair. Lia closed her eyes and rubbed her head into her palm. She swore the girl was actually purring. Still, that fearful pout returned if she looked at the window. "No need to worry about what's out there anymore. You're safe here."

Beatrice had seen the horrors of the city firsthand. The slums were filled with demons and devils warring like cats and dogs, as pointless as pigs squabbling over the quality of their mud. There wasn't a middle class so much as a class that meets in the middle between living barely and barely living.

Who wouldn't want to be taken away from all that? That thought didn't feel like her own. After all, Beatrice could attest that some prefer dirty freedom over pristine prisons.

Then she heard the tearing of fabric.

"Lia! Down!"

Chapter 5
RELOCATION

Clotho prowled along the rooftops, a blur to the naked eye. The demon had been more clever than she'd anticipated. The trail went cold in a stable, the mixture of smells and wiping the blood on old iron horseshoes distorted her senses.

It had been some time since Clotho had been on a challenging hunt. Collecting new staff was always easy, picking off strays that wandered too far from the light. This was different. This was a true hunt, a battle of wits with a predator now turned prey. The rest of that night had not borne fruit beyond one thing. The demon was avoiding a part of the slums very deliberately, even giving up chances to fully lose her pursuer just to avoid hiding in that particular area.

The demon didn't want Clotho venturing there. After a conversation with her sister fates, it became very clear why.

Clotho had her ways of staying unseen but tonight she needed the city to know she was here. She delivered her hunting call with every other leap, made sure her footsteps were heavy and her growls echoed along the alleys. Every living soul now knew a terrible fate awaited anyone who went to the old church in the slums, half-buried with its bell tower all that could be seen from the without a overhead view.

It was always hard to tell if an abandoned church was safe for the unholy to enter, most devils and demons just opted to avoid the places wholesale instead of risking burning alive from stepping a foot on ground that was still a tad too hallowed.

Except Clotho had a feeling this church had a little help in speeding along its desecration. She prowled through the broken rooms and empty halls until she stood in the nave, the moonlight shining through the stained glass of an angel flying down from the heavens with a sword outstretched. Where a preacher would normally stand was a perfectly drawn glyph, months old but clearly the purple of demon blood. A very simple way of desecrating a church, but a demon couldn't have made it this far in to make this.

A half-demon could, though.

Clotho could smell the traces of them. She'd already hit a few of their other old haunts but this one smelt the freshest. This was where the demon would look first. And realize she was already too late.

That's the trick to luring out a fellow predator. They need to be given a reason to hunt you down.

The air whistled too harshly to just be the wind. Something was flying. Flying *fast*.

The stained-glass window shattered. There was barely a moment to comprehend the demon crashing into her and hoist her into the air. Like most demons she was large and muscular, pale skin tinted purple with bat wings the length of her body. Unlike devils with horns on the front of their heads, hers were on the sides pointing upwards. Her purple eyes burned brightly within the black voids they sat in instead of whites. "Where is she!?"

Clotho had never felt so alive. She cackled like a hyena before sinking her teeth into the demon's neck. Blood, fresh and filled with emotions so sweet, fueled her as she latched on like a bear trap. The demon screeched and flew them both into the wall, then another, a wild animal throwing herself at anything to get her to let go. The momentum was unstable and the two plummeted back into the ground.

The demon tore Clotho off with a force that meant she took a solid chunk of her neck with her. She raised a clawed hand and swiped down hard but stopped mid strike. Thin strings reflected in the moonlight, with several more wrapping around her and tightening as she collapsed. She thrashed and screamed with a ferocity that would've broken chains of steel but could not even stretch the thread. "Fucking fae! Cowards! Worse than vampires!"

Clotho slunk to her feet, spitting the bloody patch of flesh out. She snarled at Lachesis appearing elegantly from the shadows, her hands playing with a web of silver threads that lead to the entrapped demon. "I had her."

Lachesis smiled coyly. "From my point of view, you were playing with your food."

"Benefits of the job," Clotho growled.

A third voice interrupted. "Except when it's in conflict with our orders." Atropos now stood with them as if she'd always been there. She sneered at the demon like she was a stain on the floor and motioned to Lachesis. With a simple few tugs the demon was standing upright, still wrapped like a fly in a spider's web. "I see this one is full-blooded."

Clotho licked the blood off her lips. "Can confirm."

Atropos was now face to face with their prey. The demon spit in hers. "Fuck *off*, you *fae **fuck***. Where is my sister?"

"Where she belongs." Atropos had the faintest hint of a smile as she pulled out a pair of thin scissors so sharp that reality seemed to bleed when she opened them. "You, however, are not. Yet."

Chapter 6
Dressing for the Role you Want

Lia's entire world had changed overnight. Which was strange since it felt like her world had started two days ago.

The new quarters were so nice, much closer to Bea's room and it was all to herself! She only spent two nights in the servants quarters and that place was clearly going for quantity over quality. It reminded her of an army barracks, dozens of beds side by side with little to no personalization or privacy to it. Now she had her own bed, a desk, even a nice view of the northern gardens. There was a stack of paper and pencils with a small note; *For recreational use.* She wasn't quite sure what that word meant so she was scared to touch them.

Lia never had her own room, she and her sister moved around too much. The best she got was ransacked children's rooms in abandoned churches. Maybe she'll actually remember going to bed now that it was nearby. This time Lia woke curled up on her pillow. She'd managed to take off her uniform but hadn't managed to put on anything afterwards.

Lady Beatrice had been a nice surprise. Lia assumed after meeting the Lady of the House that her daughter would just be a younger version of her. Cold and condescending. The head maids were like that too, she thought she'd have to start practicing a mean face to work here. All three seemed to have their own personal version of one.

Bea was nice though. She might've held herself high but she didn't look like she despised those beneath her like Ida did. Lia didn't realize Lady Ida's white hair was actually faded silver until she saw the shining silver set Bea had. In her opinion it looked much better on her lady than the Lady of the House. And now Lia's job was just to assist Bea specifically and that sounded way more fun than dusting.

Although now Lia needed to figure out how to be a handmaiden. She still wasn't quite sure how she got this job but she'd somehow stumbled up the chain to a lady-in-waiting and didn't want to give her lady any reason to toss her back. Dusting was the only maid part she'd picked up. She was fairly certain she wasn't supposed to dust Bea, so instead she'd spent the early morning in the kitchen to make her lady breakfast and immediately got distracted by the peak of high class cookery; the toaster.

It had to be magical. She'd snuck a peek inside to see if any tiny fae were doing the work but it was just some twisted metal. Now Lia wasn't stupid, she could guess how it worked. Sorta. It was just so strange that they had a dedicated tool for toasting things.

Maybe the von Closens just really liked bread. Lia should learn how to make bread for her lady, that felt like a good place to start on being a handmaiden.

"What are you doing?"

Lia yelped as Lachesis had snuck up behind her. She quickly bowed as she recomposed herself. "Sorry, I'm just...practicing?"

Lachesis leaned to look around her. There were seven pieces of toast on the counter. "Seven settings?"

The toaster dinged. "Eight."

"I see. Well, Lady Beatrice has given me permission to borrow you, but feel free to deliver her breakfast beforehand. We wouldn't want your hard work going to waste." Lachesis stole the fourth piece off the counter and took a bite as she left. "Also, your lady likes it at the second setting. And prefers butter instead of jam."

"Any other advice?" Lia asked. Perhaps on how to make more complicated foods. Or how to do laundry. Or do anything around here.

Lachesis didn't look back as she turned the corner. "Atropos makes her rounds on the hour. She hates crumbs."

That was in five minutes. Lia looked back in horror at her toasted doom. "Uh-oh."

Beatrice raised an eyebrow at the pile of toast on her desk.

A single piece had been buttered and put on a plate. The rest sat on a napkin like building material for a gingerbread man who couldn't afford the ginger in his renovations.

Confusion did not save the snack from being devoured with extreme prejudice. Such a simple delight but honestly she'd eat nothing but bread if that was an option. Beatrice smiled at what must've been the pile of trial and error. Lia was trying so hard and the honesty about her failures made her adorable.

It was a great example of what made Lia so disarming. She was just so...simple. It felt rude to say but Beatrice loved how simple her new handmaiden was. She could trust her because she did not feel complex enough to have her kindness be a facade. This wasn't a slander against Lia's intelligence. Sure, her word choices were pedestrian and her head was a tad empty, but that just added to her charm. Those flimsy curtseys and tacked on my lady's, the way her eyes would light up with excitement at things Beatrice would find commonplace. Lia was a ditzy, joyful half-elf and it made her the most unique maid in the entire House because she felt real.

And Beatrice wanted to keep that realness all to herself.

Even now her thoughts drifted to wondering when Lachesis would return her handmaiden. How odd that Lia not being at her side already felt out of place.

So apparently the House really did have a million rooms because instead of being taken outside to a seamstress shop, Lachesis led Lia to the south of the building and through a backdoor of a large dressing room. There was a shift in the air as they stepped through the door, even though they were still inside it was similar to when one would leave a house on a rainy day. That sudden shift of smells and airflow. Several women were milling about and Lia caught a glimpse of an entire shop full of clothing through a door one of them was moving to and from. She knew her nose wasn't perfect but the place smelt like it was close to the ports. That couldn't be the case though, that was on the other side of the city.

As soon as the door closed, every employee froze in place and looked at them in sync. It creeped Lia out and she stepped behind the head maid, the only thing that stopped her from just running back through the door. Lachesis pointed at two of them. "You two, with me."

The two bowed while the rest resumed their jobs as if nothing happened. Lia gave a nervous smile. "You run a tight ship, huh?"

"You could say that." Lachesis smirked. She pinched the edge of Lia's sleeve and dangled her arm. "Atrocious. Barely fits, and that color does not work well with your hair. We have work to do."

The two seamstresses whisked Lia to a set of mirrors with Lachesis looking her over like a show dog. She was ordered to strip to her underwear, which felt very unnecessary but so did half the measurements that were taken after she did so. Lia wasn't quite sure what the head maid was doing, she seemed to be in her own little world. She tried to fill the awkward silence. "Does Lady Beatrice own a pet?"

Lachesis coughed as if something had been caught in her throat. The two seamstresses froze for a second before continuing, like reality had a hiccup. "What makes you ask?"

"I just noticed she needs new curtains." Lia shrugged. "Looks like a cat tried to climb it."

"I am unable to say if Lady Beatrice has any pets," Lachesis said with the "inside joke" smile Lia had started to call it. "I'll make note of acquiring new curtains. It's good that you're already thinking in such a way, it'll make you a fine handmaiden if you keep it up." She tilted her head as her eyes lowered to Lia's chest. "I see why the outfit was so ill-fitting. Those don't quite match the average of your height, Atropos must've just gone up a size."

"Well...yeah." Only now did Lia become a bit self-conscious about her lack of clothes. She hadn't been ready to be called out for being top-heavy. "I didn't think measuring needed me to be undressed."

"Oh it doesn't." Lachesis ignored her reaction to that and snapped her fingers. "Okay, yep, I got a good idea going now."

The mirror shimmered. Lia saw herself reflected in an amazingly cute maid outfit, more akin to a well-tailored dress with an apron than a uniform. "I look so good! Did you just make this up on the spot?"

Lachesis nodded. "A creative mind always desires an outlet. I'll weave a few versions, let you have a variety to pull from. I'm sure Lady Beatrice would enjoy that too."

"This mirror is so cool." Lia did a twirl, amazed that the reflection made it seem truly there. She even could fiddle with her sleeves, although once she stopped they returned to their place like a rubber band snapping back.

"It does make my life quite easier. A step out of imagination without having to waste the resources on seeing if it works." Lachesis held out her hand and one of the seamstresses handed her a list of measurements. "I'll have this one done before you even leave. The rest by the end of the week. I suppose you won't need fancier undergarments." Lachesis smirked as a much more suggestive set of undergarments appeared on Lia in the mirror. "Although I don't quite know what Lady Beatrice has planned for you. Perhaps we should cover all our bases?"

Lia blushed at the implication. She'd never worn anything like that before. "Do you think Lady Beatrice is going to have me working in my underwear?"

"You can never guess a lady's tastes from a glance." Lachesis raised an eyebrow. "Is that a duty you'd desire?"

Lia refused to say. Her red face might've answered for her. It was probably just teasing anyways, why would a beautiful aristocrat like

Bea ask a street rat like her to do that? She still hadn't even figured out why she chose her as a lady-in-waiting. The only "interesting" thing she could think of about herself was something Bea didn't even seem to *know* and Lia did not want to risk losing her job by correcting half-elf to half-demon. There had to be better options. Maids more qualified or fancier, like Lachesis.

"Oh, to be a new handmaiden, fresh eyes and an open mind. I envy you, you know?" Lachesis said as if she'd been listening to her thoughts. She closed her eyes and sighed. "Although I envy many under our employ. Yet no matter how close I am to them, it's not the same. It's been so long since I've experienced the real thing."

"I don't really know what you mean. Like, you wish your job was simpler?" Lia asked. All three of the head maids were weird, this one was a certain brand of it. The "forget why because she seems nice and then she reminds you why really fast" sorta weird. Probably the reason why she's not Bea's handmaiden.

"Sure. Something like that." Lachesis tapped her chin. "Now a formal attire for a handmaiden will take more than a glance from me. So do give me a moment."

"Like a party outfit?" The maid gave a nod. "Can you have what Lady Beatrice will be wearing in the side mirror?"

Lachesis pursed her lips. "I think I can manage that, but why?"

"Well, shouldn't mine compliment hers?" Lia explained, "And like, she's gotta be prettier than me. Not that I can't look good, I just shouldn't look better than my Lady during a party."

"Spoken like a proper lady-in-waiting, you pick up things fast." Lachesis closed her eyes. "A bit harder with her not here, so the mirror might be hyperbolic on what she looks like. The dress won't though."

The side mirror shimmered. Instead of Lia in a different outfit it was Bea who was reflected, still miming her movements like a mirror would. It sorta unnerved Lia to see somebody else reflecting her in a mirror, luckily the other two mirrors were still her so it wasn't unbearable. Although Bea looked very cute in a maid outfit.

Then the outfit changed to a dress. If it could be called a dress. If anything was going to be called hyperbolic, it was this dress. It was poofy, looked like a nightmare to move around in, and had several attached pieces that made the entire ensemble look like a flower arrangement rather than a person. Lia was trying not to make a face and failing. Lachesis tilted her head. "Do you think the ensemble is missing something?"

Oil and a matchstick. Lia could already see three things that just looked like they were tossed on because they matched the theme. She hadn't figured out what the theme was yet. "Did Bea ask for this?"

"No, the Lady of the House had a hand in the choices. Lady Beatrice had forgone showing to her fittings so she had us make assumptions." The assumptions looked more like punishments. A potato sack would've made a better dress.

Lia was nervous but she wanted to fix this tragedy in the making. That was her purpose now, even if she felt undeserving of it. A handmaiden should do everything she can to make her lady happy. A rewarding tingle of pride ran through her at the thought and helped steel her nerves. "As her handmaiden, I have authority to make decisions on her behalf, right?"

Lachesis's smile grew with understanding, "Do you have any suggestions?"

Chapter 7
Deepest Desires

Dressed for success in her cute new outfit, Lia started getting used to Bea's routine as she honed her skills as a handmaiden. And she started to see why her lady never had one before now. She didn't really *do* much.

That was mean, Bea did stuff, she just didn't do anything that required help that often. Lia certainly was making her morning routine easier: making her bed, brushing her hair, helping with the more annoying parts of putting on a dress. It was surprising to learn Bea didn't have a servant doing this before, there were so many of them it couldn't be from a lack of maidpower. Lia got a feeling her lady did it just so she would have something to do.

There were tasks Bea wanted to keep for herself still, like applying her makeup. Lia did ask if she could do it anyway to practice, makeup was very much a luxury that she had no experience with, and her lady was kind enough to allow it on occasion. Bathing was something she wanted to do alone as well. Modesty might not be the reason for that after she fumbled asking her lady about it. Lia's burning red cheeks were probably the deciding factor that it wouldn't be within her responsibilities.

After the morning routine, Lia's day would mainly just be refilling tea and retrieving meals already prepped by the kitchen staff.

Which did mean if she wanted to get better at baking she'd have to do it on her own time. Nobody ever seemed to interact with Bea outside of their duties, not even her own mother would eat dinner with her.

She must be so lonely, Lia thought. Her lady never acted outwardly sad about it. She implied Lachesis would eat with her sometimes. Given Bea let Lia eat with her as if she was an equal, it certainly seemed like she craved the company. Lia was happy to oblige, companionship was part of being a handmaiden after all.

The one thing Bea did seem to do a lot was read. Like multiple books at a time a lot. She seemed to have a spot for each one, as if she wanted the atmosphere to match the story, so Lia ended up seeing a lot of the House in a short amount of time. Sorta felt like a self-contained town with the variety. The feeling from the seamstress shop happened more than once, where the air and smell shifted so rapidly entering a room was like walking into a different part of the city.

The theory was magic, obviously. House bigger on the inside, rooms that felt like they belonged somewhere else, Lia could connect the dots. Mixed with how some sections seemed like they were from eras even older than the previous, hallways with armors on display and rooms still lit by ornate candles, the House appeared to be a collection of preserved slices of time. It didn't change with progress but consumed it, adding society's improvements to itself while never letting go of what came before. It put into perspective what timeless truly meant in regards to fae. Although Bea preferred the sections closest to her room, where the House nearly matched the outside world. They only tended to venture into the older slices for when the ambience was desired.

In any case, Lia was fully prepared to just stand around to keep her lady company and refill her tea but Bea actually was nice enough to let her draw when she was occupied. A lot of the time Lia was doing the equivalent of doodling in class while her lady was enduring dull lectures about history or governance. Apparently drawing was what the paper had been for.

"What did you think recreational use meant?" Bea asked, clearly trying to hide a smile.

Lia cringed with embarrassment. "I don't know, like, paper for writing letters for you? Noting things I need to remember. Shopping lists."

A laugh slipped out before she hid her mouth under her hand. "That would be stationary paper, darling. Recreational is just for fun."

Lia was grateful, but that didn't mean she was just going to slack off. She actually spent the first day doodling the dress she'd discussed with Lachesis and slipped it to her the next time she saw her. Both to help Bea and maybe get on the head maid's good side. Out of the three, she seemed on the best terms with her lady. And was the least scary. Mostly. That "inside joke" smile still got under her skin sometimes.

Lia did doodle other things. Mostly Bea, she would draw the rooms she found interesting and thus her lady would end up in the sketch. Sometimes she'd draw the city if the room had a window, although that was rare. Embarrassingly, she also started drawing Bea's eyes a lot. She didn't know why but they never turned out right. The sketches looked too...realistic. It was like trying to capture the feeling of the sunset by drawing it, it just wasn't enough.

It wasn't until the last day of the week that Lia got an answer as to why they might have captured her focus in such a way.

"Are you starting a new book?" Lia asked as she brought the wine and cups as requested.

Bea was sitting at the end of a small table in a room similar to the room she met Ida in. A designated talking room if she had to guess. "That's a curious question, what implies that?"

"Well, I've never been in this room. And I haven't seen you drink wine before, so I thought maybe a genre you weren't reading before?" Lia explained.

Bea stared at her. "Darling, are you keeping track of my reading by the mood of the room I sit in?"

Lia rocked back and forth on her feet. "I mean, you do only read mysteries in the library. And don't want tea with the thrillers."

"Well, sorry to disappoint, but this is actually for a meeting with a Sir Tauron. A sad little man, but owns quite the amount of land outside city limits." Bea held up a letter that was sitting in front of her. "He's been a bit squirrely as of late, I decided an in-person meeting would speed matters up. I feel as though he doesn't write nor read my letters directly."

"Ah, so the wine is for him?" Lia asked, worried about having already poured a cup.

"When it comes to his type," Bea took an unladylike gulp, "I advise to become a wine drinker."

"When he gets here, I'll be getting him, right? What should I say?" Lia hadn't really been prepared for a non-staff person to see her as a handmaiden yet. Sure, she had the outfit but she didn't exactly feel like she acted like one yet. She had sorta just been winging it and was lucky that Bea seemed to enjoy the end result of that. "Is there a formal introduction? Do I just be myself?"

"I can provide a welcoming phrase for you to work off of." Bea smiled as her eyes glowed. As always, Lia was instantly put at ease. "I'm sure you'll be able to repeat it perfectly."

Sir Tauron was a middle-aged man who looked like he'd seen what Lia imagined a rich guy looked like and made himself into a gaudy copy of it. He definitely wasn't going hungry with the way he looked, although his stretching clothes and unclosable jacket implied either that was a recent change or he wasn't the type of rich to be able to update his wardrobe over time. Diana always talked about that, she called them old money and new crusts. Old money was the von Closens, they had enough stuff to never buy again. New crusts, well, they hadn't learned that lesson yet.

Lia curtseyed. "Sir Tauron, the Lady of the House welcomes you to her humble abode. Please follow me to be received by her lovely daughter, my enchanting mistress, Lady Beatrice." That was a mouthful. She was surprised she remembered it but the phrase Bea taught her just tumbled out like she'd practiced it a thousand times. Well, almost, Lia tacked on 'lovely' and 'enchanting'. She liked how it sounded.

The potbellied man laughed, although it was more like a grunt pretending to be a laugh. "Normally it's a lass from that coven that retrieves me for these things. Tossing a new hire onto the pyre, are we?"

Lia smiled brightly, hoping her nervousness didn't show as she wasn't quite sure how to respond to that. "I am Lady Beatrice's new handmaiden. Please follow me, sir."

Sir Tauron grumbled another laugh and followed her. Although he was a haughty man, she caught a glance of worry when he seemed to think she wasn't paying attention. Maybe he was just thrown off, she would be too if she was expecting one of the head maids and then a maid like her showed up instead. Lia didn't give off the same authority they did.

"Have you met with Lady Beatrice often?" Lia asked.

Sir Tauron was startled by the ice breaker. Yep, he definitely was thrown off by it being her. Atropos probably didn't talk much and Lachesis most likely too much. Clotho...probably didn't escort people like him. "Yes, yes, not often but more than the Lady of the House. Only had the pleasure of that beauty once."

Lia did not think beauty was a word she'd apply to Ida but that was an inside thought. "Me as well. She doesn't seem to leave her study often."

"Ah, so even within the House the Lady is stationary. Are the rumors true then?" Sir Tauron seemed to be warming up to her. Or maybe just decided she would be more likely to tell secrets, not that she had any beans to spill. Nobody told her anything around here.

"I'm not sure what that means?"

"The Lady of the House, for the Lady appeared first and the House built around her unyielding will. This is the oldest house in the city, people say she never leaves because she can't move from the spot she sprouted."

"Oh! Uh, no, I've definitely seen her move." Lia paused. "Although I wouldn't find it hard to believe she has never left to see a hairdresser."

"Ah, her hair! To see it again, like a willow tree of the faewilds itself." Sir Tauron made a grumbling noise. "A shame I have been relegated to converse with her child ever since."

Lia frowned. "Please don't speak of my lady like that."

"Oh, come now, I meant nothing by it," Sir Tauron said with a few grumbles between. He really liked to grumble.

"Then you shouldn't have said it."

The condescending look Sir Tauron shot at Lia got her to see where Bea's description of this man came from. The rest of their walk was much quieter. Except for Sir Tauron's grumbles. Those didn't stop.

Bea's conversation with Sir Tauron was more scripted than her welcoming phrase. Every bit of small talk he tried had a response prepared to snip the conversation short. Every dodge of her questions had a path read to put him back on the defensive. Lia was familiar with planning a conversation over and over in her head but she'd never seen it play out in the overthinker's favor the way it did for her lady.

Everything came back to Bea's main problem. "Sir Tauron, this is not a debate. The soirée is far too close for us to replace your plot of land for the out of city arrivals."

"Beatrice—

"Lady Beatrice," Lia interrupted. She'd had to do this a lot. He hadn't gotten the memo yet and seemed to be doing it just to piss Lia off specifically. Bea didn't seem to care. Or she just had a really good poker face.

"Lady Beatrice, right, my business is my own. I just cannot uphold my end of the bargain, I do apologize greatly to her Ladyship of this grand estate."

"Well, I've done my due diligence to be civil." Bea's eyes started to glow. Lia knew they did that sometimes but she'd never seen her do it around somebody else. "Sir Tauron, do remember the will of the von Closens."

"The will of the von Closens is the will of myself. I do my duty to uphold their wishes," Sir Tauron said in a glassy tone. That was odd, it was like he'd been taught to say that in response to that phrase.

Bea's eyes glowed brighter. The man went slack jawed and that was enough for Lia, she was definitely doing something to him. "You will be honest with me. Why are you so adamant as to not allow us to use the lot for the soirée guests?"

"I must be present to allow that. My wife has been getting suspicious of my habits, I thought if I rescheduled I could use the cover to visit my lover in the lower city."

Bea pinched the brim of her nose. "You were defying our simple request, uprooting a very important event, because you wanted to fornicate without your wife knowing?"

Sir Tauron nodded. "Yes."

"You're an idiot."

Another nod. "I'm an idiot."

Lia finally realized what was probably going on here. It slipped out before she realized maybe she shouldn't call her lady right in front of her victim. "You're like, hypnotizing him."

Bea didn't even try to deny it. "Enchanting is the term. Hypnotizing is for vampires."

"What's the difference?"

Bea made a face. "That is a good question." She seemed more interested in thinking about that than the befuddled man sitting across from her, waiting for more instructions. "I think it's about permanence. With vampires it's like a snake catching the focus of its prey. Enchantment is more of an artform. Thin layers of magic laid upon the mind. Although the two acts do intersect, I suppose."

Lia was fascinated but her eyes had not left Sir Tauron. While Bea had stopped he still had a glassy, drunken look, barely taking in what was being said in front of him. "So, you've put an enchantment on him?"

"More so tapped into one already there, but yes." Bea turned to her with her elbows on the table and her hands clasped together. "This is a part of my responsibilities, so you will see it often. Does that concern you?"

"Not at all, my lady." Lia looked away, her mind racing as fast as her heart. Bea could enchant people. That made sense, she was a fae, messing with people's heads was what they did. It explained her obsession with her eyes. Is that why she thought Bea was cute, did she enchant her to think that? What if *all* her feelings were fake? Why did that make it hot? Did she tell her to think it was hot? Dammit, now it was even hotter!

Get a grip, Lia, you clearly just think the idea is hot, she hasn't done jack shit. Not that she would ever know if she did.

Bea had already turned back to the man. "Well, I think that you can try for that another night. An annual event of this degree is more important to you than some illicit affair. Don't you agree, Sir Tauron?"

"Well, yes, yes, I suppose I wasn't quick thinking with my brain on that one," the noble said with a jolliness that was not there before. "I do suppose I hadn't considered my importance to this event. Much more important than a night with my mistress. I am always happy to accommodate the Von Closens."

Bea sighed with relief. "Good. Then perhaps we can wrap this up quicker than I had anticipated."

"Is that all you're going to have him do?" Lia asked. It didn't really seem like much of an ask, she basically mind controlled him just to skip to the end of the meeting.

Bea raised an eyebrow. "May I ask what you have in mind?"

"I don't know, something silly? Isn't that what fae do, twist your mind and embarrass your victims," Lia asked genuinely. Diana always warned her about fae being able to mess with your mind. She warned her about a lot of stuff, she was very protective. She'd probably be telling her to leave the room just in case but Lia was too curious now. "He was sorta rude to you before he got here. He definitely would deserve it."

"I mean..." Bea paused as if contemplating a thought. "...I suppose it's been more business than play these days." She sighed. "Or all business. I loathe these meetings."

"Why?"

"It's boring. And easy. Like maintaining upkeep on a garden you didn't even get to plant." Bea looked at him, eyes not even glowing. "Slap yourself. It's customary today."

Sir Tauron did so without hesitation. The red mark showed he had not held back.

Bea waved her hand. "See? He's basically a walking puppet. What point is there for me to care?"

"I guess. So, without the work you don't really feel like it's a reward?" Lia asked.

Bea laughed. "That's a fascinating way to put it. Perhaps you're right."

Despite being far under the influence, apparently Sir Tauron's personality had not been vanquished. "I must say, your handmaiden speaks out of turn more often than not. A little strange for von Closens, usually you have quite the standards for your staff," Sir Tauron said bluntly. He gave that grunt of a laugh again. "I suppose handmaidens aren't always picked for their heads, are they? Wasn't aware you were the type to have a treat stand nearby to enjoy, Beatrice. I would've curtailed my offers to your liking if I knew."

Lia looked away in shame. Then she noticed Bea's eyes glowing brightly with the mask of pleasantness long gone. "It's quite a hot day, Sir Tauron. Perhaps the wine will help."

Sir Tauron's motions were sluggish, sipping at the cup. It looked like he could barely remember how his lips worked as his eyes were locked on hers.

"No, no, you need to cool down. That expensive coat must overheat you greatly, I'm sure a good splash would make you much more comfortable."

The noble didn't splash it so much as just let it slip from his hand and drench his outfit. The wine dripped from his chin like an untrained child. The man was utterly enthralled and Lia was worried if she even gave Bea a direct glance she might follow suit. Which honestly made it even harder to resist to a peak.

"Very good. Onto business. So, we agree that you should move your outing with your mistress to a different date. Perhaps you should ask your wife, I'm sure her scheduling skills are far more adequate in that regard." Bea gave the fakest smile Lia had ever seen. "In fact, I think your wife should come to the next meeting. That way I can catch her up on your responsibilities."

Sir Tauron looked confused. Not about asking his wife to reschedule his adultery, to that he had given a genuine nod of approval. "My responsibilities?"

"Yes, yes, we'll keep you propped up as a puppet of course, but it makes more sense to let her do the thinking so your time can be more open for your sexual rendezvous. It would help our end as well, I do believe this takes up a lot of *my* time trying to work it all out." Beatrice narrowed her eyes. "I was trying my best to leave you be. I normally don't care. But I do not take kindly to insults. And just as an insult against the staff is an insult against the Von Closens, one against my handmaiden is one against me. So your commentary insulted me twice."

Sir Tauron laughed nervously. "Beatrice—

"Lady Beatrice," Lia corrected.

He nodded, showing her much more respect than before. "Lady Beatrice, I meant no offense."

Bea's gaze was locked with his. "Oh no, you quite did. You insulted me in hopes I would punish you. I know you get off on women punishing you but I must say you should save those desires for your wife or mistress. I am not interested in men. They bore me. Although in your case there may be a general consensus, perhaps you should be more clear about those needs to your lovers. I'm sure they'd find you far more interesting when they realize your attitudes are just a show, a bait to earn their ire that you crave so deeply."

Lia was amazed at how seamlessly Bea was slipping in new ideas between her comments. She spoke so confidently that even she started to wonder if what she said was being planted or just something that was already true.

After those eyes capture you, is there a difference? Lia wasn't sure if the shiver she got was from fear.

"Yes, yes, of course," Sir Tauron said with a red flush. He stood quickly. "I think we've discussed everything, yes? I need to get home for dinner, I didn't expect this to take long."

"Out of curiosity, dinner with your wife or your mistress?" Bea asked.

Sir Tauron cringed. "My wife."

"Good, good. You have much to discuss with her. If she questions your actions just tell her it's the will of the Von Closens, that should tide her over. Although I doubt she will, if anything she'll be glad to not have to pretend she's not already doing everything for you." Bea's eyes glowed one final time. "Oh, do kiss my handmaiden's foot on the way out. Both as an apology and also an awakening. Groveling at our feet is where you belong, after all."

Lia was now the one blushing as the wealthy noble fell to his knees before her and gave her foot a peck. "Forgive me, miss." She was a bit glad Sir Tauron let himself out. It would've made the walk back much more awkward. Especially if the spell wore off before he was out the door.

"You didn't have to do that for me," Lia said shyly. *Not that I didn't mind.*

"That man is always a wealth of underhanded commentary. It's more efficient for me to just ignore, but..." Bea covered her face. Was she blushing? "...you didn't deserve to be berated. Perhaps an overreaction. It is not one I am sorry for."

"So you can just make people do anything?" Lia smiled nervously as she hadn't said her true question. *Can you make me do anything?*

"To say anything would be hubris, more than you think would be more accurate." Bea closed her eyes and only then did Lia realize she had been leaning towards them. "Every fae is different. For instance most can perform name thievery, but it is an artform I am not prolific in compared to those who can steal your name just from you thinking it too loudly. Just as such, most fae can enchant somebody, if they have the time and setup."

"But you?"

"I can lightly entrance people with a glance." Bea motioned to where the man had once sat. "And even more with a glare. Still, it does help to have a practiced silver tongue to pull them down and plant my suggestions."

That was clear as day. After that display, it was obvious Bea had a tongue so silver it matched her hair. "You wouldn't use them on me, would you?" Lia asked with a nervous smile. Why did she feel like she wanted her to say yes rather than no?

"Of course not, darling." Bea gave her a devious look. "Not that you'd ever know either way."

Lia got that shiver again. She was certain that time it wasn't fear.

————◇————

By the end of the week Lia had a tailored set of handmaiden uniforms, a beautiful dress for the soirée, and her own magic mirror. She'd mentioned how cool the mirror was to Bea and found one had been set up in her room the very same day. Lia planned on making a special breakfast, specifically toast made from bread Lia had baked after several loafs of practice failures, to thank her for it. Although she was worried she was staying up too late messing with the mirror to be able to wake up on time.

After fiddling around with it for some time Lia realized it was basically reflecting her imagination. If she thought really hard about the image of something, it would appear. Now she understood why Lachesis had her strip, she assumed it was just some kind of maid hazing but being in her underwear made it easier. Otherwise it looked like she was putting clothes over other clothes. The mirror could only reflect people and outfits. She tried to think of a garden and it looked like a tiny forest had grown on her. It wasn't clear if that was a mirror limitation or if she just wasn't that good at using it yet. She spent the night 'trying on' all her new outfits, her new dress, she even got it to reflect Bea again after practicing. She wondered if she could get Bea to stay but not reflect what Lia was doing. It always seemed to even if the person wasn't her, but maybe...

Lia imagined herself kneeling in front of Bea, then knelt in front of the mirror. Bea remained in place, standing in front of her. She looked up with a smile and Bea was looking down with her own signature smirk. It was almost like she was really here. Lia wasn't sure why this was her first idea but it felt natural. It felt right.

It felt like where Lia belonged.

Obedience is pleasure, The mirror Bea seemed to say. Her eyes glowing so bright, so beautiful.

Lia heard herself whispering, "Obedience is pleasure."

Serving is your reward. Those eyes could enchant her to do anything.

Her hand slowly slipped into her panties. "Serving is my reward."

Your purpose is to serve and obey. Enchant her to think anything.

She moaned as her eyes started to roll back. "Serve and obey."

Lia snapped out of it, the mirror changing back to just reflecting her. She took her hand out and hugged herself. What just came over her? That was...that was very inappropriate, Bea was her Lady, she shouldn't fantasize things like that. Even if it felt good.

It felt *really* good.

Maybe getting this mirror was a bad idea.

Chapter 8
ROUTINE MAINTENANCE

Lia was fast asleep when midnight arrived. Midnight on the last day of the week to be specific. The maid sat up rigid as if the bell of a grandfather clock struck loudly but the House was silent as ever. Her eyes only opened halfway, still fully asleep as her body left her bed to prepare. She ignored her new outfits, putting on her original ill-fitting maid uniform, and left her room in a silent march.

In the back of her slumbering mind Lia stirred with unease. Lia wasn't a maid, she was a handmaiden. She was Bea's handmaiden. She wanted to tell her mistress, no, she *needed* to tell her.

Rule Five : I cannot tell Beatrice about the Rules of the House.

The urge was snuffed just as fast as it had ignited. It came and went again, then again, over and over as she walked, strongest when she passed Bea's room and nearly reached for the door before it was extinguished. Lia's mind gave up after that and fell back into slumber as her body marched on to where it needed to be.

The walk to her unknown destination was long. The architecture became older and older, wallpaper turned to stonework, gaslights became candles that in of themselves looked crafted from a bygone age. Traversing deep into the center of the House where ancient brickwork gleamed as if it'd been laid the day before. Lia reached a door she did not know but her body entered like she had an invitation. Inside was an office where Ida sat behind the desk, her hair signing forms, shuffling through books on the shelves, and doing other random tasks while she spoke with Atropos. They both paused at her unannounced entry.

Lia didn't acknowledge them, her empty eyes locked forward. She elegantly curtseyed, wandered over to the nearest bookshelf, and began to dust.

"Well, at least *that* is still operating properly," Ida muttered with annoyance.

Atropos glanced at the clock being dusted and narrowed her eyes. "Except she's late. Puppet, why were you not punctual?"

Lia mechanically turned her head towards them. She wasn't speaking, rather something else was speaking through her. "Unknown. This maid left her room at the required time."

"Beatrice has already moved her, it would seem." Atropos turned back to Ida. "My lady, perhaps we should remove this routine. A lady-in-waiting is much more likely to be missed than a maid."

Ida didn't respond. Lia could feel both their eyes boring into her, but she didn't care. She wasn't being addressed so she needed to clean. It was the first rule. "Puppet, report."

Lia spun around, her arms dropping to her side as her entire body went rigid. The thing speaking through her made her sound like a tin soldier. "Lia Abith, house maid, five days since last report, seven hours unaccounted for, no rules broken." Lia stirred again. House maid? She wasn't a house maid, she was a handmaiden, they needed to get that corrected.

"Seven hours. Beatrice laying her enchantments, no doubt. Still, no rules broken, so no apparent cause for concern." Ida tapped her fingers together and turned her focus back to Atropos. Lia began to dust the shelves as if nothing had happened. "A coincidence. Several coincidences. You know how I feel about coincidences, my dear."

"There are more pressing concerns than Beatrice's fascinations," Atropos said, tapping a set of papers on the desk, "I reformatted her exams to gauge the damage and her scores were atrocious. This is far worse than I had anticipated, I fear for her mind."

Ida made a 'hmm' noise. "Beatrice's mind is strong. It is for that reason we are having such difficulties. This tramp I worry about more, I still think even allowing her onto the estate was a horrible idea."

Lia hadn't settled back into slumber like before, but had not pushed past zoned out daydreaming as she worked. It was very rude for them to talk about her as if she wasn't in the room, she could still hear them when she was cleaning. Sure, it was hard to focus on most of the time but her curiosity was breaking through with them talking about Bea. She wanted to be a good handmaiden and a good handmaiden should listen when conversations involve her lady.

"It was not your idea."

"Which further proves my point. Couldn't we just reset and reassign her to another part of the House?" Ida paused as if thinking of what the worst place would be. "Perhaps the servants quarters? The gardens? Maybe just leave her in the cellars with the other one."

Lia started to panic. She didn't want to stop working for Bea, they can't change her role. She was a handmaiden, Beatrice von Closen was her lady, those were just facts. They can't just change the truth like that. She really needed to talk to Bea.

Rule Five : I cannot tell Beatrice about the Rules of the House.

"My lady, do not forget the consequences that would have occurred if you had not employed her. We already were not holding up to the spirit of the agreement, meddling further may incite scrutiny." What would've happened if they didn't hire Lia? Well, she probably would've died, living on the streets wasn't fun. That was a big consequence but it would've been her problem, not theirs.

"But why must I hold myself to the agreement? It's not like she's around anymore to enforce this...this theatrical facade." Not around anymore? Had they *killed* somebody? The only person who'd have any relation to her get hired would be her sister, but she was here too.

Lia *had* seen Diana since she'd been hired, right?

"Because of traps that may lay within both their minds. We know not what she did in preparation."

"I am aware we have gotten to this point due to my underestimations, so I concede to your caution. Yet do you truly think there are such contingencies?"

There was an eerie pause. "I am unsure if we comprehend how far ahead she truly thought. Or if this deal was not a plan in of itself." Another pause, one that made Lia realize something very, very bad. And before she could fix it, Atropos said, "Puppet, why have you stopped?"

Rule One : When the Lady of the House is present the maid must never be standing about and must busy herself unless she is addressed.

Lia had stopped cleaning. She'd gotten so caught up worrying she'd broken the first rule. Ida and Atropos were both staring at her when she turned to them with glares that made her feel she wasn't going to be around anymore. "Just finished up. Wasn't sure where to go next."

"That's not the House talking." Ida raised an eyebrow. Her eyes glowed in the dim light. "Good evening, *Lia*. Were you listening?"

"Yes," the answer escaped her mouth before she could even think. Lia was much more lucid, up until now everything had felt like a dream. Not the wonderful dream like the gardens, but a nightmare that she only now was starting to comprehend she was in. One where no matter how much she wanted to run her body seemed to have forgotten how.

Atropos frowned. "How?"

Lia didn't know how to answer that. "With my ears?"

Ida rolled her eyes. "Did you understand what we were saying?"

"No." Lia rarely understood what they were saying even if she wasn't zoning out, so it wasn't a lie. And she felt to her core that she had lost her ability to lie.

"But you managed to still listen." Ida pursed her lips. "Even the simplest of instructions and you somehow interpret them in the most asinine ways. Or maybe..." She squinted as if suddenly suspicious. Her eyes reminded her of Bea's but only in how they were the complete opposite. Bea's were like blue sapphires that drew you in. Ida's were like bloody rubies that refused to let you look away. "What are you trying to do right now?"

Lia answered honestly. "Trying to build up the courage to ask if I can go see my sister."

Ida smiled. "I see. You wish to put your worries to rest. What a wonderful idea." She motioned to Atropos. "Has Clotho finished...resituating her?"

Atropos somehow made simple nods feel vile. "Yes, my lady."

"Good. Run along, puppet." Ida nodded her head upwards. Lia's body moved for her, like strings that she forgot were there had begun to pull. "Remind your sister what she still has left to lose. And alter rule eight of the Rules of the House, you no longer need to report to us unless we directly ask."

When the strings loosened Lia did not stop, but instead moved even faster. It wasn't until she was far away, deep into the maze of hallways of the House, that she started to try to put together what just happened. It was the middle of the night. She actually remembered going to bed for once, and then she zoned back in dusting Ida's office. Had she been sleepwalking? Or sleepmaiding. Bea told her not to worry about strange dreams but that was *not* dreaming and it was really freaking her out. Should she tell her?

Rule Five—

But Ida said to change rule eight, so maybe this wasn't related to the rules anymore. Wait, what was rule eight and how was this related to this? Gods, this was hurting her head. It didn't help that taking orders from Ida felt gross. Like in the back of her mind she kept asking herself "Would Bea be ok with me doing this?" Even if that didn't really matter, since the Rules of the House clearly stated Ida's orders superseded Beatrice's.

That rule sucked. It gave Lia the ick. Actually, all Rules of the House did, she tried not to really think about them. After all, not thinking about them was a rule too.

What was Lia just thinking about? Eh, it didn't matter. She'd reached where her sister was staying.

The hallway she'd stopped in the middle of had no doors or windows. Instead she pressed against a specific brick she knew was correct, even though she couldn't quite remember why, and thus a rectangle of the entire wall dissolved to reveal a stairwell downwards. It was so strange how illusions worked here, they were so strong that you could run into them and think the wall had been real. She wondered if it was all mind tricks and she could still fall through it if she tried hard enough.

This part always sucked. She held her breath and jumped through the doorway. It felt like she'd hopped through a wall of fire, a momentary but intense burning across her entire body. She took a moment to let the pain settle and catch her breath. The entryway must've been lined with silver. The stuff didn't kill her but she still had reactions to it like an allergy. Luckily gloves solved that, at least touch wise, so she wasn't getting rashes handling silverware for Bea.

Rattling metal and raspy groans echoed off the walls as Lia gleefully hummed descending the stairs. The air was cold and damp. Lia didn't mind but wondered if she should complain to Bea about it for her sister's sake. Diana probably didn't care though, she could deal with freezing cold or blazing heat no problem. Not silver though. She couldn't handle even crossing silver.

If Diana tried to go through that door she'd be toast.

Lia was wondering why the room at the bottom of the stairs was different when she remembered Atropos said they'd resituated her. Not that it was too much different, it just didn't have any windows like the last one. A cozy little room, grey brick walls, a cold concrete floor, no natural light or light at all.

Wait. That didn't sound cozy. Not cozy at all, this place sounded dreadful when she put it into words. Maybe Lia should bring some candles next time. Yeah, that was it. Get some light to make up for the lack of a window, maybe a few pictures on the wall, the room was just a little barren at the moment. Nothing she should worry or think about. And it wasn't empty, there was the cot and couch from the old room.

Laying out on said couch was a demon, as one might guess from the horns on the sides of her head. Her large batlike wings were sprawled out as she rubbed her head like she had a bad hangover. Her hair was a mess, although there wasn't much to mess up considering both sides were shaved and just the top remained. "Lia?"

Lia ran up and hugged her. "Thank goodness, I was worried you'd died or something!"

Diana ended the hug quicker than expected and stepped back, a weird rattling noise occurring when she did so. She looked both concerned and confused. "What are you wear—what happened?"

"Oh it was stupid. Ida said somebody wasn't around anymore and was talking about my employment so I thought she was talking about you! But like, I knew you were down here, but I hadn't seen you in a while so I got worried." Lia smiled brightly. "But then Ida said I could come see you, I didn't tell her why I wanted to but you're still ok so I must've just not understood." Diana suddenly looked sad, like somebody *did* die. Her cheerfulness took a nosedive. "Did I say something stupid?"

Diana said something that Lia didn't catch. Maybe because the weird rattle happened again. It was so distracting, she swore it happened whenever her sister moved. She looked around but there wasn't anything metal on the floor, there was barely anything in the room, what the heck was causing it? "Sorry, I didn't...didn't hear you, what did you say?"

"They got you. Dammit. Dammit, I—" Diana sighed and put her hand on Lia's head. "I said I love you, sis. Please don't forget that too."

Lia didn't understand. She closed her eyes and put her hand on top of her sisters, both pressing down like they were stacking hats on her. "How could I ever forget you love me?"

"I hope to the gods they'll never make me learn."

Chapter 9
Simple Rewards

"Is something wrong, darling?" Beatrice asked as Lia set the tea down.

She wrinkled her nose. "No, just had a weird night. I think I stayed up too late."

Beatrice raised an eyebrow as she took a sip of tea. "Doing what, might I ask?"

Lia blushed heavily as she quickly said, "Nothing." She averted her gaze but still smiled. "Just enjoying the mirror present you left for me is all."

Beatrice smiled as her eyes glowed in wait for her handmaiden to glance back. *Good. I'm about to enjoy my present to myself.*

Something Lia had said a while back had lingered in her mind. Her pre-conceived notions of fae messing with people. After mentioning it Beatrice had admittedly, well, started messing with her.

It was innocuous at first. An evening of reading here or there with Lia thinking she was a cat. Putting her into trance mid-sentence to hear her trail off into a giggle with that droopy smile that made her heart flutter. It wasn't with any real purpose in mind, her initial enchantment was barely needed with her enthusiasm so Beatrice had forgone reinforcing anything. Putting Lia under was nothing more than her own harmless little fun.

Then it got a bit more...unintentionally intimate. Beatrice might've accidentally called her a good girl on reflex and the whimper of surprise got them both to blush. The next time she managed to save face. It was easier to do so when it wasn't an accident.

Today was certainly going to push that bit further.

"So, would you liiii-" Lia trailed off as she was caught in her mistress's gaze. The subtle shift in relaxed posture as she leaned ever so forward.

Beatrice stood up and put her hand under her handmaid's chin. "How do you feel?"

"Calm, relaxed, and entranced, mistress," Lia said dreamily. Every time she entered this state was a little different, especially if she caught her mid-sentence, but that phrase was the step into a true trance. A final confirmation just to be sure.

And also Beatrice liked the way she said it. "That's good. Now, do you remember how it feels when I call you a good girl?"

"Yes, mistress," Lia said with a glazed look of longing. Impressively she hadn't used the question to trigger the reward. Loyal to a fault.

"We're going to take a new word and apply that feeling to it. But not at full strength. I want you to cut it in half, over and over until it's only a sliver of what it once was. Do you understand?"

"Yes, mistress."

"However, unlike the first, this trigger is cumulative."

"I don't know what that means, mistress," Lia said with a hint of worry.

Beatrice didn't understand why she found Lia's limited vocabulary cute. Maybe it was her honesty about it. "Stacking. You just cut the feeling in half over and over, so now every time you hear it, you'll add a half back." She saw the smile on Lia's face growing. "You understand what this means, don't you?"

"Yes, mistress," Lia said with a hint of excitement. "May I know the word, please?"

"So eager. Very well, it's one you hear often." Beatrice leaned in as if to whisper a dark secret into her ear. "The word is *darling*, darling."

As expected, Lia ever so faintly shivered at the immediate use of the word. Beatrice wondered how fast that sliver would surpass the original feeling. This was going to be an interesting day.

"Darling, could you fetch me that book?"

Lia had to bite her lip to not make a noise. "Y-yes, my lady."

Bea had been asking her to do stuff a lot today. And it was making her feel...something. It was a good feeling, sure. Lia knew she liked her job, and at first she thought the feeling was pride.

"Oh, and darling?"

Lia nearly moaned that time. It definitely wasn't pride. "Yeah?"

"Excellent work lately. I'm very proud to have a darling like you in my employ."

"Thank...you." Lia had barely made it halfway to the bookshelf. It was way too close for her not to have reached it. She was barely functional right now. Why was she so horny? It was that stupid mirror, she knew it was a bad idea.

"Darling, are you ok?" Her voice sounded more amused than concerned.

Do not touch yourself, do not touch yourself—

"Darling?" Such a beautiful voice. Oh the things Lia wished it would ask of her.

Maybe just a little touching wouldn't hurt—no, bad idea, Bea is right there and what if you can't stop? She'll toss you and Diana back out on the streets! Do you want to explain to your sister you got fired for getting off in front of your lady?!

"*Darling?*"

Lia covered her mouth as the point of no return was passed. She found a second wind to get the book and nearly threw it at her lady as she made a beeline for the door. "I need to go!"

Bea's amused mood turned to actual concern. She stood up as Lia fled. "What? What's wrong?"

"Nothing! Nothing, just need to—" Lia froze in place as her arms dropped to her sides, "—watch...your eyes...so pretty."

Bea quickly moved to be next to her. She gently cupped her cheek. "Are you ok? What are you about to go do?"
"I am fantastic, change my panties," Lia answered in tandem.

"Oh." Beatrice blushed heavily and took a small step back. "*Oh,* did I make you—oh gods, I am so sorry."

"It's okay, mistress. It felt really good," Lia said with a smile, no longer caring about the proof of her shame streaking down her leg. While the shame was gone, the hornyness was not. If anything it was boiling over in this blissful state, she'd probably be a hot mess on the floor if not for her desire to stand still and watch those beautiful sapphire eyes. "May I finish?"

Bea was red as a tomato. "I suppose." She yelped as Lia began to obey. "Not here! Just...go back to your room, finish, and then clean up. Return to me after, so I can make sure you don't die of embarrassment remembering this."

"Yes, mistress," Lia said. Her mistress was so silly, she wouldn't die of embarrassment. She'd probably find it hot and then die of embarrassment of *that*.

Before she left, she heard a hesitant, almost guilty, "Good girl, darling."

That was the final push. Lia moaned shamelessly with a shudder and then quickly left to clean up. She hoped her mistress wouldn't be too mad that she hadn't even made it out the door before she finished.

Lia walked into her mistress's room and curtseyed. "Good morning, my lady."

"Good morning, Lia. Sleep well?" Bea asked, sipping at a cup of tea.

"Better than last week, at least," Lia said as she untied her apron and took it off. It'd been almost a full week since that weird night and her dreams since then had been much more pleasant. And one a tad *too* pleasant. Not that she was complaining, beyond having to wash her bedsheets. "Did somebody come by already?"

"Why do you ask?"

Lia shrugged as she took off her shirt. "You already have a cup of tea. It's sorta early and I just got here."

Bea looked between her and the teacup. "You are fascinating with the things you notice, you know that? I never would've thought of that as a clue."

"Clue? Oh, somebody did come by. Was it a secret?" Lia slipped out of her skirt, folded up her clothes, and put them on the chair.

Bea seemed suddenly distracted. Lia waited patiently for an answer. "Hmm? Oh, it's nothing to worry about. Do you mind dusting the room?"

"As you wish, my lady!" Lia said happily. Sometimes she wondered if Bea had her dust because she just wanted to make sure she had a task to occupy her. Her room never seemed to actually gather that much.

Today was weird though. Bea seemed to be watching her. She usually reads or writes or does something when she asks her to clean. Lia dusted faster. Was she being tested?

Lia was wearing the correct uniform, right? She looked down. Bra and panties, check. Wait, was her headdress on? She pretended to scratch her head to check if she remembered. Yep, still there.

Bea was hiding a laugh. She must've noticed. Lia smiled nervously. "Sorry, sometimes I forget to put it on."

"Ah yes. We wouldn't want you underdressed," Bea said with a seductive smile.

She shivered. "I wouldn't mind being underdressed for you, my lady." Bea's smile dimmed. Lia began to panic. "Oh gods that was so inappropriate, I mean, I just...ignore me, my lady."

"Stop."

Lia obeyed. She stopped moving.

And stopped thinking.

Beatrice's heart was racing. How had that gotten her to panic?

It had been a simple suggestion. Tweaking what her mind considered a uniform when in her chambers. She'd been curious to see what Lia would do.

In all honesty she hadn't expected the handmaiden to strip. Or rather, she hadn't expected her to strip so *eagerly*. And there was just no shame, she truly thought her underwear was the proper dress and somehow that removed any embarrassment towards being in nothing but that in front of her mistress.

And then that last remark. Lia couldn't possibly know. Was it just a coincidence? And why did her implied desire for it fluster her more than her actual half-nudity?

This was getting out of hand. Beatrice didn't think she'd feel so conflicted about this. Although she never thought she'd be doing this at all. It was supposed to just be getting this…this lust out of her system but it only seemed to be fueling it further. And why was there such a lust in the first place? Lia was fascinating because of how unenchanted she was, she was endearing for her natural enthusiasm. So what was causing this burning desire to craft an enchantment to make the handmaiden hers alone, mind, body, and soul?

Beatrice couldn't help but feel she wanted to inflict onto Lia the very things she was protecting her from. Shame rose within her at the thought. She knew what it was like to have her mind twisted by Ida, to have her very personality overwritten with no care for her own desires. No concern for the suffering it had wrought on her psyche.

Why would Beatrice want, nay, *crave* to do that to somebody as sweet as her handmaiden?

Lia was obediently waiting while her mistress had gotten lost in thought, her hand mid brush. It was hard to feel that shame looking at her now, so blank and yet so happy. "You have no thoughts."

That wasn't meant to be a command, but Lia repeated, "No thoughts."

Beatrice almost was in a trance of her own. Never before had she fought her fae instincts, not until this moment did she even realize her enchantments were driven by them in such a way. She lightly began to explore her body. "You want nothing more than to serve."

Lia shivered. "Serve."

"Every time you obey you'll feel a lick of pleasure." Beatrice closed her eyes and stepped back. She remembered the 'darling' incident. "No, no, I shouldn't. Forgo that last order."

"Yes, mistress," Lia said. She sounded disappointed. It must be her imagination.

Beatrice had her redress, woke her from her trance, and sent her to get some tea none the wiser. Lia offered to make her a snack, mentioning she wanted to attempt baking bread, and she agreed.

It gave Beatrice time to...quell her lustful urge.

It shocked Beatrice how fast the Seelie Soirée had arrived. She was used to her days feeling never ending, the months all but draining years from her soul. Yet ever since Lia arrived there was never enough time in the day and the weeks passed by in the blink of an eye.

Even if Ida had not truly believed in her words beyond their means to her own ends, perhaps she was correct about Beatrice's need of a handmaiden. Luckily her being wrong about Lia being a poor choice counterbalanced the ill feeling of declaring something Ida said having merit.

"Why the veils?" Lia asked as she brushed her hair. They'd long since been preparing for the event since this morning, Beatrice lightly coaching her and answering the myriads of questions that she suddenly had. "I noticed the Lady of the House had one prepared as well, will I need one?"

"You won't, it's just for us. Think of them as a sheath. We cannot exactly disarm ourselves, so the veils are a gesture of good will." Beatrice hated this the most about social events. Not all fae held themselves to such standards. The wordsmiths and name thieves didn't have to muzzle themselves and in fact blabbered on more than most. The vampires who wore veils were usually the only ones who *couldn't* mesmerize people, either as a bluff or a fashion statement. But no, the von Closens tradition was a very well-known one. It wasn't just a gesture of good will. It was a reminder, an instillment of terror that even other fae could fall victim to their gaze.

Lia finished tying some of her hair into the star pattern hair pin she'd picked out. "Ok, and done!" She led her over to the standing mirror. Her smile faltered as Beatrice took in her evening wear in silent awe. "Is that a happy face or a disappointed face?"

"Not disappointed. Not disappointed at all, I just hadn't quite realized how different this year's arrangement was." For formal events Beatrice normally was forced to wear outfits reminiscent of forestry and leaves, with sharp greens and floral patterns. This dress forgoed the ground in exchange for the sky, a rich blue sequence with an undertone of glittering fabrics that mimicked a starry night.

Lia beamed proudly. She was already in her dress, which while still having a semblance of being an attendant, it was only due to how it seemed to compliment Beatrice's. "You like it? I helped design it. Lachesis is an incredible seamstress, she basically turned a pipe dream of a doodle into a reality."

Beatrice now realized the drawing that hung from the side mirror must've been the one she spoke of. To call it a doodle was a disservice, she had almost assumed the drawing had come second with the detail it had. "You've outdone yourself, darling. Even as a fae I've never looked so ethereal."

Lia clapped her hands together with a delighted squeak. "You really do. It's an amazing outfit but it wouldn't be stunning without you in it." She gave a sad sigh as she pulled the veil down and adjusted it gently. "It's sad you have to cover your eyes, though. I thought the dress complimented them."

Beatrice smiled at Lia through the mirror as she returned to her side. "I suppose that's a sight only you will be allowed to enjoy."

Lia blushed. "I shall cherish that privilege, my lady."

Chapter 10
THE SEELIE SOIRÉE

Lia had never felt more unqualified for her job than when the Seelie Soirée began.

The ballroom sprung to life at the snap of Ida's fingers. Suddenly there were caterers moving in coordination, guests trilling in one after the other despite the other side of that door having been quite empty moments before, the band even started halfway through their song as if they'd been playing the entire time. Everyone who wasn't Lia seemed to know exactly what they were supposed to be doing and that was bad considering her job was to simply stand behind her lady until further notice.

As the heiress of the host, Bea was tasked with greeting the guests and became an entirely different person. Well, not literally. It was more that seeing her interact with other rich people and upper crusts made all the little things that made her *Bea* harder to see. Her words were rigid and scripted, she didn't speak to Lia for so long she began to worry she'd done something wrong. And it didn't help that there were a bunch of other attendants that made her feel inadequate. She couldn't understand how they managed to look so proper and trained just standing next to their masters and mistresses. Lia tried to mimic their postures and felt like she was just making a fool of herself. Most of them were humans, some with blank sleepy expressions and others more elegant and rigid, although not as rigid as the set of mannequin maids that had faces drawn on them. Lia thought they were sorta cool but she wasn't sure if they could talk.

On that point, Lia was fascinated by the guests they were greeting. Some were so small they could've stood in her palm while others were lanky like they'd been stretched out with a rolling pin. Lia couldn't stop herself from staring at a pair of black haired fae with snow white skin and a complete lack of noses. When their eyes met she quickly shifted her gaze to their attendant, whose judging sneer caused her to decide her shoes were the best thing to focus on right now.

Lia was shaking when they left, terrified she was being an embarrassment. She didn't belong here and everyone could clearly tell just by looking at her. Bea for the first time since this had begun turned to her, gently lifted her chin and lifted her veil ever so slightly with a finger to reveal a glowing eye. "You're doing great, darling. Don't fret, this is the worst part. Soon you can just enjoy the party."

The words warmed Lia like a cup of hot chocolate. She let her shoulders relax, that proper posture was exhausting. "Thank you, mistress."

Bea let the veil drop and it got Lia to realize that was what made her seem so different. Her expressions were always this muted but with her eyes covered it made her seem cold. Now with each curl of her lips and cover with her hand Lia could imagine what those sparkling sapphires were saying behind the veil.

A sight just for me, Lia reminded herself with a smile. She was already feeling better.

"Lucial Nullith, your ladyship."

And then it went right back to terrible.

Lia kept her eyes locked on the floor. It couldn't be him. It couldn't and yet the shadow on the floor was winged with horns at the top and a tilted posture that was identical to Diana's. This was a fae party, what the hell was *he* doing here?

"A pleasure, Nullith. Do feel free to mingle but if you wish to converse with me we can do so later," Bea said curtly. She was clearly annoyed that Lucial hadn't kept moving. Lia fought the urge to look up, he must've been staring and her lady didn't realize it wasn't at her.

"Right, right, etiquette and formalities and all that. We should speak when we're away from our duties." Even Lia could read the writing between the lines on that one. The winged shadow left her sightline. "Not that I have much to say."

Lia looked up but the man was gone, although he was too tall to miss even if Bea wasn't watching him saunter through the crowd like a panther amongst foxes. "And here I thought neither devil nor demon would ever step foot inside our halls."

Lia flinched. "Do you not like demons, my lady?"

"Ida doesn't but I have yet to discover what she does like. One being invited does perhaps illuminate what seemed to be occupying her thoughts as of late." Bea pursed her lips. "As for me, I prefer not to make opinions on those I haven't met. Lucial does not make a strong case favoring demon kind. He appears quite full of himself."

"He doesn't seem like a good example." He was the worst example. Lia rocked back and forth on her feet. "I'm sure there are demons out there you'd like."

Bea turned to her with a sliver of a smile. "I'm sure there are, Lia. And I'm sure none of them would ever desire to be at a soirée like this."

After the last of the guests filtered in, Bea excused herself and led Lia to a table hidden out of the way with a wine glass already filled. Apparently her habits at these events were as coordinated as everything else.

"That was exhausting," Bea muttered as she nearly drained the wine in one go. She motioned to the seat next to her. "Sit, sit, it'll make it look like I'm occupied and not to be bothered."

Lia sat down. "I don't think they'll assume I'm a guest, I don't look fancy enough." *Or weird enough for that matter.*

"There are more roles to be had than mistress or maiden. You could easily pass as my entertainment."

"What kind of entertainment would I be?" Lia asked curiously.

Bea smirked. "Considering you don't make me dread being here, one of high quality."

"Oh. Uh, thank you, my lady." Lia blushed at the surprise compliment. "You said that was the worst of it. What do you normally do next?"

"Until I find an excuse to leave? Mostly people watch." Bea nodded her head towards the party and thus revealed their tucked away corner had angles on almost everywhere notable. The dance floor, the tables of guests, the only one not visible was Ida herself. Probably a feature rather than a flaw. "I take it you noticed the variety of fae?"

"Yeah, what makes you a fae? Like a demon and devil are different, but they're both infernal. And usually you can tell which is which and even then you know they're one of the two. Everyone here just looks super different." Despite all her warnings about fae, Diana never seemed to be able to describe what one would look like beyond saying it's usually obvious. Now she understood what that meant.

"Exactly. Fae are different from mortals, thus making them fae." Bea smiled at her confusion. "It's hard to explain. The lack of consistency is almost in of itself the consistency. I could joke that we're the miscellaneous category of species."

"Ohh, so you like to watch them and like, guess stuff about how they work."

"Precisely. No fae will ever tell so why waste time talking?" Bea had been scanning the crowd until she stopped and nodded her head. "Much easier to watch and see, say, one stealing our fine silverware."

Lia followed her eyes and saw an elven looking man with silver eyes and pale blue skin flipping silverware through his fingers like a pen. Except for a split second she could see two, then just one again. After that he'd place it down and start flipping a different fork.

Bea gave her a playful look. "Take a guess as to what he's doing."

Lia had good eyes but it was too far away and too fast. She could tell what he probably was doing, but how he was doing it was a mystery. "Well, if he's stealing them, he's leaving a fake behind."

Bea nodded with approval. "Fae custom, an unauthorized trade is forgivable. Theft is not."

"Did he bring a bunch of fake forks?" Lia asked, half joking, half serious. It would be weird but weird was the vibe.

Bea laughed. "Doubtful. More likely he has a bag of something that he's turning into fakes. Marbles or maybe just clay. Or perhaps illusion magic, some fae are skilled enough for illusions to be physical clone copies, but the clones would turn to dust in a few weeks."

Lia tilted her head. "Wait, if he's here, isn't he rich? Why is he stealing?"

"A fascinating question that I like to observe and theorize. Sometimes it's just a game, harmless fun to see how far one can get away with it and will declare themselves victorious to our Lady of the House at the end. I tend to ruin their nights the most." Bea smiled mischievously and then shrugged. "Other times, it's with a little more malice. But it's still innocuous, what punishment will we lay bare upon a man who swiped a few forks? And of course, you mustn't forget the most important part of being wealthy."

"Which is?" Lia asked.

Bea took a drink of wine. "Be cheap, darling. The richer you are, the cheaper you can afford to be. Why buy what you can take, why take what you can steal, and why steal what you can talk somebody else into giving you? That's the Seelie Soirée at its core. We're all spending cheap words to reap riches and rewards."

"But some are only rich enough to steal your forks?"

Bea choked on her wine. "Gods, don't make me laugh when I'm drinking."

And so they played Bea's aristocratic version of eye spy, Lia guessing which attendant caught her lady's gaze and why. There were two nymphs talking vigorously; Lia said they were probably some kind of trade partners. Bea, however, said it was likely the equivalent of a property dispute given one looked of a forest and the other of a river. The fork thief had moved on to plates and Bea made the final call that it was a game. He was going to keep upping the ante until caught. And so on and so forth, it was a lot of fun. Lia could tell Bea loved to explain her deductions to her. Maybe she was her entertainment in a way. Or rather was somebody for her lady to entertain.

"I always wondered what people did at these. Like I knew there would be dancing but I couldn't really understand what else," Lia said, "The longer I watch, the more it feels like dancing is a side effect rather than the point."

Bea nodded in agreement. "Ironic, isn't it? The one thing most know lavish events for is one that barely half care to participate in."

"Have you ever danced at one?" Lia asked.

"No suitor has been both brave enough to ask and worthy to earn a yes. A pity." Bea swirled her wine. "Then again, I don't sell myself as approachable. Perhaps I am more like my mother than I wish to admit. I don't think anybody has ever asked her to stand from her chair, much less share a dance."

"That's a little harsh, you don't scowl like your mother." Lia gave a bashful smile. "I would be happy to dance with you if no suitor worthy arises in time."

Bea hid her mouth under her hand and raised an eyebrow in thought. "Perhaps I'll take you up on that offer, darling."

Lia didn't think that would actually work. She had no clue how to do a ballroom dance. Probably should've thought about that before asking. She hoped Bea would be good enough to cover for the both of them.

Then her eyes caught the tips of a pair of horns at the refreshment table and saw her promised dance slipping away if the demon they belonged to caused a scene. Inside she was afraid but laid over that fear was a desire to be a good handmaiden. She needed to clean up this mess quickly rather than let it become a bother for Bea. "Would you like another glass of wine, my lady?"

Bea finished the last sip. She rarely drank wine alone, but appeared to be a well-practiced alcoholic when forced to interact with those of her status. Lia wondered if that meant she could hold her alcohol well or if she couldn't and that was the whole idea. "I think you should just bring the entire bottle, darling. I'm going to need it."

"I'll bring you something to snack on too," she said with a curtsy.

Lia carefully made her way across the ballroom, trying to not have her attention distracted by the close encounters with the fascinating fae who all seemed to give her at least a passing glance. She felt like a house cat surrounded by foxes. Not exactly prey, not exactly mutuals, the house cat belonged inside and yet the foxes were invited in as well. All bound by the rules of decorum that the Lady of the House demanded of them.

The panther that was Lucial Nullith, however, had many fox eyes locked on him in wait for those rules to falter even for a moment. He approached as soon as Lia arrived as if they'd planned to meet at the refreshments in secret, looming over her with his hands behind his back and his leathery wings lightly stretching. Red slitted eyes sitting in black voids that looked more annoyed than threatening. His shirt was half tucked with his suit unbuttoned. He looked more like an enforcer than a guest. "Lia."

"Sir," Lia said timidly. She'd hoped she'd never have to talk to him. Not alone, at the very least. "How's mom?"

"Healthy." His eyes almost seemed to rotate as they narrowed. "How is *my* daughter?"

Lia winced. He didn't have to say it like that. "Diana is safe. Why are you here?"

"I was invited." Lucial glanced between her and Ida in the distance. "I am starting to get a hint as to why."

Lia swallowed her fear. Bea was having a good night and she was not letting this demon get her tossed to the streets a second time by ruining it. "This is a formal affair, sir. The Lady of the House and my lady as well would not appreciate it if you abused their hospitality to cause trouble."

"You think I'm here for havoc? Not a shock, Diana probably sold me as an outright terror to you. I know when to fold my wings." Lucial rolled his eyes. "You should be grateful I accepted. I may just be your saviour."

Lia wasn't sure what that meant but it didn't sound like a good thing. Lucial left for Ida's throne without even a goodbye. He looked even more out of place than Lia did. Not that everyone at the soirée was a fae, he was just the only demon, in fact he was the only infernal creature she could see. She had no idea why he was invited, he wasn't that important. Diana always called him a backup bloodline or something. She was glad her sister wasn't here. Putting together those two would quickly turn this soirée into a melee.

Bea was probably getting annoyed she was taking so long. Lia quickly started filling up a plate and was having trouble deciding on which wine was the one that had been in her glass as a new figure interrupted her. She wore a silvery dress, had short hair colored like a pile of autumn leaves, and butterfly wings that faintly flapped like a flag in the wind. The only reason Lia even acknowledged her was because she blocked her from leaving.

"Well aren't you a diamond in the rough," the fairy said. She held out her hand as if expecting Lia to either take it or maybe kiss her rings. "Nyssa Deburio. May I have your name?"

"I'm Lia," the handmaiden said, feeling a little bit off. "I'm sorry, but I need to-"

"Don't worry about that, worry about me. I'm so bored and you're fairly cute. Come back to my table and entertain me," Nyssa casually demanded.

The handmaiden almost started to follow, but was stopped by a tug at her mind. This wasn't right. She didn't know why but she was convinced Bea was going to be upset with her if she didn't come back right now and very quickly. "I need to return to my lady."

Nyssa laughed. "Oh, deary me, you're so confused. Here, let me explain." She booped the handmaiden on the forehead and made a popping noise with her mouth. "You don't have needs. You don't even have a name, your name is just what you are and I'm reminding you that you're my toy. And I wish to be entertained by my new toy, so you'll be coming back with me."

Toy blinked. Everything Nyssa said made sense. She wasn't sure why her new owner was explaining it to her like she was five, she wasn't a dumb toy. "Ok."

"Glad you understand," Nyssa said, taking her hand. Toy left the plate of food behind, fully forgetting anything other than entertaining her new owner. "Oh, and forget your lady. She's not important, I'm your mistress now."

"Yes, mistress," Toy said, but she was lying. Sure, the concerns of returning were now far from her mind but her lady wasn't forgotten. Lia promised she'd never forget Bea.

What a strange promise to remember. Who was Lia?

Chapter 11
PROPERTY RIGHTS

Beatrice ran her finger around the brim of the empty glass of wine. She started to wonder if it was taboo for a lady and her handmaiden to share a dance. Usually by now she'd be looking for excuses to retire to her chambers early but she couldn't help staying just to let Lia enjoy the party. Entertaining her was much more fun than mingling with her fellows.

A new glass of wine was set next to her. "Thank you, Li-"

It was not Lia, but Lachesis. "Enjoying yourself for once, Lady Beatrice?"

"I suppose you could say that," Beatrice said, "I'm surprised to see you on the floor. Usually catering requires immense focus for coordination."

Lachesis took her hand from behind her back. Wrapped around each finger was a tiny tied thread connected to each other. Her fingers were constantly moving like she was playing an instrument, the threads forming countless shapes and patterns that shouldn't be possible to do one handed. "I do admit the workload is substantial, but sometimes a personal touch is required." She eyed a passing countess. "And enjoyable."

"Cotho is running security, I assume," Beatrice said, taking a sip of wine. "And Atropos?"

Lachesis smirked. "Where do you think?"

"Standing next to my mother, her glare like a ward against the unworthy?" Beatrice rolled her eyes. Ida never left her seat during these events. She'd hear whispers of those who only saw her during soirées spreading rumors that she had never stood from her spot in decades. Ida von Closen was the Lady of the House, for the House was built around the unmoving Lady.

There was a kernel of truth to the rumors. Beatrice knew Ida moved, but she wasn't certain she'd ever left the House.

Lachesis winced as one of the threads on her finger snapped. It wasn't but a flicker before the thread was retied. "Oh dear, another one snatched. I know we have an unspoken open use policy but I'd wish our guests would let the caterers hand the entrees off first. It's such a hassle locating where they put the trays down."

A chill went down her spine as Lia's lack of return now was much more foreboding. Beatrice stood, taking a large gulp of wine. "Excuse me, I think somebody has stolen my dance."

Toy was very glad she didn't have to dance for long.

Mistress Nyssa seemed to get bored very easily. Toy had attempted to entertain her with a little dance as instructed but it wasn't easy in a dress. Afterwards her mistress asked very personal questions, but when Toy told her answering was against the Rules of the House, the fairy suddenly looked scared. She hid the fear quickly under a snide laugh and said it didn't matter, toys don't have personal lives anyways. She was right of course.

Mostly mistress Nyssa just asked her to "look pretty" and suggested new poses. For a while she rested a drink on her head, but eventually that spilt onto Toy's dress. After that mistress Nyssa just started to use her dress as a napkin.

That weirdly annoyed Toy. Everything else had been whatever, she was meant to entertain, but ruining her dress was a line being crossed. Like wiping your boots on the host's white carpet kind of rude. She didn't bring it up, it's not her place to make commentary, it just bothered her.

Hopefully Bea wouldn't be too upset.

"Toy, my shoulders are tense. Massage me."

"Yes, mistress."

Beatrice was not upset. She was enraged.

Sure enough a plate filled with foods that Beatrice would enjoy sat forgotten on a lone table. Somebody had taken Lia. How *dare* they, she clearly wasn't one of the caterers. This was nothing short of a robbery and so Beatrice had wasted no time in heading straight to where she knew Clotho would be perched.

"Hiding again?" Clotho asked as she approached, her eyes dilated as she watched the room like a hawk. Unbeknownst to even the staff, she could switch places with any of them at a moment's notice. Excellent for responding to threats but not very effective for prevention of petty theft. Although that was by design. Anybody pushing their luck beyond silly games would be allowed to leave with whatever treasures they managed to hide away.

All that meant was Clotho had new houses to ransack for reimbursement. And she had a very good memory.

Beatrice would sometimes hide up here during events that were getting too much for her but still required her to be present in some capacity. "Not today. Did you see anybody intercept Lia?"

Clotho snickered. "Snagged by a fairy. The Deburios' daughter." She gave a toothy smile. "Shall I reacquire her?"

"You don't get a reward for allowing this, you knew she was mine." The Deburios, a fairy family of name thieves. The enchantment on Lia was thin, stealing her name would easily bypass it. Beatrice was kicking herself for letting this happen as well, all that overthinking about what enchanting Lia further would do and now a fairy had stolen her unprotected prize. She already spotted the likely winged upstart and sure enough a dazed half-elf was with her. "I will handle it. Eye to eye."

Toy was very zoned out right now. Still, even as she casually massaged her mistress's shoulders, she felt off. Disappointed? No, not that. Unfulfilled. It was just hard to get into a rhythm, she was just going through the motions. She wondered if Bea would want massages like this. Maybe that was a good motivator, she could pretend she was practicing.

"Hmm, that's enough, Toy." Her mistress motioned for her to come around and casually fondled her tit. "Gods, you've got quite the pair. Maybe I'll take you home to play with."

"Nyssa, this is a civil affair, stop molesting the help," the vampire said as casually as one would ask their friend to not smoke at dinner. He joined the table after Toy had arrived. In fact a few people had, it felt like a show was about to happen. Toy wondered if she was going to need to entertain them all. She didn't know any good party tricks.

Her mistress glanced up at Toy and smirked. "Oh very well. I suppose a toy isn't appropriate for a ball. Which is okay, considering you're my chair."

Chair, who weirdly thought her name was Toy moments ago, dropped to her knees and felt much better. That's why she was so off earlier, she wasn't a toy. She was a chair for her mistress to sit on. Luckily she was light, a little too light. Perhaps her wings faint movements weren't just an aesthetic.

Chair wondered if Bea was light enough to sit on her.

Nyssa was laughing casually with a few other fae, some well-endowed mortals, as well as a vampire. The ones who weren't her entourage did not warn her of the approaching storm that was Beatrice, their curled smiles implying they'd surmised this outcome and were excited to see the show. The fairy was clearly unaware of this and seemed to think she'd suddenly gained the popularity she deserved.

And Lia, oh poor Lia, was her chair. Her outfit was stained, her hair was a mess, and the top of her dress was half hanging like it had been turned into a towel.

Be calm. Be rational. Be elegant.

Beatrice calmly approached the table. She rationally waited for Nyssa to stand as one should when greeting the host's heiress. And then she elegantly slapped her across the face with her glove.

"I beg your pardon?" Nyssa asked, shell-shocked.

"It is my forgiveness you should beg for." Beatrice put her glove back on. "You have stolen my lady-in-waiting. Return her at once and I'll graciously let that be repayment for an honest mistake."

Nyssa's attitude shifted as fast as her wings fluttered. At first confused, she now hovered at eye level with her hand under her chin and the mocking smirk of a rival. "Oh, you mean my chair?" She glanced down at Lia. "Are you certain you want her as a lady-in-waiting? She barely made for a good toy. I could offer one of our nameless instead, it certainly would be trading up."

The gathered crowd laughed. Beatrice did not. "First you disregard our hospitality, now you insult our staff. Do you have any sense of decorum? Or self-preservation?"

"Come now, don't get all worked up. We all borrow a servant here and there, if you wanted to keep her off the menu so bad then you should've kept her at your side," Nyssa said as if she was being the voice of reason, "You can't be upset somebody stole your corner piece if all you did was put it on a plate next to the cake."

Nyssa laughed. The crowd didn't join in as fervently as before, as many could sense the murder being plotted behind Beatrice's veil. She reached out and tore off Nyssa's pearl necklace with a harsh snap. She shook it in front of her stupid shocked face. "Look at that, such a beautiful set. Clearly not on a neck at this moment so it must be up for grabs!"

"You uncultured swine!" Nyssa snarled. She snapped her fingers and Lia stood up. "Chair, we're leaving."

"Lia is staying," Beatrice said.

Nyssa looked annoyed and perhaps worried as Lia seemed distraught at the conflicting orders. She sneered in a clear attempt to hide her concern. "I own her name, she won't listen to you."

Beatrice glared at her, not a hint of emotion on the rest of her face as it all was devoted to the rage in her eyes. Her veil may prevent the magic but the glow was so violent it was all but bleeding through. "Do you truly think that's enough to save you?"

Even the snotty brat faltered from a death glare like that. Perhaps if she was alone she would've conceded, but the crowd was watching and her pride was on the line. Beatrice was prepared for recklessness, but she wasn't prepared for the insanity that came out of her mouth. "Chair, if she lays another hand on me, kill yourself."

The silence that washed over the darkened faces of the crowd said very loudly, *You shouldn't have done that.*

Rather than scared, Lia looked like she was just asked to walk on water. "How?"

Beatrice knew such an order was asinine. Putting aside survival instinct being much stronger than name thievery, she'd also turned Lia's sense of self into an inanimate object. How would a chair that's never been alive comprehend killing itself?

Those were the rational thoughts. The irrational thoughts were the ones tearing off her veil. The fires behind her eyes burned so bright they reflected in the now entranced eyes of the so-called daughter of the Deburios.

"Sit," Beatrice ordered.

Nyssa obeyed. So did Lia. Even a few others did, although out of being enchanted or just afraid it wasn't clear.

"Give me her name," Beatrice demanded.

"Her name is Lia," Nyssa said blankly, the lack of emotion now making the shimmer of her voice when doing so much more obvious.

Always strange how such a simple sentence held such power. Beatrice glanced at her handmaiden. "Behind me, Lia. Now."

"Yes, my lady," Lia said timidly as she shot to her feet and hid behind her. She looked shaken, probably trying to piece together how she got here. Issues for later, for now she was where she belonged and that's all that mattered.

Beatrice looked down upon her prey. What little original thoughts were in her head were long gone as she was caught in her enchanting gaze. Against a fellow fae, enchantment was not easy. Not only was it taboo, they were naturally resistant to magic of the mind. Resistance wasn't immunity, though. A mixture of her rage and her target's fear was more than enough to overcome those pitfalls.

Still, it wasn't fear that a fae should use. That would make Beatrice like her mother. Fear only got you so far. There were far more effective emotions to exploit. "You didn't even get her last name. A poor excuse for a Deburio." She gave a mockery of a sympathetic smile. "You think that too, don't you? You don't worry about last names because you feel undeserving of your own. The Deberuios have what, seven children? How exhausting that must be, always fighting for your seat at the table, unable to meet the endless expectations. Wishing you didn't have to deal with the responsibility."

"Yes," Nyssa said with empty eyes and a hint of longing.

"Of course you do, who wouldn't? But then you'd lose all your privileges and that's all you've ever known. Change is terrifying, sometimes your chains are a comfort." Beatrice was relentless. Already Nyssa was accepting her words as truths, although she had a feeling these weren't far off from the girl's true feelings. The mind loved having an outside force to blame for acting on internal desires. "Sometimes you probably wonder what it would be like, wonder if losing them would be worth it. Free of responsibility. Free of worry. Free of thought."

"Free," Nyssa repeated happily. The fear was gone and with it any resistance.

Beatrice smirked. "Let's do that, shall we? Give you a taste of freedom."

"Shouldn't we do something?" Alder Deburio, prince of the Deburio family, was seething with rage.

His father, Coric Deburio, shook his head. "We are guests. Your sister was weak willed and this is her punishment." His calm was not any safer than his son's rage, it still burned like dry ice. "The von Closens are not a family we can make direct enemies of."

"Not even for this!?" Alder pointed to his sister.

Nyssa was on all fours, grazing at a plate of salad that had been left out for her. Her dress had been pulled down to let her breasts dangle, attempts to remedy her wardrobe or even her mind were met with fierce resistance. For all intents and purposes, the girl was content and considered these attempts threatening to her newfound happiness. She looked up at the finger pointing at her, bits of lettuce falling from her mouth as she stared with bovine emptiness. Then, she mooed.

"I will be having a word with the Lady of the House." Coric looked down upon the disappointment he called a daughter. Even before tonight she was a strain on their reputation. Now she didn't even have the capacity to comprehend how much she was humiliating her family. "If that fails to bear fruit, we shall pursue subtler avenues of retaliation. The only worth your sister has right now is that every moment she spends like this will be compensated in full. And clearly her pitiful mind intends to make that a hefty sum."

Nyssa happily mooed in response.

Chapter 12
An Owed Dance

Beatrice stormed to her room with Lia in tow. She was muttering vague curses under her breath as she threw her doors open. "My entire night, ruined. Ruined! The one time I finally find some joy in a soirée, I swear."

The distant music echoed even after Lia closed the doors behind her. She looked over her dress and wiped off the more obvious stains while Beatrice fumed. She tried to speak up a few times before finally finding an opening. "I'm sorry your evening was ruined, my lady." She braced with a nervous frown. "Did I mess up?"

"What?" Beatrice was knocked out of her tirade and gave her a confused look. "Why would you think that?"

"I don't fully understand what happened, but I just...I just feel like it's my fault. Are you mad I didn't bring you back your food?" Lia shifted in place more than usual. "Or was it the guests? I was trying my best...I think. Did I not satisfy mistress Nyssa?"

Beatrice went cold. Mistress? *Mistress?* That underhanded *tart*! For the first time the glow of her eyes did not relax Lia. "You will remove that title from her, she is Lady Nyssa at best and even then she barely deserves more than miss."

"Yes, mistress," Lia said. Her voice was more timid than the usual blank.

Beatrice did not relent. "You are mine. You are my handmaiden. You are my property. I am your mistress, your owner, and nobody is allowed to lay a hand on you but me. I own your name now but your body belonged to me long before that, understood?"

Lia was as still as a statue. "Yes, mistress."

Beatrice took a breath. She stepped back and tried to reign in her anger. There was fear under that empty stare, that alone was extinguishing her rage. She took her handmaiden's hand and felt it quivering. "Lia, look into my eyes. Don't worry about anything else, just look."

"Yes, missss—" Lia didn't finish the thought as Beatrice gently pushed her mind deeper than she normally did. Her body finally relaxed and she started to slump forward.

"Just a dip into mindlessness, letting the calm wash your worries away. In fact you feel the memories after entering my chambers dissolving into nothing, unimportant and unneeded." Beatrice guided her to the bed, having her kneel in front of her as she sat down. "Rising back to the surface, feeling much better now. Calm, relaxed and entranced."

"Calm. Relaxed. Entranced." Lia took a deep breath, appearing much less tense than before. Still, the aura of unease was lurking behind her blank stare.

"I'm sorry, darling." Beatrice lifted her chin up and kissed her on the forehead. "It wasn't your fault. You did nothing wrong."

"Are you sure, mistress?" Lia asked. She had that lost puppy look again. Gods, she was so cute.

"Very sure. It was my fault that I let such a catch walk around unprotected," Beatrice said kindly, "If anything, I'm upset we didn't get to share a dance."

Lia blushed with a shy smile. "That's ok, mistress. I don't actually know how to dance."

Beatrice raised an eyebrow. "Is that so?" As if to endorse the idea that came to her, the faded music in the distance changed to a classic ballroom tune. "Then perhaps you need to learn."

"I'll lead. It's natural for you to let me lead. Second-nature." Beatrice placed Lia's hands and pushed her feet to the proper places. She kept her tone gentle and chose her words carefully, Lia only in the lightest of a trance but still accepting her ideas as unarguable truths. "We'll go slow. Just let yourself follow along."

The two began their dance. Slowly, at half-step to let Lia learn the pattern, but she was a quick learner. While the music was more of an echo than anything else she swayed and smiled as if the band was in the bedroom playing just for them. "That's good. I think you're a better dancer than you give yourself credit."

Lia smiled. "I have a good partner, mistress."

"You make a fair point, it is easier when you have a proper partner. Letting them lead where you go. Guide how you step." Beatrice smiled at Lia with glowing eyes. "It's so much easier to let me lead. To enjoy the dance without a worry. Just letting my words compel you like the music compels your legs to move with it."

Lia looked like she was in her own little world, smiling as she absorbed every word Beatrice said. Their dance slowed to a crawl and she didn't even question when they stopped, just swaying as she waited to be led. She was so adorable. Her dress should've been hyperbolizing her cuteness but it had been callously defiled by that fairy.

No need to keep it on, then.

"I'm going to help you out of your dress now. But this isn't just covering your body. It's also covering your mind." Beatrice slipped her hand underneath the strap over Lia's shoulder. "With each piece taken you'll feel yourself become more open, more pliable."

Her smile dimmed as she said hesitantly, "Is that safe, mistress?"

"You're nervous. That's natural, it's scary to be vulnerable. It's why I'm here with you." Beatrice lifted her chin as her eyes glowed even brighter. She wasn't holding back anymore. This was for Lia's sake as much as her own. Nobody else was allowed to touch her. "This is a safe place. Just as only I may see your body, only I may mold your mind. You trust me, right?"

Lia all but melted. "Trust you."

Beatrice untied the back of her dress. "Piece by piece, a little more open, a little more suggestible." Lia was almost dancing as she was stripped, Beatrice's hand over hers as they caressed along her body from piece to piece. Even when she could've done it herself her hand waited as if eager to feel her mistress's touch guide her. It was not long before she was down to her underwear, not needing help to take that off but appeared to be unable to do so without following the impromptu routine she'd made up in her head. "Let the last of your garments fall to the floor, and with them any last bits of resistance."

Lia swayed to the rhythm as she sensually slipped out of underwear. Beatrice held a hand out to help and she took it eagerly, giving the dress a little kick as she stepped out of it. "You lead."

"Good girl," Beatrice said as she began their dance again. Lia shivered with delight. After a few sets she decided she wasn't being fair as the only one clothed. She leaned in. "Would you mind helping me out of my dress as well?"

"Of course not, mistress," Lia said. In trance her movement was more sluggish but not clumsy. Although her focus was easily distracted.

While directly behind her, carefully undoing the buttons and ties, her hands became slower and slower. Beatrice had a sneaking feeling as to why. She could feel her breath on her neck and with a shiver she reached behind her to lead her to take that last leap. Her handmaiden kissed her neck gently as she ran her hands underneath her dress and down her body, allowing for Beatrice to step out and turn to her with a seductive smile.

Lia was captivated, her mouth just ever so slightly hanging open. "You're gorgeous, mistress."

Beatrice blushed. She never was ready for those compliments to slip through. She took her hand. "You have a beautiful body yourself, darling."

"Thank you, mistress," Lia said with a smile.

"Even better that it belongs to me." Beatrice pulled her into their starting dance pose. "Say it."

"My body belongs to you," Lia said dreamily.

Beatrice nodded as they began their dance again. "Good girl. Feel that truth sinking in, your mind as naked as your body. Well, *my* body. Because?"

"My body belongs to you," Lia said with a proud smile.

Dancing in the nude gave a very different feeling of intimacy. Every step their skin brushed against each other, their movement beyond free and yet naturally they wanted to stay even closer than ever.

"Your mind is for me to fill."

"My mind is for you to fill."

Lia didn't even need to be told to repeat, she just seemed to know and was eager to obey. Perhaps it was because Beatrice's eyes were still glowing. She didn't need them by now but it made her feel even more connected with her enthralled dance partner.

"My will is your will."

"Your will is my will."

"You can stop repeating," Beatrice said, "This is your mantra. Whenever you enter a trance this will be what plays in your mind, over and over, solidifying my hold over you."

Lia nodded. "Yes, mistress."

"You learn fast, darling. Your body and mind both take to my lessons quickly." Beatrice leaned in to whisper in her ear. "You're such a good girl."

Lia shivered at the praise. "Thank you, mistress."

"Now that we're in a rhythm, let's up our moveset." Beatrice twirled Lia while holding her hands to hug her from behind. "I'm going to dip you, both body and mind. The deeper you dip, the deeper you will sink in a trance. Only resurfacing as I pull your body back up. Doesn't that sound delightful?"

"Very delightful, mistress," Lia said with a longing sigh.

Beatrice twirled her back to their stance, her anticipation matching the excitement she could see in Lia's eyes. One set. Two sets. Three sets.

"And dip down—ahh!" Beatrice dipped Lia and she dragged them both to the ground as her entire body went limp. She started laughing, which prompted Lia in her addled state to giggle and just made Beatrice laugh even more. They laid tangled together on the floor, Beatrice trying to stifle her snickers as she turned Lia's head toward her. "I think that was a little too deep."

Lia smiled droopily. "Just a little, mistress."

Beatrice didn't want to get up, instead wrapping herself closer. Lia was so deeply entranced she'd stay there forever, staring into her eyes even now with that adoration that made Beatrice feel so warm. It was a look impossible to resist, she couldn't help but lean in to steal a kiss.

What was making love but another kind of dance? And so Lia followed her lead. Simple and natural, their hands exploring as they moved from the floor to the bed. It was wonderful, it was passionate, it was...

It wasn't enough. Beatrice wanted *more*. Her eyes were glowing before she even decided to act on her instincts, putting her hands on Lia's cheeks as she pulled away from the kiss. Her jaw went slack from the sudden intensity, her body shaking from the pleasure she was being drowned in. "Sleep." Lia went limp again as Beatrice pulled her onto her chest in a loving embrace. "Deeper and deeper. Just sinking into mindless bliss. Your mind is open and ready to obey anything I tell you."

Lia was guided to kneel on the floor before her on the bed. Beatrice ordered her to open her eyes and despite already being deep in trance she was hit again with the enchanting glow. Beatrice lifted her chin, using her thumb to wipe the drool running down it. "Speak your mantra."

"I am Beatrice's property. My body belongs to her. My mind is for her to fill. Her will is my will," Lia obediently repeated.

"Good girl." Beatrice smiled at the shiver the trigger invoked in her handmaiden. "Now, for the rest of the night, you are nothing but a doll for my pleasure. Your purpose is to sexually satisfy me. Your tongue is nothing but a tool to pleasure me. Your body is for me to play with. Just as with your light trance, this doll state will be one you return to any time I demand it."

Lia was utterly enthralled by the glow as she absorbed everything she was told. "Yes, mistress."

"Good girl." Beatrice kissed her on the forehead and let her eyes stop glowing. "Now, awaken, my lovely Lia doll."

Lia continued to stare. No words were spoken but in her eyes she was saying clearly 'tell me how to please you.' Beatrice obliged the silent plea and lifted her foot in front of her. "Kiss it." She shivered as Lia kissed the top of her foot without hesitation. Her lips were gentle and cherishing. "Continue up. Slowly."

Lia obeyed. She eagerly gave her foot another kiss as she caressed her leg, sensually making her way up as she worshipped her like a goddess. She *was* her goddess, Lia was her doll and as her owner Beatrice was her entire world.

"To touch me is a reward, a privilege you cannot comprehend, so every kiss you savor. Every touch makes you wetter." Beatrice was finding it hard to sound in control as her own whimpers and moans snuck their way between her words. Lia was halfway up her thigh and she almost didn't catch her before she got too far along. She quickly put a single finger against her forehead. "Stop."

Lia froze, her head between her legs and tongue outstretched.

"Not yet. You haven't earned it yet." Beatrice lightly pushed her back with her foot. Lia looked up at her with those wistful eyes longing to please and she nearly rescinded her words to just push the girl back between her legs. "My other leg first, darling. Worship my body. Earn the right to taste me."

Beatrice got a chill from the look Lia had after she said that last part. Her eyes were dilated like a predator but that didn't make her expression any less filled with devotion. She wasn't a mindless thrall, she was a devoted doll with a purpose and she had just been told to earn it.

And earn it Lia did. She worked her way up her leg, kissing and licking past her supposed prize and up her stomach. Lia gently pushed her back onto the bed, caressing her body as she kissed her passionately. Her hand brushed along her thigh and Beatrice moaned as she was fingered. Apparently that was Lia's cue to kiss her way back down, her fingers teasing ever so gently as she still had two breasts to give her love and attention. Beatrice shivered with anticipation as the fingers were taken out and felt a pleasure she never had before as Lia began to lick.

Beatrice put a hand on Lia's head and another on her own breast as the girl ate her out as if she'd done it many times before. The yearning of her heart was burning brighter than ever as the heat in her body fueled its flames. She never wanted this to end but any thoughts of savoring the moment vanished as the talented tongue of her handmaiden quickly brought her to the brink of climax. Lia was amazing, she was relentless, and she made her mistress cum harder than she ever thought she could. She collapsed back onto the bed, only faintly comprehending what must've been Lia licking her clean. Beatrice couldn't help but giggle at the thought of her need to be a good handmaiden still driving her actions. "S-stop. Give...give me a moment."

The tongue stopped mid lick. "Yes, mistress."

Beatrice eventually collected herself. She sat up to see Lia staring forward, her once lust filled eyes now empty and satisfied with a hint of a smile as she obediently waited for new orders. She pet her head. "By the gods, you are going to be doing that every night from now on."

"With pleasure, mistress," Lia said.

"Good girl." Beatrice smiled mischievously as her doll moaned in response. "Good girl. *Good girl.*" Lia's eyes were getting even hazier as her hand flickered closer between her legs. "Good girls repeat their mantras."

There wasn't even a hint of hesitation. "I am Beatrice's property. My body belongs to her. My mind is for her to fill. Her will is my will." That was the final push for Lia to start touching herself, her breaths between sentences getting heavier. "I am Beatrice's property. My body belongs to her. My mind is for her to fill. Her will is my will."

No orders were being given but just the pleasure she'd receive from her trigger was causing Lia to follow the implied instructions. Beatrice wondered how far she could take this. "Good girls debase themselves for their mistress."

Lia started to giggle as all the suggestions were clearly starting to combine. A new version of her mantras spilled out between soft moans and heavy breaths. "I am Beatrice's fuckdoll. My tits belong to her. My cunt is for her to fill. Her will is my will."

Beatrice had to actually take a moment to take that all in. She put a hand to her chest and caught her breath. "My, my, there's a little slut hidden in you, isn't there?"

Lia tipped over, her declarations erratic as her hand was moving faster than ever. "Yes, mistress, I'm a slut. I'm your slut. My body belongs to you. Cunt belongs to you, ass belongs to you."

"So shameless. Seeing as you're my slut and I own your body, then I suppose you can't cum without my permission." Beatrice smirked at the whine that incited. She'd clearly been approaching a climax. She snapped her fingers. "Into the bed and against the wall, darling."

"Yes, mistress," Lia panted, crawling onto the bed while still muttering variations of her mantra. She laid against the back of the bed and her hand started to find its way between her legs again.

"No, no, that's mine, remember?" Beatrice said, Lia's hands obediently falling to her sides. She ran her hands along her body, giving one of her breasts a good squeeze as she teased her clit. "You love that, don't you? You're just a sex toy, a fuckdoll and you love that I own you."

"Love it," Lia said with a stupid grin. Her mind had to be a horny puddle by now. "Love being owned. Body belongs to you. Mind for you to fill."

"Good girl, repeat your mantras while I enjoy my lovely doll." Beatrice caressed her breasts. Gods they were captivating in of themselves, she sucked on one while still playing with her pussy. Lia moaned, gripping the bed sheets as she clearly was fighting to not touch anything without permission. Beatrice gave her breasts a squeeze. "You may play with these beauties, if you wish."

Lia's hands shot to her chest the moment she had permission. "Thank you, mistress."

"Of course, darling. I take care of the things I own." Lia moaned with surprise as Beatrice kissed her, whining as she pulled away just as fast. She fingered her faster. "Then again, we all give a little extra attention in the early days of ownership. Maybe I'll grow bored, leave you on a shelf without a thought in your head. Playing with yourself endlessly with no release, just to stay wet in case I decide to use you again. What do you think of that?"

Lia stopped muttering her mantras between moans just long enough to say, "I think what you want me to think, mistress."

Beatrice got a rush from that. "Oh *good girl*, such a good little doll, so obedient I don't even have to teach you what you clearly already know. You don't think, you just obey."

"I don't think, I just obey!" Lia shouted, the pleasure triggered by her praise clearly overwhelming her already edged body. Her eyes were rolling into the back of her head as she almost started to scream her mantra. "I am Beatrice's property! My body belongs to her! My mind is for her to fill! Her will is my will!"

"Do you want permission to cum?" Beatrice asked casually.

"Yes!! Yes mistress, please!" Lia begged.

She smiled. "Will you do anything? Even humiliating?"

"Yes!"

Beatrice caressed her way upwards, unrelenting with her fingers. "Tell me what you'll do. Make me believe you."

"Anything, mistress!" Lia cried out. "I'd walk around naked, back to my room, to the ballroom with all the guests, I'd go to Ida herself and tell her I'm your whore. I'd let you twist my mind until I was nothing but a doll, sucking on whatever you leave in my mouth as you toss me away until—"

Beatrice stuffed her panties into her mouth mid-sentence. "Cum."

Lia arched her back as the fabric muffled her scream of pleasure. Beatrice's eyes glowed as she collapsed back into the bed. "Sleep."

Lia's eyes rolled back as they closed. Beatrice stroked her head. "Deeper and deeper, every ounce of your will having left your body and nothing left but my obedient, loyal doll. Sinking into the afterglow, no worries, no needs, no thoughts." She laid on her side next to Lia, gently removed the undergarment from her mouth and let her take those needed deep breaths. Beatrice certainly was taking some, she was exhausted. As her breathing evened out, Lia looked so peaceful. Beatrice almost just snuggled up next to her but decided against having her sleep here. This time, at least. She gave her cheek a light tap. "Open your eyes."

Lia obeyed. Her eyes were emptier than a sleepwalker and yet they made Beatrice feel so alive. "Are you ready to go onto the ballroom floor, my mindless slut? Flaunt your body to the guests and declare yourself my whore?"

"Yes, mistress," Lia whispered in a way that made her shiver.

"As much as I'd enjoy that, I think you've earned your rest. Use my washroom to clean up, then return to your room." Beatrice felt another rush as one of Lia's ideas sounded quite tantalizing. She assumed the path between their rooms would be barren during the soirée. No guarantees, but where was the thrill without risk? Beatrice lightly pressed on Lia's chin, opening her mouth without a hint of resistance, and gently stuffed her impromptu gag back in. "You will return naked. Keep my panties in your mouth. For safekeeping."

"Safekeeping," Lia repeated. Or at least that assumably was what the muffled word she just said was.

"When you lay down, you will put them on your head and repeat your mantras until you fall asleep." Beatrice was having way too much fun, she couldn't help herself. Already she saw a future of scandalous nights with her new thrall laid out. But in the same beat there was a tinge of fear. What would Lia think of this when she awoke? Would the real her *want* this? No, she certainly would start to question her own actions and then Beatrice would have to enchant more answers. How much of Lia's personality, of that realness that she craved, would disappear because of her debased desires? It was a clear cascade to an empty thrall and as much as she enjoyed the devoted doll she was softly caressing even now, it wasn't something she would permanently trade for her ditzy handmaiden.

Still, Lia deserved a night to remember after giving her mistress one. "And as you dream, your memory of tonight will change."

Lia walked down the halls of the von Closen House, her nipples hard against the cold air as she leaned slightly forward with her steps. The only garment being the pair of panties safely stuffed into her mouth, drool trailing down her bare chest. She muttered muffled mantras like a good girl should. The excitement of being caught was not being comprehended by her mind but her body certainly felt it. She heard voices from other halls, the music getting louder at one point, more than one occasion seeing a maid in the distance until she turned before either got close enough to truly see the obedient slut exposing herself on her walk to her room. She never even considered changing paths to hide, she would've walked right past them if they'd come this way.

Eventually Lia reached her room, took the panties out of her mouth and onto her head, and laid in her bed. As she began to obediently repeat her mantras and slowly drift off into sleep, she couldn't help but feel a sliver of sadness. She knew her memory of their dance would be replaced with them dancing at the ball. They had not left together in anger but stayed out of spite, with Beatrice showing her a good time and saving a special dance just for her. It was sweet and she cherished being able to remember that.

Except Lia was a slut. She was Bea's slut and deep down under the loving loyalty was a debased desire to disobey just so she could remember that too. She wanted to remember making love to her mistress, worshiping her body, even now the scent from her panties filling her nose as she savored the memory of eating her out. She wanted to remember being edged relentlessly, begging for humiliation, her mind melting as she came harder than she ever had in her life.

But Lia was also a good handmaiden. An obedient doll, willing to do anything for her mistress. As her mantras trailed off into nothing and her eyes fluttered shut, she knew she'd follow her instructions to the letter. She lived to serve.

It had been a night to remember. Too bad Lia wouldn't.

Part 2

The Rules of the House

Chapter 13
Savory Snacks

Lia was in an amazing mood. She was all but dancing with her steps, even standing still at her lovely lady's side she swayed back and forth as she hummed ballroom melodies. For the first time she truly felt like she belonged in her role. Bea seemed amused by her high spirits as the two of them walked together down the House halls. "You seem to be chipper today."

"Very much, my lady. I never thought I'd get to go to a fancy party." Lia sighed as she closed her eyes and reminisced. "Or share a dance with a beautiful lady."

Bea blushed. "There's no need to feed my ego, darling."

Lia twirled. "I can't help it, I feel so alive today!"

"That can be rectified if need be."

Lia covered her mouth as she yelped from terror, startling Bea in the process. Atropos loomed over them with her hands behind her back. She was smiling, if one could call the tiny curl upwards a smile. Somehow it was more terrifying than her scowl. "The Lady of the House wishes to see you, Lady Beatrice."

Bea straightened up. "I suppose this was inevitable. Why send you to fetch me, though?"

Atropos held up a hand to reveal a pair of scissors. She didn't snip at the air so much as sliced it like a paintbrush. The blades seemed to cut through reality itself, a tear opening further and further until it was a fully sized portal with the door to Ida's study laying beyond its threshold. "She didn't want you to get...sidetracked." She glanced at Lia when she said that last part.

Bea narrowed her eyes. "Lia—"

"—will accompany you. Those are my orders." Atropos never seemed as happy as she did in this moment. She leaned in to whisper but not quietly enough for Lia's good hearing. "No hiding your toys away this time, little miss."

Lia admittedly was caught up in the amazing work of magic before her. The edges of the portal were nonexistent, it truly looked like a piece of reality had been cut open. Bea's expression made her refocus. Before she seemed steadfast, but now she looked frightened.

"My lady?" Lia asked as Atropos turned to step through the gateway.

Bea took her hand. "Please, don't try to speak for me, don't try to defend me, do not draw attention to yourself in any way."

"Okay, but why?" Lia frowned when she looked terrified to answer. "Bea, you're scaring me."

Bea cringed and her eyes glowed. "Don't be scared. Just let me handle this."

Lia smiled as her fear melted away. "Ok, mistress." She held her hand tighter as they stepped through together. "I'll still be right behind you."

Ida and Bea stared at each other for nearly a minute in complete silence with both their eyes glowing. It got to a point Lia wondered if fae could speak to each other by glaring. The chance to ask disappeared as Ida finally spoke. "I have just endured a very long conversation with Coric Deburio. One so long that it had started last night. You deemed to retire early and have spent much of this morning avoiding any of the staff that isn't your handmaiden."

Bea raised an eyebrow. "I'm unsure what you mean about the staff. The little need I had for them Lia supplements easily. I assume they have begun shifting their habits."

"And I suppose furniture rearranges itself when you decide on a favorite chair?" Ida did not seem amused. "If their habits are changing, it is from suggestions you have given them. So I reiterate, you know what this is about and have been avoiding the consequences. I shall give you one chance to explain."

Bea straightened up. "Nyssa Deburio disrespected me, spit on our name, and mocked our traditions. I am not sorry."

Ida did not look pleased at this explanation. "Do you even comprehend what you've done?"

Bea matched her gaze. "I reclaimed stolen property. They should've known better."

"That doesn't mean you had the right to turn the Deburio's daughter into a befuddled bovine." Ida did not shout but her raised voice was like blades of ice to the ears. "You will give her back her name this instant."

Bea didn't flinch, but Lia noticed her hands behind her back were moving rapidly, like she was channeling all her fear into one place and keeping it out of sight. "I never took it."

Ida narrowed her eyes. "The evidence to the contrary currently believes she walks on all fours."

"The laws of the courts are clear, I am not allowed to take the name of a fellow fae by force. In any case, that's the tactic of the Deburio family, I just...reorganized. If she's as intelligent as she declared she'll find herself in the back of her mind in a day or two." Bea was very clearly trying not to smile. "My guess, at worst she'll be mooing for a month."

Ida pinched the brim of her nose and took a deep breath. "I see." She turned around. "You're lucky their demands were less than reasonable. A request to undo it, perhaps I would've obliged, but a demand for your name in exchange was nothing short of insulting. A clear attempt to trade up."

Lia beamed proudly for Bea, but stifled a scream when a tendril of hair wrapped around her lady's neck. Ida's eyes glowed like bloody rubies as she turned back. "Do not think this makes your actions commendable. Any more of a similar nature and I will take away what little privileges you still have. Starting with your tramp."

Bea looked more scared of that last comment than of literally being strangled. Lia couldn't stop herself from rushing forward but the hair already let go by the time she reached her side.

"You may take her to her chambers," Ida said, turning her attention to her work as if the matter was settled.

Bea was locked in terror on something only she seemed to be able to see, her eyes slowly turning red as if the sapphires were bleeding. She barely cared to breathe until Lia incited her to. "What did you do to her?"

Ida side-eyed her. "Take her to her chambers."

Lia's legs tried to obey. She didn't let them. "Not until you tell me what you did to Lady Beatrice."

Ida's face darkened at her disobedience. Her hair slithered and curled around the floor like angry snakes. "You should be grateful I am not permitted to lay a hand nor hair on you. Beatrice will recover. If you do not obey your mistress then I cannot guarantee you will be as fortunate."

Lia hugged Bea's arm defensively. "Bea is my mistress."

Ida smirked. "Rule three of the House. Repeat."

"Ida's authority supersedes all others if conflicting orders arise," Lia obediently replied. She almost started to argue but held her tongue. She didn't want to give Ida ideas. "I'll make sure she gets back to her room safely."

"Indeed you will." Ida seemed to take pleasure in her moping. She waved her hand as Lia gently led Bea out. "Never forget that I am the Lady of the House. And you belong to the House."

Lia was not a violent person. The Lady of the House made her wish she was. She helped Bea walk back to her room, the long way back as Atropos did not grace them with a portal. That last remark made her blood boil. It wasn't even *true*, Ida was twisting those stupid rules to make it seem like she had more authority than she did.

I am Beatrice's property. Not Ida's.

My body belongs to her. Not to the House.

My mind is for her to fill. Not for the Lady of the House to overwrite.

Her will is my will. And her will is stronger than them all.

The strange mantra left Lia's mind as quick as it surfaced but it made her feel better. More importantly, it made her feel loyal. She rubbed her head against Bea's shoulder. "I'm sorry to have caused this, my lady."

Bea didn't respond. She didn't say a word the entire walk to her chambers. Lia led her to her bed, sat her down, and then went to get her tea. It was a bit concerning that she was still there by the time she returned. Although her eyes were normal again, tearful but back to the beautiful blue. She was muttering something under her breath.

"I am Beatrice von Closen. I am a fae. I am real." Bea whispered it over and over like her own mantra, every time she got to the last part she didn't sound fully sure.

"Are you ok?" Lia poured her tea, handed her the cup, then sat down next to her.

Bea stared at the cup of tea in her hands. "Is this real?"

Lia frowned. "Is there a way to fake tea?"

Bea laughed, soft at first but growing louder until the laughs became cries and Lia managed to take the cup away before she put her hands to her face and screamed into her palms.

Lia had never seen her act like this before. She didn't know what to do, but it was so distressing she had to do something. She put her head on her shoulder, took Bea's hand, and put it on top of her head.

Bea didn't exactly calm down but the act did derail her meltdown. "What are you doing?"

Lia wasn't fully sure. "Comforting you?"

"How does—in what way is this *you* comforting *me*?" Despite asking, Bea had not taken her hand away.

"I don't know." A hand on her head was how Diana always calmed Lia down but that probably meant she should've put her hand on Bea's head, not the other way around. "Is it working?"

Bea didn't answer. The hand still had yet to move. Lia took that as permission to lean on her shoulder and in doing so had a very strange urge, like a rumble being caught in her throat. Was she trying to *purr*? That's...new. Might be a "is this a demon thing" question for Diana.

Maybe purring would help. Would Bea think she was weird? Of course she would, Lia wanted to purr and felt very capable of doing so, that's *really* weird.

"So, what was that?" Lia asked, trying not to think about purring. "Your eyes turned red and you looked like you'd seen a ghost."

"My mother is quite good at making her threats clear." Bea wiped a tear away. "I don't need to imagine what they would be like. She implants in my mind exactly how she thinks it will play out. And she has a vivid imagination."

No wonder Bea asked if this was real. "Doesn't that mean you'd like, experience the threat anyways?"

Bea looked away. "Quite an effective way to make me not want to experience it permanently."

"What did she make you see?" Lia put her hand on her shoulder, but took it back when Bea flinched. "Oh. It was something with me, wasn't it?"

Bea didn't answer.

Lia leaned in front of her. "I think you need a snack. Would you like that?"

Bea refused to look at her but faintly nodded.

"As you wish, my lady." Lia stood and gave a curtsey. She knew she never did them properly but the flimsy attempts always got Bea to smile so she didn't exactly try to improve them. And sure enough the hint of a smirk broke through her sourness.

Lia spent most of her walk trying to think of what treat would cheer up a fae. She knew most of her lady's pastry tendencies, she was more fond of baked and frosted goods than ones with filling, but nothing really spoke out as special. This train of thought was derailed as she entered the kitchen to see Clotho raiding the pantry. And raiding was the right word, she was so focused on hunting for whatever it was she wanted that she didn't notice Lia coming up behind her.

Lia had always been a little scared of Clotho, but the head maid had been around for way longer than she had. She might be able to point her in a direction. She cleared her throat. "Excuse me?"

Clotho froze, her head slowly turning towards her. She grunted with acknowledgement.

"Bea's sorta upset right now and I wanna get her something to help make her feel better. Do you know a treat she likes that fits that?" Lia asked timidly.

Clotho didn't speak but the sequence of expressions that occurred Lia interpreted as; confused as to why *she* was being asked, genuine thought, a toothy smile as an idea hit her, and a head nod. She gave the impression of somebody who learned common as a second language but understood it well enough. Or maybe she was just a maid of few words.

Then Clotho vanished into thin air, leaving a confused cook holding a rolling pin in her place. Lia wasn't sure why, but she had this instinctual understanding this was a fellow servant. Even though she looked like she'd come straight from a bakery. The woman looked at her with confusion. "Where am I?"

Lia opened her mouth but another blink and Clotho was back in her place holding a tray of brownies. They smelled fresh. "Do we have a bakery in this House too? Or did you just teleport to a random bakery we own?" A more pressing question rose in her mind. "Wait, did you just steal those?"

Instead of answering, Clotho stuffed two brownies into her mouth and placed the tray on the counter before leaving without a word. Well, there were two words, said a tad too late as Lia went to grab the tray and yelped from the pain. "Still hot."

"Oh my gods, where did you snag a full tray of these?" Bea was not elegant in devouring the deserts as fast as she could.

"A good handmaiden has to have some secrets of the trade, doesn't she?" Lia wasn't sure if she would believe her encounter with Clotho. She nibbled at the corner of a brownie. "They taste sorta bland."

Bea laughed. "You aren't eating them right, then. Honestly, you really shouldn't let me eat this many, they're a tad addictive. But given recent events it's...well, it's basically emotional food. Focus on a feeling and you'll feel that one as you eat it."

It was weirdly hard to focus on a feeling purposefully. As Lia took a second bite she didn't so much taste a food but feel an explosion of emotions in her mouth. Excitement, joy, satisfaction, pride, and embarrassingly, arousal. In fact she had to sorta fight that last one as it started to win. That had been happening a lot lately, she just kept finding herself horny without a cause.

Well, there was one cause, it was always around Bea. Or when she was drawing Bea. Or thinking about Bea. Lia was ignoring the obvious on purpose, it was beyond inappropriate to think of her lady like that. At least, while being right next to her.

Those thoughts were for after hours.

"Woah, that was a lot," Lia said as she evened out. She was impressed Bea had eaten so many, she must have extreme control of her emotional state. "So the von Closens sell foods that make you feel things?"

Bea nodded. "Oh yes, we own several shops that specialize, I think the sleep gummies have been quite the financial success. Of course those are made with purpose, diluted to elicit specific feelings or thoughts. This is much more potent. And dangerous, you could end up in quite a spiral if you accidentally enhance more negative attributes."

"Sooo, I gotta make sure you stay happy while eating that many?" Lia scooched over and laid her head on her shoulder. "Cuz I'm gonna try to if that's the case."

Bea let her own head lean on Lia's in turn and yawned. "Oh? Do tell what your strategy for that is going to be."

"Hmm. I don't know, I already got you sweets, not sure how to top that," Lia said, "You're the smart one. Is there anything you can think of? Bea?"

Bea had gone silent. Lia listened carefully to hear her breathing calmly, slowly leaning further onto her as her body relaxed. Aww.

Did she think about the sleep gummies and then fall asleep because the emotion food amplified it? That's so cute.

Well, it wasn't fair to be awake then. Lia snuggled into a more comfortable position and took a big bite. This time the brownie tasted delicious, warm and calming almost. She closed her eyes as a feeling of prideful satisfaction guided her to sleep. "Sweet dreams, my lady."

Chapter 14
Temptation

"I brought more candles!" Lia said cheerfully as she entered Diana's chamber. That word what she settled on, calling it her room felt weird, her cellar made it sound like she was living with the booze. Actually that sounded like a place she'd like, maybe it did fit better than her chamber. Lia had done her best to spruce the place up with her visits. It hadn't worked yet but she was trying her best.

"I think I have enough candles for a monastery." Diana stopped as she sniffed the air and her eyes dilated. "Is that dried sage?"

"Mhm. And I brought some extra paper. You know, for recreational use." Lia smiled as her sister was already hard at work rolling a joint only a demon would ever enjoy . "I'm sorry you haven't gotten the real thing in a while, holy sticks just aren't something we really take stock of. I hope this covers the cravings."

"It'll take the edge off for sure." Diana cut a sliver of paper from one of the sheets with her pinky. She was impressively delicate with her claws when she needed to be. "I'm surprised they let you bring me stuff."

"Actually, as long as it's reasonable they sorta just let me have whatever if I say it's for you." Lia hung up a few drawings on the wall. She'd been bringing her favorites, to keep Diana 'in the loop' as she requested. Not clear what interest she had in handmaidening but it was whatever, she got to show off her art. "Well, Lachesis does. Atropos grilled me about why I wanted to give you candles for like an hour, I think she assumed you'd somehow set the House on fire."

Diana pulled out a lighter, one Lia had gotten her for her birthday and had negotiated getting back to her after the candle request. "Ain't nothing flammable around here, sis." She lit her homemade joint and took a puff like it was the last one on earth. The smell was already making Lia regret her decision a bit, she forgot how much that habit sucked in close quarters. "Believe me, I checked."

"You saying stuff like that is why I get grilled about giving you stuff." Lia shivered at the memory. Over and over Atropos asked nearly identical questions, a lot she didn't even have good answers as a half-demon. She should get a book on demon anatomy if she was so interested in such weirdly personal things. "Plus, I'd prefer you not burn down my lady's home."

"If you didn't have the wool over your eyes you'd be begging me to," Diana muttered.

"Hey, be nice!" Lia said defiantly, "I know you warned about fae a bunch but it's been sorta nice working for Bea. She's treated me very kindly and is very honest with me. Mostly." It had been a few weeks since Ida punished Bea and she still wondered what the Lady of the House had made her see. She hadn't asked, no need to make her lady relive it. Knowing she mattered to her enough to be used as a punishment had a weird endearing effect to it.

Diana paused after another puff. "Ok, so you heard that. You know Beatrice is a fae? Like you know she and her family enchant their victims?"

"Yeah, I've seen her do it to a few people. I don't mind, it's sorta fun to watch." *And exciting to think about her doing it to me.* Lia quickly stuffed that thought down with embarrassment. Thoughts for later, she still had a full day ahead of her.

"Sis, she just made you think you didn't mind," Diana said. There was a nervous glee in her tone, like she wanted to gossip but wasn't sure if nobody was listening. "They're fae, and not just any fae but the von Closens. They are masters of enchantment and deceit, worse than vampires trying to lure you out of your homes. They can make you not see things that are there, do things that you'd never do, instill their will to make you into a puppet. Lia, look at me." She did and was concerned by the intensity of her sister. "The von Closens can change what you perceive. Even about your loved ones."

Lia already knew all this, hell she fantasized about it sometimes, she wasn't getting why Diana was being so intense. "Okay?"

Diana looked at her even more bewildered. "Gods I can't tell if that's the enchantment or you're just that thick." She leaned back and laughed painfully. "Probably both."

"Hey, I'm not stupid!" Lia wasn't sure what enchantment she was talking about. She noted that for later but somehow could feel the mental note already slipping out of her pocket.

"Never said that," Diana said with that sisterly mocking tone of one hundred percent having said that.

Lia sat down on the couch. "I don't get why you hate the von Closens so much. Like, I have my own room, good honest work, three meals a day—"

"Prison's got all that too."

Lia made a face. "Are you saying working for Bea is as bad as prison?"

"Pristine prison is still prison, sis." Diana waved her blunt around in thought. "Pristine prison. Where have I heard that before?"

It felt familiar to Lia too. Deja vu, as it were. "I think Bea said it once."

She shook her head. "Can't be that, never met her."

"Maybe you should. Bea is super nice, I'm sure you'd get along if you gave her a chance." Lia smiled brightly. She would understand Diana's feelings if she only thought of the von Closens in reference to the Lady of the House. As Bea said with Lucial and demons, Ida did not make a good case for fae kind. She sucked.

"So you often say," Diana scoffed, "Not like you're working for fae and an upper crust at that. A two for one special on being two-faced."

"Oh haha, very funny." Lia rolled her eyes. "I've seen both faces. The real Bea is very caring and even then both faces treat me with respect, I'm sure you're being dramatic.

Beatrice bit her lip to stop a moan from escaping. She put a hand on Lia's head, which was between her legs mindlessly licking away. Gods the girl had talent with her tongue, even in a trance she could tease like a pro.

As declared during that night of dance and debauchery, this had become a nightly ritual. One Lia was quite unaware of. Beatrice could've enchanted her to believe this was just part of her duties, but something about having her be in trance added to the fun. The mindless devotion was unmatched, the only thought in Lia's head was to lick her mistress. Nothing but a doll whose only purpose was to make her owner cum. The scandalous thought pushed Beatrice over the edge and she came onto her handmaiden's face.

Beatrice used a finger to push her head away as she caught her breath. Lia licked at the empty space before her, her mouth dripping with juices. How did she make such a dumb act look so cute? "Stop."

Lia obeyed. "Yes, mistress."

"Clean yourself up."

"Yes, mistress." If Beatrice hadn't been watching she might've not caught Lia lick her lips before reaching for the towel she'd set out for them. For whose benefit she wasn't sure.

Beatrice laid back and sighed. "I wish I could reward you. I'm not sure how, though." She didn't know that much about Lia. Whenever she asked she would dodge the question and say she was 'poor and downtrodden'. It was strange, the answer felt like one an enchantment had fed her but Atropos' enchantment should only make them blind to the few weeks before their employment. Lia's mind seemed to reject the question entirely.

Although then again, maybe the staff would act the same way. It's not like Beatrice ever actually asked. "What would you desire as a reward?"

"Serving you is my reward, mistress," Lia said.

Beatrice rolled her eyes with a smirk. "A reward you can't remember. What would the waking you desire?"

A pause. Lia said quietly, almost inaudible, "To cum, mistress."

Beatrice sat up with a frown. "What?"

"Your handmaiden wishes to cum, mistress," Lia said. Her cheeks were bright red even for how expressionless she was.

There was missing context here. Beatrice lifted Lia's chin and let her eyes do their work. "Explain."

Lia gave a relaxed sigh as she began to confess. "I think about you every night. I love serving you but sometimes I fantasize you telling me to do something dirty. And I'd imagine I wouldn't hesitate, even if it was humiliating, because you can just look into my eyes and I'd be unable to resist. I imagine embarrassing myself for your amusement, turning me into a fuckdoll as you play with my body. I imagine my mind emptying, ready for you to fill it with your own twisted desires. But no matter how worked up I get I can't cum."

Beatrice was heating up, she almost pushed her back between her legs for a second round. But also a sting of guilt was beginning. Lia wasn't supposed to remember these encounters, much less fantasizing about them. "Why not?"

"You haven't given me permission, mistress." Lia said it so innocently, like she was reminding her lady of a responsibility she had forgotten.

The guilt stabbed further. Beatrice could almost hear herself declaring that order weeks ago. She never imagined she'd adhere to it when out of trance. "Why are you still following that suggestion?"

Lia's cheeks rose ever so slightly from a loyal smile. "Obedience is pleasure. I live to serve, mistress."

Beatrice looked away. The adorable whine now hurt to hear. Lia wasn't just enchanted, she was getting addicted. An addiction that her mistress inflicted on her just because it got her off and now she was starting to crave being used. Commands meant for the moment cementing themselves in her so deep that even her waking self was being denied release just to feel the high of obeying her mistress. It was hot and it was horrible.

Lia didn't ask for it.

Beatrice needed to make it right, in more ways than one. She could just remove the suggestion, but Lia deserved more than just a simple fix. She looked into her handmaiden's eyes with fierce intent. She went limp like a doll whose strings had been cut as she was sent deep into trance. "Lia, listen to me very carefully."

Lia lay in bed, her duties long since finished, and her hands already slipping between her legs. Almost a nightly ritual by now, she barely had the will to resist it. Every time she returned to her quarters she would just be so unbelievably horny.

Horny for her mistress.

It was shameful to admit, but Lia couldn't stop thinking about Beatrice. Eyes that could entrance but a body that didn't even need them to capture a maiden's gaze. Every one of her fantasies kept curling back to the silver haired fae. Tonight's was so vivid. Lia could almost see herself walk into Bea's room and lock the door behind her, without awareness she'd been told to be there but not questioning it either way. With but a glance every thought she had vanished and the obedient doll she truly was rose to the forefront to obey. Her lady, who she now recognized as her mistress, her owner, began to tell her what to do.

Strip. Lia obeyed. Property did not need clothes. She'd never wear them again if she was told not to.

Kneel. Lia obeyed. She belonged on her knees, at her mistress's feet. She would stay there for the rest of her life if her mistress desired it.

Lick. Lia obeyed. Her tongue was nothing but a tool to please her mistress. The drool running down her chin was no longer from an empty mind but a lustful focus as her mistress opened her legs and had her loyal doll crawl between them to perform its purpose.

Lia squirmed as she could almost taste her mistress, unsure how she'd become so imaginative lately but reveling in it nonetheless. Just to touch Bea in such a way felt like a privilege she could not comprehend and it made her so wet to think she'd be allowed to go down on her. In her fantasy, however, the only thing on her mind was lapping away like a good little fucktoy. Each lick was an order obeyed and would give her a wave of pleasure, she could imagine it so clearly and was trying desperately to make herself feel it now.

This was usually where it ended. A hot mess unable to finish. Except this fantasy, so vivid she could feel her owner's fingers under her chin, lifting it up to stare into her wonderful, enchanting eyes. Eyes that spoke to her now, the perverted little handmaiden touching herself at this very moment. Ordering her not to let up, to finger faster and faster, unable to stop, unable to disobey, unable to even think as her eyes crossed and her muddled mind emptied, leaving nothing but a horny doll shamelessly fucking itself until she was finally allowed to—

Cum.

Lia obeyed. She came for the first time in days, maybe weeks. It was impossible for her not to all but scream, "Yes, mistress!" as she swore it was like every orgasm of all the nights she'd failed to finish happened at once.

Lia took deep, heavy breaths, barely able to keep her eyes open as all her energy went to that wonderful release. But even as she let them shut the sapphire eyes were still there. Whispering soothing commands that cuddled her melted mind as she fell deeper and deeper. She gently wrapped herself in them like warm blankets.

Property has permission if its owner is unavailable to give it.

Lia drunkenly smiled as sleep overtook her. "Thanks, Bea."

Beatrice loved having a mindless handmaiden.

It didn't make sense. She never got joy out of it before, if anything she was always indifferent towards those she enchanted. But Lia just invoked a passion in her she couldn't grapple with. She kept wanting to ask Lia to do things. And only Lia, she kept wanting to use *her*. Beatrice wanted to watch her eyes go blank, her smile so unrelenting that it still stayed up, albeit droopy. She wanted to hear Lia say 'yes, mistress' in a way that only she seemed to be able to make sound full of devotion and made said mistress feel things that she could not quite understand.

And Beatrice swore the second she decided to reel herself back, to try to think with her head and not her loins, Lia had made it her life's mission to tempt her. Feigned ignorance towards tasks, leaning in ways that had no benefit to her cleaning, even overstepping in ways that seemed poised to incite an enchantment. This was proof she had addled the girl's mind, she was subconsciously craving control. It wasn't clear how she was supposed to ween off an addict who both didn't know she was addicted and her dealer was having a hard time not giving her more drugs.

"Darling, what do you think you're doing?"

Lia smiled. "Preparing your bath, my lady."

"The bath seems quite prepared. I am asking what you are *still* doing." Beatrice internally sighed. This one was becoming the most consistent. Perhaps because it was technically a task that some handmaidens would be asked of but one that she did not.

"Oh. Well, I thought since I've been your handmaiden for some time now that perhaps—"

"No."

"Com'on, you don't even know what I was going to say!"

"You want to participate in cleaning my body." Beatrice wasn't sure what was inciting her desire for this. Perhaps given in trance she'd seen her undressed, her awake mind was desensitized to seeing such a thing. And so her desire to be a quality handmaiden made her want to do this task.

Lia blushed. "I wasn't going to phrase it like that."

"You've come up with many rephrasings, the answer is still no." Every time it became harder for Beatrice to give that answer. She needed to have self-control. "I'm not a child and you are acting like one with how immature you're being."

"It's not immature, it's a proper duty of a handmaiden," Lia said, "Are you embarrassed for me to see you naked?"

If only she knew how ironic asking that was. "I am not going to humor that with an answer."

"I mean, we could make it fair." Lia smiled brightly. "I could get naked too."

Be strong, Beatrice, be strong. "I do not see the equivalency."

"You know, if I get to see you, then you get to see me? I don't mind, it'll make my job easier. Won't have to get my uniform wet." It was unclear if Lia even knew what she was suggesting. She was so empty headed sometimes. "I just think-"

Beatrice snapped her head with her eyes burning bright and grabbed her by the cheeks. Lia had only a moment of flushed excitement before her eyes emptied and a bit of drool dribbled out instead of the rest of her sentence. "If you are so determined to accompany me in the washroom then *thinking* will be beyond your capabilities."

Lia smiled blankly with her left arm straight out. The only clothing on her body was the towel that hung from it. This was normal. She was a towel holder after all.

Lia was a good towel holder. She'd be squirming with excitement for how good of a job she was doing but objects don't squirm. They don't think about the ecstasy of having their purpose fulfilled, even if her body was involuntarily showing such excitement. They don't think about their skin sweating from the steam of the hot bath water or feel the ache of standing in place for so long. They don't think at all, it's not their purpose. Her purpose was to hold this towel.

Her owner grumbled from the bath, albeit while admiring her property. "Why does this somehow feel like you winning?"

Lia just continued to blankly smile. She was a very happy towel holder.

Chapter 15
Breaking Point

Rule Five : *I cannot tell Beatrice about the Rules of the House*

Lia startled awake. She had her hand around the handle of Bea's door. She would've screamed if this wasn't the fourth time she'd sleepwalked towards her room.

This was the closest she'd ever gotten, though.

Every week, this happened *every* week, right at the end. And what's worse was she couldn't plan for it because she kept forgetting about it by the start of the next week. She'd left notes for herself, but they'd eventually confuse her and she'd toss them out. She tried to tell Diana or even Bea, who she seemed very insistent on visiting in the middle of the freaking night but every time she tried she'd lose her train of thought and not think about it until it happened again.

Lia was already making her way to where her sister was being kept. Talking to her always calmed her down. Made her forget her worries.

Forget her worries. She didn't *want* to forget her worries, she wanted to stop the problem that was making her worried. Lia wanted to tell Bea. She *needed* to tell Bea. She couldn't. So she should go to Diana, that would make it all—*no!* No, no, no, she was not letting that voice win this time, this was getting worse, she needed help.

Who could Lia ask for help if not her lady or her sister?

Clotho's room was interesting to say the least.

Lia was not surprised the head maid was still awake. She never really saw her between breakfast and dinner. That didn't exactly feel like a great reason to go to her for help, but the options had been limited. Atropos was even scarier, Lachesis talked in circles, and even thinking of going to Ida made her skin crawl. Clotho was scary in a physical sense, yes, but she never acted like she wanted to hurt Lia. After the brownie encounter in the kitchen Lia started to see her as the most straightforward of the three head maids. So out of desperation for a straightforward answer she found herself knocking on Clotho's door. Surprisingly when Lia asked if they could talk she was invited in with no question. Maybe her gut feeling about coming here had merit.

Apparently Clotho had a thing for maps. Or maybe just geography in general, there were a lotta books sprawled about the city and the surrounding land layouts. A huge map on the wall was tacked with pictures of people or beautiful architecture, each with a date written under it. Lia noticed dates with people had yet to pass. She recognized several fae from the soirée.

The one thing she didn't seem to have at first glance was a bed. It might've been buried in the maps, there was a corner that sorta looked like a nest.

Lia sat nervously on a stack of books like it was a chair. Clotho just crouched to her eye level. She smiled nervously. "Should I make us some tea?"

"Hate tea." Clotho motioned to a bubbling contraption sitting next to her bed nest. It looked like a clear glass cup and a metal pitcher on a set of scales. There was an open flame under the pitcher and a dark brown liquid dripping into the open glass.

Lia had noticed it but now realized it was not just a strangely piled hoard of unrelated utensils. "Oh, you like coffee! I always wondered where those little bags of beans were ending up."

"Want some?" Clotho asked as she took the glass cup out of the holder.

Lia shook her head. "I don't think that would be a good idea, not being able to sleep is sorta part of my problem. Diana likes coffee though, maybe you could teach me how to make it?"

Clotho shrugged and downed the entire thing like it was a shot glass. Lia swore it was still boiling when she'd taken it out. "Sorta late for cooking lessons."

"Yeah, that's not why I came here. I have a weird problem."

Clotho didn't respond but she nodded her head up and appeared to be prepared to listen.

"So, I think it has to do with a night from my first week. It's honestly so long ago I don't even remember why Ida wanted to talk to me at midnight but ever since then, I keep waking up in the middle of the night around the same time. It's always on the day before the weekend, same day as that meeting, and I'm always on my way to Bea's room." Lia took a breath. Clotho's expression had yet to change. "I think I need to tell her...something. I don't know *what* I need to tell her but I need to and I feel like if she asks the right questions I'll remember and tell her. Like...like I just wanna follow all these different rules and there's a sequence that'll make everybody happy but I don't know it and I can't ask for help with puzzling it out." She smiled nervously. "Do you like puzzles?"

"No," Clotho grunted. It wasn't an annoyed reaction, just blunt. She wasn't reacting much at all but she did seem to be listening.

"Me neither. I love watching other people solve them, but I just get frustrated." Lia continued to ramble. "Anyways, I don't understand why it's so hard. And I keep having thoughts that don't feel like mine, but sometimes I like them and other times I hate them so I can't just ignore everything that doesn't feel like me."

"Hmm." Clotho took a breath with her teeth clenched, which felt threatening except her eyes were on the floor so that might've just been a thinking face. "Can you tell me?"

Lia smiled. That wasn't a bad idea. "I suppose."

Rule Five : I am not allowed to tell Beatrice about the Rules of the House.

This isn't Bea. "I think somebody is breaking an agreement."

Rule Five : I am not allowed to tell Beatrice about the Rules of the House. You know you're trying to tell her indirectly.

Indirectly isn't against the rules.

Rule Five : I am not allowed to tell Beatrice about the Rules of the House. You're a good maid. You belong to the House. A good maid follows the rules.

I am a handmaiden. I am Beatrice's property. She deserves to know. "She needs to know."

"That's not a rule," Lia said out loud to herself.

Lia scoffed at her own words. The internal argument very quickly got external. "Then let's make it a rule. Rule Two: I am Beatrice's property. She is my owner. So she should get to know."

Clotho didn't try to interrupt. Her attention was more focused than ever.

"You can't do that. Beatrice isn't allowed to modify the Rules of the House," Lia said to herself again.

Lia rolled her eyes. "No rules against *me* adding more rules and this rule makes sense. Rule Two: I am Beatrice's property. She is my owner."

"Stop that. Stop resisting. Property doesn't resist."

"I am not resisting. I fully accept that I am property. Beatrice's property." Lia didn't care how weird that sounded, she barely cared she was arguing with herself. She was winning that argument and that's all that mattered.

The loser using her voice sounded worried. "You don't know what you're doing. You're twisting it all together, it's too much. You need to stop before you break."

"Then let Bea fix me!" Lia shot to her feet, shaking violently as she tried to comprehend the conversation she just had with herself but could feel it leaving her mind like a bath being drained. Clotho stared at her with a raised eyebrow, the most reaction she'd given the entire time. "What's wrong with me?"

Lia wished she'd accepted that cup of coffee. Maybe then she wouldn't have passed out before Clotho could even grunt an answer.

Knock, knock, knock.

"Give me a moment." Beatrice rubbed her eyes as the knocking became more insistent. It wasn't the polite tap of a knuckle but the brutish bang of a fist. She sleepily trudged towards the door. "It is past midnight, what could possibly be so—"

Clotho was standing at her door. Lia was in her arms, muttering something under her breath. Suddenly Beatrice was awake and alert. "Dear gods, what happened?"

That was apparently permission for Clotho to enter and sit Lia on the couch. The head maid acted uncharacteristically concerned, in that she was showing any hint of concern at all. "She needs air."

Beatrice gave a worried look as she sat down next to her. "I can open a window."

"Real air." Clotho cracked her neck. "Been inside too long."

"I don't understand what's wrong with her?" Beatrice finally started to discern what she was saying. It was her mantras, disjointed and confused but her mantras for certain. Was she in a trance right now? It wasn't clear, she wasn't used to her face being fearful in that state. "How long has she been saying these?"

"Not long." Clotho made a face. "Too many orders. Trying to sort herself out."

Beatrice cursed herself. This was her fault. She was trying to limit her influence and instead she drove the girl into a mental breakdown. "Should I avoid putting her in a trance in this state?"

Clotho shrugged. "Not my specialty. Not my call." She closed the door, but not before saying, "Talk to her."

Beatrice noticed Lia had stopped once Clotho left. She wasn't quite sure what to do, but fortunately Lia went first. "Am I broken, my lady?"

So she wasn't in a trance. Beatrice was glad to have set up that 'my lady' and 'mistress' suggestion to be able to tell. "You're not broken, darling. What's wrong?"

"I don't know." Lia frowned. "I think I used to know. I told Clotho and she brought me here. And now I don't. That doesn't make sense but it feels like it's true."

"What did you talk with Clotho about?"

"Like I said, I don't know." Lia hugged her knees. "I feel so stupid right now because I can't even remember what upset me."

Beatrice was nervous about asking but she was curious too. "Do you recall what you were saying when she brought you here?"

"Yeah." Lia blushed. "I mean, maybe. I don't know, it was...calming me down. Made me feel safe."

"Do you say them often?"

Lia scrunched up her face. "No? Maybe. They feel familiar." She blushed even harder. "You didn't hear what they were, right?"

"No," Beatrice lied. She could tell Lia wasn't afraid so much as embarrassed by the mantra. Not a surprise she would be hesitant to admit to her lady she was declaring herself her property to calm herself down. No need to make her night worse. "You've been working very hard lately. Perhaps you should take some time off—"

"No!" Lia seemed to startle herself as she covered her mouth. "Sorry, gods, what is *wrong* with me tonight? Forgive me, my lady. Please, I'll be fine in the morning."

Beatrice didn't like that reaction. The enchantment should only make Lia want to be her handmaiden, not to feel fear at the idea of taking time off from the role. She gently put a hand on her shoulder. "This isn't a punishment."

"Why does it feel like one?" Lia asked sadly.

"Because you're an excellent handmaiden. But an ill handmaiden does not bode well for either her or her lady, so perhaps thinking it that way will help ease your mind about taking a break." Beatrice put the back of her hand against Lia's forehead. "You're a tad warm. We should discuss this tomorrow. If you won't take the day off then at least sleep in. A good night's rest may help whatever this is pass more smoothly."

The mention of sleep caused Lia to yawn, the fatigue she clearly was hiding now obvious. She looked away sheepishly. "Can I sleep here tonight? I think I sleepwalk. Or at least...Clotho says I do."

Beatrice gently cupped her cheek. "Lia, please, be honest with me. Do you remember going to her room?"

Lia was trembling. "No, my lady. I really don't."

Too many orders. Clotho wasn't one to give warnings lightly. Beatrice had only been worried she'd been affecting Lia's mind subconsciously. Now she was terrified the enchantments she'd laid were not a foundation but an intertwined web that was digging into her brain and bleeding her sanity. Beatrice guided her to lay down and handed her a spare blanket from underneath the sofa. "Get some rest, darling. You're free to use my lodgings until you feel better."

Lia just hugged the folded blanket, closed her eyes, and sighed. "Thank you, mistress."

Oh no. Beatrice looked in the mirror and saw the glowing eyes of a monster looking back.

Chapter 16
A Taste of Freedom

It was starting to hurt that her lady never seemed to look at Lia anymore.

Bea had been distant since Lia spent the night in her room. Not literally, in fact she was at her side more than ever before but that was mainly because she had stopped asking her to do things and thus Lia just spent most of her day standing nearby. Her lady was acting off. Reserved. It sorta reminded her of how she acted at the soirée.

It was bumming Lia out so much even her libido took a hit. Not for a want of trying, she had started her nightly ritual of pleasure a few times but when she tried to imagine her mistress she just looked so...so sad. Suddenly she wasn't fantasizing about worshiping her mistress, she just wanted to hug her and tell her she was okay.

Her dreams were even worse. In them she was a doll, once loved but now ignored. Not forgotten, she was well taken care of, but what was the point of a doll that was never used? Why wouldn't her owner look at her? Why wouldn't she play with her like she used to? Had she done something wrong? Was she going to throw her doll away?

Lia didn't fantasize at night much after that. She wanted to, she was longing for how it felt before, it just wasn't hitting right. And she'd rather not do anything than feel unsatisfied.

Strangely enough, that ritual got replaced with a new one; Clotho. Apparently she had the only coffee maker so Lia kept going to her room to make some for Diana and they got to talking. As much as one could call the maid's grunts conversation. After getting past that rabid animal exterior, Clotho was actually fairly docile. If she didn't want Lia to keep bothering her she easily could've started making coffee before she arrived and not let her make it herself.

"Is something wrong with Bea?" Lia asked while she poured water into the cylinder.

Clotho was staring at the maps on the wall. She shrugged. "Seems healthy."

"But not happy." Lia took the match from her mouth and lit the candlewick under the pitcher. Hard part was over, just a bit of waiting now. She sat down and snacked on the banana bread she'd brought in preparation for that. She'd been getting really good at making bread and had started to venture into fruit breads.

"Is she ever?" Clotho sniffed at the air, side-eying said snack.

"Yeah? I mean, I've seen her be happy." Lia pouted at the snort the maid gave. "I have! She's not exactly loud about it but she can enjoy herself. Something's bothering her."

Clotho shrugged. "Hasn't snuck out in a while. Cabin fever?"

"Snuck out?" Lia asked. "Why would she sneak out?"

"Wants to go outside on her own. Against the rules, needs a fate to guard her." Clotho sounded like her mouth was full. Lia swore she didn't see her move but one of her pieces of bread was missing.

"So like, one of the head maids gotta be there if she goes outside?" Lia asked, getting a grunt that she'd learned meant 'yes'. She could see why that would bum Bea out. Not to this extent but a stack of things bothering her could be just as likely as one big thing bothering her.

An idea struck Lia. She quickly explained it to Clotho, who didn't give an answer for the rest of the time she waited. Only after Lia poured her a mug of coffee and even then it wasn't until as she was about to leave with the cup for Diana did the maid shrug and say, "Sure."

Lia smiled brightly. "Amazing. Thank you!"

"You seem more eager than before about taking time off," Bea said, still not looking at her even with her in the mirror as she brushed her hair.

"Eager for me, no. Eager for you, yes." Lia almost thought better of saying anything more but she couldn't help it. "You've been really sad lately. A day on the town should cheer you up."

Bea sighed. "Remember how I said I wanted this to be a day you don't worry about me?"

"Too bad, I'm worrying." Lia put her chin on her shoulder. "You can tell me what's bothering you, you know? Companionship is a part of the gig and you haven't been using it as much as you should."

"You don't need to force yourself to be kind to me," Bea said quietly.

Lia lifted her head and looked at her like she was crazy. "Who said I was being forced?"

Bea turned away. "Apologies, that came out wrong. Forget I said anything."

"Ok. But still, not being forced. I like being nice, it's easier than being mean." Lia leaned around her to try and get her to smile. "And it's not like I would be asking what was wrong if Ida was my lady, so do with that what you will."

Lia, Bea, and their assigned guardian Clotho walked down the streets of Webershafen together. She hadn't really realized until now she'd never left the House to explore the upper city. The very thought had been foreign but now she was beyond its threshold and her curiosity had returned in full force. It was strange how similar it was to the slums but still distinctly better. It was more maintained, cared for even. The brickwork had no potholes, the land was level and not a patchwork of buildings sinking into the very ground. People even smiled at each other as they passed by. The slums always smelt like a mixture of sulfur and blood so it was a pleasant surprise the air here only had faint industrial smoke plaguing her. Not that it was great, just preferable to her demonic sense of smell. Clotho must've had an even better nose than her because she tended to cringe when the wind picked up.

Bea was dressed for an outing, Lia as well with only the skirt of an apron being a part of her outfit, but Clotho still wore her maid uniform. She somehow made that work. Probably because nobody would be brave enough to make a comment.

Their destination was technically a cafe on the edge of a market district, although Lia had brought a picnic's worth of supplies in a wicker basket. Bea had her public mask on, both literal in the veil she wore and figurative in her rigid properness. She walked elegantly, gaze locked forward as she said to Lia, "I still do not understand why you insisted on Clotho to be our guardian."

Lia smiled brightly, deciding they were probably far enough out of view. She bowed to the head maid. "Thank you for escorting us. I'll do my best to keep our lady out of trouble."

Clotho grunted, ruffled Bea's hair and patted Lia on the shoulder, then disappeared into the crowd. An impressive feat for somebody dressed as a maid.

Even the veil couldn't hide Bea's rare look of complete confusion. "What just happened?"

Lia lifted her shoulders gleefully. "I just negotiated two hours of unsupervised time off. You'll keep watch over me and I'll keep watch over you. We'll meet back here and pretend this is where we all spent the day. As far as Ida knows, all her rules were followed."

"What on earth did you bribe her with?" Bea asked.

Lia shrugged. "Nothing. I just asked and she seemed to agree it would be good for you."

Bea's eyes seemed to bore through her veil staring at her as if she was insane. "Truly?"

"Yeah, I mean, I *was* bringing her snacks a bunch but that's because we've been talking. Well, I've been talking. Clotho is a really good listener, like the way she listens makes it seem like she hates what you're talking about but that's not true, if she hates it she'll just leave." Lia paused. "I think. I don't know, I just don't bring up fashion anymore. She just sorta...left the room when I asked if she ever tried to grow her hair out."

Bea laughed. A long, genuinely baffled laugh that felt like the first real emotion she'd shown in a while. "Alright then. I suppose we shouldn't waste your hard work."

Lia smiled brightly. Maybe Bea really was the one who needed a day out instead of her, she already was acting more like her usual self.

"Oi, Lia? Is that you?"

The two of them turned to see a devilish man trotting up. He wasn't as short as an imp but he shared the trait of red skin and a forked tail, a winged devil. He lifted his bowler hat to them. Two holes were cut in the brim for his horns to poke through. "I haven't seens you in weeks. Was wondering if you finally gots Diana off the twigs, bad for me business but good for her lungs I'd wager."

"I'm terribly sorry, but...who are you?" Lia asked. She didn't quite remember who she last bought twigs off of for Diana but she was certain she'd remember a hat like that. Or the smell, which did imply he sold twigs as he smelt as smoky as a burning bush.

The man paused, then glanced at Bea. His smile didn't drop but seemed to further curl, clearly more forced than genuine. "Apologies, must've mistaken you's for somebody else. Easy to do these days, dare I say." He bowed so fast the smokey smell wafted harshly at them both. "Enjoy your day, your ladyship. Please forgive me rudeness towards confusing your servant."

The man vanished as swiftly as he appeared. Bea didn't seem annoyed but more like she was ashamed. She once again refused to look at her.

"What's wrong?" Lia asked.

Bea forced a small smile. "Just a reminder of something I need to make up for. Nothing to worry about."

Lia did worry though. Sure, it did bother her that a strange devil seemed to know her but a forgotten face was nothing to get worked up over. Yet her lady had been upset by it and Lia didn't like how it made it feel like it was somehow her fault.

So much lately felt like her fault. "So, shall we continue to lunch?"

Bea pursed her lips. "Yes, but I think I have a more enjoyable idea than a cafe."

Lia stared out over the open sea from their perch. "This is so cool! Does your family own this lighthouse too?"

"No, just an old hermit who decided to let me use it whenever I desire. And then forgets when I leave that he ever did so." That made sense, the bearded man seemed only concerned with Lia's existence until Bea had a few words with him. It was interesting how she used enchantments so subtly. For somebody who could have anything from a glance her lady seemed very inclined to remove even the implication that she asked it. So separate from the rest of the world that she didn't seem to want it to know she was there.

And yet in the same vein, Bea seemed to crave being as close to the world as she could get away with. Lia leaned over the side of the brick ledge. "You can see so much of the city from here."

"Trying to spot your childhood home?" Bea asked after flinching from her lack of fear.

"Uh, no, I didn't...exactly have one." Lia could see several churches she vaguely remembered staying at. Cathedrals were easy to spot from a view like this. "I was, you know, homeless."

"Oh, apologies, I didn't mean that as an insult." Bea cringed and held up a spyglass. "I was just offering to help."

"You have this for people watching, yeah?" Lia said, looking through. She felt like a pirate as she started with the shipyards loading and unloading crates of trade.

"A peaceful pastime of mine, yes. Although it's much more invigorating at night, those out and about in the hours of twilight usually have more interesting activities to deduce." Bea pulled up a chair for herself, which got Lia's brain to remember what her job was.

"Sorry my lady, I got distracted." Lia put the spyglass down and started rummaging through her wicker basket. "No table up here, but the ledge sorta works as one. Just give me a second to set up."

Bea reached down and lightly lifted her chin. "Darling?"

Lia's entire train of thought derailed off the ledge of the lighthouse. "Hmm?"

"A day for yourself, remember?" Bea gave her a gentle smile paired with a playful chastising look.

That train was not getting back on any rails at this rate. Lia blinked as she tried to form a response despite that. "I know, I just...wanna make it a good day for you too."

Bea sighed. "I suppose those aren't exclusive concepts." She reached into the basket and pulled out the wine with a raised eyebrow. "Interesting view of what a good day is for me."

"We were going to a cafe, I assumed they'd already have tea." Lia blushed. "We're lucky I brought food at all. Basically just cheese and bread in here."

"Then we have the essentials," Bea said with a smirk.

The wine was poured, the bread and cheeses were set out on a small silver plate that Lia was careful not to touch directly, and the two enjoyed the strange impromptu meal at the top of the light-house.

They ate, they talked, they watched the bustling city below together. It was almost like a date. Lia shouldn't really think of it like that, she was still a handmaiden and Bea was still her lady.

If it *was* a date, which of course it wasn't, but if it was, Lia was enjoying it.

"Can I ask a question?" she asked between bites of cheese.

"You just did," Bea said with a smirk as she took a sip of wine.

Lia rolled her eyes but still giggled. Should've expected that from a fae. "Oh shush, I'm serious, can I?" Her lady nodded. "Why don't you leave the House?"

Bea paused and said cautiously, "I suppose I should try to go out more often."

"No, no, like why don't you move away?" Lia asked. After learning her lady had a tendency to sneak out it was a question that had been on her mind. "You hated being at the soiree around other upper crusts. And when you're forced to do your aristocratic duties or studies you just seem to be miserable."

"You think I would fare better as something other than an aristocrat?" Bea asked curiously.

"The opposite actually, you're way too good at it." Lia took a few nibbles of a piece of cheese. "The problem is you don't get to be Lady Bea. In the House you're just the von Closen heiress, the daughter of Lady Ida. Everything you do is to further her wants and needs. The only person who sees you as just Lady Bea seems to be me." She finished snacking before finishing her thought. "Your mother is so controlling, but even worse, she's holding you back. So why not leave?"

Bea swirled her wine, deep in thought as she contemplated the question. "I've considered it. So many times I've snuck out of the House and thought 'why not just never return?'. And even more after arguments with my mother." She sighed. "Ida would not support such a decision. No matter what path I take, such freedom would cost me everything I've ever known. Disconnected from my fellows I may be now, but if I left I'd be utterly alone."

"Well, you wouldn't be alone anymore." Lia smiled brightly. "You'd have me."

"I would?" Bea asked with a frown. "But my status would be gone and I'd not have a penny to my name. I don't even know if I could house myself, much less a lady-in-waiting. Why would you want to come with me?"

"Why wouldn't I?" Lia looked at her like she was being silly. "I don't care if you don't have status or money. I'm your handmaiden, wherever you go, I go too."

"What have I done to earn such loyalty from you?" Bea asked herself in quiet disbelief. Although it almost sounded like she knew the answer and she didn't like it.

Lia shifted around nervously. All those little comments were starting to get to her lately, she wanted her lady to understand she truly enjoyed being her handmaiden. She obviously couldn't tell her about the super inappropriate fantasizing but there were other reasons she could admit to ease her mind. "If you want an actual answer, it's because you make me feel wanted."

Bea tilted her head. "Come again?"

"When you first took me as your handmaiden I couldn't figure out why. I wasn't qualified and there wasn't anything about me that seemed to be desirable to somebody of your status," Lia said, "You said I was interesting. I tried to figure out what *about* me you found interesting, but you just seemed to like, well, me."

"I don't think that's too odd of a desire? You're quite the catch," Bea said.

Lia blushed at the compliment and then shrugged. "I guess it's odd to me because I was sorta...born unwanted. You could say I was living on the streets because I didn't come out right." Her sister would tell her she wasn't made wrong, she was just a surprise. Sometimes people do things they regret when they're surprised. "And here you come in, saying you'll keep me safe from said streets for seemingly the same reason I thought was why I deserved to be on them. It made me want to do everything I could to earn my place at your side, I wanted to be there because *you* wanted me to be there."

Lia was hoping she wasn't bumming Bea out with this but she couldn't stop the words tumbling out now. "Whenever I'm around you I feel...a lot of things, but I feel so safe. Like I'm wanted and cared for. I think if we were both tossed to the curb I'd still be safer at your side than being a supposedly well-off maid for the Lady of the House." She was holding back a bit, it was more than just feeling wanted. Her fantasies weren't the only time she liked feeling owned by Bea. The idea of belonging to her in of itself was this strange sense of security she couldn't get enough of. "So yeah, it doesn't matter if you wouldn't really be a lady anymore or not even have a way to support the both of us. Your handmaiden will be there for you for as long as you want her. And said handmaiden really appreciates that you want her at all."

Bea didn't respond, instead staring out over the city with a strange wistful expression on her face. The wine was running dry and the food had become crumbs. Lia was a bit worried she'd weirded her lady out until she asked in a curious tone, "Hypothetically, if we ran away together right now, how do you imagine that'd play out?"

"Hmmm. Well, we'd probably want to skip town. Your mom seems like the jealous type, she'd never let you be more popular than her. Get on a boat, go somewhere nobody knows the von Closens beyond the name. Just a glance at a ship captain from those eyes of yours is all we'd need." Lia tilted her head back and forth as she ran through all the possibilities. "Your eyes honestly would make it really easy. Make a landlord give us a house for free. As your lady-in-waiting I'd sell you as a new foreign aristocrat, we'd meet with all the local upper crusts who'd want to size you up, and put them under your spell. You'd be a lady of status again in no time."

Bea had been suppressing a laugh during her explanation that finally broke through. "What a devious plan to help me rise to power. But let's say we're not the only fae in this new town and such a tactic would be seen as an invasion into their territory. Or perhaps acknowledge that enchantments won't sway public opinion overnight. What then?"

Lia tapped her legs while trying to think of a good second solution. She half-heartedly shrugged. "I could sell my art?"

"So plan B is we go from high society to starving artists?" Bea asked with a smirk.

Lia laughed. "No, no, like, high society loves art. You'd be a "wealthy" benefactor and I'd be your pet artist. Enchant a few rich assholes to overpay for something I've made, they brag about having the works of such a sought-after artist, and suddenly our status is legit. Oh wait, this totally reminds me!" She went into the wicker basket and pulled out the paper and pencils, as well as a clipboard to make it into a sorta makeshift sketchbook. "I'm glad I brought these, I totally want to get a drawing of this view."

"Would you like me to move?" Bea asked.

"Unless you wanna hold that pose for a while," Lia said jokingly.

Bea tilted her head in thought and held out her wine glass as she turned to look over the city. "Very well, then."

"Wait, really?" Lia tapped her feet nervously. "You want me to draw you?"

"I'm not holding this pose for my health, darling." Bea glanced at her, which prompted her to start sketching immediately.

Lia would be lying if she said she hadn't drawn Bea before, but her lady had never been really aware of it, much less posing for her. The further she went along the less stressful and more fun it became. Every once in a while they'd both look at each other at the same time, causing Lia to giggle and Bea stifling her own laugh trying to hold her stance. Near the end Bea was changing her expression between glances in a clear attempt to make her laugh even harder. "You're gonna make me screw it up, just look all wistful and demure."

Bea looked at her funny. "Those terms don't coincide, darling."

Lia waved her pencil at her. "Sure they do, they're fancy, you're fancy, just look fancy!"

"As you wish," Bea said, turning her head away and looking incredibly fancy. She didn't really have to try that hard, she had to put effort into looking not fancy if anything.

Eventually Bea got to relax as Lia filled in the background details. She stored it away before she could see. "I'm gonna improve it later, just got all the basics down. Don't worry, your part is done. You turned out beautiful." She blushed at her lady blushing. "I mean, like, the drawing turned out nice! Not that you aren't beautiful, just the drawing was beautiful, which, like, is good, it's accurate and I'm going to stop talking now."

"I am glad to hear my new portrait is 'accurate', then," Bea said with a playful look. She glanced at the sky. "I suppose we'll have to get moving soon if we don't want Clotho to miss us."

"Yeah, I guess so. This was fun though." Lia smiled brightly. "I think we both needed it."

Bea continued to stare out over the city. She appeared to be looking towards the upper districts where her House lay in wait for their return. "It was a nice change from the status quo."

Lia cringed. She could already sense the lingering despair lurking beneath Bea's better mood. This was supposed to fix it, not just bury it for an hour. "Is there a part of the status quo your handmaiden can help make a bit more bearable when we return to it?"

Bea looked away. "It's nothing you need to worry yourself with."

"My lady, if you don't want me to worry, then can you please just tell me what's wrong?" Lia asked politely. She scooched her chair over to be directly next to her. "You don't think I haven't noticed that you barely look at me anymore? You seem scared to ask me to do anything. Sometimes you even flinch when I talk to you."

Bea had become very still. She seemed to be trying to choose her words carefully. "If I tell you, you may be upset with me."

Lia put a hand on hers. "I promise I won't."

"Promises like that are dangerous to make to a fae, darling." Bea took a deep breath. "If you insist. Could you please tell me what your life was like before you were hired?"

"I was poor and downtrodden," Lia said.

Bea nodded. "You say that quite often. But can you tell me what your life was like before your employment? A day, even a week prior?"

"Of course, I was poor and downtrodden." Lia frowned at her own repetition. She just was thinking about her upbringing a minute ago, the last year shouldn't be this hard to remember. The churches she stayed at were all meshing together, the streets she lived on had no names she could recall. And the week prior to her employment there was nothing but this strange feeling of loss. A sorrowful dread that was feeding into her panic as she winced and put a hand to her head. "I was poor and downtrodden. I was...I remember living on the streets. Why can't I remember anything specific?"

"It has to do with how you came into our employ. Our staff is constantly being cycled so Clotho goes on hunts when we need to replenish." Bea refused to look at her. "It's an unspoken agreement with the city. Catch and release you may call it."

"That doesn't sound bad?" Lia said, confused at the relevance.

"It's not good either." Bea gave her a look. "You do understand that we are not hiring people, yes? We take them. We dress them up, put them in the roles we need filled, then toss them back when their minds have reached their limits."

Lia was starting to see the part of the picture her lady clearly was trying to get her to focus on. "Have I been taken?"

Bea gave an almost imperceptible nod.

"That devil—"

"You knew him, most likely. It's easier to make you blind to your past than to write a new one," Bea said shamefully, "Easier to lock your memories away so we can write in what your new role will be."

Lia took her time thinking about all this. Bea seemed to be waiting for her to react in some kind of way. "Can I have my memories back?"

"I don't have them, you do. They're out of reach, not out of mind. I doubt Atropos will be willing to release them." Bea perked up. "But your wits are not beyond you. Would you like to talk to that devil? Perhaps refine the blurrier memories with questions?"

"No, not really. I don't know if I'd trust what he'd have to say." Lia wasn't actually worried about that. She was worried about something much bigger.

I said I love you, sis. Please don't forget that too.

Lia didn't want to risk bringing Diana up. Not before she got the full story. Or before she knew if bringing her up would make her forget her. "I can see why you'd think I'd be upset but I don't get what part's making you upset."

"Because of the part I've played in this regard. You have performed your role of companionship well. I am ashamed of what I've done to somebody who showed me nothing but dedication and eagerness." Bea braced herself like she was about to tell her she was dying of a disease. "Do you recall when you asked if I'd ever use my eyes on you?"

Lia's heart started to race. Her worries flew out the window real fast. "Yes?"

"Normally Atropos does more than just make you forget being taken. You said you felt you had no training and you were right, I stepped in before they could." Bea closed her eyes. "I requested it to be left to me."

This wasn't going the way Lia expected. Sure, some of her expectations may have bias towards those very inappropriate fantasies, but even with that she thought it would be a little playful. Not this somber tone, like her lady committed some unholy sin against her. "So, you've been enchanting me instead?"

"Consistently." Bea still wouldn't look at her. Now she understood why. "I am a fae, Lia. A fae and your lady, so this shouldn't be any problem for you. However, I believe that if you don't incite me, I will have no cause to do so." The sentence cut off as if she were about to say "anymore" and decided against it.

Lia couldn't help but feel like that wasn't a threat, but a desperate plea. "Why?"

Bea looked fine but she sounded like she was barely holding herself together. "Does there need to be a why? I have found your service satisfactory. I don't think you need them."

Lia didn't believe her. "Why the shame?"

That broke her. "It's started to affect your mind. Unintentional orders are twisting, enchantments melding, even out of trance you're all but craving to be put back under. I don't want to devolve into a thrall. I just want you to be my handmaiden, my Lia." Bea couldn't wipe the tear running down her cheek fast enough to hide it. "I'm sorry. I'm so sorry, I never thought...well, that's just it, isn't it? I've never thought about it. And now it's all I can think about. I don't want to break you."

Lia wasn't sure what to say. What she ended up saying was probably the wrong thing but it was the first thing that came into her head. "Did you make me think I was a cat?"

Bea was thrown off. She coughed a laugh through her teary tone. "That's your first question?"

"I mean, if you're looking for unintended side effects," Lia wasn't sure how to explain sudden urges she started having around Bea. Some she assumed was just getting closer to her, but others she honestly thought were just a demon thing she'd never run into before, "sometimes I want to purr."

Bea looked fascinated. "I admit early on I did have you believe yourself to be a cat." She hid a smile. "Sometimes I'd have an evening reading and you'd fall asleep at the foot of my bed. I haven't done so since the soirée."

Lia blushed at the image of her curled up on Bea's bed like a pet. "Why?"

"You tend to tear up my curtains," Bea said curtly, "I'm not sure why you'd still desire to purr."

"I mean, I didn't even know I *could* purr. Like, if you taught me how to whistle, I wouldn't just unlearn whistling unless you specified, right?"

"I suppose." Bea raised an eyebrow. "When exactly do you desire to?"

Lia blushed heavily, not making eye contact. "You know, like, when purring is an appropriate response." She wasn't ready for the surprise chin scratch and couldn't stop the little purr from escaping.

Bea managed a smile, even giving a light laugh before her face turned sour and she snatched her own hand away. "No, no, this is exactly what I mean. Gods, why am I so weak to temptation?"

Lia held her hands up. "It's ok! I didn't mind—"

"You didn't mind because I made you not mind. Do you not understand that?" Bea didn't even try to hide the tears starting to swell this time. "Please tell me I haven't pushed you to the point you can't even comprehend what I'm doing."

"My lady," Lia put her hand on Bea's, "you haven't pushed me to do anything. Not anything I wouldn't have already done."

Instead of relief, Bea stared at her with despair. "So I truly have broken you."

It had been a wonderful day and Beatrice had ruined it.

Lia had done everything she could to cheer up her dower mood and that only made the guilt stab further. She just didn't understand, how could she? Beatrice may not have lied but she omitted so much she might as well have. If Lia knew the truth she'd run. And she wouldn't blame her.

Perhaps Beatrice should let her run. Right here, right now. Remove as many chains as she could, let Lia fearfully flee into the crowd and be free of her horrid captor. She'd have to convince Clotho not to retrieve her, though. Their strange new acquaintanceship may make her more stubborn to let it go.

Lia trailed next to her with a look of despair. The poor girl, still thinking this was her fault. Beatrice wanted her to know it wasn't.

But no matter how many times she tried, Lia refused to accept it. She was too loyal. Beatrice had done her job too well.

The two were interrupted from returning to their meetup with a traffic jam of pedestrians and wagons. Apparently a cart driven by several imps had decided to park themselves on the sidewalk, forcing a conversion of wagon and walker as now half the street was taken up. The imps were tiny and multi-colored as a package of wrapped candy with blue, red, and green ones just to name a few. They all wore flat caps and square sunglasses, though, so they looked to be a part of the same group.

Beatrice decided she'd rather cut across the alley then deal with the traffic jam. Apparently she wasn't the only one, as there were more imps traversing it. It wasn't more than two steps in did she notice the same caps and sunglasses. Suddenly this appeared to be an unwise path to take.

"My lady, we should keep moving," Lia said, strangely insistent on not letting Beatrice turn them around. She stuffed something into her dress.

It was about halfway through the alley when an imp stepped in front of them. Beatrice glared with her glowing eyes in a way that should've made him leave but he just smiled and tipped his cap to her. "The Deburios send their regards."

Beatrice wasn't sure what she was expecting after hearing such a foreboding remark. Lia hitting the imp sneaking up behind her over the head with a plate was certainly not it.

"Nab her!" the one in front screeched before the plate struck him across the face like a frisbee. Neither attacks had much weight to them but the imps writhed in pain like the plate had been boiling hot.

Lia dropped her basket, grabbed Beatrice by the arm, and pulled her past them. "Keep moving!"

There was a flurry of wings flapping from behind them as they sprinted for the open street. "Won't there be more?"

"Imps always assume you'll run back the way you came, they were totally waiting for you to turn around. If we're lucky—"

Beatrice felt the icy burn of iron snap around her neck as a raspy voice whispered, "You aren't."

Chapter 17
FLY LITTLE DEMON, FLY

If that had been a mugging, Lia did everything right. Diana taught her a bunch of little things and she'd even *been* mugged before, she knew how to handle it. She'd never been kidnapped, though. Her actions weren't as great for a kidnapping.

Firstly, smacking their assailants with a silver plate would've been great if they were muggers. Devils, especially imps, don't like people who put up a fight and certainly not ones who were packing silvered anything.

Instead, Lia had started off her kidnapping by burning the faces of her captors. Not a great idea.

Secondly, Lia dropped her basket before they ran. Muggers want things, you give them things and they'll call it a success. Murder was like mugger paperwork, they don't wanna deal with it. These imps didn't want things, they wanted Bea. And an imp was a fast devil when he wanted to be, despite the tinier wings they were super-fast fliers even in close quarters, so they were never going to outrun them.

Thirdly, Lia had no idea what they got around Bea's neck but the second it closed she screamed like she'd been stabbed and collapsed. Lia wasn't going to leave her lady behind so they got them both.

Now they were bound with bags over their heads, sitting together in a cart as they were taken to who knows where. Lia had a
fairly good sense of smell, not demon good but she knew if any of
the imps were back here she'd smell them. They all smelt smokey like
their clothes were dipped in fireplaces. "Bea, are you ok?"

Bea groaned. "Nope. I am not ok. I am…whatever the opposite
word is."

"What did they put on you?" Lia asked.

"Iron. Not just iron, glyphs on the metal, I can feel them. The
world is so blurry now, my eyes hurt. Mind is like molasses." Bea
sounded really loopy. "Darling, is it night already?"

"No, my lady."

"Why's it so dark?"

"I assume there is also a bag over your head."

"Oh." There was the sound of a face rubbing against burlap.
"Why's there a bag over my head?"

"We've been kidnapped, my lady."

"Right. *Right*, the fucking Deburios. Gods it's hard to think
straight right now."

Lia wasn't certain she'd ever heard a real curse from Bea before.
"What did you do to them again?"

Bea cackled. Like an actual, cute tiny witch cackle that Lia had
never heard her make before. "Made their daughter think she was a
cow. Not sure why they're upset, she seemed happier that way."

Lia couldn't help but giggle with her. "I remember that. You
were so mad, why did you do that?" Bea didn't respond. "My lady?
Bea, are you ok?"

"Huh? Yeah, yeah." Another pause. Lia wasn't sure if this was
the collar causing her hesitance. "I did it because she took you."

Before Lia could ask what that meant the door opened and the smoky smell filled the cart. There was a scrappy grunt.

"Two? Order was for one."

"Order for the fae but the girl was with her. Put up a fight so we nabbed both."

"Girl a half-elf?"

"Mhm." Lia did not like how excited he sounded confirming that.

"So I guess we might get a bonus after all. Take 'em to the hold." There was a flap of wings. A tiny hand grabbed Lia by the arm and started directing her out. "And keep them glasses on. Von Closens are the eye ones, I don't care what sales pitch that dibs devil gave, I don't trust that collar to prevent a glance slipping through."

The bag was ripped off Lia's head as soon as they were inside. Apparently leading bagged people was hard for imps. The smell was awful, a mix of sulfur and whale oil. She didn't know what this place used to store but she knew it would be decades before it lost the smell of it.

Bea was kept bagged, the imps motioning for Lia to take her hand to guide her. She obeyed, there wasn't much they could do. Neither of them were fighters and Bea's trump card had been removed from the game. The first floor was nothing special, but there were at least a dozen imps spread about. Most were in a corner playing cards, far away from the staircase that they were being led to. Either this was a gang or a family. Or both.

The only other thing that caught her attention was on a table they passed sat a lone sandwich that looked forgotten. Even amongst the stenches Lia could pick out the special ingredient. It must have some deadroot, which for devils basically meant that sandwich was an edible.

For demons deadroot was…a lot.

The basement was filled with rusty workshop tools and rotting crates. The corner was sectioned off like an old saloon jail, which they were promptly locked in with a padlock. The imps snickered about a job well done as they left up the stairs.

As soon as the smokey smell was far away Lia took the bag off of Bea's head. The blue of her eyes was almost completely overtaken by her pupils as she blinked out of sync. She looked like she was high but the leaching blue veins around her neck did not imply it was an enjoyable trip.

"Are we still kidnapped?" Bea asked. She continued to stare forward as if moving would hurt.

"Yes, my lady." Lia examined their jail. The bars were part of the building. If this was an old workshop it probably would've been where they used to store valuable supplies. The imps were repurposing it as their prison. Angel steel, not a cheap thing. Fae hated iron, infernal hated silver. Both hated angel steel and that hatred was mutual. "Do you think Clotho will be able to find us?"

"Not with the smell."

"It explains why they chose this place. It would hide them from just about anything with half a decent nose." Lia looked around the empty cell for anything else and sat next to Bea as there was nothing to find. "I wish they gave us water, you look like you need some."

"I doubt they care for my comfort," Bea mumbled. Her head didn't move but her eyes shifted to Lia's chest. "I saw you stuff something in there. What was it?"

Lia cringed and pulled out the crumpled set of pages she'd torn out of her sketchbook and stashed in her cleavage. It was the quickest place she could think of when she decided she was going to drop the basket. "I didn't want to lose my drawings."

Bea weakly took one, giving a faint smile. "I didn't even think about that."

Lia shrugged. "It's not like it'll help us."

"It means we don't have to go looking for them. That's helpful in the long run," Bea said. Her smile was lopsided as she stared at the drawing.

"You make a fair point, my lady." Lia thought it was funny that she was the worried one right now. The line between thinking ahead and overthinking was one Lia never could tell so she didn't care to do either. Bea was really good at it but that usually came with a trove of worrying. Right now she barely seemed concerned they were even being held captive. "What did you mean when you said the Deburio took me?"

The drawing fell out of her hand. Lia quickly stashed it away again and guided her hand back down. Bea was shaking. Okay, so apparently Lia was *very* wrong as now her lady was having a panic attack. "It's okay, I'm right here, just breathe. You don't have to think about that right now."

"No, no, I just...forgot this is all my fault. I'm not used to being this slow-witted, it's hard to focus on more than one thing right now. Your art is of quality, I almost thought we were back there and not...here. To think the serenity of that drawing occurred not even an hour ago." Bea's fancy talk was coming back but it was already falling apart at the seams. Maybe thinking out loud was easier but not as elegant. "Nyssa Deburio. I was careless. She took your name at the soirée, stole you from me when I wasn't paying attention. Made you think you were a chair. I had you block the memory, it was stressing you."

Lia smiled. "Well that's sweet that you got me back."

"No. It's horrible. I got pissed off because somebody else was controlling you and it wasn't because you were being humiliated. I was jealous it wasn't *me* doing it." Bea cringed as the glyphs on her collar pulsed. "It's so clear to me now. I was jealous and so I punished her, then made you mine forever. I didn't even give your name back. I didn't need it. I just felt I deserved to have it. That I deserved to have you. Now we're going to pay for my sins."

"That's not fair, you can't think *this* is a reasonable response," Lia said. She worried Lucial was involved in this too, fae hiring imps wasn't too strange but fae hiring a demon who hired imps felt just as likely. The fact she was a 'bonus' didn't bode well in either scenario. "It's not your sins, it's a rich family being dicks."

Bea shook her head. "You don't understand what I've done. I deserve this."

"The Deburios—"

"Not to them, darling. To you. I need to come clean. You need to know...how I've ruined you." Bea closed her eyes. "I know about your late-night fantasies."

Despite being captives, only now did Lia suddenly want to be anywhere else. "I don't know what you're talking about."

"Lia, I had you tell me. You're not dreaming, you're remembering. You fantasize about the moments we've shared because you can't remember them but your body does." Bea blushed. "You're so passionate. Gods if I didn't feel so horrid for admitting this I'd be able to compliment you for your talents."

"We've done things together?" Lia asked. Her dreams, her fantasies, were all of them real?

"You've done so much and made me feel things I never thought I could feel." Bea chuckled. "You kept craving to be used. And I couldn't stop using you. Perhaps we're both addicts. I'm sorry. Sorry isn't enough. Cheap words aren't worth the forgiveness I wish to reap. And thus this iron around my neck is my just reward."

Lia was feeling many things right now. None of them were the anger Bea seemed to be begging for. She'd thought she'd never even kissed anyone and now she knew locked away in the back of her mind was her first kiss, her first time, her first...her first *everything*! The way Bea spoke of her like some fiery affair was somehow the part that was the hardest to believe. That somehow Lia could be a passionate lover devoted to pleasing Bea.

Lia wanted to be that person. She *was* that person, she just couldn't remember. And the barrier from reclaiming those memories was this angel steel cage and a piece of iron around her lady's neck.

They were getting out of here.

Step one was getting the jail unlocked. Step two was a work in progress. Lia wasn't sure if they could sneak by the imps, there were a lot of them and Bea was delirious at best. Although a fever dream plan from her would be smarter than the plans Lia was coming up with. Like the deadroot "plan" that didn't feel like a plan so much as a stupid idea that might benefit them. Setting a bull loose would make their escape technically easier in a way too, it didn't make it a plan.

It didn't matter, step one was her focus right now. The bars were open enough for her arms but not enough to slip through. There was a padlock on the door, she'd have to constantly be in contact with the angel steel to try and pick it. Luckily, angel steel hurt less than she expected, usually silver lined openings like that would burn but she only felt a warm tingle sticking a test hand through the bars. Sorta felt like standing in a church. Oh, *angel* steel, that's clever.

Lia took a glove off and flicked her index finger against her thumb to extend a claw. She reached through the bars and began to get to work on the padlock.

Bea flopped her head back so she could see her. "What you doing?"

Lia fidgeted her claw in the keyhole. "Picking the lock."

"That's...that's not how that works." Bea tipped over. "You need...stuff. Lockpicking stuff."

The lock clicked. Lia smiled as she opened the prison gate. "Even easier than church locks."

"You've broken into churches?" Bea mumbled.

Lia cringed as she hid her claw retracting. "Holy water is a good black-market trade in a pinch."

"I'm starting to think I don't know you at all." Bea suddenly started to weep. "I don't, do I? I never...never tried. Every moment out here I've learned something new, you're so interesting and I never cared to ask."

Lia didn't like Bea talking like this. Earlier she was being over-dramatic but now she sounded like she wanted to die. "My lady-"

Bea sat back up and cut her off. "I'm not your lady, I'm your *warden*. Even with this prison open you cannot leave, for the shackles I have on your mind keep you trapped at my side." She sounded like she'd lost her mind, making her voice scrappy for no reason.

Lia ignored her ramblings and knelt down to look at iron around her neck. "We need to get these off you, they're messing with your head. I don't see a lock, though."

"It won't have one." Bea laughed through the tears. "Makes sure if I...manage an enchantment I can't just...make somebody free me. You should run. This is your chance, you should just run away from me like any sane person would."

Lia really wished she'd stop saying that, it was actually starting to hurt her feelings. "I'm not going to abandon you."

"Because the enchantment won't let you. I won't...I won't let that be your end. I won't let *them* have you. You don't deserve...my fate." Bea's eyes glowed. They were filled with pain as if the sapphires were cracking under pressure. Her shackles burned with searing light. "Take your name back. Never let anyone have it again. You are Lia. Now run. Don't die for me. Just...run. You're...you are free." Her eyes rolled into the back of her head as she slumped forward.

Lia felt the order swimming around in her head. It was weak, a vague command, borderline begging. The last of her strength just to unlock the chains on her mind. Still it was hard to resist. It was always hard to resist Bea. Enchantments had nothing to do with that.

"As you wish, my lady." Lia lightly laid her down and decided that the really stupid plan was the one she was going with. It wasn't how Bea intended her to interpret that command, but she wasn't thinking straight. Lia could take a couple liberties. It was probably going to get her killed but she wasn't afraid. In fact, she didn't feel fear period.

After all, Beatrice ordered her not to die. And Lia lived to serve.

Lia poked her head up from the stairs to look around. As expected all the imps were in that gambling corner of the room around the wall, the smell of the smokey clothes they wore filling her nose from that direction. She saw the sandwich on the table, still uneaten.

As she recalled, the table was in plain view of them but they were still on the other side of an entirely separate room. She listened for some kind of opening. She didn't know what they were playing so she decided to just wait until they cheered and hoped she'd have enough time.

Lia's nerves started to get the better of her as she waited. She tried to ignore them by mentally preparing herself. *Don't let it get out of hand. Let Bea's order guide you. Don't die. Run. Just remember to run towards her first.*

The imps got silent, with a few building oohs. The second they all erupted Lia crouch sprinted to the table and scarfed down the sandwich like it was her last meal on earth. It was disgusting, she had no idea what half the things on it were but she knew they didn't belong together whatsoever. Gods she was going to murder whoever called this horrid thing a meal.

That violent thought told Lia it was starting. Her hands, head, and back burned as if fire ants were running along them. She tried to keep her task at the forefront of her mind, focusing on it instead of the urges rising from within. The beat of blood pumping filled her ears, only drowned out by somebody shouting, "Hey! How'd you get out!" That kicked it into overdrive. She snapped her head towards them with a fanged snarl, her eyes dilating into slits now able to see the confused fear sprawled on the imps faces. The pain on her head and back exploded along with the sound of fabric tearing.

The last random thought Lia had before the braver imps dove for her and instinct took over was, *aww, this is going to ruin my outfit, isn't it?*

Beatrice weakly opened her eyes. Lia was gone. It had been a long time since she truly felt alone. While at the House she always felt like she was being watched. When in the city the busy world pressed against her even if it never truly cared to know she was there. And the last few weeks, she had Lia. Every day Beatrice felt her presence, even in the moments she was somewhere else.

Now Beatrice was alone. It never hurt like this before.

Perhaps the Deburios would be merciful. They would humiliate her surely but not kill her. Death was such a lowly form of revenge. Take her name, make her believe she was a potted plant for a month, and then send her back to her mother. It was quite distressing that the second part sounded worse. At least she might like being a potted plant. Lia certainly made being a towel holder look enjoyable.

Oh, sweet Lia. The very thought of the Deburios keeping her as some bonus made her sick to her stomach, but then it just made her hate herself more. Maybe, if Beatrice thought higher of herself, she could've believed she'd done it for the right reasons. *If you love something, you have to set it free.*

Beatrice was no hero. Lia was just a prize so precious that if she couldn't have her, nobody could. She didn't deserve sympathy for selfishness.

The morbid thoughts were interrupted by a ruckus happening from above. Devils were shouting curses and what sounded like furniture was being tossed around. Beatrice wondered if the fates had found her. Or maybe devils just played rough in their down time.

"Hold her down!"

"You try holding a demon twice your size!"

"She ain't a fucking demon, she's just a girl!"

"Tell that to her!"

"Sorry about this."

Beatrice sat up at the sound of a window being shattered. She must truly be losing her mind, because that last one sounded like Lia.

The ceiling outside the cell caved in as a blur of red and black crashed through it like a cannonball. Beatrice's vision was doubling and trying to stand caused the chains to burn her again. From what she could make out it wasn't a demon fighting devils so much as one that was tossing them off herself like they were angry cats she didn't want to hurt.

The demon rushed over to her prison, batting away a devil diving at her with her leathery wing. The door was still unlocked but this was a woman on a mission. She winced as if the bars were red hot but she ignored the pain. The door didn't open so much as was just torn off its hinges.

Beatrice stared awestruck as the demon grabbed the shackle around her neck and snapped it open like a twig. She lifted her up from under her arms and placed her on her feet.

Her fangs were sharp, her horns curled upwards from the sides of her head, and her eyes had those demonic slits. But her skin was pale like a human, the eyes still had whites instead of the black demon eyes sat in. And only one girl's smile could have fangs and still make Beatrice feel the urge to smile back. "Lia?"

Lia pulled her in for a hug. At least, that's what she thought this was until the wings that were as tall as her extended outward. Her voice was still just as sweet, but it sounded like a second deeper version spoke under it as she said, "Brace yourself, my lady."

The two of them launched out of the cell, through the hole in the ceiling, and out a window that had been shattered, presumably by Lia throwing a devil out of it. The sudden change in altitude mixed with the fatigued relief from being shackled meant by the time they were as high as bell towers Beatrice was fading into unconsciousness.

This had to be a dream. Perhaps if death was like falling asleep, then dreaming was just how it felt to die. Unreal and fantastical if one was lucky.

Beatrice was very lucky that her dying dream had Lia in it.

Lia wasn't so much flying as gliding now, her wings locked in place. It reminded her of hanging off the side of a cliff, the strain of holding on while being unable to readjust. Even trying to get another flap and they'd quickly go from gliding to falling without style. They were almost back to the House. Almost safe.

At least, Bea was almost safe. Lia couldn't help but feel she was returning to a prison now. And she'd just wasted her chance at freedom on saving the warden's daughter. She wondered if the enchantment was why she had no regrets.

A waft of a familiar smokey stench hit her nose. *Oh no.*

Lia screamed as a bolt of fire missed her ear by an inch and nearly let go of Bea. Listening for it she could hear leathery wings, at least three sets rapidly flapping. She didn't think any would follow, they must really be scared of failing to deliver. Imps were so fucking annoying, she wanted to just rip those stupid front horns off and shove them—

Demon thoughts, those are demon thoughts, stop it! Lia was already running out of steam and she couldn't waste it trying to fight. She needed to signal to the fates they needed help. It wasn't clear if the idea she went with to do so was actually a reasonable one or if it was just the demon brain trying to run the show still.

"Sorry, Bea," Lia said as she lifted her up and bit her neck. Not hard, just enough to draw blood. It was sweet, but for a fae it also had a surprising iron taste. Actually that was probably a bad sign about the lingering effects of that collar. The smell of blood was strong now, much stronger than the smokey smell of the approaching imps. Maybe a little too strong.

Don't lick it, don't lick it, you need the smell to stick around, DO NOT LICK HER NECK.

Lia licked her neck.

LIA, YOU FOOL!

The potshots the imps were taking were getting more accurate with every try. The two of them were losing altitude fast, Lia couldn't fly up to dodge so every maneuver got them closer to the ground. They were so close. She could see the House, they just needed to—

A bolt of fire hit her wing and they plummeted like a rock. Lia pulled Bea close and enveloped them both in her wings. They skidded along a patch of grass, it burned painfully but she knew her wings were the most durable thing about her right now. As they came to a stop the sound of the imps landing hit her ears. She hugged Bea tighter and prayed for a miracle.

Lia didn't think a miracle would sound like a rabid jaguar yowling. The devils screamed, wings were flapping as if trying to get away, there was a sound of leather ripping and what she swore was bones snapping. One by one their cries were cut short.

Long, heavy breaths were the only thing breaking the silence. Lia was scared to look but she couldn't resist lowering a wing to peek. She hadn't realized she'd landed in the northern garden, the bushes having broken their fall. The three devils lay dead as doornails, bodies bloodied and throats torn. Hunched over one was Clotho, her eyes focused and her sharp teeth stained red. A long, thin silver blade was attached to the top of her arm. She ran her forked tongue along it as it retracted. The blade didn't disappear so much as Lia's eyes refused to acknowledge it as soon as it was put away, implying it had always been there.

Clotho snapped her head at the hint of movement. In a blink of an eye she reached them but it was like slow motion to watch. Prowling forward as if she was trying to remember she walked on two legs, her gaze never breaking like a predator locked onto prey. She now loomed with her head tilting as if deciding this was friend or food.

Lia swallowed her fear that Clotho didn't recognize her in this demonic form and moved her wing to reveal Bea unconscious in her arms. "Please. Help her."

Chapter 18
If it Comes Back

Beatrice woke with a horrid headache worse than any hangover she'd ever had. Her throat was dry, her eyes ached as if they'd been squeezed. She rubbed her neck and felt bandage fabrics wrapped around it. Cold iron was a horrid metal to experience on its own, shackles designed for fae felt like ones that had been dipped in fire and then cooled in acid before being locked around her neck. Torture would've been more merciful.

If Beatrice was dead, the afterlife looked like her bedroom. Which meant her mother would be here. Maybe she was in hell.

There was a cup of tea on her nightstand and a piece of buttered toast with a bite taken out of it. Both clearly had been sitting out for a while. Her memory was fuzzy, she had been quite intoxicated from the shackles.

The last thing she remembered was too insane to be real.

The door opened. Lia walked in, no wings, horns, or claws to be seen, just a supposed half-elf happily humming in her standard uniform. She was holding a tray with towels, a teacup, and a bowl of water, which she set down at the nightstand. She tossed out the old tea and stuffed the toast into her mouth as if she'd decided it still being there was permission to eat it.

Beatrice only noticed the chair next to her bed when Lia sat down and began to dip the towels in the water. She smiled even brighter when their eyes met. "Good morning, my lady. Or good day, I guess, we are nearing lunch."

Beatrice tried to respond. A croak was all she managed, to which Lia shushed her and placed the wet towel on her forehead. "Atropos said leyline iron is like blood poisoning, you need to rest and let your body flush it out." Lia softly caressed her cheek when Beatrice winced hearing that name. "Don't worry. I'm doing my best to keep fate from bothering you. Just rest, my lady."

Beatrice drifted off into sleep once more. The feeling of her hand on her cheek never left.

Much of the day was just Beatrice drifting in and out of lucidity. Most of the time Lia was there, switching out towels or trying to get her to drink tea. Sometimes she was talking to her. Beatrice wasn't sure if she'd been responding or if Lia was just having a one-sided conversation. One time she was startled awake by loud shouting and saw her handmaiden fuming, standing with her arms crossed at the threshold of the door. Lia became very upset that whoever she was arguing with had woken Beatrice up and declared that permission to slam the door shut.

There was one time Lia wasn't there. That one felt the longest. And the loneliest. Beatrice might've cried. She wasn't really sure. Lia was always there after that.

"Were you a nurse?" Beatrice managed to ask during one of her more lucid moments. It was a strange question but she had this wild memory of Lia being a demon earlier so nothing was off the table at this point.

"No. My sister got really sick once, though. Dopple-flu, nasty thing to catch, it's like a virus that hates you and chooses which symptoms will make you suffer the most. Lasted like a week, I think after that I can nurse anything to health." Lia smirked. "At least you're not as whiny as she was. She needed chains to keep her in bed."

It was the afternoon now. Beatrice had been lucid for longer than a minute and was trying to put everything that happened together. All she managed to say was, "You saved me."

"Of course I did." Lia replaced the cold tea with a fresh cup. "Although without Clotho my efforts wouldn't have been worth much. If anything, she saved us."

Beatrice put her hand on her forehead. "I thought I told you to run." *I swear I set you free.*

"You did." Lia sat in the chair next to the bed. "You didn't say not to come back."

"I really have broken you," she mumbled glumly.

Lia shrugged. "Maybe. Not sure why it bothers you so much, I feel like I should be the one who's all moody about it."

"How are you so cavalier about this?" Beatrice sat up and tried her best not to look as though it hurt much more than she had expected. "Truly, your optimism is unbreakable even in the face of all I've told you. And your skills learned from your street life does not imply an easy upbringing. How are you so...so *happy*?"

"It helps to be around somebody who makes me happy. Not that you seem to believe me when I say that." Lia crossed her arms. "You acted like without the enchantment I'd just abandon you. Is that how you think of me? Like I secretly hate you all the time."

Beatrice winced. "Lia, that's not what I meant."

"If you want me to be mad at you so badly then it's going to be about this, because that really hurt my feelings. Like even if it was true, do you really think I'd just leave somebody I didn't like to *die*?" Lia asked. "And then I thought about the other stuff you said and all of that hurt too. You called me an addict. You're so caught up in assuming my feelings are fake that you never even considered what it meant if they weren't."

Beatrice cringed. "No! No, that's not—Lia, your feelings aren't fake, that's the entire problem, they're being influenced by suggestions and enchantments you're unaware of. I made you feel that way."

Lia shrugged. "So?"

Beatrice stared at her. "What do you mean *so*?"

She held up her hands with another shrug. "So? If you make me like it and I like it, what's the problem? That's how liking things works, you get introduced to them and then if you like it, you like it."

Beatrice knew that logic was not sound but her mind was not performing well enough to deconstruct it. "I don't think that applies when enchantments are involved."

Lia pouted at that remark and that was hurting more than the leyline iron. Beatrice weakly reached to put her hand on her leg but only managed to get to the edge of the bed. "Darling, what I said while under the influence was...hyperbolic. I fear even now I may say something hurtful that I do not mean, can we table this until my head is clear?"

Lia looked like she was trying to keep her pout up but a smile broke through as she put her hand on hers. "As you wish, my lady."

Beatrice felt a brush of calluses and turned Lia's hand over. There were lined burns, mostly healed but still scabbing. "Gods, what happened?"

Lia cringed. "I didn't think about the angel steel after I..." she looked quite embarrassed, "I'm fine. It'll heal, I swear, I was just being stupid."

This brought back to the forefront the part of their escape she still couldn't see as anything other than a hallucination. Beatrice avoided eye contact, just to make sure she didn't accidentally incite an answer, "Half-elves don't get burnt by angel steel. What exactly are you?"

Lia stared at the ground. "I'm half-human, my lady."

"May I ask what the other half is?"

A moment before a heavy sigh. "Demon, my lady."

So it wasn't just a hallucination. "I would like to point out that I have seen you in the nude and did not spy a pair of wings."

"They sorta...sprout? Hard to explain, can't bring them out easily. Needs a mix of high emotion and a dash of deadroot. It buffs the demon blood but it makes it hard for me to think straight." Lia shifted in her seat uncomfortably. "Violence isn't my thing. I just don't really match well with what I am."

Beatrice coughed a laugh. "Indeed. Never did I think such an unyielding smile could be paired with such sharp claws." She remembered the other demon quality that had appeared. "Do you have horns?"

Lia was very interested in her shoes. "Maybe."

Beatrice tentatively held her hand out. Lia didn't even hesitate to lean in and push the top of her head into her palm. At first she didn't feel anything, but as Lia moved her head from side to side she found two very subtle bumps right in front of where her headdress sat. Two adorable little demon horns, hidden away in her hair. "Those are so very cute."

Lia blushed. "They're dumb and make brushing my hair a pain."

"Can you style it for them to be seen?" Beatrice asked.

She shrugged. "I'm not sure, but I don't like being seen as just a half-demon."

Beatrice gently brushed her hand down her face and lifted her chin. "Horns wouldn't stop me from seeing you as my sweet and humble handmaiden Lia."

"So, I am still your lady-in-waiting then?" Lia asked with nervous hope.

I set you free and you came back. That means you're mine. Beatrice closed her eyes. It was all she could do to resist. "Yes, darling. I'm clearly in need of one as good as you."

"Thanks, Bea." Lia put her hands under her head and kissed her on the forehead. A girl who through enchantment Beatrice had done so many things and yet, somehow a simple forehead kiss felt like the most intimate moment she'd ever shared with her. Lia pressed her forehead against hers. "I'm so glad you're ok."

It left Beatrice stunned, allowing Lia to lay her back down gently. "Even though you're feeling better, I would try to get all the rest you can. The Lady of the House wished to see you the moment you woke."

The serenity was broken at that revelation. Beatrice hadn't even thought about the rageful storm that awaited her after such a fiasco. "Oh gods."

"Yes, it's quite a shame you weren't awake when I came in here. I'll just have to check again in, say, a couple hours?" Lia brightly smiled as she stood up. "Enough time to eat, get dressed, and mentally prepare. If you were awake, that is."

Beatrice took a moment to realize what she was implying. Which was further evidence she most certainly needed this time to reconfigure herself, she was thinking at a snail's pace right now. Most of her processing power was being devoted to yearning for a second kiss. "Thank you, Lia. For everything."

"No need for thanks, my lady." Lia curtseyed. "After all, I live to serve you. Whether you like it or not.

Chapter 19
Waiting on the Lady

"Why am I doing this?" Diana asked as she did Lia's hair. She was actually really good at using her claws as a comb.

Lia sat on the floor in front of her with her arms wrapped around her legs. "I wanna see if the horns can be shown."

"Yeah, exactly, so why am I doing that?" Diana asked again. "I thought you hated these."

Lia was embarrassed to answer. She didn't exactly hate her horns. She just hated people making assumptions when they saw them. And it just drew attention out in the slums, devils and demons ignore you if you're just some half-elf that a breeze could knock over.

"Did Beatrice make you do this?"

"No! No, I just thought I'd try it out." Lia put her chin on her knees. "Also, I'm sorta just hiding out until Bea talks to the Lady of the House."

"Lady of the House?" Diana asked. "Oh, you mean the mom. I forget Beatrice isn't the top dog, you don't talk about her mom that much. All I know is she's the one holding the leashes on that freaky maid trio, what's she like?"

"A bitch." Lia stifled a laugh and cringed. "Sorry, that was rude. I just don't like her. And I hate how I can't remember that when

I'm in the same room as her, it's so annoying, she's gotta have like, a reverse enchantment."

"The word you're looking for is glamour. A fae defense mechanism, makes you not want to hurt them. From the sounds of it she's so vile it's just always running." Diana chuckled. "So, that's the upside. You're a thrall but at least your mistress isn't the meanest one here."

"Bea's not mean and I'm not a thrall." Lia sighed. "Believe me, she doesn't want me to be one."

"You say that like you're disappointed." Diana stopped combing. "Don't tell me you *are*."

"No. Maybe." Lia cringed. Thrall made it sound worse that it was, but if she was enthralled by her mistress, then what else would she be? "I'm a prisoner, right?"

"Yep." Diana didn't even skip a beat as she continued to brush her hair.

"Why didn't you tell me?"

"I tried." Diana stopped combing and rested her palm on her head. "I really tried, sis. I failed you."

"It's not so bad." Lia closed her eyes. "I get to be around Bea. She's kind to me."

"At least she's a merciful warden."

"Sometimes it feels like we're both inmates." Lia frowned. "Are you a prisoner?"

"You won't remember if I tell you." Diana laughed painfully. "I doubt you'll even remember me saying this."

"I still remember you love me. You were worried I'd forget, but I haven't." Lia hugged her legs tighter as she remembered she and Bea were in a lot of trouble right now. "Yet."

The silence soured their shared time together. Eventually Lia tried to break past it. "If we're prisoners, we need to make the best of it, right?"

Diana snorted. "I guess."

"And if we're worried about enchantments, it's best to stick with people who want to keep our memories intact."

"Where's this going, sis?"

Lia was having trouble phrasing it. Especially in a way that would get an actual answer. She couldn't bring up what had happened, Diana would call her an idiot for not escaping. "Is it okay to belong to somebody who makes you happy?"

Diana grumbled like she was trying really hard not to say something vulgar. She sighed. "So long as you do it on your terms."

"What does that mean?" Lia asked.

"It means that you and me are very different. I don't think I'd ever feel happy if I did but you're asking so you're feeling it and...fuck, I don't know, I'm not a prize to be won but you want to put a fucking bow on your head." Diana pulled her head back so that she was looking up at her. "Just make sure you know what you're getting into. Don't let yourself be taken."

Lia spoke before thinking and cringed right after the words tumbled out. "But what if I want to be?"

"Then you make that godsdamn clear. Make the first move. Give yourself." Diana hugged her from behind. "I want you to be happy, sis. I can't lie and say I don't wish this wasn't what made you happy. But at the end of the day, with the hand we've been dealt, the only play I have left is to just be glad that you are."

"How are you feeling?" Ida tapped her fingers against the table. Beatrice was surprised that she wasn't filled with unyielding fury. In fact she seemed more contemplative than anything else.

"Better than before." Beatrice rubbed her neck.

"Good." Ida leaned in. "Do you think you are healthy enough to recall what occurred?"

Beatrice winced. She wanted to search through her memories. "I assume Lia and Clotho have already debriefed you."

"They did. I want your perspective." That explained why Ida wanted to see Beatrice alone. She told Lia to lie low until she returned, she still was unsure what the consequences of this endeavor were going to be for either of them. In all honesty it was surprising they hadn't already been inflicted.

Beatrice took a deep breath. "I was foolish. I wished to have a peaceful outing alone. I sent Clotho away, giving the Deburios' minions a window of opportunity. My memory after the leyline iron is hazy but I am certain I would've perished if not for Lia. She insisted that I not be fully unsupervised and thus was also taken. Our captors had not prepared for her as thoroughly as me and thus afforded her the opportunity to escape. I told her to run and get help, instead she freed me and from what I understand alerted Clotho to our location." She was lying about why she told her to run but that wasn't important. Lia saved her and she deserved to be rewarded, not punished.

Ida just stared. Not with anger, nor disappointment, nor any emotion Beatrice had ever seen from her. It almost looked like acceptance. Or maybe relief. Both were ones that she had yet to emote as far as Beatrice knew. "Do you know what has surprised me the most? All three of you have taken the blame." She put her hand to her temples. "I wasn't too surprised about Lia. I was curious about how you would spin it, but Clotho was quite unexpected in her admission of fault."

"Clotho took blame?" Beatrice asked, surprised.

"Yes, she admitted that she was overconfident. At least that's how she put it. Assumed that a small time frame of being out of sight wouldn't be of consequence as she went to 'let off some steam'. She did not anticipate the imps tactic of covering your scents and given she had not seen what occurred she had no clear way of finding you again." Ida made a grumbling noise. "Lia said she'd tricked Clotho and was trying to allow you to have some wanted free time alone. She also claimed you had no part in planning that and thus all punishment should be given to her."

Beatrice panicked. "You can't, she didn't—"

"You will be silent or I *will* punish her." Ida paused to let her threat settle in. Beatrice begrudgingly remained quiet. "Good. And you thus prove my point. If you were trying to use your handmaiden as a scapegoat and enchant her to think it was her fault, you'd have no cause to admit blame. After hearing everything, I must conclude this to be an unfortunate tragedy. One that we all will work to avoid in the future."

"You will not be leaving the House until we solve this Deburio debacle. Clotho will be making up for her failure in that regard. You will be required to always be within sight of somebody until she has made it clear we are not to be trifled with. That is your punishment." Ida closed her eyes and sighed. "Your handmaiden will count, inside our walls at least. You need not worry about outside our walls as you won't be leaving. That is my ruling, you may go."

Beatrice was shocked at how reasonable that was. This didn't go the way she thought it would at all. "Why are we getting off so lightly?"

Ida raised an eyebrow. "Do you wish to be punished more severely?"

Beatrice did have that concern pushing this, but this was far too out of character. There was something she wasn't letting on. "Forgive me, but you have to admit that it's not so much a punishment as it is a precaution."

Ida glared at her, then closed her eyes. "Do I truly have to explain my disgrace for you to be satisfied?" She stood up. "Fine. I made a case for you to have protection when leaving the House. Not only was the one time you actually agreed to it the time you were abducted, the only reason for your survival was a handmaiden that I also was heavily against you having. This entire event has made me look the fool. And petty punishments would only make me appear to be a sore fool at that."

Beatrice never thought she'd see the day Ida admitted fault so readily. She pushed her luck even further. "In that case, I think Lia should be rewarded for her efforts as well."

Ida narrowed her eyes with an unamused expression. "Lia was allowed to keep her mind after she backtalked to Atropos during your recovery. Let's call *that* her reward."

Lia knocked on Clotho's door. The darkness did not break when the door opened just a crack. Her tone was quiet and tamed. "What?"

"Thank you. For saving us." Lia held out the zucchini bread. She'd found it to be her favorite variety of bread so far and thought to make some for the fate as a gift. "I'm sorry you're being punished for my idea."

In the blink of an eye the gift was snatched from her hands and the door slammed shut. It opened a crack again and half the bread was slid back out. Lia frowned and tried to push it back but the door was already closed again. "Share it with the miss."

Lia knew better than to argue, but was confused as to why she wouldn't take the entire loaf. Luckily Bea seemed to understand after she shared the bread and explained what she'd tried to do.

"We all took blame. So we all share the apology." Bea softly laughed. "A fae custom that she's allowing you to partake in. Further fascinating me as she appears fond of you."

"I think she's lonely." Lia nibbled at the bread. It was delicious, she really was proud of her baking skills by this point.

"Considering most are afraid to even speak to her, I'm not shocked." Bea finished her piece and gave a heavy sigh. "We are beyond fortunate to have come out of this unscathed. Not just the event itself but also surviving the wrath of my mother."

Lia nodded in agreement. "I know, she looked so mad but she barely even said anything to me. I explained what happened and she just told me to go busy myself. I thought she'd like, make me live out a nightmare or something." A thought came to her. "Maybe she felt like I already was living one and couldn't top it."

"What nightmare were you living?" Bea asked.

Lia frowned. "I thought you were dying and the last thing you thought was that I hated you."

Bea sighed. "Right. I did promise we'd discuss this, didn't I?"

Lia stood up and moved in front of her. "Yeah, and I've had a long time to think about it. So I'm going first and then you can...can do whatever you decide to do, ok?"

Bea straightened up with a look of curiosity. "Very well then. You have the floor, as it were."

"My lady. Bea." Lia tried to fight her nerves, she practiced this in the mirror a few times but it didn't compare to the real deal. She closed her eyes to make sure Bea didn't think she was making her say this. "I, Lia Abith, give you permission to enchant me in order to make me the best lady-in-waiting I can be for you. I have enjoyed my time as your handmaiden, do not think you have impaired my mental state, and even if you have, I don't care. I have never felt happier and that is more important to me than worrying how I got there."

Bea didn't respond. Lia couldn't help but open an eye to peek.

Those sapphire eyes were glowing brightly in wait. "Sleep."

Chapter 20
Prized Possessions

Lia opened her eyes. She was calm, relaxed, and entranced.

She was naked. This was okay.

Bea was in front of her, eyes glowing with a hand caressing her cheek. She was also naked. That was *very* okay. If her dreams were truly memories then her memories didn't hold up to reality. Ethereally beautiful in the moonlight like a fae from legend. "You're gorgeous."

"How do you manage to slip those in, even in trance?" Bea asked.

"No thoughts means the new ones slip out," Lia said, literally feeling the words slipping from her mind as soon as she said them.

Bea hid a laugh. "This is why I love this state the most. Just lucid enough to be honest but still a toe dipped in mindless bliss." She moved her hand under her chin. "But you're waking up, aren't you? Your mind stepping back into your body, no memory of how you got here but no capacity to be concerned about why."

Lia felt like she'd been lounging in the back of her mind and was given a mental hand to stand back up. Gentle words accompanying the fae eyes that drew her back to the surface.

Bea looked guilty. "When you resurface you will tell me the truth if I ask a question of you." She paused. "Answering truthfully will make you feel warm and happy. Even if you feel shame for your answer you will feel euphoric for telling me. Now, wake up."

Lia blinked, her brain finally able to catch up on what words were said and not just how smooth they'd been to listen to. She then cringed. "What does euphoric mean?"

Bea's face scrunched up. She was so trying not to laugh at her but also smiled like she thought it was cute she didn't know. "Excited. It means very excited."

"Oh! So if I tell you that I think you're laughing at me for not knowing that—" Lia stopped as her entire body tingled. Her face was heating up and she nearly started hopping between her feet as a giddiness sprouted within her. "Oh my, that's...that's nice. It's like I'm being hugged by—" she stopped but the urge to keep the tingling going coerced her to finish the thought "—by you, my lady, oh wow that really does work."

"I suppose that means I don't need a test question. I was so proud of the one I came up with." Bea ran her fingers along Lia's horns. "Is there a reason you changed your hair to let these be seen?"

Lia whimpered. "Hey, that's not fair and yes, you said my horns were cute so I wanted you to see them." She stomped her foot while failing to prevent a smile forming from the euphoria coursing through her. "Damnit, I couldn't even stop myself at the yes, it just feels too good!"

"Don't fret too much, I had already guessed that answer," Bea said with a sly look, "but I also guessed you'd not want to admit it directly. Thought it was a clever test question, it's impressive you noticed I left the option for a simple yes."

"Well yeah, you're a fae, you do clever wordplay, it's what makes this fun," Lia said.

Bea's playfulness became a little more uncertain. She looked away. "So, you find this fun? I blanked your mind, stripped you bare, and made you aware only so you can know you're telling me your darkest secrets. You don't have a problem with that?"

"It's humiliating and I love it." The euphoria running through her cut down any inhibitions very quickly.

"Yes, yes, I suppose it's like one of your fantasies." Bea glanced at her. "When exactly did you start fantasizing?"

"First week. After you messed with that noble guy who insulted me." Lia spoke the fact before she even truly remembered it, like the truth just wanted to tumble out. She frowned as Bea looked confused. "What?"

"I hadn't even done anything to you yet." Bea pursed her lips. "I mean, I had enchanted you by then but if anything your commentary that day is what started my path. I assumed my lustful decisions during the soirée were what formed these feelings."

"I've been fantasizing since day one." Lia was starting to accept she just didn't have a filter anymore. "Maybe not intensely but I always liked your eyes. And when I learned what they could do, it didn't take long to start imagining stuff." She had a realization. "Wait, did you do this just to scare me? Like you thought if I woke up naked and unable to lie I'd tell you I wanna go home and you'd be able to prove your point?"

"Not an inaccurate assessment." Bea no longer was acting dominant, she shifted around like she felt silly. "Your declaration was very sweet and I wish to honor it. But I also wanted you to properly comprehend what you're getting into. Or getting back into. Having you strip is tame compared to what else I've had you do." She blushed. "I've had you be unaware of me as I explore your body. I turned you into a naked towel holder. Every night since the soirée I've had you go down on me before bed like a mindless sex toy."

Lia's heart started racing. "Can you let me remember?"

Bea was awestruck. "I admit to using you like a sex object and you wish to *remember*? Why?"

Lia's legs were shaking as she had her hands between them and was fighting with all her might not to go any further than that. "Because it turns me on." She stifled a moan, words tumbling out to feed the pleasure of honesty. "This really turns me on. Losing control, my mind at your mercy, it's just so hot and you're basically teasing me right now and don't even realize it. Gods I really want to touch myself and I'm telling you that because being horny and euphoric is probably what being on drugs is like so if I keep telling you things that I'm embarrassed about but are true it feels amazing. I'm so horny, Bea. Like all the time, even when you think I'm not, it's so hard to think when I'm around you because I just am caught up in imagining all the things I want you to do to me—"

Lia locked with those wonderful glowing eyes and her lustful confession derailed. She sunk deep into bliss, her mind already drunk in pleasure just pulling her down so fast her legs nearly gave out. Her hand began to slide to her side until another one gently guided it back. "Don't stop."

Even if Lia had the mind to argue she wouldn't have. She shamelessly began to play with herself as she listened to her mistress.

"I realize why you fantasize now. That first night, I told you to dream and ever since you've been clinging to that order so you can obey when I ask you not to remember and yet never truly forget. Clever." Her words were the only thing she could hear. Even Lia's own moans did not reach her ears. "So let's have you remember what you refused to forget. You'll take it one at a time, realizing what you missed. Slow at first, reveling in it." The gentle hand showed her the rhythm, even when it left Lia could still feel it guiding her to caress her pussy. "Then faster and faster, one after the other, your mind in sync with your body as you know when you reach that last memory you'll cum. You don't even know what that memory is but you know it'll make you cum until every thought you have left is streaking down your leg. Because I told you it would and obeying is more important than anything else."

And remember Lia did. She remembered the simple ones, the first night in the garden that still seemed so surreal, the more intimate moments of the first enchantment being laid. She remembered taking off her dress and working in nothing but her underwear while Bea obviously gawked. Accidentally cumming in the library after being teased with a trigger all day. Then they got more intense, unveiling the sexual context of the first dance they shared that had been censored out, Lia worshipping her body and then Bea teasing her until her mind all but broke from pleasure.

Then it was a flipbook of orders and questions, dazed smiles, mindless wishes that she could kiss Bea as she told her what to do. Weeks of her eating her mistress out, being used like an object, every fantasy revealing to be reality, she knew she was approaching the end fast as she could feel herself begging to cum but knowing she had not yet earned it.

And then Lia was aware of the last memory. She knew it was the last because it was the present one. That while she giggled and moaned, playing with herself while her mind relived all this depravity, her mistress had been enjoying the rest of her body. Bea had kissed her neck, nibbled at her ear, explored downward, and now was playing with her tits as she became aware of it all.

And just as her mistress said, realizing it made Lia cum. Bea had to basically catch her as her body gave out, shaking heavily as her eyes rolled back feeling the euphoric climax only those enchanting eyes could ever reward her with. Her mind fought to stay topside just to feel it longer but the ecstasy of emptiness called to her like an old friend. She had to be moaning or screaming or making some kind of noise and yet she couldn't comprehend anything outside of her mind shattering from an orgasm that would not relent. It was too much but Lia couldn't get enough even as she sank deep into mindless bliss. Wave after wave of pleasure dragged her further down until there was nothing left of her aware to even register it.

The cold air against Lia's wet skin jolted her awake. She was mid-drying herself off, the sound of the bath draining behind her the only proof that she'd actually used it. She didn't remember how she got here.

Had it all been just a wonderful dream?

Lia quickly finished drying off. A nightgown had been laid out for her. She recognized it as one of Bea's. Not only that, she hadn't thought about how this wasn't a servant washroom. This was Bea's personal bathroom.

It had been real.

Lia snuck through the door as quietly as she could. Bea was at her desk, dressed for bed and scribbling into her journal. She didn't even turn when she heard Lia close the door behind her. "All cleaned up, are we?"

Lia blushed at the indifference. "I can only assume, my lady."

Bea's ears perked up and her properness vanished with a cheerful relief as she turned. "You're awake!" She held out her hand and Lia trotted over to take it. "I was worried you'd never want to resurface with how deep that sent you."

"I know, it was unbelievably amazing." Lia smelled the soap in her hair. Bea must've had to take care of both of them while she was out of commission. "I'm sorry you were forced to clean me up. That's supposed to be my job."

Bea smirked. "Who said you didn't?"

Lia blushed heavily. "You mean I've—"

"Been mindlessly following orders for the last hour?" Bea hid her face away. "I was unsure if forcing you to surface would ruin your fun. I assumed by the drool you were enjoying yourself."

"Was I...doing my job well?" Lia asked. She wasn't sure how to phrase that.

"I admire your devotion to your duties, you seemed inclined to follow them even in trance. Although, you almost walked into the hall naked on more than one occasion." Bea's hand couldn't hide her laugh, which Lia shared imagining herself being so shameless. "I think you were trying to retrieve supplies to clean up the mess we made. A simple order to not leave my bedroom sufficed as a solution. We actually bathed together, the last thing I asked was for you to finish cleaning yourself up."

Lia pouted. "Aww, how come when I'm awake you won't let me wash you but if I'm entranced you will?"

"It's embarrassing? Having a handmaiden wash me, cloth me, it makes me feel like a child who can't do anything. Entranced it was more like just using a tool." Bea turned bright red. "Not to say I think you're a tool."

Lia smiled. "I don't mind being your tool."

Bea playfully smacked her. "Don't say those things!"

"Why not? I am only being honest, my lady," Lia said, remembering the lingering order as her body tingled with euphoria. She was very happy to know that had been left on, although it was tamer than before. A reward rather than a coercion.

"Because it's very hard for me to resist following up on them and you just cleaned up." Bea looked both excited and guilty at the same time. "Lia, what are you?"

"Your property." Lia covered her mouth. "Sorry, that just came out."

Bea's excitement didn't falter. "Do you think it's incorrect?"

Lia blushed. "No."

"And more importantly," Bea took her hand, "Is that what you want to be?"

Lia stared at her. Both because she was thinking and also Bea's eyes were glowing in such a loving way. Like they still were commanding her but only to feel adored and cherished, which she was happily obeying. "Why ask?"

Bea looked away, causing Lia to stifle an involuntary whine. "Because I can make you say yes. Both as your lady and mistress. Asking makes it that much more special to me."

"You misunderstand," Lia knelt down while still holding her hand, "why ask when the answer is obviously yes? I live to serve you,

Lady Beatrice. What else would that make me than yours and yours alone?"

Chapter 21
Live to Serve

Lia kicked her feet with excitement. "So, what's first on the brainwashing agenda?"

She'd been waiting for this the entire day. Bea had all but been torturing her by only mentioning it once the night before and feigning ignorance the next morning. More like teasing actually, she swore Bea could tell when she was thinking about it and would make some off-hand remark about "retraining" her. Her lady refused to go into details and it made her imagination run wild. By the time Lia was invited into her room and asked to sit down for said training she was more giddy than a girl who already knew what presents she was about to be surprised with.

"Glad to see you're eager, today is going to be quite intense." Beatrice smirked. "Not that you'll mind, I'm sure. But I need to remove and then reapply my enchantment over you."

Lia frowned. "Wait, remove? I thought we were adding stuff."

"Darling, I was not being dramatic when I said I was worried about your mental state. You were having memory lapses, apparent sleepwalking, even mood swings. Things I said that accidentally conflicted with previous orders caused very distressing reactions." Bea rubbed her neck. "Not to mention I have no idea what orders still have a hold over you after my order to free yourself. Since unintended enchantment interactions are precisely what I want to avoid this time, I'm going to use this as an opportunity to start fresh." She raised an eyebrow. "Why are you smiling like that?"

"Because you're already trying to be a better mistress just for me. It makes me feel special." Lia blushed with a hint of excitement. "I hope that doesn't mean you'll hold back."

Bea gave a somewhat predatory smile as she lifted Lia's chin. "On the contrary, I'm going to break you down, carve new truths into the core of your being, and rebuild you as my loyal, obedient doll. How does that sound?"

Lia felt euphoric as she whispered, "Hot."

"Good." Bea moved the chair in front of her and sat down. "But I'm still going to do this with surgical care."

Lia straightened up. "I'm ready."

Bea's eyes glowed for barely a second. The apprehension made it confusing as they stopped and she took a deep breath, sounding exhausted. "So far so good. I left some simple triggers, but have removed almost everything else."

Lia frowned. She was a little more relaxed but nothing much else. "Already? You didn't even say anything."

"Nothing that you can remember. Your trance self did suggest I take a souvenir as proof." Bea gave a sly smile as she held up a pair of panties. "It's been an hour, darling. Had to be thorough."

Lia turned bright red as her hands went to her waist and realized it was much more airy down there. "Hey!" She shivered. "Gods, that was so seamless. No wonder I haven't noticed up till now."

"Yes, which is probably why your memory started collapsing. No more, from now on you'll remember everything." Bea glanced at the souvenir that was her underwear. "That is, unless I deem you forgetting will be more fun."

Lia shivered at the thought. *Awesome.*

Bea took a deep breath. "Alright, I'm going to go slow. But to be honest, enchanting you causes me to go into a bit of a trance myself, I get into a rhythm. I truly want feedback as we go along, so try to speak your mind as often as you can. For the short time you'll have a mind to speak, that is. This is a journey together."

"Ok, ok, I'm sold, just hit me already!" Lia was kicking her legs with excitement.

Bea's eyes glowed very lightly. "Now, how do you feel?"

Lia instantly relaxed. Everything became slower, a calm clawing at her adrenaline as her kicks came to a halt and her arms hung at her sides. "Woah. Feels...tingly without the setup. Warming. Like drinking a cup of hot chocolate."

"That's good. Just let that warmth consume you. Let the tension in your body fade, your excitement thin to serenity as you take deep, calming breaths. Just staring into my eyes." They glowed slightly more. "What do they look like to you?"

"Enchanting," Lia said with a giggle. She didn't mean to but it just slipped out. "Normally they're beautiful but when they glow it's like...like stars. Sparkling stars in the night sky." She caught herself leaning forward and readjusted. "I...I wish I could draw them, sometimes. I try to remember but I know I'm not getting anywhere close."

"Ah, but to draw them you'd have to look away. And no matter how hard you try, you can't. Every time they just fill more of your mind like the ever-expanding night sky they remind you of. Each sparkle a thought of yours popping." Bea smiled warmly as

Lia started to giggle more, her popping thoughts tickling her brain. "And the more my eyes sparkle, the more space is made for my words. Words that fill your mind, guiding you so you don't have to worry about anything but watching the pretty eyes, the sunless sea that has captured your gaze. A lovely loop of watching so you can listen, listening so you can watch."

"Watch. Listen." Lia slumped back into the couch as Bea gave her the lightest of taps. She wasn't sitting in the chair anymore and instead loomed over her. "Getting hard...to think."

"You don't need to think, darling. Don't you love the sound of that? Free from thought as my words fill your mind. Letting me think for you as you enjoy mindless bliss."

"Yes," Lia whispered. "Love it...so much."

"Tell me why. Gather all those thoughts you have left and use them up explaining why you're so excited for them to be gone."

"It's freeing. Like letting somebody else plan your day." Lia blushed, still aware enough to be embarrassed but not enough to stop. "And I like how helpless I feel. How you *make* me want to be helpless...crave giving up my will. Unable to disobey, willing to do anything, it's wrong but...it's hot."

Bea caressed her cheek. "Do you want it?"

"Yes."

She ran her hand down and under her chin. "Do you need it?"

"Yesss."

Those beautiful sapphires glowed brighter than she'd ever seen. "Then be a good girl and sleep."

Lia's eyes fluttered shut. She could hear words being whispered into her ear, feel her body being caressed. She was asked to do things. She obeyed. The eyes were with her even when she couldn't see them, her empty gaze focused on nothing but those sparkles. Was this what she always saw while in a trance? The thought slipped out as soon as it appeared. It didn't matter. Nothing mattered. The eyes mattered.

"Awake."

Lia opened her eyes. She was naked. She remembered stripping, she remembered making it a little show too. The act had been as unthinking as breathing. Is that what mindlessness was like? No wonder she wanted to go back so often. "Woahhh. Remember...but like, not during...feels like a dream. Good dream."

"You're still giving feedback? That's so cute." Bea shared a smile with her. Then her eyes glowed again. "You're doing great, darling. Now, sleep."

Lia obeyed. She was sinking, the lake becoming an endless ocean of empty bliss. The words were beyond her understanding but she knew they were making this world for her to enjoy. She never wanted to leave. Never wanted to—

"Awake."

Lia opened her eyes droopily. They were on the bed, Bea lying at her side. "Hi?"

"Hi." Bea kissed her and then her eyes glowed bright. "Sleep."

Lia fell back into the ocean of emptiness with the only thing on her mind being the fleeting feeling of the kiss on her lips. Sinking deeper and deeper, her body so relaxed and limp as the current seemed to carry her. So soft and gentle, caressing her body as she sunk ever so deeper.

Then again, rudely snatched from the arms of bliss, "Awake." Beatrice caressed her cheek, wiping off a speck of drool from the corner of her mouth. Lia didn't even say anything, she just looked into her eyes and obediently waited for them to send her back. A moment that felt like eternity passed before she obliged. "Sleep."

Lia sank so deep she forgot where she was. She forgot what she was doing. Awareness dissolved in the waters of apathy. Drifting along the bottom of her mind in a serene peace.

A voice called out to her, alluring as a siren. It began to ask her questions. Lia was happy to answer.

"Who are you?"

That one was easy. "Lia Abith."

"What are you?"

A half-elf, she should've said but she couldn't bring herself to lie. "A half-demon."

"What is your purpose?"

That made her stumble. "I don't know?"

"Would you like to know?"

Lia smiled with relief. "Mhm. Yes, please."

The voice sounded amused. "Okay. But we have to fix the answers to the first two questions."

"Are they wrong?" Lia asked fearfully. She didn't want to make the voice upset with her.

"Of course not. They are core truths, they belong to you forever. Nobody should ever be allowed to take who you are away." If words could kiss the voice was kissing her forehead. Any worries that had bubbled now popped and made Lia giggle. "In fact, we're going to make sure we keep those answers safe and sound."

"Now, open your eyes." Lia didn't realize hers were closed. She did so and saw beautiful sapphires staring back. "And *sleep!*"

What once felt like the deepest recess of her mind opened up to swallow her whole. Deeper and deeper, never losing sight of those eyes no matter how far she sunk into nor how far her own eyes rolled into the back of her head. Falling like a feather until finally free of any thought but the ones the voice gave her. The light from the eyes illuminating what she needed to see.

"You've gone to a place in your mind even you didn't know was there. A place you can't reach without my help. A safe place. You feel so safe here. So relaxed. So open," the voice whispered, "We're going to put these answers into a box. Do you see one?"

Lia was holding a jewelry box now. She didn't remember picking it up but it was in her hands just like the voice said. "Yes."

"We're going to open it and place those valuable answers inside. Once we do, nobody will be able to change them." Her hand obeyed and started to open it. Even now she wasn't in control, just letting the voice puppet her. "It'll be safe from everyone. Even me. Doesn't that sound good?"

"Yeah." Lia expected it to be empty, but there were actually a couple things in the box. One was an old pair of earrings, ones she swore she was wearing right now. The ones Diana gave to her. That seemed right, she wanted that to be safe.

The other was a necklace with a heart locket on it. It must be important if she put it in here, but why didn't she recognize it? Somehow not recognizing it hurt.

"What's wrong?" The voice sounded concerned.

"What else is in here?" Lia asked.

The voice didn't respond immediately. Every moment of not hearing it made her worry more until it returned and made it all better. "You must've stored away other things you didn't want to forget. That's a good thing, keep them in there. We'll take them back out when we're done, ok?"

"Ok." That made sense. Lia didn't want to forget Diana loved her. So a symbol of her affection was in the box.

That didn't explain the locket. But she didn't care anymore, the voice said it was a good thing and she believed her. She put the answers in the box, smiling as they seemed to manifest into objects for her to remember. A ring with *Lia Abith* engraved on it and a well-drawn picture of her, even having the horns in her new hairstyle. Who and what she was.

"Close the box."

Lia closed it tight and with it the answers were locked away.

"Now I'm going to put it away and we can go over this again. So we don't alter them accidentally while clarifying those questions."

The girl obeyed and let the box return to wherever it had appeared from. Out of mind but not out of reach.

"Now, who are you?"

"I don't know." It didn't bother the girl, she knew where the answer was. She'd just locked it away for safekeeping after all.

"You are a doll. Repeat."

"I am a doll." The doll moaned as she felt a lick against her clit. This made sense, the voice seemed to puppet her very thoughts, what else would she be?

"Good girl." The words made her shiver with pleasure. "What are you?"

"I don't know." The doll was excited to learn.

"You are property. Repeat."

She wasn't as quick to obey. Even her excitement couldn't fully dull her confusion. "I'm property?" The doll was disappointed to feel nothing in response. She must've upset the voice with her hesitance. "I'm...property." A faint lick, a tiny reward for an unconfident answer.

"It's okay. Topside you're eager but deep down it's hard to admit." The voice didn't sound mad, like it was being very patient with her. It made her want to please it even more. "But you're not just any property, you'll be my property. My special little plaything. I'll take good care of you, all you have to do is repeat it until you remember it's true."

"I'm...property. I'm p-property. I'm property." Each time the doll said it she felt another lick, each one better as she said it more confidently. It wasn't more than a few times before she was saying it over and over as the phantom tongue edged her relentlessly. "I'm property! I'mpropertyI'mpropertyI'm—"

The doll stopped. She had been told to stop when it became true and despite her body demanding to finish she obeyed the voice instead. After all, she was nothing but property. Property obeyed its owner.

"Good girl." The doll didn't even need to shiver. She was already swimming in the pleasure of obedience. "I think you might understand now, yes?"

"Yes."

"That's yes, mistress."

Of course, how could she forget? "Yes, mistress."

"Good girl. You've been so obedient, I'm proud of you, darling." The doll squirmed from the praise. "What is your purpose?"

The answer was so clear now. "Whatever you decide it is, mistress."

"*Good girl.*" The doll moaned, she couldn't help it. "Your purpose is to serve and obey."

"My purpose is to serve and obey." The doll whimpered with surprise as her clit was teased relentlessly by the tongue rewarding her obedience. "I am a doll. I am property. My purpose is to serve and obey."

"Cum."

"Yes, mistress!" The doll came on command. It was quick but it was perfect. It was perfect because she obeyed and the pleasure from that almost overcame the act itself.

"Good girl. Now I'm going to bring you up, just a little. Out of the safe place but still deep in mindless bliss." The voice sounded so pleased with her. "I want you to give your answers. With each one you'll remember the truth beneath it."

"I am a doll." *You are Lia.*

"I am property." *You are a half-demon.*

"My purpose is to serve and obey." *And that purpose is one you chose.*

"Do you remember your mantras?"

"Yes, mistress," Lia said, her name back in her grasp. She was Lia, she was a doll, and she was having the best time of her life.

"Repeat them."

"I am Beatrice's property. My body belongs to her. My mind is for her to fill. Her will is my will." Lia was heating up more and more with every word. The moment the mantra left her lips she recognized the smooth voice belonging to Bea, her lady, her mistress, her owner.

"Obedience is pleasure."

"Obedience is pleasure."

"You don't think, you just obey."

"I don't think, I just obey."

"You are a toy. You exist to be used."

"I am a toy. I exist to be used."

"You love to be used."

"I love to be used."

"You *need* to be used."

"I need to be used." Lia whimpered. "Please use me, mistress."

"I am, darling. I have been, this entire time." Lia started to squirm as at this revelation. "You probably want to know how, but you don't need to. You could be my footrest, you could be massaging me, you could have your pretty little head between my legs mindlessly licking away, but the only thing you desire is knowing you obeyed, that you fulfilled your purpose to serve. The pleasure of being used is all you need, it's all you want, it's all you crave."

Lia wasn't thinking so much as absorbing everything being told to her like a sponge. She didn't even know if she responded. The mantras echoed in the emptiness that was her mind.

It was pure bliss.

"My, my, that really pushed you over, didn't it?" Her mistress said, but it didn't really register. It wasn't an order. It wasn't important. "Well, let's not waste a trance this deep. Repeat your mantras, darling. Repeat them until they're all that's left."

Lia eagerly obeyed.

Beatrice wrapped her arms around Lia as she played with herself, mindlessly repeating her mantras. She'd sunk so deep her words swung from monotone to a drunken giggle, fully indifferent of anything being done to her body. Beatrice felt a heat between her own legs as she couldn't help but kiss and suck on her handmaiden's neck, inciting gleeful moans before returning to repeating her truths. If it was anybody else, she would've called this overkill.

Since it was Lia, she was calling it foreplay.

Beatrice put a hand over the one Lia had between her legs. "Sleep."

"Her will is my—yesss, mistresss," Lia said as she slumped into her embrace. She continued to play with herself, with a helping hand guiding her.

"Such a good girl. So blank, so obedient. Dipping down one final time, savoring the mindless bliss before we bring you back to awareness." Beatrice smiled at the little whine that incited. She was more than ready. "Now, feel yourself rising to the surface. Slow, steady, the same pace as the fingers circling."

"Yes, mistress," Lia whispered.

"When your eyes open you will still be in trance. Fully aware but unable to disobey." Beatrice shivered as Lia whined louder. "Up and up, almost there, three, two, one, and open."

Lia opened her eyes. She was calm, relaxed, and unbelievably horny.

"How do you feel?" Beatrice asked, her words so alluring as she whispered into her ear.

"Wonderful, mistress," Lia said. Internally she blushed. She didn't recall ever calling Bea mistress like *that*. Not that she didn't want to, she really liked how that sounded. It felt good, it felt *right*.

"Was it everything you ever dreamed of?" she continued.

"Yes, mistress." Lia couldn't describe the pleasure of what that had felt like. Even now, as she realized she was still in a trance for she wanted nothing but to listen and obey. The only thing that seemed like her own will was her quietly saying, "Thanks, Bea."

"You're welcome, darling." Beatrice kissed her cheek. It was only then Lia became aware enough of her body to realize she was playing with herself, she just assumed she was just embarrassingly turned on by all this. "You did perfectly. Accepted all my commands, all my little suggestions, your mind, body, and soul now completely under my spell. I think such obedient submission deserves a reward, don't you?"

Lia wanted one so bad yet couldn't help but say, "Serving you is my reward, mistress." She couldn't tell if the enchantment made her say that or if that was just the truth. Or both.

"Good girl." A shiver went down her spine as Bea whispered those two words into her ear. She would do anything to hear her say it again. She wanted to be a good girl. "Now, you've gotten me all worked up. I think that makes you responsible for satisfying me, yes?"

"Yes, mistress," Lia said, her excitement growing.

"Glad we agree. Feel free to interpret how to fulfill that order in whatever way you think is best." Bea sounded like she was trying to hide her own anticipation. "You may begin."

It was like a switch being flipped. Lia immediately spun around and took Bea's head in her hands. She allowed herself a single moment of staring intimately into her enchanting eyes, the fae they belonged to stunned by her intensity, before leaning in and kissing her in the way she'd wanted to since their outing in the lighthouse.

Her mistress was still surprised by the way this had gone but melted back into the bed with eager acceptance.

Lia was a little surprised herself. She hadn't exactly been told to kiss Bea with lovesick passion but she couldn't help herself. She grinded against her as she slowly ran her hands from her head down her neck and then settled on her chest to squeeze, all while their lips were locked in lovemaking. Clearly it had ignited something in Bea because she seemed to forgo her own idea of letting Lia please her and quickly took the reins by wrapping her legs around her to flip their positions.

Lia didn't mind letting her lead. She lived to serve.

She loved to serve. She loved to serve Bea.

Lia loved Bea.

Lia was in love with Beatrice von Closen.

It was the truth, a core truth that she'd uncovered. The locket had opened and Bea was the picture that lay inside as she always had been. She knew it, she felt it, she showed it with all her heart in this wondrous moment she hoped would never end. A mistress and maiden entwined like secret lovers having an illicit affair.

A handmaiden could dream that her lady loved her back.

Chapter 22
OBEDIENCE IS PLEASURE

Beatrice never wanted to leave the House again.

Why would she need to with her favorite doll at her side, begging to be used. No longer did she fear Lia craving to be controlled but instead happily obliged to feed that urge. The maiden had given herself to her mistress and said mistress had never felt more complete.

The unexpected part was that Lia was much more perverted than one ever would think of such a sweet girl, but only while in a trance. Not that out of trance she wouldn't love it, but it appeared part of the thrill for her was having Beatrice coerce her desires from her enthralled self and surprise her waking self with humiliating pleasure.

Sometimes those desires were a tad much. Lia had a bit of an exhibitionist streak. She vehemently denied it, but Beatrice had received far too many requests from her trance self to be humiliated with an audience. Not to mention Lia had started automatically assuming she'd get to be a nude towel holder whenever her lady decided to take a bath, she *really* liked that one.

Admittedly, so did Beatrice.

"It's not the same as mindlessness, it's like...it's like you're doing what you love and you're always satisfied from how good of a job you're doing but you also don't even worry about doing a good job because you're just a thing and that's what you're supposed to do," Lia had tried to explain. Now that she was allowed to remember her time under she couldn't seem to stop talking about the different ways it felt. Changes in her sense of self fascinated her, she'd actually come up with a list of how much she enjoyed specific inanimate objects.

Objects that had a clear purpose, chairs, towel holders, tables, were Lia's favorite in terms of lack of sentience. Things like mannequins or dolls she felt were more akin to being in trance, apparently even specifying being inanimate only made it feel like mindlessness. Perhaps as the purpose of a doll was what its owner decided, it forced Lia to be aware enough to comprehend what her owner wanted her to be. A chair just was happy if it was being sat on, a simple binary fulfillment. Strangely enough, statues leaned towards being an object. Apparently a statue's purpose was to be looked at so that was all Lia desired when thinking she was one.

Beyond the fact they'd spent days on end fooling around while twisting Lia's mind for both their pleasures, Beatrice was finding her descriptions and reactions illuminating towards the intricacies of enchantment. She felt like she was getting better at them purely through the level of nuance Lia incited just to make her experience more special.

For instance, Beatrice was able to instill commands to Lia mentally now. She still needed eye contact but she didn't need to speak if the commands were simple enough. And with this discovery she started to realize this was not limited to her handmaiden. While redundant at first glance, it meant she could instill commands without being so obvious.

Although Lia was walking proof that with simplicity comes interpretation. The two of them had spent most of this morning practicing them on her to see what she would do. *Leave and forget* was one she was practicing the most, it felt like a useful skill to have.

"It sorta felt like walking into a room and forgetting why I did, so I walked back out to try and remember," Lia explained after several test runs. She indeed would only leave the room, then return and request a reminder as to what she'd just been asked to do. Beatrice opted to not inform her what the commands were until several tries, as knowing them in of itself might skew her reactions. "This is fun. I'm sorta becoming a practice doll, huh?"

Beatrice smiled as her eyes glowed, draining the thought from her handmaiden. At this point she could put her into a trance with but a word, yet it didn't compare to the direct feeling enchantment gave her. "You're already a doll, darling. What I deem that doll to be is all that changes."

"Yes, mistress," Lia said dreamily.

"But you've been a very good girl in helping me practice, I must admit." Beatrice caressed her cheek, inciting a shiver. "I think you've earned the reward I've planned out for today."

"Serving you is my reward, mistress."

Beatrice smiled seductively as her eyes glowed brighter and dragged Lia's mind down into a much deeper trance. "I know. That's why I know you'll love it."

Lia stood patiently in the library waiting for Bea to return. She was naked and playing with herself, just like any other day. She had been alone for some time now, she wondered what her mistress was doing that was taking so long.

The door quickly opened and closed. Lia turned with a smile only to see a maid staring at her evocative display. She gave the fellow servant a nod of acknowledgment and went back to her normal duties.

The maid apparently did not see this as the end of their meeting. "Who are you?" The maid stormed up to her. "What on earth are you doing?"

Lia smiled brightly as she twisted her nipples. "I am a slut in waiting. I must keep myself wet and ready at all times in order to be prepared for when my mistress needs me."

The maid opened her mouth, then closed it. "I see."

"It's an amazing job. I'm sure if you work hard enough you could find a similar position." Lia presented her tits. "Would you like to partake? My mistress says I am to service anyone who asks until she returns. She's very generous like that, I'm so glad she's the one who owns me."

Whatever train of thought the maid had clearly derailed at this proposal. She looked around as if fearful of a trap. "Just like that? You don't have any qualms about me being just a fellow servant?"

Lia shook her head. This maid was so silly, thinking would care. That would mean she could think and a good doll didn't think. A good doll obeyed. "Of course not! I'm just a fuckdoll. I was made to be used. Please feel free. Otherwise, I suggest you return to your own duties. We live to serve after all."

The maid's eyes were locked on her tits. "Is it one way or—"

"Oh! Do you wish for me to eat you out?" Lia dropped to her knees and pushed her arms together. "My tongue is but a tool for pleasure."

The maid almost sat down but Lia said quickly, "Not there!" She cringed. "Sorry. That's my mistress's chair. I'd prefer you not have to move halfway through if she comes back, you know?"

"Oh. Interesting," The maid said, "I'm sure she wouldn't mind."

"Of course she wouldn't, my mistress is very kind, but *I* mind." Lia looked to the door as if Bea would be there right at this moment. "She likes that chair. Please use a different one."

The maid had a testy look. She sat down. "No. I want to use this chair. I want you to go down on me in your mistress's chair."

Lia's annoyance was being overridden by her purpose. She was a doll, she was to service anybody who asked, these were orders by her mistress. She thought it would be a good idea to reserve her mistress's chair but a good doll doesn't think, a good doll obeys. "As you wish. Please lift your dress so I may perform my duties."

"Good girl." The maid lifted her dress, revealing she was not even wearing panties. Lia didn't even ask, her mind was filled with an overwhelming need to lick her pussy. It was her world, her purpose, and she dove in to fulfill it. The maid moaned loudly as she put a hand on her head. "Oh yes, that's it. Such a talented tongue, no wonder she made you a permanent plaything."

A part of Lia shivered at the thought but her mind was consumed by the need to lick. She would spend as long as needed to make this random servant cum, using every technique she'd learned if need be, for hours if she demanded it. Luckily it wasn't hours before she reached a climax.

Good dolls get rewarded. Lia shuddered at the rush of pleasure for fulfilling her role. She had a goofy smile as she pulled away. She loved her job.

"That was quite efficient of you. Although, I think I've stained your mistress's chair. How does that make you feel?" the maid asked with a devious smirk.

Lia blinked. *A doll's feelings are irrelevant.* But pleasing her mistress was her entire world. "I don't know. I'll probably clean it up before she comes back."

"Wonderful idea. Your tongue is a cleaning instrument is it not?" The maid stood up and gestured to it. "Don't let me stop you."

The idea sunk into Lia's open mind. She was a good doll. A good doll cleans up for her mistress. Without hesitation she crawled forward and lapped at the chair like a cat, eager to clean it for her mistress.

"Such a good slut." *I am a good slut.* "So eager to obey." *Obedience is pleasure.* "Eager to be used." *I love being used. I need to be used.*

Lia hadn't even comprehended she was being fondled by the maid as she whispered sensually into her ear until she gave the final lick. She leaned back and smiled brightly as the maid kissed her neck from behind, satisfied at a job well done.

And then reality slapped her across the face.

"Something wrong?" The maid, who Lia had just casually gone down on and then licked her cum off a chair, asked.

Lia blushed heavily as she covered herself. Had Bea really just left her here like a tossed aside toy? Told her to fuck anybody who decided to swing by? "I...I'm sorry, I might need a minute."

"A slut in waiting needs a minute? Oh very well. May I partake of your breasts as you do?" The maid asked casually.

Lia wasn't sure if she could get any redder after being called a slut in waiting but her mouth just responded happily, "Of course. I am but a doll to be used." She held her tits out like she was offering them on a plate. She was aware of everything now but couldn't stop her body. And what's worse, she didn't want to. Knowing it was wrong didn't stop her from rubbing her legs together as the maid leaned in and sucked on her nipples. Every part of her felt so much more sensitive than she remembered, it was like even the hint of a lick would drive her up the wall with pleasure. Lia's eyes started to roll back as she said on reflex, "Thank you for using me."

The maid looked up at her with a smirk. "Do you like that? Being used."

Dolls don't lie. "Yes."

"You were left out like a cheap toy. Whored out to little old me. That makes you wet, doesn't it?"

Lia moaned. "Yesss."

She lightly caressed her thigh and teased her pussy. It was even more sensitive than her tits, she was squirming just at the brush of her fingers. "You haven't even touched yourself but a slut like you is probably ready to cum. Would you cum if I ordered it?"

"Mistress controls when I cum." Lia was still aware but her brain was so lost in the pleasure she might as well be a mindless doll again.

"But you're meant to service me. You're a fuckdoll, ready to obey." Lia nodded in agreement with each sentence, panting as she let her body be played with. "A fuckdoll should cum on command and thus I command you, cum!"

"I obey!" It was a strange and intense experience since she hadn't quite been on the verge just yet. That didn't matter to her body as pleasure shocked through and she came as she was ordered to. She tipped over, faintly muttering. "Please give this slut a minute to recover. She...cannot uphold her duties...at the current moment.'

"Oh, if you insist," a different, smoother and more familiar voice said, "I suppose I don't want to break my doll beyond repair."

Lia plopped her head to the side to see the maid was gone and in the chair was a familiar fae fanning herself. "Bea?"

Bea smiled as she handed her a glass of water from the table. "I'm sure you have questions, but please drink up. Consider it an order if you're that disoriented, I don't want you dehydrated."

Lia obediently drained the entire cup and gasped for air after, still breathing heavy from exhaustion. "What just happened?"

Bea smirked. "A trial run compromise on one of your more, ahem, *extravagant* requests. In this case, somebody other than me taking advantage of you, with my permission of course. A true test of being a loyal and eager fuckdoll."

Lia remembered that. Well, sorta, she was certainly in a trance when she brought it up. And might've mentioned Bea enchanting the third person after and having a three way. Gods, thinking back she got really descriptive with that, no wonder Bea had been toying with the idea. "The maid—"

"Was me. At first I thought to just vet the staff for a candidate who would be more or less willing to play the role. Or rather enjoy it as much as you do, as I can make any of them willing and I know that gets you off so do keep an eye out for candidates. But I then realized you perceiving me as somebody else entirely was just as effective and I wanted to start small." Beatrice stretched with a satisfied sigh. "It was quite a treat to see how you would serve somebody other than me. I didn't realize your tongue was so tailored to my tendencies until experiencing the default, as it were."

Lia was feeling way too many emotions as she was trying to process the trove of information just thrown at her. The only thing she managed to focus on was how much work Bea put into all this, just for her. She couldn't help but shyly smile. "Thanks, Bea."

"You're welcome, darling." The handle to the library door turned. Bea's eyes glowed with an almost predatory smile, as if excited to see who just volunteered to become their willing third. Then they went wide with fear. "Hide!"

Before Lia could even ask why or more importantly, *where*, Bea pulled her close and hid the nude handmaiden beneath her dress. She heard the library door close and what sounded like the fabric of a dress dragging along the floor.

Or perhaps, hair. "I'm surprised to see you outside of your study, Mother."

Lia now understood quite clearly the problem and became very, very afraid. Not the fun kind, the 'wasn't going to be around anymore' kind.

"Given your recent improvement in staying put, I decided to take a page out of your book and go for an unsupervised walk." Ida made a dissatisfied huff. "I don't quite see the appeal."

The moment Lia heard Ida's voice, the confirmation that the Lady of the House was truly here, a strange tingly sensation ran throughout her body. The fear of being found melted away as she focused on her role. She was the maid, she needed to clean. That was the first rule after all. The Lady of the House was not addressing her and she needed to busy herself.

Although, Lia was not allowed to leave beneath her lady's dress, her mistress had been very clear about that. That certainly limited her options. Still, the rules were clear, so she eagerly got to work.

Beatrice was slowly turning bright red as she felt the tongue of Lia methodically cleaning up along her leg. Her mother was standing right there, judging her every action and fully unaware of just how debased she was truly being. They'd been lucky the angle of her seat gave enough cover to let such a half-baked hiding place work but if Ida got any closer they would certainly be caught. What on earth was Lia thinking?

Her tongue was answering that question quite clearly.

"Although you seemed to be fine with a handmaiden supervising you so maybe I'll try again tomorrow with Atropos. See if that improves the experience." Ida narrowed her eyes. "Speaking of, where is Lia? I thought I told you to always be within sight of somebody."

"Lia is...getting me tea. She'll r-return shortly." Beatrice took a shaky breath as the tongue got further up her thigh with each lick. She wasn't certain she'd be able to resist a moan if Lia made it to her clear destination.

"Are you feeling feverish? You look red," Ida asked. Her hair retrieved a book from the wall, probably the true reason she came here but still strange she decided to not send a proxy.

Beatrice gave a shaky nod. "Yes. I think...it's been a long...week. Still on e-*edge* from the attack. Maybe I should lie down for the afternoon."

"Agreed, perhaps the effects of the leyline iron have lingered." Ida left the library swiftly, but to Beatrice felt like an eternity.

As soon as the door closed Beatrice nearly kicked Lia out from under her garment. "Are you trying to get yourself terminated? And me locked away forever?"

Lia looked utterly confused. "I was just doing my job."

"Your job isn't to eat me out!" Beatrice scolded. Not right *then* at the very least. "I know you have a kink for almost getting caught—"

"I wasn't doing that!" Lia said defensively.

"Then what on earth *were* you doing?" Beatrice asked sarcastically.

"Cleaning?" Lia didn't sound confident in her answer.

Beatrice stopped. She wanted to be mad, that small debased part of her wanted to shove Lia back under to finish what she'd started, but the confusion in her eyes was putting all that aside. "Lia, is that truly what you thought you were doing?"

"I think so. I don't know, I zoned out like I always do when doing my job. Your leg was dirty, I only had my—" Lia cut off as she seemed to now comprehend what she had done. Her face was red as a tomato. "I did that...with your mother right there."

Beatrice wrapped a robe she'd brought earlier around her handmaiden. "Let's retire to your room before our luck runs out."

Chapter 23
THE RULES OF THE HOUSE

Lia would've cleaned up if she knew Bea was going to go in her room.

It was a complete mess, drawing paper and pencils strewn on the desk, dirty clothes in a pile against a wall, totally unacceptable for a handmaiden and it was even worse to let her lady see it in such a state. She quickly tried to make her bed to look like there had been an attempt as Bea looked around. One of the walls by now was covered in drawings. Lia wasn't used to having so many and couldn't bear tossing any out or even storing them away. They were all precious to her.

"Why don't you use the closet?" Bea asked with curiosity. She points to all her outfits hanging off the magic mirror, slightly ruining its intended purpose.

Lia cringed with embarrassment. "Oh, it's sorta dumb, but if I can't see something I'm probably gonna forget it. Out of sight, out of mind, you know? So I try not to put things that are important in places I'm not gonna see because I'm very much not gonna remember they exist after a bit."

Bea raised an eyebrow and looked at the desk. "That explains the paper on here. I'd think to put supplies in a drawer to make space."

She opened one and frowned. She reached inside and held up a stash of crumpled paper. "What are these?"

"Hmm?" Lia looked in the drawer. There was a bunch of drawing paper crumpled into little balls and tossed inside. "I don't know. Probably just notes I left for myself."

Bea was reading them aloud with a concerned expression. *'Ask Bea about that thing.' 'You did it again, don't forget to ask Bea about it' 'Lia for the love of the gods if you're going to throw out this note can you at least do it in Bea's room?'* She looked through the drawer to find a good dozen crumpled pieces of paper. "How often are you throwing out notes from yourself?"

Lia frowned. Those notes sounded more urgent than she remembered, although just as unhelpfully vague as when she tossed them in the drawer. "I mean, I haven't found any lately."

"That's good." Bea closed the drawer. "That means this is working."

"What's working?" Lia asked.

Bea had a mischievous smile. "It is time to clean your mind."

Lia wasn't expecting that but she already was slipping out of the bathrobe. She tried to stop, mainly just to ask why, but habit overrode curiosity. This was something she didn't usually get to do until after hours. "I must clean my mind of doubt and thought." Lia knelt in front of the mirror and smiled. "I am a doll. I am property. My purpose is to serve and obey my owner." She stared into her own eyes with intent excitement. "A doll does not need to think. A doll needs only obey. This doll will obey and sleep."

Somehow the trigger surprised her every time. Her eyes unfocused as the words kept tumbling and her hands moved between her legs, teasing ever so gently. "This doll is deeply entranced. Its mind is blank and ready to be cleaned. It cannot resist. This doll will repeat its mantras and pleasure its body as it cleans its mind. This doll will obey."

"I am Beatrice's property. My body belongs to her. My mind is for her to fill. Her will is my will." Lia continued to masturbate as her mantras turned more and more degrading. "My mind is being rewritten. I am helpless to resist. Every night I will clean my mind to make her hold over me stronger and I love it. I gave up my will because it made me wet." Lia could feel herself scrubbing her own thoughts into nothing. Brainwashing really was like a bubble bath for the brain. "I am an obedient fuckdoll. I was made to obey my mistress. My mouth, tits, and ass belong to her. I love to be used and humiliated for her pleasure. I play with myself now because she demands it. I only cum when she permits it, she only permits it when my mind is clean."

Beatrice didn't intend for this to be turned into a show but she admittedly had a hand between her legs as she watched Lia brainwash herself.

This was something Lia normally did by herself before bed, as ordered by her mistress. Said mistress had not actually *seen* her do it and thus had not been privy to what mantras the maiden had been coming up with. Beatrice had not come up with the ones past the first four, she'd allowed Lia to come up with her own and then believe they were given to her by her mistress. She already had a creative mind, being aroused seemed to help expand it further.

In her mind, Lia thought she was reinforcing her suggestions and strengthening the foundation of the enchantment. Which she technically was, that part was for her own fun. She had relayed to Beatrice how much she enjoyed being unable to stop herself from performing the nightly ritual, but she was not aware of its secondary purpose. The "cleaning of her mind" was actually a deep cleanse of missed triggers and unintended suggestions. A nightly reset, as it were. This was why Beatrice had been so intense with how she'd set up the enchantment this time, the foundation gave a clear baseline for Lia to return to. The nightly self-reinforcement made the enchantment stronger and more importantly, kept it clean and tidy. Lia was a loyal, obedient doll, lovingly maintained and cared for by her mistress.

Beatrice was doing everything in her power to make sure Lia did not trip into a web of commands that would twist together over time. And yet, today eerily felt like finding the first thread. So that meant her doll needed some more specialized attention.

"My mind is clean." Lia came as abrupt and quick as she'd spoken those words. Not exactly a finale but then again, this wasn't meant to be watched. Her goofy grin implied she'd enjoyed it.

"Lia, stay in your trance and kneel in front of me." Beatrice could already see her starting to move toward her bed.

"Yes, mistress," Lia said. She didn't even get up and instead crawled to kneel in front of her. Still, her eyelids drooped as she looked moments away from falling asleep in place. Another reason why it was saved for the late hours, it was exhausting for the half-demon to handle all at once.

"I want us to go over what happened. Do you recall which commands incited you to lick me clean when my mother walked in?" Beatrice asked.

"Yes, mistress."

That wasn't a good sign. "Have those commands been cleaned away?"

"No, mistress."

Beatrice pinched the brim of her nose. So something did linger. "Which command was it?"

"My body belongs to you. My tongue is a tool to clean you," Lia recited with pride.

"Are you sure? That doesn't explain why you suddenly decided to do it right then. That command doesn't remove your awareness." That wasn't a suggestion so much as just something Lia thought about herself. It shouldn't have incited her to do anything.

"I was fully aware. The Lady of the House was present. I needed to clean."

Beatrice frowned at the phrasing. "Needed to?"

"It's the first rule." Lia winced. "I'm not supposed to tell you about the Rules of the House. Sorry, please forget I said that."

Beatrice raised an eyebrow. That was new. She'd never heard any of the staff mention Rules of the House before. "Lia, what are you?"

Lia shivered with a dreamy smile. "Your property."

"And an owner should know everything about her property. Including the rules they follow."

Lia looked conflicted, wincing again as if the idea bothered her. Her smile was softer now. "I suppose so."

Beatrice's curiosity was growing. Perhaps this was the base rule-set Atropos instilled in new hires. She might need to remove it if it was causing strife. "Okay, what are the Rules of the House?"

"The Rules of the House are the rules set by the Lady of the House. A good maid obeys them over everything else. I belong to the House, therefore I must be a good maid and obey its rules at all times without hesitation or thought." Lia frowned. "I'm supposed to be a handmaiden and belong to you. I am sorry I didn't tell you about that like you asked me to. I think I tried."

Beatrice pursed her lips as her eyes drifted to the drawer of forgotten notes. The single thread, maid versus handmaiden, the House versus Beatrice. Could such a simple discrepancy have caused her inevitable spiral? "You are forgiven. Please list the rules so we may make sure there's no other conflicts."

Lia nodded. "Yes, mistress. The first rule is when the Lady of the House is present the maid must never be standing about and must busy herself. The second rule is that Beatrice is my owner. I am her property."

There was no way in hell that Atropos would make that the second rule. Had Lia turned it into a rule? Affection ignited at the thought Lia put being owned by her so high on the list. But with it was a concern that suggestions she had given were inserting themselves into this strange ruleset. That could lead to contradictions.

"The third rule is I am not to understand the conversations of the Lady of the House unless I am being addressed." Interesting wording. Perhaps to prevent eavesdropping.

"The fourth rule is that Ida's authority supersedes all others if conflicting orders arise." That was a problem. And weird, it implied this was not Atropos but Ida's doing. Beatrice had assumed for so long that she didn't ever get to Lia to lay one.

"The fifth rule is I am to keep Beatrice happy." That fifth one muddied the waters even more, although if she added the second perhaps she added the fifth. What *were* these rules for? This couldn't be a basic ruleset enchantment, it appeared to be designed for Lia specifically. It would explain why Ida or Atropos hadn't seemed to have their usual grip on her when she first found her, but why? It was much subtler than their usual approaches, less overpowering but more widespread. It was like they didn't want her to know she was enchanted.

Or maybe they just didn't want Beatrice to know. "The sixth rule is—" Lia stopped. Her eye twitched. She sounded like she was in pain as she fought to speak. "I...am not...supposed to tell Beatrice...about the rules. The seven...s-seventh—"

"Oh my gods, stop, stop!" Beatrice took her hands. Lia was shaking as she gripped them tight. She hadn't realized how literal she had been about that rule.

This wasn't a normal enchantment, this was something that had to be sitting deep within her mind and now was lashing out as they tried to uncover it. Lia spoke fast and panicked as she tried to contend contradictory orders. "I am not supposed to tell Beatrice the rules. Beatrice is my owner, an owner has the right to know the rules of her property. Ida's orders supersede Beatrice's as a mistress, so she cannot know. But an owner is higher than a mistress. But—"

"Lia, you're going to break! Look into my eyes!" She did so and her speech began to slur together as her eyelids drooped. "That's right, let your mind sink into serenity. Just step back into bliss. Calm, relaxed, entranced."

"Yes...miss...stresss." Lia trailed off as she relaxed, her head clearly fighting to stay up just to keep locked onto her eyes. "Calm...relaxed...entranced."

"Let all your worries flow out. All your thoughts, all your woes, your mind is blank. Sleep." Beatrice sighed with relief as Lia went limp with a vacant stare. She must've sent her truly deep. "I don't need to know what these rules are. In fact, you should tell me how many rules I am not allowed to know about, just so I don't mess with them."

A slight wince. "Ten."

Beatrice wondered. "How many rules were there when you started?"

Another wince. "Eight."

So she'd added two. Rules two and five appeared to be candidates for which ones, but Beatrice didn't want to torture Lia like this to inquire further. "Okay, coming back to the surface. Don't hurt yourself, take all the time you need to come back to your senses and wake up."

Lia leaned her head back and stretched her arms, giving a little yawn as she blinked a few times. "Oh. Uh, hi?" She smiled nervously, rubbing her legs together. "Ah. I see you had a little fun." She frowned at her expression. "What's wrong?"

"Run us a bath. We need to clean up and talk." Beatrice couldn't help but embrace her. *Gods, Lia. What did my mother do to you?*

Lia knew something was wrong when Bea let her wash her without arguing.

Already being naked made it easy to convince her to just get in at the same time. But when Lia began to absentmindedly clean her mistress, she didn't get any pushback. It nagged at Lia, just a little bit. Even with how intimate their companionship had become, Bea still was adamant that she could wash herself. The lack of a fight was worrying.

Bea kept her hands around her knees as Lia scrubbed her back. She clearly needed cheering up. "Would you like me to resume my role as your towel holder after I finish?"

Bea flinched. "I am unsure if I should enchant you at the moment."

"What?" Lia put her head on Bea's shoulder with a pout. "Why? Did I do something wrong?"

Bea stifled a pained laugh. "I doubt you could do something wrong if you tried." She sighed. "Darling, do you know the Rules of the House?"

She nodded as she returned to scrubbing. "Yeah, they're the rules I was taught when I first started. Like, even before you made me a handmaiden."

"Who taught them to you?" Bea asked.

"The Lady of the House, of course. Her house, her rules."

"And what are the rules?" Bea sounded cautious.

Lia shrugged. "Not supposed to tell. Maid trade secret."

Her tone stayed wary. "Are you aware that the sixth rule is you aren't allowed to tell me the rules?"

Lia frowned. That sounded right, but only when Bea said it did she actually remember the wording. "I never thought about how it specified only you, that's so weird. "

"I'm guessing you didn't notice due to a rule past that one. I was unable to coerce any beyond the sixth." Bea curled up further.

"Lia, these rules aren't just something you've been taught, you've been enchanted to obey them to the letter."

"That's preposterous. The Lady of the House has no need to use enchantments to keep her servants in line, they are obedient and loyal to her regardless," Lia said proudly.

Bea rolled her eyes. "Listen to yourself, when do *you* use the word preposterous? That's a line that's been fed to you." She looked down with shame. "I think that's why you suddenly tried to lick me clean when my mother walked in."

"I'm certain your mother didn't give me any rules like *that*." Lia hadn't been quite so sure if Beatrice hadn't, though. A shameful part of her hoped that she did.

"Not intentionally. The first rule, when the Lady of the House is present the maid must never be standing about and must busy herself. But you still have the underlying suggestion that your tongue is a cleaning instrument and given your limited options, you decided to clean...well, me. You combined the suggestion and the rule by accident." Bea cringed. "It's not all you've combined. I made you my property."

Lia shivered at the thought. "Yes you did."

"No, think about rule two. Think hard."

Lia closed her eyes. The second rule was she was Beatrice's property. "Wait, that wasn't rule two. Rule two was 'I am not to understand the conversations of the Lady of the House unless I am being addressed', right?"

"That's rule three now," Bea said quietly, and Lia could remember that being correct. "I don't know why this surprises me. I don't know why I didn't even consider Ida would eventually enchant you, the entire staff is enchanted, but..."

"I'm off limits." Lia covered her mouth. "Sorry, that just came out."

"And I feel it in my blood that it's true." Bea looked concerned. No, she looked terrified. "Why do I feel like she's broken a promise I don't recall her ever making."

"Could she have enchanted us to forget?" Lia asked.

"You, perhaps. Not me." Bea sighed. "Everything she does is because she can't control me."

"She can implant memories though." Lia still vividly remembered the day Ida did that to her lady. It seemed like an easy leap that it could go the other way.

Bea shrugged. "It's easy to give, it's rude to search, but to take is hard. It's why I always just…reorganize. Redefine truths, twist logic, reinforce ideas, I let the mind do the work for me. My mother, however, instills her own truths. Add things to fit her narrative. When she puppets a staff member she isn't so much controlling them as instilling a copy of her mind over theirs. For those brief moments they believe they are her and in some ways they truly are. Atropos employs similar methods for training. In a way, we have had the same staff for my entire life. The faces change but the personalities are all cut from her cloth."

"So, why can't she just do that?" Lia asked.

"She used to. Not instilling herself but sometimes she'd try to instill a more pliant personality in me. Turn me into a proper daughter, as it were. Imagine thinking you like a certain food and yet you cannot stop feeling as though it tastes awful every time you have it, that's how it felt to clash with instilled memories. So I built a defense for it." Bea couldn't hide her smile. "Actually, it's how I'm protecting you as well. Your name is locked away. Your sense of self, who you are, it can't be unwritten. It's difficult to overwrite memories that are already locked away, it allows for your mind to have something to check against. Memories that contradict them will be seen as foreign."

"That's why you say that mantra, isn't it? Those are three truths that you locked away and she can't change."

"Who I am, what I am, how I am. She can never take that from me. And so as long as I can say those words, I know that what I am experiencing is me." Bea blushed. "I made your name and what you are core truths."

Lia thought about it. "I sorta remember that. Although..."

"Although?"

"There was another core truth in there. And if that's something I wanted to hide from Ida, maybe I put it there when I was getting enchanted by her." Lia was technically lying. There were two core truths she'd added. But she wasn't about to confess her love in a dire moment like this. She wanted to put her worries to rest first.

And there was only one way Lia knew how to do that. "We need to talk to my sister."

Chapter 24
Demons in the Dark

"**Y**our sister is still alive?"

Lia looked at her with bewilderment. She had been leading her to a part of the House she rarely visited, a section of wine cellars and storage closets if she recalled correctly. One the servants traversed often but was out of the way for most of her daily activities. "Yeah, why wouldn't she be?"

Beatrice made a face. "Well, after learning of your...predicament, you never seemed concerned in regards to her. No desire to see her or let her know you were ok. I assumed that meant she was no longer with us."

"Well, I actually got worried that if I brought her up to you, the memory would get stolen. I didn't fully understand what you meant when you were first explaining the enchantments and it felt like a risk, you know?" Lia explained. "But before that I just didn't see a need to, I'm safe and she's safe. There's no reason to worry about her or bring her up in conversation. If I get worried, I should just go visit her and it'll all be ok."

Beatrice didn't like the phrasing of that last part. It felt very enchantment coded. "How come I've never seen her if she's part of the staff?"

"Oh she isn't," Lia said with a laugh. "Gods, Diana in a uniform? She'd hate it. Plus she hates your family. Like a lot." She paused. "Right, probably should warn you about that, she's not gonna like you at first. It'll just take time, we can whittle her down if we're persistent. Promise you won't just make her like you? I know, I know, a good thrall would be willing and eager to help make more thralls for her mistress and I certainly am eager, but she doesn't like enchantments like I do. It's sorta why she doesn't like your family. So I humbly request you don't enchant her, I want you two to get along. Unless you don't care, in which case I suppose I cannot stop you and will try to make her as comfortable as I can as you bend her mind to your will."

Beatrice had been caught off-guard by Lia's self-indulgent tangent about helping enchant her sister if her mistress desired it. Although the way she said it was like she was certain her mistress wouldn't truly do it, she was getting off on the idea that she just could. This was a full-blown fetish at this point. "Wait, wait, go back, if she isn't a staff member, how is she here?"

"The Lady of the House has graciously allowed her shelter as a part of my employment." Lia winced, that tone of pre-made phrasings resurfacing once more.

Beatrice sighed. This was meant to give them answers but it felt like Lia was dragging her into something that would only invite more questions. Still, this was one of her core truths she locked away to keep safe. So at the very least her sister was real.

So what were the enchantments hiding from Lia?

Beatrice knew that her mind didn't want to perceive servant corridors. All of them had passive glamours, forcing her eyes to gloss over the obvious hidden doorways. This was different, a true illusion. A physical one at that, she never knew the House had any of this nature. Lia was unperturbed by it and easily triggered its dispellment by pressing a specific brick. "You must visit her often."

Lia nodded. "I try when I can. Technically it's in the contract I'm allowed to visit her whenever, but I don't wanna abuse that just to get out of working, you know?"

"Contract?"

"Hmm?"

"You have a contract?" Beatrice doubted they'd be so lucky, but if there was a physical contract it would be invaluable to help out her employment into perspective.

Lia blinked. She seemed to be trying to hold onto the thought as if something else was tearing it from her. "I think so? Maybe it's just a verbal contract, I don't remember signing anything."

And thus the hope of illuminating legal documentation was up in smoke. Still, a contract wasn't something to take lightly when it comes to fae. If Lia even vaguely felt there was one related to her employment, it was likely one truly did exist. And that was not a normal staff procedure.

Lia hopped through the door and shuddered. Her face was sweating like she'd just run a mile. "Sorry, lined with silver. You should be fine."

Beatrice didn't even ask. None of this was normal staff procedure.

Going down the stairs it became clear what this originally was, a wine cellar. Which made sense, considering it was near the servants quarters and kitchens. When they reached the bottom she saw it was barren beyond a cot and a couch. It had indents as if there used to be large barrels stored down here, aging ales perhaps. Some candles that had long since melted beyond usefulness were strewn about, as well as a few mugs stained with what must've been remnants of coffee. The sage smell covered any clues as to whether it had been. There were a good two dozen drawings tacked on the wall like one would do for a child, although she recognized Lia's art style. Several of them had Beatrice as the focus, it almost looked set up like a timeline of her employment.

Laying back on the couch with a book over her face and her wings outstretched was a full-blooded demon.

"Diana!" Lia said gleefully as she rushed into the room.

The demon startled awake, the book flopping down onto the floor. "Wassat? Is it nightfall already?"

Lia picked the book up with a look. "Since when do you read history books?"

"That's the one that tooth maid threw at me when I whined for entertainment. Least it has pictures." Diana rose to her feet. The shackle on her leg clinked as the metal links dragged along the ground.

Beatrice stared with horror. This demon was a prisoner, locked away and chained to the wall. "Lia, is this..."

Lia nodded with far too much enthusiasm for the situation. "My sister, yeah. You can obviously guess which half of the family she's on. The Lady of the House allows her to live here so long as I'm employed."

"Allows. Fucking allows, she says." Diana had black instead of white for her eyes with purple iris and black slits down the middle that were now dilating like a predator. She glanced between her and one of the drawings on the wall. "You're Beatrice, aren't you?"

"Yes?" Beatrice lowered her voice. "Darling, why is your sister chained up?" Apparently demons have good hearing and she did not like the look she got when she called Lia 'darling'. Suddenly the chains didn't feel short enough from where she was standing.

"Chained up?" Lia looked confused. She wasn't in her right mind, Beatrice could see it now. A subtle shift in demeanor when they'd crossed the threshold. "I suppose she doesn't like leaving these days, but that's ok. It's safer down here anyways."

"She won't understand. She never does." Diana stood up and gave her sister a hug. Lia smiled obliviously as she hugged back. "But you..." Quick as a panther she pounced. Before Beatrice knew it the demon had her hands around her throat. "This is all your fault! You just had to have my sister, huh?! You couldn't leave us alone, let us live our shitty lives in peace!"

Whatever effect confounding Lia was not strong enough to hide her sister murdering her mistress. "What are you doing?! Diana, stop!"

"Sorry sis, but you ain't thinking straight." Beatrice was too stunned to fight back. Not that she would be able to overpower Diana in any worthwhile sense, deteriorated she may be but she still was a demon. One that appeared to know her eyes were her weapons as she had her own shut tight. "I'm pissed you're not the head bitch but taking you out just might just break the spell."

"Stop it!" Lia took a broom from the wall and smacked her on the head with it. "Let! Her! Go!" The broom was not persuading her. "She had no choice, we had to! I promised!"

That got Diana to let go. Beatrice gasped for air as she looked at her sister. "What are you talking about?"

Lia winced as if she had a horrible headache. "I promised. I promised, I promised, I..." She stumbled as if she was about to faint. Diana helped her stay on her feet. "I...what were we...right. Visiting." She brushed Diana off and then pulled Beatrice to her feet as if she hadn't just prevented an attempt on her life. "You shouldn't be on the floor, it's dirty. Makes my life harder later because those are my chores you're adding too."

Beatrice was astonished at how quick Lia was to fall back into ignorance. "That is quite the enchantment."

Diana sat on the couch. "You're telling me." She threw her head back and ran her hand down her face. "Sorry. Fuck, sorry, I just saw those fae eyes and it was nothing but red. So stupid, killing you ain't gonna help with shit."

Beatrice didn't like the implication that if that wasn't the case Diana would gladly try again. The idea she was related to her sweet and gentle Lia at all was very hard to believe. This woman was gruff, expletive, and violent. Her face was sharp and her eyes filled with a desire for bloodshed. No, it was a clear desire for *Beatrice's* blood to be shed. The only thing the sisters had in common was their hair. It was the same color, that deep violet that looked black unless in certain lighting. Seeing it on a demon explained a lot, it appeared much more natural against purple hued skin. "I would hope my kindness towards your sister would earn me some points in my favor."

Diana's snarling expression told her that was not the right thing to say. "You kidnap her, twist her mind, and I'm supposed to be happy you gave her a nice bed?"

"I didn't take her." Beatrice felt like a liar. She didn't take her but she sure as hell didn't throw her back.

"And I gave myself voluntarily." Lia pouted. "Diana, this is why I asked you. I like her."

The demon rolled her eyes. "My fucking luck Lia falls for a fae." She waved her hand. "Alright. Fine. Won't murder you. Yet."

Lia crossed her arms. "Diana."

"It's always a yet, sis, never say never about murder."

"*Diana.*"

The demon chuckled. "Yeah, yeah, I swear I'm chill now."

Beatrice was starting to understand how Lia had formed a friendship with Clotho. She had years of practice. "So, Dia—"

She snapped her fingers at her, which sounded like a whip snapping. "Nope, I'm Diana to her. You don't get my name, you fucking fae."

"*Diana!*" Lia said with a boldness she did not often show. "Stop baiting her. Be nice."

Diana the demon cringed from the little sister scolding, then gave a forced, fanged smile. "Just call me Abith."

Beatrice tried not to huff. This was fine, this woman was very stressed and had very good reasons to dislike her right now, she was allowed to be rude. The last thing she needed was Lia's sister to despise her. "Very well. Abith. Can you please explain to me what you're doing down here?"

Diana made a face. "You don't know?"

"I didn't even know you were alive until today, much less in my House." Beatrice put a hand on Lia's shoulder, who faintly appeared to be zoning out. "We were trying to uncover a ruleset enchantment that neither of us knew of and in doing so Lia led me to you."

"Sorry, but I ain't got a clue. All I know is your mom lets Lia visit me whenever she asks. Not sure why. Maybe it helps keep Lia in line. I'm alive and cared for, so she doesn't have to worry about me." Diana pulled on the chain. "She just can't comprehend the fact I'm not allowed to leave. If I play along, I get to talk to my sister. If I don't, I waste the little time I get talking to a brick wall that makes up a conversation in her head."

Lia smiled as if agreeing with something neither of them could hear.

"I don't remember being captured. Just woke up down here." Diana glared at the hand on Lia's shoulder. "From my view, all this trouble was because *you* wanted a handmaiden."

"She's a lot more to me than just a handmaiden, but I see your point." Bea looked at Lia and wished she was able to be truly a part of this conversation. "I hope you'll believe me when I say your situation is very unique. I've never heard of us taking staff family members as collateral. The enchantments instill loyalty, why even bother?"

Diana started what was most likely a witty response before she abruptly paused, then leaned back with a more inquisitive look. "You know, that explains the shitty job they did. First night here they accidentally included some deadroot in my dinner. Managed to break out, but those freaky maids laid a trap. I didn't realize they'd already gotten Lia."

"All three involved themselves in your capture?" Beatrice asked. She remembered how often Clotho was going out when Lia first appeared. To hear Atropos left the House was worrisome. She was as rooted as Ida.

Diana nodded with a shrug. "Yeah. Mainly the hunter one but the other two helped with the trap."

Beatrice looked at her handmaiden, fully oblivious to this entire conversation but looking like she was beyond happy her sister and her lady were talking and not trying to kill each other. "If the only function you have is to keep her in line, then Lia is the key to discovering what purpose this is all for."

"You're all she talks about, so I got no clue." Diana shrugged. "Well, there are times she comes down here not understanding things that the enchantment is hiding. Seems to calm her down. Although she hasn't had that in a while, she's been more herself lately. A lot more aware of her situation, just not mine."

Beatrice knew the obvious answer for that one but was not going to speak of it, lest Diana reach the 'yet' of deciding to murder her for bedding her sister. "This is a strange question, but would you happen to know a demon named Lucial Nullith?"

Diana's face grew dark. "Don't tell me that fucker is involved."

"You know him?" Beatrice had been a tad worried she'd assumed a demon would know the only other demon she'd ever met, but his appearance at the soirée was still a strange one.

"He's my dad." Diana sighed as Beatrice couldn't help but glance at Lia. "Not hers. Our mom's a demon, her dad is dead, and my dad is dead to me. How do you know him?"

"I've met this Lucial once. At a soirée, a small time after I took Lia on as my handmaiden," Beatrice said, "I wondered why he was here. Lia didn't indicate she recognized him."

Diana shrugged. "She wouldn't, she was barely a toddler when I dipped."

"I recognized his name," Lia said, entering the conversation for the first time in a while. Beatrice wondered if she was going to have to recount everything to her later or if she would remember these more lucid moments. "I didn't want him to bother Bea so I talked to him while I got her food. He said Ida invited him. And that he'd be "my saviour", whatever that meant."

Diana snorted. "Saviour. What that means is the bitch is using us as a bargaining chip. Not that he'd care about—" She stopped herself and gave her sister a pained look. "Sorry, sis, didn't mean it that way."

Lia sadly smiled. "No, you're right, I'm not exactly worth much to him. I guess you are. Sorta."

"What would he have that Ida would want?" Beatrice asked.

"Fuck if I know. He wants me back because he's shooting blanks, I'm his only chance at a bloodline. He's not exactly high up on any chains, I think he's a member of some demon mob running a port racket he weaseled into a few years back. Gang accountants are more important than his worthless ass." Diana waved her hand. "Still, the mob is the mob, maybe she's looking to expand into it using him as a pawn. Doesn't interest me either way cuz it ain't fucking happening."

"But if Ida gave Lia to him?" Beatrice pointed out. "Not only that, but most likely enchanting her to be loyal to him?"

Diana flinched. "Fuck." She sat up. "*Fuck*. That's clever. And with how it's played out here it would fucking work, I fight the leash and Lia's neck is the one getting strangled."

That would somewhat explain the Rules of the House. They could just switch out names and make Lucial who she was loyal to. It didn't fit as neatly as it first appeared, however. Why was Beatrice not allowed to know? Did Ida just assume she would be against this course of action?

Beatrice wasn't sure how she would've felt about it back then. Or rather, she hated how she was almost sure she wouldn't have cared. Before Lia, enchanted servants and maids were just a part of being a fae. These days she felt sorrow for those trapped in the House. They did not feel the pleasure of servitude like Lia did. Only the fear of disobedience.

That didn't matter. What mattered was that she cared right now. "Lia, sit down." She obeyed. Beatrice's eyes glowed. "Sleep."

"Yes, mistress." Lia's eyes fluttered shut.

Diana wrapped a wing around her sister as she tipped onto her. "What was that for?"

"A precaution. Atropos knows everything the staff knows. I've been working under the assumption Lia is not included in that but many assumptions as of late have begun to bite me." Beatrice straightened up and tried to look more distinguished but not condescending. "You said you broke out before. Lia mentioned this deadroot as well, given how it affected her I can only imagine how it bolsters you. If I acquired it for you, would you be able to escape again?"

Diana glared at her suspiciously. "Why do you care?"

Beatrice held her gaze. "I don't. But Lia certainly will when we leave and I explain your predicament." She was being more callous than she actually was, she did care. Beatrice cared more now than she ever had in her life. Diana clearly wouldn't believe her. Sometimes she had to be who people thought she was. "I ask again, would it allow you to escape?"

Diana gave a guttural growl that turned into a scoff. "No. Last time I had a window and even then, that fucking animal in a maid outfit was on my trail in seconds. If I make a fuss and am not putting distance as fast as I can with this fucking house, I'm gonna get caught. It'll be bloody, sure, and maybe I'll get away, but they'll punish Lia if I do."

"Agreed. Stealth would be the better avenue." Beatrice tapped her chin. "I wish we knew more about the situation."

Diana shrugged. "You talk to Dibs? He's got his nose in everybody's business."

Beatrice thought about it. "Strange devil, bowler hat with his horns through it?"

"That's him. Hell, if you want deadroot he'd probably get it for you too." Diana patted Lia. "She knows where he's set up. Even if she doesn't quite remember she'll find him, she has a knack for it." The demon looked at her sister, delicately running a claw through her hair. "I guess I'm at your mercy. You clearly got Lia under your spell."

"Have you considered the reason I have yet to even try to enchant you is because she asked me not to? I could easily force these answers out of you but I don't because I respect her wishes." Beatrice narrowed her eyes. She let that settle in before continuing. "Lia may be my handmaiden but that does not mean I do not care about her well-being. If she desires for you to be free then your freedom is what I shall acquire."

"And if she wants to be free?"

Beatrice looked away. "I doubt you would believe me if I told you what Lia wants in that regard. If she requests freedom I will not deny it to her." She side-eyed her. "But will you be able to accept it if she doesn't?"

Diana met her gaze. "Are you asking for a real answer or just somebody to blame when you can't accept it either?"

Beatrice flinched. She didn't expect a remark to hit quite so close to home. Maybe Diana actually didn't see her the way she viewed fae like Ida, why she seemed more aggressive. The unknown was always scarier. "A bridge to burn when we get to it, perhaps?"

Diana chuckled. "Sure. Save the tears for when we decide who's the one tossing the torch."

Lia sat against the wall on her bed, still taking everything in. "My sister is a prisoner."

Bea sat on the edge and nodded.

"And I can't remember her being a prisoner, because I've been enchanted not to notice."

Another nod.

"And you think that telling me in my room instead of the prison may be a workaround?"

A third nod.

Lia scrunched her face. "I mean, I understand you right now. So I guess, if you're telling the truth, your idea is right."

"Why would I lie about something like that?" Bea asked.

"I don't know? Why would the Lady of the House kidnap my sister and chain her up in the basement just so I can be a maid?" Lia frowned. "I visit her so much. Have I even been talking to her?"

Bea nodded with a shrug. "Yes, actually. Although Diana said if she ever tried to explain anything you'd ignore it. Sometimes even making up a one-sided conversation to replace it with."

"That...sucks." Lia hugged her legs. "Bea?"

"Yes?"

"I'm a shitty sister, aren't I?"

"No, darling. If anything you're impressive. You weren't fighting my enchantments, you were begging for my help. And instead of listening I pushed you away." Bea held up the crumpled notes. "I feel like an imbecile. How many times did you try to tell me? How many times did you sleepwalk to my room in hopes that I would deduce what was happening, that I would find your sister and help her?"

"You're not blaming yourself, right? If I'm not allowed to feel shitty about this, neither are you." Lia moved behind her and put her head on her shoulder. "You weren't visiting her every other day and not realizing there's a freaking chain around her leg."

Bea softly smiled. "I suppose we were both fools in our own ways."

There was a silence between them. Lia broke it by asking, "What are we going to do?"

"We're going to free Diana." Bea took a deep breath. "We are going to find a way to free her, discover what Ida's plot with Lucial is, and keep you safe from both their clutches."

"Thanks, Bea. I might've not known I was trying to get your help, but deep down I must've known you would've." Lia hugged her from behind. "But could you promise me something?"

"Yes?" Bea asked nervously.

"Promise you'll keep me." Lia buried her head into her shoulder. "I don't care how I got here, I want to be yours. I live to serve you, not Ida, not Lucial, you."

Bea lightly shook. "You deserve to be free."

Lia hugged her tighter. "What's the point of freedom if I'm not allowed to give it to you?"

"And if I'm not worthy of it?"

"You are." Lia kissed her neck. "I am honored to belong to the wonderful Beatrice von Closen."

Bea turned around with teary eyes. "How am I to accept that I own somebody I love?"

Lia blinked. She'd said it. She'd finally said it, even after everything she'd never actually said the words. "You said you love me."

Bea looked at her like she was stupid and took her hands. "Of course I love you! Every day you say you live to serve and it takes every piece of my strength not to exploit you. I want to ravish you in ways that would make the gods blush. I want to selfishly hoard you like a priceless gem. I want you to be my most prized possession but what if my love isn't enough to protect you? If you are so adamant to be owned, then just as any other possession you can be stolen. *Stolen!* Do you truly trust me not to lose you?"

Lia paused. She gave it a good five seconds, so that Bea would think she truly thought about it. She didn't need to, she already knew the answer. Bea was such a worrywort, though. It was best to pretend for her sake. "I do. With all my heart, which now belongs to you too."

Chapter 25
Following the Strings

Beatrice was starting to realize how hellish their luck had been once they were forced to actively hide their actions.

Suddenly Atropos seemed to be everywhere. Always watching, always judging, only deeming not to be present when one of her sisters were instead. Or whenever Lia started "serving" her mistress, which Beatrice thanked the gods for. At least they hadn't had an audience for their sexual shenanigans.

It was agreed that Beatrice was not to visit Diana with Lia unless absolutely necessary. After some very careful prodding into Lia's mind, it was confirmed that neither Ida nor the fates had a direct line to her. There were implications of reporting information to them at a moment's notice, although both in and out of trance Lia swore she hadn't done so since the first week. The euphoric honesty had become a litmus test for these sorts of situations. Even if Lia believed something to be true, if she didn't feel euphoric when declaring it, they would deem it a possible alteration.

Lia wasn't pleased about possibly being an unwitting snitch but it couldn't be helped. If they tried to circumvent the rule or change her routines to avoid her knowing too much it may draw attention. The current advantage they had was that Ida seemed satisfied with both their compliances and thus was not checking on her. They had to make sure they didn't incite that to change.

This put Beatrice on edge more than anything else. She could just order Lia to act natural, but she didn't have that luxury. How was she supposed to pretend it was all fine? How was she to kiss her love knowing she was specifically doing it so the fate would leave and give them privacy to discuss their plans? A small part of her feared that she would notice her kisses were a little too forced.

Lia certainly noticed. "You know, we could just actually do the thing we're pretending to do."

Beatrice hadn't fully processed what she said, her mind was focused on her door. She still was unsure if there was a way to spy on them in her bedroom. "Hmm? Sorry darling, what did you say?"

"I said I'm worried you're going to burn out if you don't take some time for yourself." Lia laid her head on her shoulder. "You're super stressed about everything, but it's not like Diana is going anywhere any time soon. We haven't had any real fun in days, I'm getting pent up over here."

Beatrice sighed as she wrapped her arm around her. "I know, I know. I just feel both overwhelmed and aimless, no matter what we plot with your sister we won't be able to act on anything if we cannot discover a means of egress." She smiled at Lia being cute trying to hide the fact she didn't know the word. "Exit, darling. We need to find a way to leave the House unattended and more importantly, without alerting anyone. I prefer not to have our first unexcused absence also be the first attempt to free her."

"You've snuck out a bunch before, right?" Lia asked.

"From what I have learned, I was not as unseen as I first assumed. We need a method that they don't think I use," Beatrice said.

"Have you ever tried sneaking out of the seamstress shop?"

Beatrice frowned. "What seamstress shop?"

"You know, the one Lachesis runs? Well, I think she runs it, she sorta just rolled in with me and borrowed the place for a day." Lia shrugged. "I mean, it's technically in the House, but there were other customers there, I assume it has to lead outside somehow."

Beatrice stared at her as she felt like an utter fool. All this time she'd been climbing over the walls and she never considered that there would be portals to the city within them.

No, she *had* considered it. There was just one problem that made pursuing the idea pointless. "I thought Atropos controlled all our glyph gates."

Lia lit up. "Glyph gates? That sounds cool, are they like magic teleport doors?"

"Something like that. If you recall Atropos's scissors can make portals, I am under the impression that she can make a fixture into a permanent one." Beatrice motioned to the window. "The soirée actually had people gather in separate lots and were transported to the front door of the ballroom for instance. It was why we spoke with Sir Tauron, his lot is one we use for that purpose."

"Oh! That explains a lot, it really felt like Ida snapped her fingers and teleported them all outside," Lia said, "So that means Atropos can give control of them to Ida. I bet she could've made one for Lachesis too."

Beatrice nodded. "They definitely wouldn't expect me to use it. But I doubt it is functioning at all times, so this may not help if we require Lachesis to open it for us."

Lia got a strange look. She didn't make eye contact as she quietly asked, "What if you enchanted her to open it whenever we wanted her too?"

Beatrice tried not to sound too cruel as she was probably about to kill Lia's idea. "While Atropos would be a pipe dream, Lachesis is a master enchantress. She'd be resistant to say the least. I still think we should take advantage of your companionship with Clotho."

"Clotho would fight it too much. We might have the best chance of getting her but bad odds at keeping it secret. And getting Lachesis would make it the easiest to leave undetected, we can just slip out through her shop." Lia had been very against betraying Clotho, but her confidence in this new plan was clearly more than just a desire to avoid that. "If only I could enchant her. She'd be on guard around you, but around me she acts a little more...open." She made that face again. "Sorta too open, to be honest."

"Too open?" Beatrice asked curiously.

"I think she feels what her thralls feel. She talks about it like she wishes she could feel the full thing. Like looking back she was definitely hinting about you enchanting me, but not to make fun of me for being oblivious. She sounded...I don't know, jealous?" Lia blushed heavily. "Maybe I'm not the only one in the House who is into being enchanted for fun."

"So you think if she's not bracing for it her desires might let a subtle enchantment slip through. I can see why you being the enchanter would make it easier, she wouldn't be expecting it." This was a side of Lachesis that Beatrice certainly had never seen. The idea that the most manipulative of the three would enjoy being controlled sounded like a joke the fate herself would try to make. Still, Lia's judgement of character had already surprised her when it came to

Clotho. Perhaps there was merit in trusting it again. "You know, you just might be able to."

"You can use me to enchant other people?" Lia asked with both fascination and a hint of excitement. "Like, sending me out to expand your collection of thralls sorta thing?"

"Already making grand plans I see, but it's only a theory. It was something I was actually working on as a surprise for you. Because I have started learning to induce commands into my glances, I was hoping to master creating a glamour to allow your eyes to become reflections of mine to do the same." Beatrice had been trying to figure out how to combine the two techniques and create a sort of passive aura for Lia. She wasn't good at glamours, so it had been on the backburner as an idea. The intentions were more pleasure than business, having Lia unwittingly commanding those she came across opened many avenues of teasing her in the way she loved, but if she could somehow catch a fate with their guard down perhaps they could instill a simple command. "I was thinking, 'obey and forget'. I've mastered 'leave and forget' but that doesn't help us."

"Why not just 'obey Lia'?" Lia asked genuinely.

"I still doubt this will work at all, but I think even she may notice how obvious that one is. And the first one should give you a window to instill a suggestion into her." Beatrice gave a sympathetic smile at her handmaiden's face dropping at the mention of memorization. "We'll go over the wording together and I'll even put you under so you'll be able to repeat it perfectly."

The two of them plotted and planned like this the rest of the day. Changing the wording, going over what Lia needed to precisely do, plans to pull out if things went to the wayside. The more they planned, the more fearful Beatrice became. Every new piece was also a new point for things to go wrong. "Darling, I still don't know if I feel okay with you doing this alone. Are you sure we can't enact your plan with me in the wings?"

"I've never seen her act this way around you, it has to be just me." Lia took her hands. "I can do this, Bea, I swear. For you and for my sister, I will make sure this plan works."

"And for you." Beatrice put her forehead against hers. "Don't forget yourself. I want you to be safe."

Lia closed her eyes and smiled. "I belong to you, my lady. What I do for you is already what I do for me."

Step one of the plan was the one part Lia actually didn't believe would work at all, getting Lachesis alone in a room with her. Bea said that if they tore her dress in a very obvious way the maid wouldn't be able to resist dropping everything to fix it. Sure enough Lia didn't even get two words out before she was whisked away for an emergency repair job, along with several questions as to how it even happened. Apparently Lachesis had pride in the quality of her work and found the very idea of it tearing an insult to her craft.

"I was doing something for Bea," Lia said quietly. She was sitting in the corner of Lachesis's room in an oversized nightdress. Her room looked sorta like Bea's, if Bea had really liked sewing and wanted to remake anything even remotely made from fabric in her room from scratch. There were several tapestries on the wall of different landscapes and cities, all presumably created by the maid herself.

"Ahh, getting rough with her requests, is she?" Lachesis asked. She laughed at the panic from Lia. "You think you two have been subtle? I think the only one who isn't fully aware is the Lady of the House and even then it's because Atropos doesn't wish to recount the noises she's heard."

Lia sighed with relief. It was just a comment about them fucking, not planning to fuck her over. "A House this big, I thought we'd have privacy."

"No privacy in the House of our Lady, sadly."

The conversation was dying. Lia needed an avenue, Lachesis wasn't as talkative when she was sewing. "Why does Bea call you three fates? Can you see the future?"

"Clotho can't, she's too young. Eyes on the prize, mind on the present. Atropos might as well live in the future with how far ahead she tries to think. If I were to boast I'd say I'm a prolific prophet of cause and effect. Still, it's not like it used to be, the good old days of vast prophecy and overarching inevitability has been cut down by the fast-moving world. It was much easier to chart from start to end without all the noise society has become these days." Lachesis took a pin from her mouth. "We haven't lost our sight. For example, you can see the horizon, but if you stand in the city and no longer can see it, does that mean you've lost the ability? Or is it that you now have to be more clever, to stand in the right places that let you see past the right buildings, find the path that leads to what you know will still be there waiting."

That was a lot. Lia wasn't fully getting it, but then again, Lachesis wasn't exactly straight forward. "So there's too many paths for you to see the future anymore?"

"I'm saying that fates don't see the future. They make the future from what they see." Lachesis smiled coyly. "Like how a fate can distract her sister long enough to let a little bee find a special flower in the garden."

Lia blushed. That was so long ago, it still felt like a dream to her even now. "So you "foresaw" that?"

Lachesis shrugged. "Perhaps I also foresaw her missing you entirely, if she'd been a little too fast. I had a simple outcome I was seeking and thus saw the simple possibilities, but the further you go out the harder it gets. And the world is just so...so loud these days. You need fixed points. You need a horizon of the future to chart your path through this damn city we call life."

"What fixed point do you usually see?"

"The death of the Lady of the House."

Lia blinked. "What?"

Lachesis nodded dully as the thought bored her. "Oh yes, it happens at least once a year. Our lady is a very powerful woman, so the possibility is consistent enough to be our horizon. Atropos makes it her duty to prevent it. This year she's cutting it close. The paths of life and death are almost identical."

"So, if the path is the same, what changes the outcome?" Lia asked.

Lachesis made her 'inside joke' smirk as she looked up at her. The expression never felt more unnerving than it did now.

"May I ask why you decided to make sure I ran into Bea?" Lia smiled nervously as she obviously changed the subject. "Did you just think she'd find me interesting or did you…"foresee" us becoming close."

"I didn't orchestrate your inevitable affair if that's your worry," Lachesis said, "I am curious what actually happened. I can only surmise so much from secondhand gossip."

Lia was annoyed she dodged the question but didn't care as she saw an opening. "I only recently was even able to remember. She enchanted me before she even knew I was there."

There it was, so fast she almost missed it. The glint of excitement in Lachesis's eyes at the mention of an enchantment. "Really?"

"I was out in the gardens. Wandering around, no real clue what I was doing. So zoned out I was dusting the bushes just to pass the time. Oblivious to her sneaking through nearby." Lia was leaning towards her as she spoke, keeping direct eye contact. "I heard a noise. She jumped out at me and all I saw was the bright beautiful glow of her eyes." Lia triggered the glamour. She could almost feel her eyes glowing, it weirdly tickled her brain. Lachesesis's eyes became ever so glassy as her eyelids slightly drooped. "And just like that I was entranced. Already willing to do anything for them."

"Anything," Lachesis repeated. Not a question, but a statement.

Lia got her. She actually got her! "It was impossible for me to resist. And I didn't want to. I loved looking into her eyes and feeling them drain my will away. Can you imagine how liberating that felt? Letting all your thoughts out and having somebody else lead your mind."

"Yes," Lachesis said with a smile.

Even now Lia was nervous, but she was in too deep. "Stand up."

Lachesis stood.

"Kneel."

She knelt.

Lia's heart raced. She lifted her foot. "Kiss."

Her smile didn't seem as droopy as before, but she gently kissed the top of her foot.

That seemed like proof enough. "You will allow Bea and me to use your glyph gate whenever she requests. You will not find this strange and will deem to forget you allowed it after our return."

"As you wish, little demon." Lachesis looked up at her with a gleam in her enchanted eye. "Is that all you want from me?"

No. Lia didn't feel compelled to respond but still couldn't help but feel that thought had been planted. "What are you willing to do?"

Lachesis smiled dreamily at her. "Anything."

Lia hesitated. She'd done everything right. She should just wake Lachesis up, go back to Bea, and be glad this all worked out. She shouldn't be rubbing her legs together as she imagined telling her mistress how she pulled it off. She shouldn't be thinking about how beautiful Lachesis truly was. She shouldn't be heating up at the thought of how she was a thrall collecting more for her mistress to play with. How as her mistress's favorite doll Lia should be allowed to play with any that came after.

Lachesis waited patiently. She'd talked about wanting to experience the real deal. Lia could give her the full tour.

"Eat me out." Lia covered her own mouth but the thought had escaped and implanted in the fates head.

Lachesis didn't even flinch. She smiled seductively. "With pleasure, little demon."

Lia was too shell-shocked at her own actions to stop her. Before she regained her senses she was already stifling moans from the head maid mindlessly following her scandalous order. She giggled to herself about reporting back to Bea, telling her she'd truly captured a new thrall for her. Lachesis was under their power and Lia loved the reward it was reaping.

Then she heard a voice wrap around her mind. *"I must thank you. I've wanted a taste of Bea's little toy for ages."* This couldn't be her actually talking, because her mouth was certainly still occupied between her legs. *"Don't fret, your mistress still has her sway over me. I am nothing but a doll for her pleasure."*

So am I. Lia moaned. They were just two dolls, fucking for the pleasure of their mistress.

"Some dolls, though, like their strings. And they nudge and tug, subtly guiding the hands that control. There is power in submission. And I am powerful."

Under the surface Lia was panicking. She knew this was wrong but at the same time it just made her wetter. Being eaten out was not helping her think clearly and she could feel herself on the edge of not thinking at all. It was like Lachesis had sunk deep into bliss and pulled at the strings Lia had foolishly thought she had control of to drag her down with.

"Ohohoho, you like this too. *I knew I made the right play siding with the romantics."* Lachesis continued to expertly tease her. Lia would fully believe her tongue was what was sending these messages into her mind. *"Still, never hurts to protect an investment, so I'm going to give some tips on how to properly submit. From maid to handmaiden. Fucktoy to fuckdoll. After all, we live to serve."*

"We live to serve." And that was the final piece that sent Lia over the edge.

Chapter 26
Wrapped around her Finger

Beatrice paced in her room for hours, wishing there was something more she could do than just wait. Even planning their next move felt like celebrating victory too early. How she had been persuaded into letting Lia attempt this was a question her worried mind constantly demanded of her now. Lachesis was the maid she talked to the most and paradoxically understood the least. Neither success nor failure seemed to be comprehensible, in that Beatrice could not imagine what Lachesis would do if Lia failed and thus couldn't feel any sense of ease pretending that it wouldn't happen.

Beatrice wanted to have faith in Lia. Faith only got one so far when facing a fate.

The door opened. Lia shot inside with a bright smile as she tackle hugged her. "I did it!"

Beatrice felt a wave of relief. "Thank the gods." She hugged back tightly. "We are never doing a plan like this again, I cannot stand the idea of you being without my support."

Lia in a rare moment of forwardness kissed her on the lips. "I know, I was *terrified*. But I pulled it off! And look," she stepped back to show the wine bottle she held, "the test order worked. I had her get this for me and forget she got it. Thought we could share it and celebrate?"

Beatrice shouldn't have been surprised, Lia's adrenaline must've been through the roof trying to keep her cool. She was as hyper as a kid on a sugar rush right now. "I suppose a victory glass isn't a bad idea. You can tell me all the details."

One glass turned into two, which soon turned into four. Beatrice did not have much of a tolerance but Lia was insistent, out-drinking her easily. The bottle was gone before she even finished her tale. And by then its erotic turn didn't even phase her, instead she encouraged her to give the scandalous details. And give details Lia did.

"You ordered a fate to go down on you?" Beatrice asked with drunken shock. "Gods, I wish I could've been there to see it."

Lia smiled back. Hers was more seductive than the usual bright. "Turns you on, huh?"

Beatrice laughed. "Don't judge me, this entire tale was more erotic than I expected. Is that why you were so certain about Lachesis?"

"Yeah, I felt like she sorta wanted it. I recognized that desire for mindlessness from the way she talked to me. Not forever, just like a brain break, you know? And maybe curiosity." Lia ran her fingers through Beatrice's hair. "Have you ever wondered what it was like to be under your enchantments?"

Beatrice shrugged. "Not until you, darling."

"Really?" Lia asked with a tone of wanting explanation.

"Oh I don't know, you just have a look about you that makes me wonder. Although perhaps I just like seeing you under mine," Beatrice said, feeling the wine loosening her tongue in reluctant admissions. "You somehow make expressionless arousing. And cute, so very cute. It makes me want to put you under at any random moment to see your face drop, just for a second."

Lia turned on the record player. A sensual tune that Beatrice had no recollection of owning began to play. "I love when you surprise me and put me under. I bet you'd love it too. I'm so glad you let me remember being mindless now, it's impossible to describe."

Beatrice sighed with longing. "You do often try."

Lia started to dance to the music. "I know but no words could ever get it right. The closest I can compare is it's sorta like falling asleep, like that moment between awake and sleep. Super calm, unable to move but you don't want to move, you don't want anything. You're just asleep and enjoying every second of it." She ran her hands down her body. "Still, describing it is like describing sex. You just gotta experience it to get the full picture."

"That's a...a beautiful way of putting it." Beatrice was beyond tipsy, her eyes locked on the swaying dance. It had almost come out of nowhere and yet it felt so natural for her to be dancing. Like a doll performing a routine on reflex. "What're you...what are you doing?"

"Enchanting you, silly. So you can see how it feels. I just had to show you, it's a bliss that should be shared with everyone at least once." Lia continued to sway like she'd practiced this routine, slipping out of her uniform in a sensual tease. "Back and forth my body moves, lulling your mind into a peaceful serenity. It feels so nice not to think, doesn't it?"

That made sense. Beatrice smiled softly as her thoughts tumbled out, one by one. "Feelssss nice." She paused. Her words weren't coming to her as fast. "How are you enchanting me? You only had...had one chance with my...my..."

"Your glamour? There are many ways to ensnare the mind. Your eyes are like cheating, though, I gotta do all this work. Little bit of fae wine, little bit of love, and of course, the hypnotic focus. I don't have your eyes, but luckily I have these," Lia said with a sly smile as she let her bra fall and shook her now free hanging breasts. She already had an amazing body, but she was so hypnotic now. Beatrice couldn't tell if it was the wine, the enchantment, or if she was just this skilled at dancing. Any shame of staring was long gone and Lia clearly knew her breasts had fully captivated her. She pushed her arms together to show them off. "They're beautiful, aren't they?"

Beatrice swayed to the rhythm. "So...beautiful."

"Perfect for a slut like me." Lia was on her lap now. "Just a little dance and they stopped almost all the thoughts in your head."

No question on that one. "Yes."

"Sluts act stupid for a good pair of tits." Lia was relentless. "So if you're acting stupid for my tits, what does that make you?"

"I'm...a slut." Beatrice was drooling as Lia rewarded her for her obedience by smothering her in her breasts.

Lia pulled away and giggled as she wiped the drool off her mouth. "Not just any slut. A stupid slut, like me. It was stupid of me to try and enchant Lachesis. Lucky it worked, but luck doesn't make me less stupid. Just like how putting me in a proper dress doesn't make me less of a slut."

Beatrice didn't take to that as quick. "You're not...stupid." *You didn't say she wasn't a slut.*

"Oh, mistress, you're too kind. But we both know I'm not the brightest. And we both know you love that about me." Lia swayed in front of her again, distracting her from the fact she called her mistress. She only called her mistress when she was in a trance. Beatrice didn't put her in one, right? Maybe she did. It was hard to care either way. "I can see why. Your face right now is amazing, like I can almost see your thoughts draining out. I gotta figure out how I look, it must be such a turn on seeing me go blank if it's anything like what I'm feeling watching you. Wait, you totally should get to look!" Lia turned her towards the mirror. "Look at yourself. What do you see?"

Beatrice saw she was drooling again. She didn't even try to wipe it away. "A stupid slut."

Lia giggled. "Two stupid sluts. Make sure to include yourself."

"I did." Beatrice shivered. "Don't want...to call you stupid."

"Aww, you're so sweet to me, mistress. That's why I gave myself to you, you know? Because I know you'll take care of me." Lia turned her back to her. "But we're in this together and you gotta be honest. We're *both* stupid sluts. We're stupid sluts who only think with our cunts and that's why Lachesis got to me and now I'm getting to you."

Beatrice knew that. She must've realized it at some point that was what had happened but only now did she feel herself fighting. Her response sounded like a half-awake whine rather than actual resistance. "Nooo."

"Yesss," Lia cooed in response, booping her on the nose, "You taught me a bit, but she's taught me so much more. Like how to get rid of that pesky resistance. You're fighting it now, right?"

Beatrice drunkenly nodded. "Yess. Need to fight. Need to...to stop her."

Lia pouted, her tone feigned distress. "Fight it, mistress. Your doll is being stolen, you need to save her, to take back what's rightfully yours."

It was a trap. Obviously it was a trap and Beatrice was falling right into it as her eyes weakly glowed with what little will she had left. She couldn't think straight but she wanted to save Lia. Except Lia didn't want saving, as she turned Beatrice's head back to the mirror and she was hit with her own enchantment like the stupid slut she was. "What do you see, mistress?"

The answer was splayed out in front of Beatrice as she watched her own face go slack and a heat rose within so strongly that her hand moved between her legs. "A stupid slut who thought with her cunt."

Lia kissed her cheek. "Perfect! Just keep touching yourself and saying that until it's the truth."

Beatrice stared into her own eyes, repeating the humiliating mantra over and over as she sunk into a trance of her own making. She fought to stay topside, to regain control.

You are in control. That's why you can't stop. You want this.

Beatrice couldn't tell if that thought was planted or not. The way she played with herself was proof she no longer cared. She wanted this.

"You're almost ready." Lia turned her head away from the mirror and shoved her face between her breasts. "But I can't take the reins. I'm just a doll, it's not my place to hold your strings. So we're going to give them to Lachesis, just for a bit. We're going to listen to her words and let them become our thoughts and it's going to be the best night of our lives. It's so wonderful to give in, mistress."

Beatrice grinned goofily as she was allowed up for air. "Yesssnoo, no, Lia please." She only managed to resist because the mention of that maid infuriated her. Reminding her this intimate moment between her and Lia was tainted with ill intent. "Remember...remember your truths. Remember who you are." *A slut, stupid slut like me.*

"I haven't forgotten, mistress." Instead of having her reality restored, Lia just cheerfully recited, "I am Lia Abith. I am a half-demon. My sister loves me. I love you. Nothing has changed."

Beatrice tried to not get distracted by the fact this was the first time Lia had said she loved her, with the heartwarming addition that she made that fact as important as her sense of self. The depraved desire to be smothered again was stealing enough focus as is, giving into the sweetness of her affection would be her doom. "Then why are you obeying *her*?"

"Because she's helping me serve you better," Lia said proudly.

"But she's using you!"

Lia shivered with delight. "I love being used. My purpose is to be used."

Beatrice whimpered, from fear or arousal she didn't know anymore. The stupid suggestions meant to enhance Lia's pleasure were being used against her. And no matter how much it infuriated her Beatrice couldn't help but be just as turned on as her handmaiden was. Conquered by her own thrall, turned into a mindless toy to be played with. Lia always looked so happy going under. Beatrice would be lying if she said she'd never wondered what it was like, to truly sink into mindless bliss. To just give up control and finally have a moment of rest.

"Relax, mistress. Let my tits extinguish your thoughts." Lia smothered her again. With that the last bit of Beatrice's resistance was shattered. "I can tell you're only holding out because you're worried about me. I promise I'll love this. We both will. Do you know why?"

Beatrice smiled like an idiot as she pulled away. She'd tasted the ecstasy of emptiness and given in. "We're stupid sluts who think with our cunts."

"Exactly, mistress. Now, be a good slut and go blank for me." Lia smothered her again and Beatrice's mind obediently came to a complete halt.

Bea and Lia played with each other's pussies, mindlessly repeating their mantras together. "We're stupid little sluts who think with our cunts."

Lia loved Bea's mindless face, cross-eyed with her mouth slightly hanging open. She didn't know how long they'd been at it but she knew they'd do it until told otherwise and love every second of it. If they weren't under orders to keep a low profile, she would've set them up in the hallway just to get that extra kick of humiliation. Maybe Lachesis would order them to do that after. A fuckdoll could dream.

The door opened. Neither of them cared to stop or even look at who walked in on them playing with each other. There was a soft laugh, a sound of clothes being removed, and then Lia felt a hand on her head. "Well done, little demon. Your mistress would be proud." Lachesis stepped into view and put her hand on Bea's head. She was stripped down to her corset, her stockings and sleeved gloves still on. "Are you proud of your doll, Lady Beatrice?"

"We're stupid sluts who think with our cunts," Bea moaned in response, unaware and uncaring of anything other than her mindless pleasure.

"Oh my, you really worked her over." Lachesis tapped Lia's cheek, snapping her out of her mantras. She looked up at the maid obediently, ready for new orders. "I need her awake to talk, but she won't be able to think straight being this pent up. It's your duty to relieve that tension, is it not?"

"Yep! I'm nothing but a toy for her pleasure," Lia said happily as she crawled around her and all but dove between Bea's legs and started to tease her clit. Between that and Lachesis whispering in her ear Bea seemed overwhelmed as her eyes rolled back and her jaw went slack.

Lia lifted her head with a worried pout. "She's going to be ok, right?"

Lachesis glanced down and gave a smile that made all of her doubts melt away. "Of course, little demon. I keep my promises. Plus—" she lifted Bea's head up, who uncharacteristically giggled in response as her eyes crossed. "—doesn't she look like she's having fun?"

Lia couldn't tell if she felt concern or just envy looking up at her mistress having her mind twisted and her body fondled. She smiled blankly. "Can I go next?"

Lachesis patted her head. "How can I say no to a face like that?"

Beatrice was calm, relaxed, and entranced. She was waking up to an afterglow she didn't remember earning but her body certainly did. Lia was across from her, her eyes rolling into the back of her head as she played with herself. She was being rewarded, Beatrice knew, for satisfying her mistress. The word slipped out before she could even remember what was going on. "Cum."

Lia obeyed, arching back with a pleasurable moan. She sank back against the bed and giggled to herself. "Thank you, mistress."

"Well, aren't you generous?" Lachesis whispered into her ear. Beatrice shivered, her hand already reaching between her legs. The head maid sat on her bed across from her and snapped her fingers. "Lia, eat me out while I have a talk with your mistress."

Still not fully recovered from her reward, Lia mindlessly obeyed and crawled over to her. Lachesis looked down at Beatrice as she began to lap away. "You may awaken fully, my lady."

Lachesis snapped her fingers and Beatrice was suddenly aware of everything. She blushed heavily as she covered herself. "How *dare* you!"

"Interesting reaction, considering you sent your toy to tame me first," Lachesis said. She smiled with a soft moan, rubbing Lia's head. "Gods, I can see why she ended up in your room every night. Girl's got a tongue enchantments can't teach."

"Release her!" Beatrice tried to enchant Lachesis but instead of glowing her eyes crossed. A stupid grin grew in her face. "I'm a stupid slut. Stupid sluts aren't allowed to enchant their betters."

Lachesis rolled her eyes. "Oh calm down, she's enjoying herself. Aren't you, little demon?"

Lia raised her head with the happiest grin. "Very much, ma'am."

She wrinkled her nose. "Ew, don't call me ma'am, makes me feel like I'm older than Atropos. Miss is fine."

"Okay, miss." Lia went back between her legs and started happily lapping away once more.

Beatrice crossed her arms as she glared at her, trying to hide her arousal. She noted that Lia still viewed her as her mistress, so Lachesis was not trying to take that title away. This entire thing was so unlike what enchantments usually were like to her, she truly didn't understand what was going on. "I made it quite difficult for others to enchant her. How did you manage it?"

"I didn't enchant her. You did." Lachesis smirked at her confusion "That's my gift. I cannot tie my own strings but everyone else's are within my grasp. Letting Lia here try to covertly enchant me and then using her as a conduit, it was a simple matter." She shrugged. "I was surprised at how fast she got to you, though. I suppose you have an envy for her submissiveness hidden in you somewhere. I can relate, it's hard being the controller all the time."

Beatrice pouted. "That's...that's not entirely accurate."

"Hmm? Oh please, enlighten me."

"Lia knew me well. And yes, I did have a sliver of curiosity." Beatrice blushed. "But when I realized what was occuring she also used my panic to save her against me."

Lachesis looked proud. "You really do love her, don't you?"

Beatrice glared at her. She was reminded that Lia's first admission of love had been tainted by this entire encounter. "Is that why you're doing this? To torment me for having the audacity to love a commoner?"

"Who do you think I am, the Lady of the House?" Lachesis rolled her eyes. "You were just being honest, don't fall back now. We both know that this is turning you on as much as it is her. It's why you can't bring yourself to stop me, you'll ruin her fun."

Beatrice glared at her. "I can't stop you, you've blocked me from enchanting you."

Lachesis laughed. "Would that have stopped you with Nyssa Deburio? You all but assaulted her, I'm certain if she was here instead of me a lack of enchantments would not stop you from choking the life out of—oh, oh, hold on, she's getting me there already." Lachesis took a heated breath and waved her hand. "Feel free to keep touching yourself, just let me enjoy this."

Beatrice hadn't even realized she was playing with herself and her shame was quickly drowned out by a wave of mantras consuming her mind. Her eyes crossed and her mouth hung open. *I am a stupid slut who thinks with my cunt. I love whoring out my handmaiden just to get off. Being toyed with turns me on and every time I say otherwise I hope to be punished.*

Lachesis pressed down on Lia's head as she came and quickly caught her breath. "You know I can hear those mantras, right? You have some dirty thoughts for an elegant lady."

"I...don't...think those," Beatrice fought to say, "You...put them...there."

Lachesis smiled. "Oh really?" She moved her fingers like she was playing a piano. Lia stood up and wandered out of view. "So what I'm hearing is, you want to be punished?"

Yes. "N-no."

"Lia, please punish your mistress."

"Ok, miss," Lia said from behind her.

Beatrice had no idea what this was going to be but shoving the handle of her feather duster up her ass was not her first guess. Lia even covered her mouth to muffle the painful cry of pleasure that came out of her. Tears fell down her cheeks but she hated more how fast her fingers were moving now. She was helpless and she loved it, she almost asked for it again.

Lachesis sighed. "It's not even been a minute and you're already becoming a hot mess. How am I supposed to have a talk with a horny puddle?" She smiled with a soft laugh. "I suppose I'm not really helping. Let's try again."

With a snap of her fingers Beatrice's mind went quiet.

When Beatrice resurfaced after who knows how long she was calm and satisfied again. Her body ached like she'd moved around a lot and her ass hurt. Lia was rubbing her own with a similar look of discomfort. She was now kneeling at the foot of Lachesis, facing Beatrice with her signature bright smile. Oblivious of how doomed they were.

"Why are you doing this?" Beatrice asked. She hated to admit it, but she truly could think much more clearly now. She was humiliated, she was helpless, but the worst part was she'd failed to protect Lia. She'd sent her handmaiden to face off a fate alone and now they both were suffering the consequences. And apparently that was the exact thought Lachesis was trying to invoke.

"To show you how dangerous it is to not set up defenses. And I think I know why you haven't." Lachesis patted Lia. "For one, she's loyal. Really loyal, a master of twisting wordings to benefit her the most and thus out of loyalty she twists them to benefit you. Mix that with how your style of enchantments are through pleasure rather than pain, most fae would hit a brick wall trying to take her."

"But?"

"But, she has nothing she can use on her own. You've prepped her to resist your mother, sure, but you haven't given her many avenues to regain control if she fails. In fact half of your suggestions don't even specify you needing to say them. That's a habit I'd really advise getting into, open ended triggers are the cracks that break even the strongest foundations." Lachesis smirked as she caressed Lia's cheek. "She *really* loves being called a good girl."

Lia purred a moan in response, rubbing into her palm like a cat. Beatrice swallowed what little pride she had left in order to save her handmaiden from this humiliation. "You've made your point. We shouldn't have tried to enchant you and our lack of preparation proved our hubris. I apologize. Please, don't inflict any more torments on Lia because of this. She was only trying to please me."

Lachesis had an unreadable expression. Lia turned to her and smiled proudly. "I told you she'd do good."

"That you did." Lachesis sighed. "A deal's a deal. Let's wrap this up."

"What? What is she talk—" Beatrice trailed off as Lia crawled over to her, her dangling breasts pulling her focus. She didn't even need the dance anymore to put her in a light trance. Beatrice was drooling by the time Lia was in front of her, erotically swinging them back and forth in front of her. *Sluts act stupid for a pair of tits. I'm a stupid slut.*

"Now, Lia, are there any ideas you have to please your mistress?" Lachesis asked.

Lia had a face of genuine thought as she guided Beatrice's head and let her drunkenly suckle on her nipple. She didn't have the will to care about anything else anymore. Then a wide smile grew as Lia motioned for Lachesis to lean in and whispered into her ear. She stifled a laugh. "My, my, what a suggestion. Go ahead and put her under. I'll do the legwork after."

Beatrice was fairly under already in her opinion, whining as she pulled her wonderful tits away. Lia quickly replaced it with a passionate kiss and whispered, "We did it, mistress."

Beatrice smiled, oblivious of what that meant but Lia was happy so she was happy. "That's wonderful, darling. You're such a good girl."

Lia shivered. "Thank you, mistress. Now empty your mind and we can celebrate."

Beatrice eagerly obeyed.

Beatrice opened her eyes. She was sitting on her bed, no Lachesis in sight. Lia was waking up at the same moment next to her. Both of them were still naked.

"Lia?" Beatrice asked tentatively. She wasn't quite sure if this was a trap or not.

Lia seemed like she was back to normal. She looked worried as she hugged herself. And embarrassed. "Was that real?"

"I do believe it was." Beatrice racked her brain to try and remember what happened past the blackout. She was vaguely horny but that wasn't a helpful clue. She was thirsty, really thirsty. "I don't remember us doing anything. What was your idea?"

Lia was starting to breathe heavily. "Don't remember. It's...is it hot in here?"

Beatrice was getting hot too. That vague arousal had been slowly increasing and now that she noticed it her entire body started to heat up. The two of them were panting like dogs on a sunny day. She wanted to satisfy this sudden wave but she couldn't remember how. The concept of touching herself had been cut from her mind. And the arousal was doubling with every second, it was like an itch she couldn't scratch. "Lia...how do you..."

Stupid sluts know how to play.

It wasn't clear to Beatrice what that foreign thought meant. Being practiced in this role Lia caught on immediately and didn't even hesitate. "I'm a stupid slut."

Beatrice almost said it herself, but she finally had a stranglehold on her pride again. "I am not going to say that." She didn't fully believe herself.

"I'm a slut. Please, I'm a stupid slut, please let me play, I need it," Lia whined without a hint of shame. She haphazardly smacked her leg. "Bea, I don't think it works until we both say it."

"I am not saying that! I won't...let her win." Beatrice had tipped over on the bed and curled up as if dealing with a cramp. She was ready to fight further but Lia's desperate whines broke her. "Fine, I admit it, I'm a...slut." Nothing changed. She didn't mean it. "I'm a slut. I'm a stupid slut!"

Thankfully that was all the humiliation that was required. Beatrice certainly felt stupid as she suddenly remembered how to play, as it were. Except how to touch herself was still being kept locked away, all that had been unlocked was how to satisfy Lia. "Did that...work for you?"

Lia didn't seem to hear her. Her eyes were locked onto her dripping pussy with a primal hunger. She dove between her legs and started to eat her out ravenously.

This was *supposed* to solve everything, Beatrice knew this but instead it just seemed to make her hornier to a point it was getting painful. Not only that her thirst was growing with every lick. A mental dam that all the pleasure was beating against. It was hard in this depraved state to think of the obvious act this was leading them to do, but it wasn't until Lia gasped for air that it became clear.

"Still...horny...not enough. Need...need something...more." Lia said between heated gasps. Beatrice looked at her pussy and felt the primal urge that saw in her moments before. She knew what she had to do. Beatrice didn't even explain, too horny to waste time, she pushed Lia back and resisted the urge to dive between her legs. Instead she turned around, putting her pussy over her head before getting her pleasurable reward.

The moment both their tongues were in each other, the mental dam broke and with it her mind.

Stupid sluts think with their cunts.

Beatrice was becoming much more animalistic. Her thoughts weren't in her head, they were between her legs and being twisted by the talented tongue of her partner. Lia's grunts were getting deeper, as if her demon instincts were filling the void left by her own mind leaking out. They weren't so much building up to a climax as they'd already been built up and were ready to burst. It would barely take a push to—

Stupid sluts cum their brains out.

Beatrice came harder than she ever had in her life, welcoming the splash of juices as Lia came as well. They both went limp, what was once her mind streaking down her leg as what was once Lia's mind dripped from her face.

Good sluts lick up their messes.

Beatrice wanted to be a good slut. Her tongue started mindlessly to clean. From the feeling of the tongue running along her own leg, Lia was being a good slut too. The mood was more different now, calmer as their body's relaxed from such an intense release. Soon they were done with their legs and repositioned to clean each other's faces, mindlessly giggling together as the licks tickled.

Good sluts love each other.

Beatrice felt like the best slut in the world.

It was hours later when they came to their senses. Beatrice was spooning with Lia in bed, basking in the afterglow of a passionate night together. She wanted to be mad at Lachesis but it was hard to be mad at anything in a serene moment like this. She remembered everything, a lust filled haze of memories, sure, but ones she at least could recall still. Even the ones that weren't there before, of Lia giving her instructions, teasing her as she did. Even mindless she still had cherished Lia like she was the most important thing in the world. Beatrice wrapped further around her love, but frowned when she started to shake. "Lia?"

Lia sounded far from ok. "Bea, I didn't....I couldn't resist her..."

Beatrice flipped her around to see the devastation on her face growing and pulled her in close. "No, no, it's not your fault. She has years of experience on us both, it was my fault for underestimating a fate."

"But it was my idea to enchant her and—and she must've wanted that, I fell for it. It was wrong but it was hot, I couldn't help myself, I was so turned on and I wanted you to feel what I was feeling and she used that against me. She used *me* against you." Beatrice was trying really hard not to make Lia feel worse by laughing, even distressed she was adorable. They'd been humiliated, wound up and set loose on each other like horny schoolgirls, and all she cared about was how she might've upset her mistress. "I love being used but I don't want to be used to *hurt* you. I'm a horrible handmaiden, I betrayed my lady just...just to get off—"

Beatrice almost put her under but a point about the dangers of reliance on enchantments was just taught to the both of them. Instead she just hugged her tighter and caressed her head. "Shhh, I swear I'm not mad. Not at you, anyways, and not right now even then. I'd never be mad about a lustful night with a beautiful girl."

Lia buried herself into her chest. "You're just saying that."

"Because it's the truth." Beatrice could tell Lia was exhausted. She kissed the top of her head. "Get some rest, darling. We both need it."

"Okay. Still sorry." Lia closed her eyes and further snuggled into her. "Still love you."

Beatrice smiled warmly. "I love you too."

Chapter 27
GUIDELINES

Despite literally being her job, Lia sure knew how to make breakfast in bed feel like an apology.

"Darling, you do recall I said I wasn't mad, yes?" Beatrice was technically lying. She was mad Lia wasn't still with her in bed when she woke, she made for a very good pillow. Her proclivity for breads and pastries had earned forgiveness for that, however.

Lia shrugged as she poured tea for them both. "I know. It's just breakfast."

Beatrice raised an eyebrow. "You wrote 'sorry' with a frowny face made out of berries on the crepes."

Lia avoided eye contact. "The recipe could've called for that, you don't know."

Beatrice stifled a laugh. "I'll try to acquire you a cookbook with a happier theme."

Lia tapped her hands against her legs. "You're sure you're not mad I went down on her?"

"Considering you were being controlled, that's something that should upset *you* before it upsets me," Beatrice said. She recognized the expression Lia was trying to hide. "Are you ashamed you enjoyed it and think I'll be mad at you for that?"

Lia was very interested in the floor. "Mhm."

Beatrice lifted her chin to look in her eyes. "Ashamed that you'd do it again?"

"I..." Lia became cutely stern. "I wouldn't."

"No? So if I just let my eyes drag you under right now and ordered you to become her plaything for a day, you'd hate it?"

Lia pushed past her hand to hug her. "I didn't say I'd hate it. I said I wouldn't do it again. Not without your permission. I'm *your* plaything, I shouldn't have ever let somebody else give me orders."

Loyal to a fault. Beatrice sighed as she hugged back. "We were very lucky she was merciful." She lightly pushed her away and gave a calm but stern look. "Now, I have one very important question. Were the "slut" truths your idea or hers?"

Lia blushed heavily and cringed. "Mine."

"Good." Beatrice kissed her cheek. "As humiliating as that was, at least I don't have to contend being aroused by something Lachesis came up with."

"You...liked it?" Lia asked suspiciously. Ironic that her entranced self had been overconfident in how much her mistress would enjoy it, but awake she didn't seem to believe her.

Beatrice rolled her eyes. "I could deny it but with my luck I'd probably be triggered into stripping nude, walking into the hall, and start proclaiming I'm a lying slut to the passing staff." That thought made her shiver, albeit not without concern that this was a new kink forming. She wasn't sure how she felt about that.

"Actually, I removed any lingering enchantments, even that mental block that stopped you from enchanting Lachesis." Lia appeared to be trying to not seem too prideful. "I convinced myself that as your handmaiden it was my responsibility to clean your mind as well as your body. So the triggers are gone, Lachesis has no hold over you. She might still have access to me but I can't even put you under now, not without doing the whole hypnotic dance trick again."

A master of twisting suggestions and out of loyalty she twists them to benefit you. "You say that like I wouldn't fall for it again. You're quite the dancer."

Lia blushed. "I've been practicing. I'm a little annoyed that my surprise got used to trick you."

"It certainly made it a surprise." Beatrice smiled. "Perhaps when this is all over I'll allow you to try again. But I'd like to remove her access to you as well. You're mine alone, after all."

"I'm not quite so sure we should do that just yet." Lia held her hands up in a panic. "Wait, wait, I swear that's me talking, I'm just saying if we remove Lachesis's hold over me then it might remove your hold over her and then we'll have been humiliated for nothing."

Beatrice stared at her. "I do remember her saying something about a deal and you saying we did it. Would you mind explaining?"

"Sooo, technically, Lachesis is under your enchantment still. She's just fully aware of it." Lia nervously smiled. "After she, well, dragged me under and played with me a bit, she told me if you showed humility she'd let our plan work. I guess my trance self was confident you would and sure enough you did, so we can use her shop to escape the House whenever we want now."

Beatrice pondered on that. Lachesis wasn't just giving them a pity win. Now she'd tipped her hand as to how her powers worked it was clear being under a simple enchantment like that gave her much more power over the enchanter than the enchantment would over her. This deal benefited the fate more than anything else.

But at the same time, she wasn't warning Ida. The maid had no need to admit she couldn't enchant people on her own, she must've been implying that she needs either Beatrice or Ida no matter what happens. By not snitching she was indirectly telling them she was putting her flag in their corner. Which meant her lessons were ones they really needed to take to heart. "So, in a way, the entire time you were acting that way thinking it would lead to us accomplishing the plan."

Lia looked embarrassed. "I know, it's super dumb—"

Beatrice waved her hand. "No, it's the exact point Lachesis was making. You're willing to do almost anything if you think it'll help fulfill whatever order I've given you. Doubly so if you think it'll make me happy and earn you praise. That's dangerous if left unchecked. Imagine if I told you to make something the best night of my life and somehow the enchantment twisted that into you killing me afterwards so that no night beyond it would ever be better."

"I would never do that!" Lia said defensively.

Beatrice cringed. "Extreme example, I admit, but you see what I mean? And that's assuming nobody has tricked you or is influencing you to think in such an illogical manner. Such as if Lachesis had been lying and you'd just been a pawn in turning me into a puppet for her."

Lia gave a few nods as she contemplated on that. "I guess we need to give me a guardrail. Like the rules of the House, with how I start to get fidgety when I try to fight them."

"The rules of the House are just as bad. You can add rules, that's not something she intended. We can't have it be something that relies on exterior input, I need to give you control over your enchantments."

Lia frowned. "Doesn't that ruin the point of them?"

"Failsafes, darling, for emergencies." Beatrice smirked. "I've already been pondering a few ideas, one of which is making sure you don't consciously remember it exists. A defense mechanism rather than a lever you pull in a panic. You'll still be completely helpless and at my mercy, just how you like it."

"Good," Lia said with a smile. "You know, maybe add something for if I think you're not in your right mind. It'll cover both you being controlled and people pretending to be you."

"Smart. You're a lot smarter than you act sometimes." Beatrice cringed. "Sorry, I didn't mean to imply you act foolish."

Lia blushed. "I suppose I act ditzier than I am from time to time. I like how it makes you smile."

"Do you know what else makes me smile?" Beatrice's eyes glowed. Lia didn't even get a response out before she was caught in her gaze. Her cute entranced face brought a smile to hers. "Now, before I start, did Lachesis leave any surprises for me?"

Lia smiled brightly. "She told me if you didn't check I was supposed to write "stupid slut" on your forehead while you slept. Otherwise, no."

Beatrice rolled her eyes. "Now that just sounds childish."

"Agreed, mistress." Lia cringed while still holding up her grin. "Is it bad if I would've found it funny?"

"Immature and humorous aren't exclusive concepts." Beatrice smiled deviously. "After all, when the opportunity arises we will be taking revenge on her. Which will be both immature and hilarious."

"And humiliating, mistress?" Lia added.

Beatrice nodded. "Very humiliating, darling. I'm sure she'll have as much fun as we did."

<u>Forgive and Forget</u>

Chapter 28
CALLING DIBS

The slums weren't aptly named. Beatrice thought they should be called the sags.

The slums sagged like an overworked peasant. Buildings, streets, entire blocks sinking into the ground like the earth was trying to claim it for Hell. There wasn't much street traffic, at least not as much as one would expect. The infernal population preferred the sky after all.

That meant that the ground was left for the truly destitute, desperate, and disabled. Dewinged demons and down on their luck devils, this was dangerous for even the locals to traverse. Beatrice hid within her cloak as she walked, she thought about it more than once but never truly ventured here. Unlike her mother, she had no passive glamours to speak of. Apparently a trade-off for the intensity of her enchanting eyes. She was vigilant for anybody giving them too much attention and ordering said watchers to lose interest. A fae in the slums was asking for trouble.

Lia didn't seem afraid at all. And that wasn't a lack of caution, she was so in tune with navigating safely amongst back alleys and shortcuts that she was more leading Beatrice than anything else.

"Even if you don't recall living on them, your feet appear to remember these streets well," Beatrice said as they snuck through a crumbled building. She was breathing heavily. Climbing was not her forte.

"Yeah, I feel like I've gone this way a bunch. Probably to buy Diana twigs, to be honest." Lia took her hand to help her over the rubble and frowned. "Oh wow, you're shaking. Do you need to sit down?"

Beatrice shook her head, despite her legs demanding for her to say yes. "I'm...fine. We can...can..."

Lia narrowed her eyes. "Have you been doing the eye thing this entire time?"

Beatrice tried to catch her breath before answering. "Well, I need to...be discrete—"

"Bea, that's going to tire you out!" Lia did not seem to think climbing a broken wall was the answer to her fatigue. She pointed to a crevice. "There's a bed in there, let's get you off your feet."

"But—"

"No arguments, my lady. You need a break."

Beatrice didn't have the strength to disagree. Instead she was more baffled as to what Lia meant by a bed being inside a crevice. With her help getting down it became clear it was actually a shattered stained-glass window buried under the rubble. This was an underground church. Literally, as if the ground had swallowed it and the city just built on top of it afterwards.

"Aren't churches a bit of a problem for demons?" Beatrice asked.

"Sorta. Active ones for sure, might as well take a dive in liquid silver. Abandoned ones it's hard to tell how holy a place still is. Abandoned by the city doesn't always mean abandoned by the gods," Lia said, "They don't burn me, but I do feel weird in them. Gives me the creeps most of the time, depending on the sect. Like I can almost feel I shouldn't be there. At least until I desecrate them."

Beatrice didn't need to ask how she did such a feat. They passed by a blood stained glyph center of where the pastor would speak. There was glass shattered along the floor along with more blood as if a fight had occurred. "It looks as though somebody has done so already."

Lia glanced over. "Huh, you're right. Looks like my handi-work, actually. This place does feel safe to me, it probably was one we were staying at." She led Beatrice into a side room with the aforementioned bed. It was in decent condition and thus gave her a much-needed respite. "Honestly, we probably used this one a lot. It's harder to find ones with beds than you'd think."

Beatrice had to admit she was glad she had a moment to catch her breath. Lia's stamina was a marvel, she barely had broken a sweat. She wondered if the demon half helped in that regard. It certainly helped in keeping up during their more, well, energy-heavy activi-ties.

"You know, I was thinking about the Rules of the House. Which is sorta hard considering one of them is to not think about them, but out here I don't feel as obedient." Lia tapped her head. "I wonder if because they're house rules I don't really feel like following them while not in the House. Huh. Maybe we should try to get around them out here rather than in there."

"That's actually quite clever." Beatrice was always fascinated by how Lia interpreted enchantments. While she still worried being so receptive would make her vulnerable, in practice it appeared to give her an uncanny knack for intuiting loopholes.

"Yeah, but that's not what I was thinking about. Do you know which rule bothers me the most? The first one. Everything else feels like it's meant to control me and prevent you from even learning about it, but the first one is just about cleaning?" Lia said. "Doesn't that sorta feel like a test rule? Like she was trying to see if she could get away with it?"

Beatrice was starting to see her point. "She also seemed quite unhappy with me taking you as a handmaiden. And strangely unwilling to actually punish you even when opportunities arise. She's trying to outwit somebody."

Lia raised her hand. "Wait, what if it's like a warning bell? If I stop following the rules of the House she'll know because I'll stop cleaning when she's around."

"Perhaps. The idea of it being a test rule rings more favorable. Especially considering the reason you follow them is supposedly to be a good maid. But do you know what bothers me the most?" Beatrice did not like admitting this, but Lia thought about these much differently than she did. Her perspective was too valuable to not get her input. "Why was my awareness of this endeavor not allowed? Lucial fits perfectly except for that factor."

Lia tilted her head. "Well, you would've stopped it."

"No. I wouldn't have." Beatrice cringed at the confusion on her face. Sometimes she forgot how highly Lia thought of her. "Until recent events put it in perspective, I did not realize how much you've changed me. Changed how I view our staff, view my magic, even how I see myself. I assumed a simple binary morality of enchantments, but you've taught me there is a spectrum that includes ways I am much more inclined to. But back then, I wouldn't have cared. I was lonely but I was disconnected from almost everything. The idea would've been a tad cruel in my eyes but not one I would make a fuss over. If Ida had just told me your purpose, I would not have taken you on as a handmaiden. The very thought makes me shudder. So why didn't she?"

Beatrice continued. "Why did she decide my input was not only unnecessary, but not allowed? Why when I made my decision did she react like I had been plotting against her? I say it feels she is trying to outwit somebody. I cannot help but feel that somebody is me. That I have been battling against her without even realizing it and yet..."

Beatrice's attention was caught by a carving in the wall. A heart scraped into the side of the wall, a childish but sweet gesture.

Lia seemed to think that was the end of her thought. "It might be faster if I go to Dibs myself. If this was one of our old hideouts it's probably safe for at least that much." She frowned. "Bea? Is something wrong?"

Beatrice couldn't stop staring at the vandalism. It bothered her like a scratch she couldn't quite itch. Perhaps it just made her happy to know love was amongst even the downtrodden.

Until she finally discerned the faded lettering.

B + L

Lia used her fingers to follow Beatrice's eyes and rubbed against the stone wall. "Aww, that's sweet. Maybe there's another Bea and Lia out here." The same thought Beatrice was having must've come to her. "Wait."

Lia kept tracing her finger along the indent of the heart, over and over. She then flicked her finger and her fingernail sharpened into a small claw. Before Beatrice could even ask how she did that she traced it again, the depth lining up as she mimicked carving into the wall. "I made this. I can feel the memory of drawing it."

"Give me your hand," Beatrice ordered. Lia presented it to her and she placed her own over it, guiding it along the *B*. A tinge of familiarity tugged at her, a strangely giddy tension as if she'd never even held her maiden's hand before. "I think you helped me make it too."

They took a step back together to gawk at the piece of their past neither remembered carving. Beatrice squeezed Lia's hand, almost afraid if she let go she'd disappear. She didn't know what to say nor wanted to comprehend what the evidence implied.

Lia hugged her arm. "Bea?"

"Yes?"

"I'm scared."

We're both scared, Beatrice thought. Saying it aloud would only scare Lia more. "Will you be brave if I ask you too?"

Lia tried to smile but the fear was still under it. "For you, my lady."

Beatrice kissed her on the forehead. "You belong to me. So being brave for me is being brave for you."

Lia decided to visit Dibs with Bea. They both had too many questions and neither wanted the other to be out of their sight.

It was weird how terrified Lia was of having her memory tampered with. She'd all but begged for her senses to be twisted, her mind addled, turned into an object even. Even Lachesis overpowering her, while distressing, still gave her a thrill.

This just felt wrong. A violation, stepping over the line of something that can never be uncrossed.

Lia loved Bea. She promised she'd never forget that. She stored it away in the depths of her mind to make sure. Only now did Lia realize she never remembered *making* that promise. Somebody had tried to make them forget. No, not tried. Succeeded. And it was obvious who did it.

But why?

A bell rang as they entered the small shop. The devil called Dibs spun around and clapped his hands together. His face dropped. "Fuck." He ducked behind the counter and started rustling through the shelves beneath it. "I swears I didn't mean to mess with your plots and plans, your ladyship. I'm just a humble black marketer, only demons and devils be lovin' or hatin' on me wares, no need for fae to bother bruising me."

Lia ran up to the counter and leaned over it. "No, no, it's okay. We're not here to hurt you, we just want to talk."

"Really?" Dibs poked his head up just enough for his eyes to meet Bea's. Lia noted he had a horseshoe in a death grip like a holy symbol against his chest. "You sure your ladyship over there ain't here to melt me brain for confusing her new toy?"

Bea raised an eyebrow and glanced at her. "Do I really seem that callous, darling?"

Lia thought for a moment. "I'd say no, except I have seen your mean face and that one does make me think you'd be willing to turn a brain into soup."

She frowned. "When do I make that kind of face?"

"Usually when you're talking to your mother. Or when somebody is being rude to me." Lia paused. "So like when you're talking to your mother."

"Ah," Bea said, hiding her expression behind her hand, "*That* face." She recomposed herself. "So, you know who I am. How long have you known Lia?"

Dibs gave Lia a look for permission. She nodded. "I don't know either, sorta why we wanted to talk with you."

"Ah. That's a shame, Lia, you's were always my favorite procurer of holy water. Known you for maybe a few years now, always needing holy sticks for your sister," Dibs said with jolliness that seemed more genuine than his salesman tone. Lia smiled brightly and he gave a little lift of his hat with a blush. Then he glanced at Bea. "Never truly got introduced to you, but there were a few time I saws you. Always with Lia. I slips a sneaky little horseshoe in her pack that first time. Assumed a fae caught her when Diana wasn't looking and the burn would wake her right up." Dibs cringed. "Lia came back the next day and yells at me. You weren't there. From the sounds of it, you *really* wanted to be."

"So we did know each other." Lia turned to her lady with a sympathetic smile. Bea had been coping through denial. The idea that Ida was able to breach her defenses was more than a strike at her ego, it was uprooting her entire sense of safety. "Sorry Bea, but it looks like your memory really was messed with."

Bea nodded grimly. "I don't deny that, darling. I just wish to have all the pieces before I make any conclusions."

"You's trying to put some timeline together? Well, I can help you there, for a price." Dibs shrunk down when Bea glared at him. "Or you's could just buy something of my wares and I'll add the info as a bonus, free of charge."

"Information first. Then we will see if it is worth a purchase." Bea was being smart, Lia almost said they were going to buy something anyway but Dibs didn't know that.

"Okay, okay, you drive a hard bargain and I wager I don't really know much. Haven't seen either of you's in months. And that last visit you bought out me entire stock of holysticks. I asked if you's was leaving town and yous said "I hope we won't have to." and that was the last time I saws you."

Stocking up on Diana's vice did make it sound like they were planning on leaving town. Was Bea helping them hide from something? Maybe Lucial really did want Diana back. Perhaps Bea warned them of Ida's plan and was trying to help them escape first.

Bea was staring at the horseshoe with a dower look. "That dibs devil dealer. Here I thought they were speaking nonsense." She narrowed her eyes. "Did you procure a set of leyline iron shackles for a gang imps?"

"I can't discuss my other clients." Dibs was sweating. He covered his mouth as her eyes glowed but couldn't stop his words. "Yes, mistress, I dids do that."

Dibs shrunk down. "Your ladyship, you have to understand I hads no idea, I don't asks those sort'sa questions. Sure, I gets an order for shackles, spots a fae in the wild on pickup day, a devil can see the details of that." He had his hand over his horseshoe again. "Normally I'd not involve in what my customers do, but I tolds them that if they nabbed a half-elf along the way, I'd take her off their hands. Lia was always good to old Dibs, gods knows what they would've done with her if they'd been looking for a highest bidder. You can understand me actions, right?"

Bea was making *that* face. Lia took a tentative step toward her. "My lady, he's not the one who attacked you."

That didn't seem to dissuade her. "He sold shackles that burned my flesh and muddled my mind."

"And they would've got it from somebody else if he hadn't. He's just trying to get by." Lia knew that wasn't why she was pissed. Dibs was not smart in implying he was the reason the imps took them both. "Bea, don't hurt him. If not for you, at least for me?"

Bea's expression relented. Her eyes did not. Dibs timidly rose, then without warning he was knocked flat with a self-inflicted sucker punch. She smiled and closed her eyes. "Be glad my handmaiden is merciful."

Dibs heaved painfully from the ground. "So...iron horse-shoes...don't work like crosses...good to know."

Lia was impressed. She noticed Bea was getting more powerful by the day, the commands she could give without speaking were getting super complex. Once they were out of the fire of this situation she couldn't wait to see what ideas they could cook up with her new abilities.

"So, I've givens all I know, would you's wants to do some purchases in trade for such valuable information?" Dibs leaned over the counter and flicked his bowler hat up with a well-practiced salesman smile. "I can call dibs on anything you need, and I'll sell it to you, for a good price too."

"We need deadroot, a good amount of it. And a bundle of holy sticks." Lia shrugged at Bea's raised eyebrow. "Diana is getting grouchy, this'll keep her off your back."

"The twigs I gots, let's see if the roots be blooming for yous today." Dibs tucked the horseshoe into a pocket over his heart and started searching through his wares. "Interesting duoship you got going here, mistress and maiden as it were. Don't usually see hand-maidens with Von Closens, be practitioners of catch and release if memory serves."

"Hard to release a catch that keeps coming back to the hook," Bea said curtly.

Dibs chuckled. "That's our Lia. Persistent little half-demon, ain't she?" He plopped a bundle of sticks that looked like a disassem-bled tumbleweed onto the counter, then started shuffling through what looked like a fish tank overgrown with different fungus and moss. "She's a rarity, you know? Demon blood is potent, they don't so much as go half'n'half as just pop out a demon, get a few traits from the other. Lia's the first I've seens be able to pass off as half-elf, didn't thinks half-demon was even a thing till I mets her."

"Really?" Bea put her hand under Lia's chin to turn it towards her. The faint glow lingered but it appeared she was holding herself back. "I wasn't aware I owned a rarity."

Lia blushed as she nervously rocked back and forth on her feet. "I'm not that special. Just unexpected."

"I think I have the final say on your worth, darling." Bea placed a few coins on the counter and handed their purchase to her. "Price-less, in my opinion. Accepting that is an order, and I expect you to obey it well."

Lia was left feeling a myriad of emotions as Bea elegantly exited on that note. Her face was unable to turn red any further as Dibs raised an eyebrow at her and she quickly followed her out, whisper-ing, "As you wish, my lady."

Beatrice decided to take them back to the church instead of the House. She and Lia sat together on the bed in silence, holding each other close. It wasn't clear who was comforting who. They were both filled with terror by this point.

"More answers, more questions," Lia said.

"It's quite the annoyance, isn't it?" Beatrice said. She glanced at the heart. "I suppose this does explain one thing."

"What?"

"Why I was so drawn to you. Even in the gardens you made my heart flutter and by the next day I couldn't help but hunt you down to make you mine." Beatrice laughed to herself. "Or maybe that's just you. You're quite the catch."

"If only we could remember how it went down the first time to compare," Lia said with a smile. She noticed the face Beatrice made. "Wait, I know that look. You're thinking about trying that somehow, aren't you?"

"In a way. That's why I brought us back here. You said it yourself, the House seems to not affect you as harshly outside of it and this is a place that we have a connection to." Beatrice looked away. "But what if we remember and we don't feel the same?"

Lia frowned. "Why wouldn't we? We were in love."

"Were we? Or had we only merely begun to fall?" Beatrice ran her hand over the faded heart carved into the wall. "I'm in love right now, I don't want to be dragged out of it at the mercy of some...some childish crush that wasn't quite sure yet."

Lia frowned. "Is that what you think this started as?"

"What? No, no, that's not what I meant." Beatrice hugged her tighter. "I know how I feel right now and I never want to stop feeling like that. What benefit is there to risk losing it?"

Lia smiled at her as if what she said next wasn't terrifying. "You're scared I'll stop loving you back."

Beatrice cringed and then nodded. "I wouldn't blame you. I fear we'll remember that I couldn't stand up to my mother and you were a victim of my cowardice. That we'll know we went through all of this because I didn't love you enough to save you the first time." She closed her eyes. "Can't we just be glad that we have each other now? And not start a second chance with the knowledge of how much pain I've caused you."

Lia laid her head on her shoulder. "You weren't weak. Even without my memory I know you must've tried your best."

"How can you be so sure? Lia, truly, how can you have such optimism?"

"Because you're so scared to lose me you'd rather let your mind stay wiped than risk a memory making me dislike you. If you're this clingy now, I can only imagine how you were the first time." Lia kissed her. "Plus, I'm not the one with fae eyes, so it's my memories we're gonna have to dig up. And I want them back. I promised I'd never forget you, I want to keep that promise."

Beatrice couldn't resist her puppy dog eyes. "Then who am I to deny you?" She went in for another kiss, one that turned to two, that turned into a vigorous session of making love before she abruptly cut it off with the bright glow of her eyes. "Sleep!"

Lia ragdolled into her open arms. "Deeper and deeper, sinking into a deep sleep. Letting the feelings burning in you right now lead you to similar ones long since lost." Beatrice stroked her hair as she whispered commands into her ear. "I know how you love to dream what you aren't allowed to remember. Those euphoric emotions rise in you and you eagerly dream about what inspired them."

"Mhm," Lia muffled into her chest. Too asleep to even add 'mistress' on the end.

"There's many feelings you have attached to this place. And I want you to dream about them. I order you to dream about them, to let every detail that occurs rise to the surface to entertain your peaceful slumber." Beatrice kissed her neck, inciting a faint giggle. "You're such a good girl, I know you'll obey that order eagerly."

Lia curled up in her embrace. "Mhm."

"Now sleep, my love." Beatrice laid her head on hers. "Sleep well and dream big."

Chapter 29
Catching her Eye

Lia snuck into the back alley that led to Dibs Delight's with her hand tightly around the vial of holy water. The stuff was hard to acquire for the slums, considering almost anybody who wanted it would also burn up if they stepped foot into a church.

Dibs popped from up from behind the counter as the bell rang from her entry. His salesman smile became more genuine. "Lovely Lia, my favorite procurer of the holy and hellish, what have you got for me today?"

Lia put the vial of holy water on the counter and braced for bad news. "Is this enough to trade for a bundle?"

Dibs reached under the counter and pulled out a pair of tongs to carefully pick up the vial. He examined it closely, holding his hand near it as if to check for its warmth. "Hmm. No." He sighed at her frown. "Diana already go through her last bundle?"

"She sold her last twigs for food. It's making her...grouchy," Lia said.

Dibs' smile waned. He disappeared into the back and returned with a bundle of tiny sticks wrapped together in twine. "Keep the water."

Lia frowned. "But it's—"

"You think I didn't notice you two's had to skip out your last hidey hole? Times are rough on all of us," Dibs said. He poked the vial towards her with the tongs. "I'd rather keeps a Lia in me life than be a stickler about, well, sticks." The bell rang behind her. Dibs looked around her. "Welcome new friend! Just be a moment."

Hooded figure was the most accurate way to describe the new customer. Lia was fascinated by them as she took the bundle and left. Their hood wasn't far enough to create such an impenetrable shadow but she couldn't see anything past the brim, not even a chin. A shady customer no doubt but such a strange way to hide their identity. It had to draw more attention than anything else.

Lia couldn't help but feel their hidden gaze had been locked on her.

Lia hummed to herself as she entered the alley and then froze. Two demons were flanking the crevice that led to their shelter. It didn't look like they even realized it, just hanging around an empty alley to talk, but there was no way for her to sneak by.

It's okay, she told herself, *this happens all the time. Just usually the other way around.*

Diana had trained her what to do, she just needed to pretend she was passing through. Go somewhere else, wait them out. She looked like a half-elf, they had no reason to give her a second look.

"Is that a bundle you got there?" one of them said as she passed by.

Oh. Right. They would give *those* a second look. Lia started walking faster. She ran into a wing that wrapped around to block her. "I don't think those are healthy for a little thing like you."

"We'll be glad to, heh, *dispose* of them for you," the other said.

Diana would kill Lia if she got hurt over something stupid like resisting a mugging just to keep some holy sticks.

On the other hand Diana was already going to kill her for sneaking into a church and stealing holy water, so she was sorta in for a penny. Tossing the holy water into the demon's face was probably considered being in for a pound.

It was also really stupid because there were two of them.

"You bitch!" the demon snarled as covered his face and swung a claw blindly. She easily dodged but screamed as the other grabbed her by the side, his claws piercing her skin. She was certain the second demon was going to cut her throat out just to make it even, but out of nowhere he let her go. As Lia stumbled back to dodge another swipe, the demon just stared past her looking confused. No, not confused, he looked...sleepy?

The one clawing at his burning face growled at him. "What the hell is wrong with—" he glanced at where the first one was looking. "-oh fuck."

"Leave."

The sleepy demon grabbed his injured friend by the throat and extended his wings. At first he struggled but he seemed to decide being allowed to leave was worth his pride of being dragged as a ride along. The two shot off into the night sky.

Whatever could make two demons dip was not something Lia was going to win against. She still couldn't get to the entrance before being spotted. Maybe whatever super scary thing behind her was would just ignore her. Like ignoring an ant. Bad analogy, ants get stepped on, but no time to make a better one. Lia took a deep breath and turned around.

And suddenly everything was fine.

It was the same hooded figure from before. It was still weirdly impossible to see beyond the hood except now two sapphire eyes within sparkled in a way that made every worry melt out of her head. Lia gave a droopy smile. "Hi?"

The figure slowly approached, staring at her intently. Lia didn't mind, it meant she could look at those eyes longer. "Are you ok?"

"No, I think I'm bleeding out," Lia said happily.

"What? Oh my gods! Put pressure on the wound!" The figure ordered in a panic. Lia obeyed. Her blood was warm. The figure looked around. "Do you live nearby?"

Lia pointed to the secret nook that led to their home. "Right there." She frowned. That was a secret. Why was she telling this person that? "What are you doing to me?"

The figure guided her inside. "Keeping you calm."

That made sense. Lia liked feeling this rather than remembering she was bleeding. That meant she'd remember the pain. "Ok. Thank you."

She stifled a laugh. "That's cute, you're welcome."

Lia was led to her bed to sit down and she zoned out hard. With Diana having been gone for a few days she'd been on edge, but even then Lia had never been this calm. She could fall asleep so much easier if she felt like this. It was only when the stranger put down her hood that she tuned back in just to say blankly, "You're hot."

The hot girl blushed and then cringed. "Oh, right, sorry." The glow of her eyes faded.

Lia blinked a few times. She blushed heavily and took interest in her shoes. "I mean, that wasn't a lie." She then yelped as she realized she no longer had a shirt on. The wound had been dressed and bandaged the best it could with what was on hand.

The hot girl stifled another laugh. "Well, since I coerced that thought out of you, I'll share that I think you're quite beautiful yourself." She held her hand out. "I'm Beatrice. And who might you be?"

"Lia." She shook her hand. It was smooth and uncalloused. "Where's my shirt?"

Bea cringed. "You tore it when taking it off. Sorry, it was my bad wording."

"Oh. It's whatever." Lia didn't want to admit that was her only shirt. She pretended not to care she wasn't wearing one. "Why'd you save me?"

"Isn't saving a beautiful girl enough of a reason?" Bea asked.

Lia shrugged. "Not around here."

"Well I'm not from around here."

"I can tell. You talk too fancy."

Bea laughed again. It was such an elegant laugh, but not condescending like she expected an upper crust would sound. "Maybe you can teach me how to speak like a commoner. Make it easier to blend in."

"Why would you want to be in the slums? It sucks down here." Lia may be content with what she and Diana made do with, but it didn't mean her life was an easy one. The idea somebody would casually want this situation was a bit weird even to her.

"Some prefer dirty freedom over pristine prisons." Bea sighed. "I'm sorry to have intruded upon your...home?" She cringed at the unintended insult. "I shall take my leave."

"Wait!" Lia ran up to her as she turned to leave. "Before you go, can you do that eye thing again?"

Bea looked confused and concerned. "Why?"

"It's been a stressful few days. It was nice to be calm." Lia blushed. It really had been, Diana had been gone for almost a week now settling some scores and being alone for that long made her anxious. Her sister always came back in the end. It didn't make waiting any less scary.

"I'd never think somebody would want to be enchanted." Bea glanced at her with her glowing eyes. "Is relaxing all you want?"

Lia slumped back against the wall and sighed. She said something and Bea responded but she didn't really catch anything. In one ear and out the other. Before she knew it she was drifting off to sleep in a way she'd never been able to. And the entire time she thought about Bea, lost in her eyes but after time able to appreciate the full picture.

In the morning Lia woke with a blanket laid over her and the phantom feeling of a kiss on her cheek. She didn't expect that to make her heart sink a little, knowing it was probably the last she'd ever see of the odd, beautiful stranger.

Beatrice lightly stroked Lia's hair as she mumbled in her sleep. She hoped that was a sign this was working.

Knock. Knock. Knock.

The raps against the wood of a door echoed along the abandoned church walls and sent a chill down her spine. It was firm, determined, and much too confident. Somebody knew they were here.

Knock. Knock. Knock.

Three more raps, impatient and demanding. Beatrice lightly laid Lia down, kissed her on the forehead, and covered her with the blanket like she was concealing a body. "Be safe, my love. I'll be right back."

Knock. Knock. Knock.

Three last raps. They felt final, fated to be the last declaration until the unwanted guest was received. The door to the church was as buried as it could be. The other side should be nothing but rubble and soil battling for supremacy. Beatrice opened the door and even after guessing she still flinched.

"Good evening, Lady Beatrice," Atropos said, her posture as poised as ever, "We have much to discuss."

"Knock knock."

Lia had been drawing Bea on the wall with chalk from memory and jumped as her artistic subject popped her head up from the crevice opening. "You came back!"

Bea climbed up, putting a wicker picnic basket on the floor as she did so. "You asked me too."

"I did?" Lia gave her a hand climbing.

Bea cringed. "Oh, that must've been sleeptalking after the enchantment took hold." She blushed heavily. Lia did as well. What else had she said while she was under? Bea held up the basket. "I brought food. And a shirt."

Lia was beyond embarrassed. "I mean...I have other shirts."

Bea raised an eyebrow, glancing down at the blanket she'd make-shifted into a poncho and then back up. "Oh really?"

"No." She quickly took the clothes from her. It was a tunic, a real one rather than the patches of cloth she'd called a shirt before. "Thank you."

"It's the least I can do." Bea smiled. She then frowned at the sight of her own face on the wall.

"Sorry, I didn't think you'd come back," Lia said timidly, "I didn't want to forget what you looked like."

Bea stepped up to it with a look of awe. "You captured me quite well."

"Except the eyes. They don't look good enough." Lia stole a glance and confirmed to herself that she hadn't truly captured the blue sapphires.

"Perhaps I'll bring an easel next time. Commission a portrait," Bea said.

Lia's heart fluttered at the mention of a next time already. "Well, let's enjoy this time first, yeah?"

Bea held out the basket with a smile. "Let's."

They set up a little picnic outing on the roof. The food was amazing, Bea seemed embarrassed about not knowing what to bring but Lia didn't care. It was real food, baked and prepared and everything. It was hard to resist devouring it all in one go, although her savouring the meal seemed to catch Bea's attention.

"You don't have to nibble, you can eat whatever amount you desire," Bea said, eyeing the tiny bites in half the foods she'd brought.

"Oh. Uh, sorry, force of habit." Lia looked away nervously. "Good food is hard to come by. I like to make it last as long as I can."

Bea cringed. "I didn't think about that. Apologies, I didn't mean to mock you."

"No, no, you didn't, I really appreciate it." Lia took a large bite of a pastry. "I promise to gorge myself next time."

"Right." Bea looked up into the sky. The sun had long since set and the stars were brimming above them. "Next time."

They continued to eat and talk. Or rather Lia would talk and Bea listened with a warm expression as she'd sip away at the wine. It was like a little date. Lia wasn't sure if she could call it that. She'd never been on one to compare it too.

The wine started to run dry. The food became crumbs. The two of them sat side by side, stargazing together. Bea pointed out constellations and the names they had. Lia leaned on her shoulder while she did. It was a wonderful night to share with a beautiful girl.

It was too bad Lia had to ruin it. But all good things come to an end. "You're a fae, aren't you?"

Bea's smile died.

Lia finished off her drink. "Are you here to take me?"

Bea didn't answer. She didn't look threatening, just ashamed.

Lia tapped her fingers together. "Can I say goodbye to my sister first?"

"I'm not going to take you." Beatrice put her head between her knees and laughed. "Gods, did I really think...what, if I showed a girl one last good day I'd suddenly feel better about kidnapping her?"

Lia didn't try to run. Those eyes wouldn't let her get far in any case, but Bea wouldn't use them to stop her. Not that she had any proof of that. She could just tell. "How many people have you done this too?"

Bea hid her face. "You're my first."

Lia giggled. "Really? You did all this for the first try?"

"I didn't exactly intend for it to be one. I never had the urge like that, when I enchanted you in the alley I just...couldn't help myself. You had such a cute droopy smile and sounded so happy answering questions." Bea laughed. "And then as I tried to leave you were all but begging to be put back under. I felt like I'd found a perfect thrall. But after this, I don't think I want a thrall."

Lia put her hand on Bea's. "What do you want?"

Bea stared into the night sky. She looked utterly ethereal in the moonlight. "A paradox of a person, I suppose."

Lia wasn't going to miss her chance twice. She positioned her head to be in the right place and closed her eyes.

"What are you doing?"

"Not looking in your eyes. I wanna make sure you know that I want to do this. And not that you made me want to do this." Lia leaned in to kiss her. She'd been aiming for the cheek. She hadn't considered Bea might turn her head.

Seeing as the unintended kiss on the lips quickly turned into making love in the moonlight, Lia was very glad that she hadn't.

The morning sun was shining through the windows. Lia snuggled in Bea's embrace, reminiscing about her first night of making love that she hoped would not be her last. She smelled something familiar, a waft of sage. Like somebody had just lit a holy stick. She sat up in a panic. *Diana!*

"Darling?" Bea yawned as she sat up and rested her head on her shoulder. "What's wrong? Bad drea—mmph!"

It was too late. By the time Lia turned Diana had her arm around Bea's neck and a hand over her mouth. "Even a whisper and I'll snap your neck."

Lia held her hands out. "Wait, wait, don't hurt her!"

"She's a fae, sis. Fucker's got her talons in your mind." Diana clearly didn't know it was Bea's eyes that did the work, not her words. "Don't know what one of you is doing down in the slums but you ain't leaving in one piece."

Lia could feel the pleas from those blue sapphire eyes starting to drag her down. Ordering to save her. She covered her eyes and shook her head. "No Bea! Don't do the eye thing, she'll kill you!"

There was a small gasp, probably Diana switching to cover her eyes. Bea choked out a terrified plea. "I...was...invited!"

"After planting that invite in her head!"

"Diana, if you don't let my girlfriend go I'll hate you forever!" Lia shouted.

The commotion stopped. Lia peeked through her fingers. Diana looked mortified and confused. Bea just looked stunned.

"Girlfriend?" Both said at the same time.

In trying to keep Atropos far away from Lia, Beatrice ended up leading her to a worn-down confessional booth. The barrier was long since broken, leaving the fate open to see her sins laid bare.

"The Lady of the House does not know I'm here. It is a maid's duty to clean up messes before her lady can see them." Atropos sat down. "Clearly you've surmised that deals have been struck and your memories of them stolen. I see no other reason to be in this ghastly place."

Beatrice tried to hide her relief. Atropos didn't know their plans, she didn't know about the deadroot. "Are you here to inform me of my stolen past or just warn me that knowing would make things much worse."

Atropos didn't smile so much as the corners of her mouth curled ever so slightly. "I'm here to make a counteroffer. Information and warnings can be on the table."

"Counteroffer requires me to know the first offer. So let's start there." Beatrice held her gaze. "Why does my mother want Lia?"

Atropos mockingly scoffed. "We don't want Lia. *You* wanted Lia." She let the statement settle before driving it home. "This entire charade is your doing, Lady Beatrice."

Beatrice did not reward her theatrics with shock or denial despite both things boiling within her. "Why?"

"How should I know? I'm not the one who demanded to have her." Atropos rolled her eyes. "Her sister's unexpected exit complicated things. You found Lia before we could properly set up, but you took her as your handmaiden. I advised the Lady of the House to just let the cards play where they fell and react as needed."

"If this is all my doing, why was her sister locked up? Why not make her a fellow servant?" Beatrice couldn't have been that callous, even back then. She refused to believe her first path from indifference was not paved with love but littered in cruelty just to make Lia hers.

"It was agreed that her sister would not be enchanted or be forced to be a part of the staff. It was also agreed Lia would have access to her whenever she desired." Atropos scoffed. "You clearly had a soft spot for the girl. Wanted to make sure she was appeased so as to lengthen her stay."

"Do not speak of her in that tone," Beatrice said coldly. She reigned in her emotions, she was showing her hand. "This doesn't explain the actual offer. Why would acquiring Lia also make locking our memories necessary?"

"You were weak. Soft. Instead of claiming her as a thrall you kept leaving the House to convene. The Lady of the House gave an ultimatum, claim the girl for the House or leave her for the streets. You couldn't live knowing you brought her here but couldn't live without her. This was the compromise. You get your Lia, you don't endanger yourself visiting her, and you don't have to remember that you were the reason for her employment. A myriad of other caveats were worked out, as you can guess with her sister's current predicament."

"You speak of this deal as if it was an honest compromise and upheld to the letter. And yet at every turn my mother has tried to dissuade me from even seeing her," Beatrice said coldly.

Atropos nodded. "We both know how Ida gets, it was a poor reaction on her part and one you self-remedied. You should thank me for convincing her to let you have your toy and leave you be."

Beatrice hated how well that explanation fit. Ida was the type to scrap everything if it didn't go exactly as intended. Perhaps she was going to make Lia her handmaiden that day and the fact Beatrice declared it first just threatened her desire for absolute control. It would explain her outburst, her sudden withdrawal. It fit much neater than their previous assumption. "What of Lucial?"

"What of him? He's an idiotic demon who wants to be as big as he feels he deserves, we have our reasons to speak to him." Atropos raised an eyebrow. "Concocting wild fantasies of Lia's fate at his hands, are we?"

And there it was, the grain of sand still stuck between the supposed fitting pieces. A coincidence. When it came to Ida and her favorite fate, there were no coincidences. "So, what is your counteroffer?"

Atropos clasped her hands together. "Firstly, the context I provided is free. There was no telling what assumptions would be made nor what specific memories either of you may have already reclaimed. I prefer not to have to clean blood being shed from a long jump to conclusions."

Which meant there were things Atropos wasn't telling her. Fae didn't lie, not often. Hiding in truths was always the preference. "Noted."

"My counteroffer is that so long as you stay where you belong, I will never interfere with Lia within our walls."

"How is that a counteroffer? If anything that sounds like a rephrasing of the original deal," Beatrice said.
"Because you're worried that if you throw her back and is out of your reach, you'll be unable to protect her from us." Atropos gave the allotted time for her words to settle. Did she know what they were doing? Or was this just a prediction? The inevitable thought that Beatrice was ignoring this entire time.

If she helped Lia and Diana escape, would she go with them? And what consequences would that choice incur.

"I cannot make this offer on my sisters' behalves, but that would be a short-term problem. My offer is that if you choose to release the Abiths back into the wild, I will not stop you nor will I do anything to reclaim Lia or her sister. We don't want them, little miss," Atropos said, "I'm not going to lie and say that orchestrating her escape will be easy. But so long as that escape does not end with your absence, I won't be a barrier." She smirked. "And we both know that would cover for my Lady of the House. So long as you aren't too brazen, my indifference will make her blind to your actions."

Beatrice had never hated Atropos more than this moment. This offer, this ultimatum, made their admittedly poor plan both feasible and guaranteed to fail if she didn't agree. The head maid would be watching every step and could ruin it at a moment's notice if she so desired. The only way Lia and Diana could ever escape would be if Beatrice stayed behind.

In the end, Lia wasn't the prisoner, Beatrice was. Would she inflict her life sentence onto the girl she loved just so she wouldn't have to suffer it alone?

If what Atropos said was true, she already had.

"I don't want to forget you," Lia said, nuzzling into her girlfriend's shoulder. Everything was murky, her words a script she didn't remember writing. Was she dreaming? She was supposed to be, maybe that's why she felt like it. This one was different, the memory faded and burnt. Embers of a long since doused fire.

Bea wrapped her arm around her and any worries of dreams faded. "I know, darling. And if we're lucky you won't. But I have my doubts Ida will play fair. We need to plan ahead."

Lia didn't understand. Her dream self didn't seem to like it. "We can run away, like we talked about. We've been dodging them so far pretty well."

"I waited too long. The fates have our scent, we'll never slip away with their gaze locked on us. This is the only way." Bea kissed her head. "It'll be alright, my love. We'll win in the end, I swear it."

Lia looked up at her. "I love—"

Bea put her finger to her mouth as her eyes glowed. "Hold onto that. Bury it deep, deeper than you ever have before, deeper than you even realize you can. And promise to me you'll never forget it. Promise that if you ever think I've forgotten, you'll remember to tell me what I already know."

Enthralled by her gaze but fully aware, Lia kissed the fingers on her lips and then pushed the hand on top of her head. "I promise."

Bea's eyes stopped glowing. "Good. That's the last enchantment I had planned. I hope it never comes to that, our situation would be quite dire if it did."

"I know I promised not to tell you right now, but," Lia put both their hands against the wall, "can I show you?"

Bea smiled warmly. "Always, darling."

Lia flicked a clawed finger out and together they carved a heart into the wall. Each putting an initial, albeit with the claw as the tool to make them. A final show of the love they shared and would hope to never forget.

If only they knew.

Lia opened her eyes and found herself wrapped in her girlfriend's arms. She wondered if this was still a dream and in wondering that decided that it wasn't. She gave a sleepy smile. "Hi."

Bea smiled back in a way that didn't feel as happy as it should've been. "Hi."

Chapter 30
Promises

Diana took a long, overindulgent puff of the twig she just lit and blew out enough smoke to fill the room with that unyielding sage smell. "So. You two fell in love and that's why we're here?"

Lia nodded. "Pretty much, yeah."

"And Lucial?"

"Still not sure. I think Ida was hunting us to use as a deal involving him and that's why we were running. Bea thinks Lucial was a coincidence." Lia sighed. "I don't know why, but she thinks this is all her fault still."

"She's scared." Diana took another puff. "Scared and surprised."

"People do things they regret when they're surprised. That's what you always told me."

"Yeah. Like when you brought a fae down here and told me to play nice."

"So that means you regret attacking her?" Lia asked in a subtle jab for an apology.

Diana grumbled. "Let's just agree I was surprised." She raised an eyebrow. "Also sorta shocked you can remember that. You wigged out after it went down."

"Oh! Right, forgot to tell you, this is a test run of our final step. We figured out the wording of Rule Seven. *If the rules, the House, or the von Closen's actions ever cause me worry, I am to visit my sister and put my worries to rest. Seeing my sister should make me happy. Anything that saddens me should be ignored.*" Lia smiled brightly. "Bea tried to explain how she overrode it, I don't exactly understand why it worked. Basically I'm only able to see stuff down here that doesn't upset me and so she enchanted me to have not seeing the truth upset me...so the rule cancelled out? I don't know, she said it wasn't the biggest concern because it only seemed to apply to this room, but it was a good sign that the Rules of the House can be eventually overwritten."

The twig sputtered in her hand as Diana stared at her. "No more tiptoeing? I can talk to my little sis for real?"

Lia nodded. "It's good to see you again. Really see you, that is."

Diana quickly snatched her up in a full-on demon hug, wings and all. She'd deny it but Lia could tell she was shedding a few tears as she painfully laughed. "Good to see you too, pipsqueak. Got a lot of catching up to do."

"And we can do that real soon. We're putting our plan into motion." Lia hugged her back. "It's almost over. All we gotta do now is rig fate in our favor."

Lia was very proud of her plan to deal with Clotho. It was very easy to make breaking a coffee maker look like an accident. And by extension, breaking Clotho.

The one problem with the plan that made Bea the most nervous was the inability to plan for her reaction. It was gonna *cause* a reaction for certain and they could wish that she'd leave to get a new one, which would take a couple days at least with how expensive that thing looked. Sure enough after two days of the fate becoming more and more fidgety and cranky, she was all but ordered by her sisters to go acquire a new one rather than wait for it to arrive. They had two days at best. It was more than Bea assumed they'd get.

Lachesis was next. Lia had started assuming she was on their team, but Bea was certain she would not just stand by if she noticed. They needed to give her plausible deniability. The enchantment Lia had on her was the obvious solution, as it was designed to let them use her glyph gate to leave. They just needed to add some additional steps as to what Lachesis would be doing while they used it. The more they planned exactly how they would do that, the more she wondered if this was Bea hitting two birds with one stone and taking revenge on the fate. Enchanting her to not leave her room until the next day was one thing. The specifications of what she was to *do* while in her room to busy herself was a bit over the top.

Although in a way, it certainly would give Lachesis an excuse to hide behind. Any passing staff would certainly hear the moans if not the mantras they came with.

Atropos was last. Bea said she handled it. That's all she would say for the longest time, avoiding the subject heavily. It worried Lia, not because she didn't know the plan, but the look her lady had whenever she asked about it. Bea told her when the time was right, she'd tell. Apparently that time was the day of their planned final egress. After dealing with the maiden and the mother she finally learned how they were going to deal with the crone.

"I made a deal with Atropos. She's going to ignore our escape. There's just one part of it I have yet to uphold." Her eyes glowed. And while they entranced her mind like always, Lia didn't feel calm or relaxed. She'd looked into the stars that glittered within that glow so often that she could almost read them, and this night the stars told a tale of pain to come. "I'm sorry. I'm so sorry I made a promise I couldn't keep. I love you too much, and I know you love me too much to not come back."

Lia didn't understand. She hoped she didn't understand. She didn't like what she wasn't understanding.

"Lia, after you leave with your sister, you will never return to the von Closen House."

No. No, no, no, you can't. You promised you'd keep me, you promised, you promised, Beatrice von Closen you promised! Lia wanted to scream. She was trapped in her own body, unable to even whimper a request. "Ok."

Bea looked away. Lia refused to say anything positive to these ridiculous commands and she hoped that was causing her to feel guilty. There will be no "with pleasure"s and "yes, mistress"s for this horrible plan. "I won't make you forget. Even though I wish you would, just to ease the pain."

Lia said nothing. She wasn't allowed to say what she wanted to say.

Bea kissed her. It was soft, one-sided, and felt as incomplete as Lia assumed the rest of her life was about to be without her mistress. "You belong to your sister now. I'm giving you back to her. She'll take care of you. Maybe she'll find somebody who can purge you of all these...chains."

They were meant to chain us together.

"I need you to be at your best. I'm doing this for you. You will not be aware of these commands until you have left the boundary of the estate." Bea looked her in the eyes and they shone brighter than ever before. Sapphires as blue as the tears that they wept. "Wake up, my love."

Lia blinked as her train of thought derailed. Why did she feel so angry? She frowned as Bea broke into tears. That quickly took priority as she pulled her in and hugged her tight. "It'll be alright. It's almost over."

For some reason that just made Bea cry more. She didn't understand why she was crying so hard.

Lia didn't understand why she was crying with her.

Beatrice entered the cellar where Lia was giving Diana the final bits of the plan. She gave a fanged smile at the sight of her. "Just in time, I'm about outta twigs."

"I suppose that's a good motivator for success." Beatrice opened the sack and pulled out the bag of fungus. It faintly glowed like a dying firefly. "You're certain *this* will help?"

Diana barked a laugh. "Like you wouldn't believe. I could take a dip in a silver bath and stare down the Lady of the House without even flinching."

"Why do demons not employ it on the regular?" Beatrice asked. Demons were somewhat resistant to enchantment. Not in the fae sense of a natural defense, more so their emotional states were not as easy to twist into subservience.

Diana shrugged. "Diminishing returns. Tricks our bodies into thinking they're dying, you can only have so many last stands stored up, you know? Better as a backup plan than an enhancement drug."

"Could you cut the back of my outfit?" Lia asked, turning away from her sister. She saw the look Beatrice was giving. "Wings. They're gonna tear it, might as well give a clean opening."

"Will she become resistant to enchantments as well?" Beatrice asked.

"Nah, the human half is still too vulnerable. If anything, she might be a tad more susceptible." Diana carefully ran her claw along the shirt, ending up with two make-shift wing holes. "There we go."

Lia held out her hand to Beatrice and smiled brightly. "Ok. I'm ready."

"No point in waiting any longer." Beatrice portioned out half of the deadroot and plopped it into her hand. She gave the rest to her sister and took a healthy step back.

Lia nibbled at the edge of the plant. The effect was startling to say the least, her eyes dilated as she stuffed the entire patch into her mouth. She shook her hands and danced in place like she was having a sugar rush, her fingers starting to look much sharper as she did. The dilation had rebounded to demonic slits as her horns visibly grew longer. A giggle one might call manic slipped out as a pair of wings truly sprouted from her back through the holes Diana had made for them.

Diana didn't change quite as drastically, given she already had the full demonic package. There was an atmospheric change to her though. An aura of adrenaline as she broke the chain around her leg like it was nothing. Her hands burned from what was most likely silver but it healed just as fast. She cracked her neck with a gravelly laugh. "Dibs you beautiful devil. You really know how to make a vice into a repeat customer."

Lia was bouncing off the walls. Literally, she used her new wings to leap between them in a way that made it seem gravity had tipped over for her. Diana caught her mid leap and without hesitation Lia chomped on her hand. Her sister didn't even flinch, instead using her latching as an opportunity to reel her in. "Could you put a leash on the wild child?"

Beatrice was so taken off guard by their behavior, she didn't even realize Diana meant an enchantment at first. She supposed her hatred of them was probably being overridden by the crazed half-demon gnawing on her hand. Her eyes began to glow. "Lia, look at me."

Lia was a winged blur. Attacking her with love would be an apt description as her kisses were making it quite difficult for her to even get a word out. Every instinct was being overstimulated, Beatrice hadn't even considered one of them would be her libido. "Lia, you need—darling this is not the time—" She rolled her eyes and let them glow so bright even Diana got a glassy look for a moment. Normally that should've knocked Lia into a deep trance but she just stared like a cat ready to pounce. Still, it got her to stop. "Calm down. Stay in a trance if it helps you focus."

Lia pouted with a whine. She closed her eyes and took a deep breath. She then quickly got off of her and cringed. "Sorry, mistress."

Beatrice stood up and brushed herself off. "That was quite the reaction. You seemed more in control the last time you had this."

Lia shrugged, her wings raising ever so slightly with her shoulders. "I had your order to focus on, usually things go a lot more chaotic."

Diana chuckled. "It's because she's not used to the urges. Demon adrenaline is like steroids, why do you think every one of us looks like we lift weights? It's why half-demon isn't really a thing, demon blood is supposed to win, not compromise. So when our resident half-demon gets something that amplifies the blood, aka jacking up every demonic instinct she usually barely feels up to max...well, I mean, did she tell you what happened the first time she ate deadroot?"

Lia snapped her head towards her sister. "She doesn't need to hear about that."

"What? It wasn't anything bad, you just flew off in a frenzy and I found you passed out in the back of a butcher's shop—"

"Please stop talking."

"—drenched in pig's blood, you musta ate through half a farm's worth. See, nothing bad, just—well, okay, yeah, I guess you sorta started crying when you came to your senses, but you were barely nine, you just didn't understand—"

"Shut it!" Lia tackled her.

Beatrice laughed as the two tumbled onto the couch, Diana having that smile of a sibling who knew exactly what they had been doing as Lia fought to silence her. It was nice to see the two of them being able to act normal with each other again.

Nice to know Beatrice was going to leave Lia with somebody who cared about her.

Chapter 31
Dirty Freedom

It felt like the House knew they were trying to escape.

Every servant entrance was locked. Every hall seemed to be longer than it should've been. The paths made no sense anymore, every hallway started to look the same, that feeling of being watched growing with each turn. Lia was in a light trance to keep her focus but even then it was hard to ignore every deadroot boosted demonic instinct in her screaming to claw the eyes out of whatever horror was digging them into her back.

Apparently their plan to use Lachesis's glyph gate was even more necessary than they thought. They never saw windows, which Diana started to complain about loudly. Well, not exactly. She more of just complained about having to carry Bea. Flying was faster and dignity did not get priority in a prison escape.

They passed by several servants, the first few looking confused. Then the next batch looked disappointed, their eyes starting to glow red. Finally, at the end of a long hallway with dozens of knight armors on display, a maid twitched like an ice cube was pressed against her neck, the red glow in her eyes visible even from there. She stood up straight and proper. "Beatrice, I am only going to say this once. We can just forgive and forget this entire ordeal if you just put everyone back where they belong."

Diana almost tossed Bea to Lia as she snarled with her fangs bared. "I ain't going back in the basement!"

Lia shook Bea as she set her down. "You said Ida wouldn't know!"

"She doesn't. Atropos is the nerve center but if she's kept her word, she's cut off communication. This isn't the Lady." Bea looked back to the maid. "Just the House."

The maid snapped her fingers. Every suit of armor turned its head towards them. "And the House prides itself on being tidy."

Lia felt a switch in her brain. Her human half and demon half had the same response and that's all the demon blood needed. The single thought coursed through her veins. *Destroy.*

The Abith sisters became a demonic whirlwind. Lia was high on the adrenaline as she toppled armor after armor like dominoes, tearing off limbs and using them to eviscerate even more. No real bodies meant the human half had no qualms and the demon half was having fucking *fun*!

Honestly it went too fast. Soon enough there wasn't a set left standing. The maid had dipped long before they even decided to deal with her. Diana laughed as she patted Lia's back with pride. "You know, if we weren't trying to escape, I'd say we should do this on weekends—"

Diana roared with anger as the tip of a blade pierced out of her stomach. She backhanded blindly and both were shocked to see Bea on the other end of it. She tumbled across the floor, her eyes both empty and red as rubies.

"What? How?" Lia shouted. She glanced at one of the armor sets they'd disassembled. Within the empty black of the knight's helmet two red eyes suddenly glowed brightly.

Got you.

The House shook as if an earthquake hit. Tendrils of hair shot out from the brick walls, hundreds wrapping around Lia tighter and tighter. Her vision blurred before being covered completely, her breath was squeezed out of her. No amount of demonic blood could cope with a literal lack of air and thus the world faded to black as she passed out.

Lia jolted awake. She was standing in Ida's office. Diana and Bea were at her sides, both their eyes empty as they stared forward. *No. No, no, no, this can't be happening!*

"Oh but it is, puppet."

The Lady of the House rose from her desk, her hair carrying her in front of Lia as she smiled with triumph. Her eyes glowed bright and Lia felt every bit of her will to fight drain away. The glamour removed the entire concept from her brain. She couldn't strike somebody as superior as Ida. It was like thinking she could fight the rain, it was just dumb to even try. "You had everything. Your sister, your love, all could've moved along if you just stayed where you belonged."

Lia wanted to run, to scream, to do anything, but she couldn't remember how. Ida left her aware of her helplessness. She wanted her to know what her punishment was to be.

"It was a good attempt, but one you will not be performing again." Ida stepped up to Bea and lifted her chin. "I warned you.

You've lost your privileges and the first thing to go is the right to a handmaiden. Or even remember the one you had."

Bea suddenly seemed aware she was in danger, her eyes filled with panic and horror. "No, don't take my handmaiden away! Please, I...I..." Her arms fell to her side as she stared off into the distance. "Who was I just talking about?"

"Not much of a fight. Are you sure she loved you? Just one wipe and she doesn't even remember your name." Ida laughed. It filled the room like a horrid reverb of mockery. A living nightmare.

A nightmare. Lia frowned and looked up at her captor. "What *is* my name?"

The laughter died. "What?"

"My name. Say it." Lia had been so uneasy just moments ago and it wasn't just for the obvious. Bea didn't call for her by her name. She didn't even say darling. She just called her a handmaiden. And the glare in Ida's eyes was telling her she was right to question that. "This isn't real. You're adding stuff but Bea locked my name away, you can't even say it."

Everyone's eyes glowed red as they all spoke in unison. "I despise that little trick she came up with." Dozens of tendrils shot from the shadows, wrapped around Lia, and lifted her into the air. Every limb started being stretched in different directions. "Knowing this isn't real won't make the pain hurt any less. After all, we need to keep your mind occupied while your body subdues the others."

"No!" Lia screamed.

And then something else screamed. No. Something else *roared.*

The door slammed open. It flew inside, tearing through the tendrils like a possessed pair of shears, cutting down the doppelgangers of her loved ones as if they were made of paper mache. Ida looked terrified, more proof that this was fake as the real her would rather die than show fear. A fanged smile that could almost be called bright was all Lia saw before a screech of terror from the vile fae shattered the nightmare entirely.

Diana was not good at defense. She always made sure offense made up the difference. Now the opposing team was her sister and her sister's girlfriend. And non-lethal was hard with claws.

Lia wasn't too hard to handle, even claws out she was basically a house cat trying to take down a tiger. It was making it hard to keep an eye on Beatrice, though. No matter how many times Diana smacked them out of her hands, the girl kept picking swords off the ground and patiently waiting for another opening to drive it through her chest. It was getting really hard to resist breaking her hands just to get her to stop doing that.

Diana wasn't stupid. You don't fight the thralls, you break the spell. Usually by breaking the fae. Problem was the fae was a fucking house, the entire place would have to burn down to make that happen and she didn't have enough matches right now. She needed to get them outside.

She needed to watch out because she noticed the sword in Beatrice's hand a tad too late that time.

Except Lia caught Beatrice by the wrist, twisting her arm behind her as she started whispering into her ear. The enchanted fae weakly fought against her grapple, a very uncanny sight as both their faces were still expressionless. Like two dolls being played with in a mock fight.

"Let go. I order you to let go," Beatrice said with a blankness that did not match her struggling.

"Those words are not yours. I obey my mistress alone," Lia said just as blank. Diana was never a fan of enchantments but her sister looked straight up possessed right now. Even her eyes were showing their demon side. Luckily that side wasn't red so she seemed to be in some form of self-control. "You are Beatrice von Closen. You are a fae. You are real."

"I am Beatrice von Closen and I order you to stop telling me that. I am a fae and I don't need to know that I am real!" Beatrice wasn't struggling so much as she was convulsing now. The red was draining away. "What...what's going on?"

Lia let go. "Ida got to you. She got to me as well. I have removed her hold."

"You did?" Beatrice gasped. "Oh my gods, it actually worked."

"What worked?" Diana patted her wound that was already sealing. Deadroot was kickass for real, too bad it was a once in a while gift and not a full-time boon. "And are you gonna stab me again?"

"It's a defense mechanism I put into Lia. It broke her out of her enchantment and must've helped me out of mine." Beatrice ran her hand along her cheek. "The deadroot must've allowed it to take control over her trance self once it was triggered. Gods you are a marvel of a girl, Lia."

Lia stared at her. She didn't look blank, but focused. Deadly focused. "You promised."

Beatrice flinched and then looked guilty as hell. "Are you going to undo *that* order too?"

"No." Lia's empty eyes still somehow glared as her claws curled up in anger. She never acted like this, especially not to Beatrice. "You made my purpose to protect her mind. Not her heart."

"I'm sorry, my love. It's the only way." Beatrice seemed to remember they weren't alone and sighed. "I'm slowing you down. You two fly to find an exit, I shall take a subtler path and meet up after."

Diana knew she was lying. Beatrice was looking at Lia like this was the last time she'd ever see her. "You know she's gonna come back, right?"

"Yes," Beatrice said with despair as she kissed Lia on the cheek, "I know."

Lia was flying. Flying fast, much faster than before. As if they'd left something very important behind.

They must've found a window. She remembered glass shattering. She remembered her wings starting to retract as she landed like a meteor onto the street, skidding along the sidewalk.

It wasn't until Lia looked upon the House that all her senses finally returned and the horrible memories of what she was ordered to do rose to the surface. "We have to go back!"

Diana was already holding her back with a hug. "Woah, woah, calm down girl, you've been put through the mental wringer."

"No, no, no, you don't understand! She's not coming with us, she's staying behind!" Lia broke free but couldn't bring herself to move past the boundary of the estate. She put her hand up and couldn't even make herself swat at the air that lay beyond the metaphorical barrier. Like how a mind prevents people from purposefully burning their hands on a hot stove.

Bea had done the worst thing she could ever do. She set Lia free.

And stole her right to choose.

Chapter 32
Pristine Prisons

Lia glumly prepared dinner. They'd managed to steal some supplies before they escaped to keep them going until they could resettle. For now they were hidden away in an abandoned church in the slums, half destroyed and looted. She hated it. The benches were so rotted that they'd been sleeping on the floor. It wasn't the church that had a reminder of Bea carved into the wall but at this point she was starting to think that pain was worth it if she could just have a bed again.

Diana stared out the window, watching with intent. She blew golden smoke from the burning twig she puffed. "You don't have to cook every meal, you know?"

Lia shrugged. "It's my job."

Diana took another puff. The sage smell burned at Lia's nostrils, she didn't know how she withstood smoking that stuff being a full-blooded demon. "You ain't my maid."

Lia sadly cut the carrots and tossed them into the soup. She hated carrots. "I want to do it. Why does everyone keep making decisions for me?"

"Sis, you literally just got given the ability back to make decisions."

"Then let me make dinner!" Lia shouted. She was shaking with everything bottled up inside her trying to burst at once. "I *like* cooking! I *like* making food for my loved ones, it makes me feel *happy*!"

Diana flicked the twig out the window and put her hand on Lia's head. "Hey, hey, I didn't mean it like that. Cook all you want, you just don't have to—"

"I don't care if I don't have to, I want to!" Lia cried. She hated how well the stupid hand thing worked on her still. Her anger was already melting into tears. "I'm not some broken doll, I'm a handmaiden. A maiden whose mistress threw her away, but still a maiden."

Diana gave her a look. "You know that's not what Beatrice did."

"She could've left! She could've come with us, but no, she tossed me out. Put up a wall and told me never to come back." Lia closed her eyes and wept. "She's trapped with that horrible woman and I can't even try to save her because I love her too much to disobey."

Diana let Lia cry the tears she'd been holding in since they'd escaped. Bea had betrayed her. She'd promised to keep her. She promised and she broke it like she broke her heart.

"Look, I'll be honest with you. It's not that I think you shouldn't help with things." Diana took her hand off her head and wiped a tear away. "The reason is...your cooking sucks."

Lia sniffled. "What?"

Diana looked at the pot as if it was poisoned. "You don't know how to cook. I need something that stays down."

Lia crossed her arms and gave a pitiful huff. "Bea never complained."

"Then Bea is tasteblind." Diana raised an eyebrow. "What did you make for her?"

"She liked bread. I'm really good at bread." Lia pouted. "I miss having a toaster."

Diana smirked. "Which do you miss more, Bea or the toaster?"

"Don't make me decide that, I should be allowed to have both!" Lia said defiantly.

Diana continued to watch out the window as Lia made her apparently inedible dinner. She sighed at her sour mood. "You said Bea gave you to me?" Lia shrugged with a nod. "So that means any order she gave, I can undo?"

"What? No, you can't do that." Lia frowned. "Can you?"

Diana made the face of mischief only a sister could. "Slap yourself."

"No." Lia stuck her tongue out at her. "Sorry, doesn't work like that."

"What a rip-off, a thrall that disobeys and talks back at that." Diana rolled her eyes and lit another twig. "So was it just metaphorical? Or did Bea just forget to put my name on the mental paperwork."

"I don't know. It's weird, everyone talks about how I'm good at loopholing my own enchantments but I feel like I don't get to pick and choose when I do it. Like I find them when I'm trying to obey them better, not fighting them." Lia sighed. "It's easier when I'm in a trance. You don't think you're loopholing on purpose when you can't think much at all."

Diana didn't respond at first. She was staring out the window with a stern look, the twig she'd just lit being prematurely snuffed between her fingers. "So if say, a fae put you under, I might be able to work some loopholes into her commands?"

Lia shrugged. "That's not a terrible idea. Why?"

Diana peered out the window again. Her eyes dilated like a cat ready to pounce. "Because I think the crone we didn't deal with has caught our scent."

Beatrice was living in a prison of her own making.

A test of character had been presented to her. A life locked away was her fate no matter what. Would she doom another soul just to make her life sentence more palatable? Or let the soul go free, so that only one of them had to suffer.

The correct choice had been made. Beatrice knew she'd never have the will to make it again. That almost made it hurt worse.

Lachesis walked into the library study, put her elbows on the table and her head on her hands. "You've been more routine than a wind-up soldier."

Beatrice stared at her studies, not comprehending anything. Thralls had eyes less dead than hers. No punishment had been given for her helping Lia escape. No punishment was needed. The act caused her enough pain as it was.

The only implication that Ida was even aware of their escapade was Beatrice needed to be kept in sight of a head maid at all times. Lachesis had taken charge of said task. "Are you missing your little toy?"

"Lia wasn't a toy." She was her most prized possession. And Beatrice gave her up so that nobody else could have her.

Lachesis smiled coyly. "This is precisely why I helped."

Beatrice looked at her without moving her head. "Because it would make me miserable?"

"Because I was speeding up the inevitable." Lachesis waved her hand. "The Lady of the House is withering away. Your defiance has been a stalemate most fae would fold against, but our Lady is not most fae."

Beatrice lifted her head and narrowed her eyes. "What's your point?"

"You and your mother are going to clash. You'd never make a move with Lia at your side, but without her, who knows? Only us fates, I suppose!" Lachesis cackled. "The game is almost over. The Lady of the House thinks she's won. But I think there's still a few hands to play. And Lia is a lovely wildcard."

Beatrice scowled at her. "Lia's not a part of this anymore."

"Oh, silly little Bea. Thinking just because she sends her beloved pawn to the corner that means she's not still fair game. After all, a corner pawn is far from harmless. All you've done is allow her to choose what piece she becomes." Lachesis now looked vicious. "Lia is going to come back. I've put my bets on it. And Atropos did as well, but I feel her intentions may lean more towards cleaning up Clotho's failure than the remains of your shattered heart."

"What?" Beatrice stood up. "We had a deal. She wouldn't interfere."

"Oh, I assume Atropos said she wouldn't stop Lia from leaving. Did you make sure to include a caveat that she wouldn't take steps to prevent her from coming back?" Lachesis became amused at the horror dawning on her face. "How many times do I have to tell you the importance of wording? Especially with my sister. She is as clever as me but with none of the heart. Even djinn are jealous of her callous interpretations."

"What do you know?" Beatrice asked. "What is Atropos going to do to her? Where is she?"

Lachesis just smiled. "Why should I tell?"

That smile irritated her. It was daring her to do it, goading her to enchant Lachesis. A trap that took pleasure in knowing how obvious it was. Yet the maid was holding back on details that involved her love. Beatrice put so much energy into her next command she could see glowing blue reflecting in her eyes. A weaker mind might've shattered from the weight of it. "Tell me everything you know about Lia. About the deal, about Atropos, about my mother. *Now.*"

"Finally." Lachesis smiled wide as her eyes went vacant. She almost looked high. "I have such a tale to spin, my lady."

There was a knock on the church door. It was light but desperate, as if unsure this was the right place. Lia ignored it as she hid in the kitchen, the only other room in this tiny chapel they'd called a hideout. A creak of hinges paired with the noise of the outside world before it was snuffed shut along with the door.

"Lia? Lia, are you here?" The alluring voice of her lady called out. Even knowing it was a trick wasn't enough for Lia to resist peeking just a smidge.

In the center of the chapel stood Bea, looking scared and filled with regret. They locked eyes, even in that blink of a peek she saw her and held out her arms open wide. "Lia!"

Lia couldn't resist. Days without her mistress she ran happily into the obvious trap. Part of her hoped that this truly was Bea, the other just wanted to believe the lie. A lie that sadly fell apart as fast as the trap it hid was sprung.

All her thoughts came to a screeching halt as she was tightly hugged. Instead of her loving mistress she was grappled by the unloving Atropos, her words already dancing alongside her thoughts. "Shhh, it's okay now. You're safe and with Bea. All you have to do is stand beside her, like you always do. Just stand still, docile and obedient, waiting for orders like a good handmaiden should."

There was no evidence of this being true but it was just enough to get Lia to hesitate, to let the fae past the door and within moments of smithing the enchantments so elegantly she stood blankly, living in the world that Atropos dreamed up for her. Standing at her mistress's side, a place she longed to return to, waiting for orders. She could still somewhat see and hear the real world beyond the illusion. But a lovely daydream was much nicer to focus on than a living nightmare.

Atropos ran the back of her hand along her cheek. "Even I assumed you weren't this idiotic. You enchant Lachesis, indispose Clotho, all the trouble hiding but you don't even bother locking the door. I wonder why?"

There was a subtle waft of air as something large silently descended from the rafters. "Because you're the meanest of the three and I don't feel bad about what's gonna happen to you." Lia stared blankly ahead with the faintest smirk as she heard a violent smack and Atropos crumpled like a tissue.

"Gods these bitches freak me out." Diana dropped the broken plank of wood and waved her hand in front of Lia. "You under? Really don't think we're gonna be able to try this twice."

"Probably." It wasn't the same as Bea's skill. A poor imitation, a lack of intimacy. She felt agreeable, not obedient. She'd probably break out of it in a minute if she tried hard enough. Which meant she was much more inclined to agree with her sister than the bitch who'd put her under.

Diana leaned down to be eye level with her. "You don't know?"

Lia smiled. "It's hard to know things when I'm under."

"Smartass." Diana laughed and put her hand on her head. Lia closed her eyes on instinct and the tension that had been in her since Bea forced her away finally relaxed. Her sister was here, ready to solve everything for her. "You owe me big time for this, so I'm gonna take advantage real quick of you having to listen to me. You'll give me a shoulder massage whenever I ask. You'll also just think you do it because I'm the best sister ever and amazing."

Lia internally rolled her eyes. "Yes, sis."

"That's best sis ever to you."

"Yes, best sis ever."

Diana smirked. The power was clearly going to her head. "Say you're a dork."

That didn't take long. "I'm a dork."

"A lovesick dork who misses her girlfriend."

"I'm a lovesick dork who misses her girlfriend." And who was worried they were running out of time.

"I'm starting to see the appeal of this." Diana led Lia to a chair and sat down across from her. "Okay, let's get to work tearing down the walls your girlfriend put up around her."

Lia smiled brightly. "Gladly, best sis ever."

Chapter 33
The Von Closen Legacy

The maid's eyes turned red as she scowled. "What in the *hell* do you think you are doing?"

"Downsizing." Beatrice stared her down and the red faded until there was nothing but blank obedience. "The Lady of the House is not your mistress anymore. Don't panic, leave quickly, be free."

The maid nodded, gathered her supplies, and stormed off as if she had a train to catch. Beatrice had learned from the first few that she needed to get them off the property before letting the enchantment end. Recently freed fae fodder apparently have a tendency to scream and not be very palatable to instructions on how to leave.

Beatrice had been on a rampage through the House. She waited until nightfall to clear out the servants quarters and was now finding the few stragglers left. It had been so easy for something so catastrophic, a simple breeze knocking over a skyscraper of cards. The staff wasn't an example of the von Closen legacy, it was a monument to Ida's inability to control anything without constant and invasive influence.

With each one her rage furthered. The entire staff was an enchanted web built on their misery. There was no joy for them, there was no benefit to their servitude. They could be told to feel anything and instead they were made to be aware of their helplessness. Beatrice had received more devotion from Lia than she'd ever encountered from the hundreds of enthralled servants that had passed through this godforsaken house.

"May I at least know what has inspired this tirade?" another maid asked as she approached.

"You already know, you horrid hag!" Beatrice shouted. "A year! A year of my life, stolen and for what? You couldn't handle the fact I was in love? You tried to *kill* Lia? Why, because it would make somebody else the most important person in my life?"

The next maid she found scowled at her. "Oh don't give me the Lachesis version of this tale, you know I am not that petty."

"You *are*. You are the pettiest person in the entire city, the only reason you still live is because even death is not beyond your malicious spite," Beatrice said before freeing her from Ida's grip.

"I didn't care about Lia. I cared that you were going to run away with her! And then I'd truly lose everything!" The next one shouted, continuing this strange argument of mind-controlled mouthpieces as Beatrice freed them with each of her retorts.

"As if you care about our bloodline. You never intended to give me the reins of our legacy."

"Legacy? You think I wish for your survival because of our *bloodline*? Beatrice von Closen, a day does not pass by without me wishing you were never born. I thought I was making an extension, an emissary. Not a thief and usurper!" The maid put her hands over her face. "You took my eyes, child. They used to be green as emeralds. Now they are red for what remains are just bloody wounds left from where your birth cut them out."

Another maid had appeared behind her as she freed the first, just to say, "The House is my domain and within it I still hold my power, but you, you can leave. You can leave to the world and enchant your way through anything you want, meanwhile I am trapped here, unable to even step foot outside without feeling my entire life draining away. I have searched and searched and I feel I have been on the precipice of a solution but then...then you found that *tramp*."

"I found somebody who understood me! Somebody who truly loved me, who I love back and you were going to take her from me!" Beatrice shouted at a poor kitchen maid she stormed in on.

Her eyes turned red as she scowled. "She was taking *you* from *me*! She filled your head with dreams of life beyond our walls and if not for Atropos's foresight you would've fled the city with her. Out of my reach, leaving me to wilt into nothing like a mighty tree in a drought never ending."

"I was ready to annihilate that half-breed's psyche but you, you threatened to do the same to yourself. Mutually assured destruction, a stalemate." The enchanted maid scoffed. "You made an offer. Allow her to live, to be with you, and you'd return to your proper place."

The last maid was in the middle of the hall, her eyes already red in wait. "I of course tried to go back on my deal the moment you let your guard down, I was at least cautious enough to only wipe a year. I hadn't realized your threat was an actual mental trap, one that clearly assumed I would not hold back, and thus wiped a year from you as well. Truly asinine that you waste such talents on some peasant street rat, you forgot what you'd done and any traps you may have left for me."

"So you upheld the deal until you could figure out how to get rid of her without setting off any more mental snares." Beatrice narrowed her eyes. "You didn't talk to Lucial using Lia and Diana as leverage. You wanted to get rid of her without breaking the deal and decided selling her off to her own father was the safest bet."

"It was quite clever, you must admit. For no matter what your feelings, I could tailor the tale to allow for her transfer. And while I could not fire her, I could let her serve a different master." The maid sighed. "I hope this little talk has helped you get this out of your system. You must know Clotho allowed you to release all of the staff just so she could have fun recollecting them, yes? You've accomplished nothing but earning my ire."

Beatrice smiled viciously. "We'll have to see what fate has in store for me first."

The maid was freed, leaving Beatrice to stand alone in wait. Her mother wasn't wrong, Clotho could've stopped her at any time. But she was always a little too eager to let people get away with things if it made her own job fun in the long run. Three quarters of the staff had been released before anybody even knew what was happening, why not let Beatrice snip the rest just to make a fresh start of hunts?

Sadly, the game was over. Clotho needed to start cleaning up, as it were. And sure enough, she now stood at the end of the long hall with a look of what might've been pride. Or at least respect for the audacity. She started at a walk, then a run, then a full-on animalistic sprint after seeing Beatrice hold her ground. That look was plastered across the maid's face, pride and respect of a foe she was ready to eviscerate.

Dear gods, she isn't going to capture me, she's going to make sure I can't even walk. If this didn't work, Beatrice was truly done for. Her eyes glowed bright with the deadly glare she gave right as the fate was all but on top of her. "Switch."

Clotho was impulsive but she was still a fae and a fate at that. A fate that would certainly be bracing for such tactics, but her face made plain that order was not the one she expected. And the hesitation was just enough to let the simple ask slip through. In the blink of an eye where the maid once stood was a confounded kitchen maid. Given her position she was already caught in Beatrice's gaze and said fear melted into complacency. "The Lady of the House is not your mistress anymore. Don't panic, leave quickly, be free."

The maid bowed and fled, now relieved of duty and thus out of the fate's reach. Purging the staff had a secondary purpose. Ensuring the servant that Clotho switched with was the one Beatrice had locked in the cellar they'd turned into a temporary prison for their demon guest. She felt bad for using the poor maid like that, she enchanted her to be calm but it didn't make it feel any kinder. To compensate, she'd given her some of Ida's more pricey jewelry to wear and thus escape with to pawn off. It was the closest thing she could equate to a severance bonus.

The dog was in the kennel. Now to deal with the hag holding the leash.

Diana went through the portal first but she couldn't stop Lia from following before giving the all clear. The moment she'd been awoken from her trance it took all her strength not to sprint towards the House on foot as even then she could feel the mental wall tumbling down.

"I'm shocked you got those scissors to work," Lia said, looking around. They were in the basement cellar where they'd kept her sister locked up. Weird choice at first but nobody would expect the prisoners to break in through the jail cell.

"You talked about those magic mirrors a lot, so I just went with it the same way. Cut at the air thinking about this place. Probably helped I was stuck here for so long, super vivid in my mind." Diana held up the now broken magic item. One cut and they'd all but snapped. "They didn't like me using them. Guess that old crone's night just got even worse."

They both turned and froze at the sight of a maid they'd somehow completely missed. She stared at them like she was waiting for them to address her.

"Who are you?" Lia asked, holding a hand out before Diana bonked her on the head like she clearly was about to do.

"Ophelia, miss. Are you why I am here?" The maid asked with a hint of confusion in her voice. Oddly calm for a person not knowing why they're locked in a cellar.

Diana scoffed. "Doubt it. Unless Beatrice planned on this."

"Lachesis is good at predicting things, she might've helped." Lia smiled warmly as she helped the maid to her feet. "Who told you to wait here?"

"My mistress did. She gave very clear instructions to wait here until she spoke with me again. She told me to remain calm." The maid motioned to the tray of food. "I was told I could eat if I got hungry. I'm sorry if that was meant for you."

Lia's smile waned at the title. "She's in a trance. Bea put her down here for some reason." It seemed rather out of character. Bea wasn't so cruel as to throw somebody in the dungeons and even then, the maid didn't seem to think of this as a punishment.

Diana grunted. "You sure her mistress isn't Ida?"

"The Lady of the House doesn't care if her thralls are calm." Lia noticed the glitter of her necklace. "Ida wore that at the soirée. Where'd you get it?"

"Mistress told me to wear it. Along with a few rings, actually." The maid gave a nervous smile. "She made a comment about keeping them once I was let go, but I'm not quite sure what she meant by that. Been waiting here ever since."

A chill ran down Lia's spine. "Diana, we need to go." She looked between the portal and the stairs, unsure of which to flee to. "We need to go like right now."

Diana looked baffled at her sudden panic. "Why's an over-decorated maid got you worked up?"

"Because I remember this plan. It was one of our earlier ideas to trap—"

The maid vanished. And in her place was a very pissed off Clotho.

Everything happened in a split second. Clotho was about to strike out of reflex and hesitated when she saw Lia was on the other end of her blade. She growled at her like a wounded animal. A snarl, a bluff, and demand to get back so her weakness wouldn't be known. But she didn't look hurt. *She doesn't want to attack you.*

Diana had not seen this soft side of Clotho. All she saw was a fate who'd hesitated and blitzed her through the portal. She grappled her as her wings stretched out, giving her sister a stern look. "If you don't come out of this alive I *will* kill you!"

The glyph gate fizzled shut. Lia hadn't even realized it had been closing, but Diana clearly had. She snapped out of her shock and rushed up the stairs to find her girlfriend before it was too late.

Lia ran through the halls of the House without fear. The one thing she remembered about that plan was the reason they couldn't enact it. Bea had said almost as a joke they could just fire all the staff to guarantee Clotho switched with the right maid.

And sure enough, that was exactly what Bea had done. The House was eerily empty, her steps echoed the vacant halls she ran down. Had Bea learned about what Atropos was going to do? This did feel like the type of reaction she would have. But it was insane, this wasn't something she could take back, she'd have to face Ida head on.

Lia couldn't let her do that alone. But what was she going to do about it? That stupid glamour Ida had made it so hard to even remember to stay mad, much less act against her. Not to mention if her enchantments were that strong through her proxies, they would be impossible to resist in person. There was no way she would make it within ten feet of her without ending up a brain-dead thrall.

But a thrall *could* make it past those last ten feet.

An idea popped up in the back of her head. An idea that she hated, an idea that was insane, but she felt like it would work. It had to work. For Bea, it needed to work. She was running towards Ida's study with a determination she'd never felt in her life, it *will* work.

"Oh will it?"

Lachesis stepped in front of her from out of nowhere. She had that damn "inside joke" smile as if she'd been reading her thoughts. "Hello, little demon. Off to save your love like a hero of old?"

"Yes, I am," Lia said definitely, "Are you here to stop me?"

"I'm here to further protect my investment." Lachesis held out her hand. "Do you trust me?"

Lia braced herself. "No."

"Good." Lachesis snapped her fingers and the world melted away. It wasn't even a fight, the fate had already won and was just now revealing her victory as she sent Lia into a deep trance. "Your plan is clever. But it won't work, not without me. After all, a puppet with a plan still needs somebody to hold up her strings."

"It will work." Lia didn't say that. She was fast asleep. Something *else* was awake. And it said again, "And I'm not your puppet."

Lachesis had a vicious look of pride. Strangely, just as Lia's eyes blankly stared past her, the fate's eyes almost seemed to stare back in the same way. Like two ghosts within them glancing at the other. "Ohohoho, hello beautiful. Do you have a name?"

"Names can be stolen. Thoughts can be changed. I am a purpose." Lia's eyes, glassy and unfocused, still narrowed with anger. "I can feel you tying your strings. Explain them or I will cut them."

"So *violent*. Not at all like the Lia we know. Oh how I wish I had time to analyze this defense mechanism Beatrice set up. I wonder how I missed it, stashed away in those lurking demon instincts perhaps? No wonder Lia was ready to charge in, you were fueling her gut feelings that it would work." Lachesis stopped her appraisal and gave a bow of respect. "I cannot lie to an enchantment so well crafted. So I will forgo my nature and speak plainly." She glanced up with a smirk. "After all, a 'purpose' will never be able to recount my disgrace in doing so. Even in these trying times, I do have a reputation of mystique to uphold."

Beatrice admittedly had put more thought into getting to this point than actually achieving it. She'd grabbed a sword off a statue, burst into Ida's study, and lunged at the spot the Lady of the House never seemed to move from. A tendril of her hair darted out and caught her by the throat.

"All the pageantry for such a poor finale." Ida tossed her against the wall like an unloved doll. Beatrice heaved heavily from the pain, her eyes on the sword left behind at the door. The hair wrapped around it and handed it to the hag. "Unlike you, I prepare for when my words are not enough to solve an issue."

"Ha! Do you even have anything but cheap words to resolve this? Your enchantments barely work on me for more than an hour at best, so that's unsustainable. I'd ask for you to just kill me but you've gone to such lengths to keep me alive I'd say your pride alone shields me from an execution." Beatrice started to cackle like a mad witch. "The great Lady of the House at the mercy of being unable to control her own daughter. How long will the mighty legacy last if I refuse to help it?"

The red eyes of Ida glowed brighter than the fires of hell. Her grip on the sword tightened and there was a moment where Beatrice believed she'd truly pushed her over the edge. Her smile did not waver and instead grew at the thought. *My death is yours. Kill me now and gift me victory.*

"May I interject a wildcard into this final bout, my ladies?"

Both von Closens turned to the open door to see Lachesis enter with Lia, a string wrapped around her neck like a dog on a leash. "Good evening, everyone. Lady Beatrice, I found your misplaced toy." She bowed to Ida. "The poor girl was so confused, I gratefully reminded her she was property of the House. I also noticed my sisters are absent. Indisposed dealing with our misplaced demon guest, most likely."

"No," Beatrice said with horror. She nearly dove for Ida but stopped as Lia stepped between them. Her eyes did not seem to even register her. "No, no, no, why?" She turned to Lachesis with fury. "Why must you twist my heart like this? Play us like a pair of cheap violins to serenade this hag with our misery?"

"I am fated to persist, my lady." Lachesis sighed. "But just because one is cursed to always win, does not mean one gets to choose which side is the winner. Only that said side will always be yours."

"Well put," Ida said with a cruel smile.

Lachesis sighed more dramatically. "I was rooting for you two. But I can only do so much."

"That is enough." Ida's face became less amused. "Locate your sister. Not Clotho, even I can hear her snarls from here, but my Atropos. I do not wish to rob her seeing the fruits of her labor flourish."

"As you wish, my lady." Lachesis gave Lia a kiss on the cheek as she loosened the thread. "Don't forget the Rules of the House, little demon. Make sure to defend your owner from any harm."

"Yes, miss," Lia said blankly.

Beatrice frowned at that, then quickly returned her expression to anger as Ida ran the back of her hand across Lia's cheek. "As always,

Lachesis subtly provides a solution to a rising predicament. My first mistake was underestimating how deeply you cared for this tramp. Good leverage is so hard to find these days." She gave Beatrice a curled smile. "So, let's draft up a new arrangement. One that will make you far more amiable to our legacy, as you say. And in return I shall not make this girl's life a living hell."

That made Beatrice's blood boil but she couldn't help but notice something was different about Lia. She had seen the girl in a trance so many times, in so many ways, that she could recognize what certain mindsets looked like. She knew loving obedience, she knew fearful control, she even knew the look of when she perceived herself as an object, but this looked like...waiting. Lia had been given an order and was waiting to act on it.

Why had Lachesis said owner? Ida never cared to call herself an owner, she held her title as lady so highly that Lady of the House became more well known than her actual name.

Lachesis had made a move. A subtle one, so that if Beatrice failed she could still side with Ida. Fated for the winner's side to always be hers, as she said. What else had she said, what clues of indirect incitement were in her words? But her love's capture had taken precedence over remembering what she had thought to be a cruel final monologue. Beatrice was failing at the game she'd stopped playing assuming she'd already lost.

And so Beatrice put her faith in Lachesis as apparently Lia had, and bluffed. "I will not give in to such underhanded tactics. I made a deal with Atropos that Lia was no longer involved, she did not return under my orders. Release her and let this stay between fae, eye to eye."

"You still think this is a negotiation? How quaint." Ida motioned to the entranced half-demon. "Let's start small. Lia, please tell me your worst nightmare. A few hours of you screaming should be a good taste of what's to come."

Lia smiled blankly. "No."

Ida glared at her with a hint of bafflement at the audacity. "What was that?"

"No." Her smile did not waver.

Ida turned to her, allowing for Beatrice to have an opening, one she was wasting on being fascinated at Lia's defiance. "You are nothing but a piece of property. You do not have the capacity to disobey your mistress."

"Correct," Lia said cheerfully, "You are not my mistress. You are not my owner."

"The Rules of the House—"

"Fully functional. And no longer within your power to control."

"You...you couldn't have..." Ida grabbed her by the collar. "I made it impossible for Beatrice to alter them! What rules are you following?"

Lia's smile was unrelenting with positivity. "Rule Two : Diana is my owner. Rule Five : I am to make Beatrice happy. Rule Eleven: an owner is higher than a mistress and has priority over orders given by a mistress. Rule Twelve: Rules not set by property are to be disregarded, as declared by their owner. Thus only rules two, five, eleven, and twelve are applicable anymore. Transference of ownership to Beatrice commenced as soon as I saw her."

"You couldn't. You couldn't have!" Ida glared at Beatrice as her hair began to curl like a swarm of vipers hissing in anger. "You taught her, didn't you? To stoop so low as to let your thrall learn our ways, I swear after this is over you will suffer—"

It didn't even register to Beatrice as an attack. A casual but swift swipe, like a maid would do against a spot they'd missed, Lia slashed Ida across the throat with a clawed hand. She continued to stand still, emotionless in a way that one could call vicious, as the Lady of the House stumbled back and choked on her own blood.

"Why?" Ida asked, more a question to the universe rather than to her executioner.

"I will not allow her to suffer. I am to defend my owner from any harm," Lia answered curtly.

Ida's hair fell still like strings that had been cut, leaving a mess of frizzled threads that cocooned her as she fell to her knees. She reached a blood hand out to Beatrice. "Please...this isn't how I wanted it...how either of us wanted it..." Her pleading red eyes the only thing she could see through her mat of hair that seemed to now be weighing her down. "We can start again...you can be...forgiven."

Beatrice was cold and indifferent. "And you can be forgotten."

The Lady of the House collapsed, the cocoon of hair dispersing like a shattered tumbleweed to reveal not a trace of a body beyond the faded white threads stained with her blood.

Beatrice looked at Lia with an unwavering sense of awe. How she even got here was a tale she was eager to hear, but in this moment all that mattered was that she was. That they were free. "Handmaiden turned hero, loyal to a fault. No matter how hard I try, you always come back."

"Always." Lia's fearful tone didn't match her soft smile. Despite being in trance, she asked, "May I make a request, mistress?"

Beatrice nodded. "Of course, my love."

"May I forget?" Lia's bloodied claw shook. "May I forget what I've done?"

Free from Ida, but not from the suffering she yet wrought. Beatrice winced with how much pain was in such a simple question. She took her hand, uncaring of the blood staining her own, and gently coaxed her to retract her claws. "I don't want to start our new lives with me making you forget again."

"Ok." Lia paused. "Can you make me feel ok with it?"

"Of course, darling." Beatrice kissed her cheek and then let her eyes glow. "But not in the way you're thinking."

Lia was hiding in the back of her mind. She didn't want to wake up. She didn't want to feel the blood. She didn't want to feel anything.

In trying to keep her thoughts empty, darker ones began to fill the void. Lia was a murderer. She'd purposefully twisted the threads of her enchantments so that she could kill somebody. The excuse that she was being controlled didn't even help because it was her own orders she was following. She knew it was the only way she'd not reveal her plan, the only way the glamour wouldn't stop her. The only way she wouldn't hesitate.

Blank bliss was beyond Lia, she could only shield herself in layers of apathy. She couldn't even cry, because if she let one emotion through she might be crushed by the weight of everything else.

Then, in the abyss of her mind where she thought nothing could reach her, a hand was gently placed on her head. She never told anyone why such a thing calmed her down. It was so stupid, something she should've grown out of. In the slums, in the early days when they were constantly moving and Lia was too young to understand, there were times when they would have to hide from other desperate demons and the like. With the right place Diana could encase her wings around them to blend into the background, but she would be forced to cover Lia's mouth in case she'd cry. While that clawed hand was fierce and locked, the hand on her head would be gentle. It was a silent reminder that this was still her sister, that she was keeping them safe. Soon the young Lia started putting her sister's hand on her head whenever she was scared, seeking that feeling of safety. It was childish but to this day she couldn't help but still feel calmer when Diana did so.

This hand was too small to be her sister's. It was smooth and uncalloused. It still made her feel safe, like somebody was there to protect her. It accompanied the voice that dismissed all her dark thoughts that she felt trapped with.

Lia was a demon.

Half-demon. And that doesn't make you a monster.

Lia was a murderer.

You were protecting your mistress. You were saving your love.

Lia had blood on her hand.

We can wash it off together.

Lia wanted to forget.

Then first you have to forgive yourself.

Lia wanted to cry.

You have permission. And a shoulder that's always there for you.

And so Lia cried. She sobbed on the shoulder that had been offered to her, feeling every part of her sorrow from the deepest parts of her soul. She cried for her sister, for her love, and for herself.

Eventually the tears ran dry. Lia was asked if she wished to stand, but she didn't feel ready. She was told she could take as much time as she needed.

So Lia laid down, the hand gently lowering her, and with that permission finally was able to sink into emptiness. It wasn't blissful, not when she had all these emotions still lurking above her, threatening to drag her back to feel them full force. But the empty was peaceful, as it always was. No worries. No thoughts. Just—

Sleep. And you may wake when you are ready, my love.

Chapter 34
Mistress and Maiden

Surfacing from a trance that lasted so long and was self-controlled made waking difficult. It was like trying to get out of bed after sleeping off the worst illness. Just remembering how to move her own feet was a challenge. Settling back into a body that she hadn't cared to feel for…a while. She wasn't sure how long. Long enough.

I'm ready, Lia thought to herself. She wasn't sure. *I'm ready to see Bea.* That, however, she was sure of.

Lia took a deep breath and opened her eyes. She was standing in Ida's office, specifically next to Bea sitting in the chair behind the desk. The mark of her murder was long gone, both the floor and her hand clean of blood. Dozens of forms and reports were scattered in front of her, a few of which Bea was holding up to read. She looked exhausted. Somehow Lia knew the teacup on her desk never stayed filled for long.

There was a knock at the door. Bea rubbed her eyes with a heavy sigh and flicked her hand towards it. "Gods, is it already time?"

Lia's legs moved for her. Not in any sense of enchantment, more so just going through the motions of her role as handmaiden. Clearly she'd been doing this for some time, even with her back at the helm her body wasn't used to needing her input. Lia opened the door to find Lachesis on the other side. The head maid gave her a nod, although she immediately walked into the room so it wasn't clear if she truly was addressing her or just nodding out of habit.

"Our Lady of the House," Lachesis said, giving a curtsy.

"You sound chipper. Enjoying your new role?" Bea still hadn't looked up from her papers. Lia returned to her side, deciding to wait until this was over to speak up.

"Absolutely! The House hasn't changed in a century, I am most excited to help you with your tapestry in the von Closen legacy." Lachesis glanced at Lia, who quickly tried to pretend she was not paying attention. Her eyes narrowed ever so slightly before looking back. "Reorganizing has been a chore, though. Your purge of the staff means it'll be some time before we can replenish, too fast and we may catch the city's ire. Not to mention your new restrictions slow us down regardless."

"The benefit is that in my House we will only have to do such a thing once," Beatrice said. "It will be nice to have a staff that lasts longer than a month. I can actually start to learn people's names."

Lachesis raised an eyebrow. "Clotho will not be pleased. You know how she feels about her hunts."

"While Clotho may be gnawing at her new leash, she does not tend to bite the hand that feeds her." Bea tapped her fingers against the desk. "I'm certain during this transition we will find tasks that require her services. Perhaps ones more stimulating than unsuspecting lost souls in the slums."

Lachesis was only looking at Lia now. She'd started to regret waiting to say something and was failing at hiding her awkwardness. "I do suppose she only felt invigorated hunting rogue demons and runaway fae in these recent weeks. Perhaps if we give her similar challenges she will find joy in the long run, my lady."

"Speaking of, any updates on Atropos?" Bea asked.

"Neither Clotho nor Diana have been able to locate her. And I doubt either will, her gifts of deceiving the senses are unmatched even by your late predecessor." Lia flinched at that last part. Lachesis smirked. "My lady, perhaps we should table this meeting for later."

Bea rolled her eyes. "Why? I still have a dozen things I need to go over. Ida was so intertwined in everything, I feel like I'm plugging holes left and right caused by tearing her out."

"Because it appears a little demon has finally resurfaced."

Bea stopped. She didn't turn, but held her hand out tentatively. Lia couldn't help but take it. "Lachesis? Leave."

"With pleasure, my lady." Lachesis all but skipped out of the room. She wiggled her eyebrows at them as she closed the door. "I'm glad that my investment was worthwhile."

Bea shot to her feet the moment the door clicked. Papers scattered over the floor as she took both of her hands. "Lia, my love? Are you awake, are you ok?"

Lia didn't answer at first, because she truly didn't know. Somehow both an eternity had passed but she still could feel the blood dripping from her hand. She weakly smiled. "As much as one can be after what I've done, my lady."

"I am so, so sorry for everything I've put you through. For sending you away, for stealing your memories, for making you feel you had no choice to do what you did. You of all people should never have been forced to commit such a sin." Bea pulled her in and hugged her tight. She shook lightly as if she was about to cry. "I hope to the gods you'll never have to do it again. And I promise to never ask such a thing of you."

Lia returned the hug. This was the final thing she needed. It was all better now. "I'd do it all again for you, Bea."

Bea leaned back and her teary eyes had one clear desire. Lia didn't even need a command, she wanted this ever since she was forced away and now pounced on the clear permission to give her mistress a passionate, loving kiss. After so long without her it was the best reward she could ask for.

Bea reciprocated like a woman who'd been waiting every day for this to finally happen and pulled her into the chair as they continued to make love. It was big enough to share, so long as Lia sat on her lap. She didn't mind one bit.

"How long have I been in trance?" Lia asked, cuddling on her shoulder as Beatrice tried somewhat to do her new duties. After going so long without even a moment shared with her lover, it was very hard to focus on them now.

"A week. At first you wouldn't do anything without orders, truly anything, I was worried you were going to stop breathing if I didn't tell you to do so. After a day or two you started performing your handmaiden routines." Beatrice motioned to where she had stood earlier. "I was pleased to have you by my side while I handled the aftermath, even if you weren't truly aware of it. I comforted you as much as I could, every spare moment I had."

"Comforted me?" Lia asked, a hint of excitement.

Beatrice laughed. "Not like that. The temptation was daunting, though. Forehead kisses and hugs were all I allowed myself." And one moment of weakness with having her disrobe and hold a towel during her bath again but that was her little secret.

"Aww, ok. That's very sweet of you." Lia pouted as if not taking advantage of her was disappointing. Perhaps only a secret for now. "Why not just order me to wake up?"

Beatrice cringed. "I don't know if you remember, but you were in quite the state. I thought it was best to let you cope however you could and eased you into a sort of meditative sleep. You didn't need to surface until you were ready."

"It helped a lot. I don't think I ever would've come back up if you hadn't been there." Lia nuzzled into her shoulder. "Thanks, Bea. I love you."

Beatrice's heart fluttered. It had been so long since she heard those words and it was worth the wait. "I love you too, darling. I'm never letting either of us forget that ever again." She cleared her throat. "Your sister will be glad to know you're awake. She's been helping me keep Clotho in line, as well as other fae who are trying to take advantage of Ida's demise. I think she enjoys being my enforcer just a tad too much."

"That's a great job for her," Lia said with a laugh. She turned her head to the mess of papers on the desk. "So, you're the matriarch of the von Closen House now. What does that make me?"

Beatrice smiled. "You can have any role you wish. I'd even let your only duty be to enjoy your life, if you so choose. But I have the sneaking suspicion that there's one position you're still quite fond of, though."

"At your side, on my knees, and without a thought in my head?" Lia rattled off without hesitation.

"Lia!" Beatrice playfully scolded.

"Being honest makes me euphoric, my lady." Lia giggled and then kissed her cheek. "If the new Lady of the House would allow me to return to my position as her personal handmaiden, I would be most pleased." She whispered into her ear. "And if my mistress would like to reclaim her doll, said doll would also be very, *very* happy to be owned by her again."

Beatrice smirked. Her eyes glowed blue as she glanced over. A soft moan slipped out from Lia as she went limp, her eyelids fighting to stay open just to keep staring. "This is truly what you want, my love?"

"More than anything, mistress," Lia said dreamily. Her wonderful smile now droopy, making her so utterly adorable.

Beatrice put her hand under her chin to help it stay up as she sent the love of her life deep into a trance. One that would never stop making her feel cherished as it would wrap her mind in threads that would become a tapestry of her love for her. An enchantment that would forever entwine them together as mistress and maiden. "Then who am I to deny you?"

Epilogue
No Rest for the Wicked

Nyssa rested her head on her hand as she stared into the mirror. The maid behind gently brushed her hair. She was not a maid yesterday. She was their most valued maid today. As far as they were aware, at the very least.

"I'm sorry I failed you, my lady." The maid kissed the top of her head. "I know this is not an ideal circumstance."

"I shall make do with what I've been given, my love. At least Beatrice was kind enough to clear a path through this tart's mind." Nyssa's eyes glowed red. "Don't fret. We have plenty of time to conquer this family before we retake what is rightfully ours."

Acknowledgements

There's many people who helped this story get to where it is. My wonderful beta readers who endured my first attempt at smut, my friends who encouraged me to self-publish, large quantities of caffeine. Special thanks to Kira, who without her constant encouragement and guidance about this genre I wouldn't have ever even had the courage to share it. Thank you to Aditya and Danielle as well, you were very brave to endure this sharp turn in my usual manuscripts I ask you to read. I also must thank my editor Roxana and cover artist Haya for their wonderful services, as well as my friends for the amazing artwork they provided.

And thank you, dear reader, for getting this far. While there may not be many of you yet, you are the reason I write. There is no point in putting words on the page for me alone. Every emotion I invoke in you, positive or negative, is one I felt while writing it. Sharing that experience is what drives me to write more. So thank you for allowing me the opportunity.

About the Author

Sova Erickson is an author from the American Midwest with a lot of time on their hands and too many stories in their head waiting to be put on the page. Whenever they aren't being possessed by the sapphics to tell their tales, they are being both player and dungeon master in Dungeons&Dragons, as well as enjoying numerous genres of video games.

They also have two loving cats who do everything in their power to prevent Sova from finishing their manuscripts. The cats have asked to remain anonymous and deny all accusations of their crimes.

Sign up for their newsletter at www.sovaerickson.com

Connect with the author on their socials:

Bluesky: @fae-author.bsky.social

Instagram: sovaerickson_author